GHOSTLY
RETURN

To Di

Best Wishes

BRENDA HURLEY

Brenda Hurley   2·5·22

Matador
Unit E2 Airfield Business Park,
Harrison Road, Market Harborough,
Leicestershire. LE16 7WB
Tel: 07534 489333
Email: books@troubador.co.uk
Web: www.troubador.co.uk/matador

ISBN 978 1803130 163

British Library Cataloguing in Publication Data.
A catalogue record for this book is available from the British Library.

Printed on FSC accredited paper
Printed and bound in Great Britain by 4edge Limited

Typeset in 12pt Adobe Jenson Pro by Troubador Publishing Ltd, Leicester, UK

Matador is an imprint of Troubador Publishing Ltd

GHOSTLY RETURN

To my darling and understanding husband Roy

The last time Louis had blended with a mortal was sixty years ago. Six decades since he'd rescued a vulnerable young woman at the edge of existence.

Six decades in which he'd floated between worlds, watching, waiting. Until now.

This opportunity, so unexpected yet so welcome, had plunged him into a relationship which was no longer confined to dreams. He was about to begin a new life with Katie, his darling girl, but first he had to find a way of stepping into a dead man's shoes and learn to be a man of the twentieth century.

1

He felt deathly cold. The restrictive cocoon that wrapped around his spiritual body was both tight and chilly. It was a sensation that he hadn't felt for so long that, at first, he didn't recognise it. Yet here he was, shivering, with a clammy skin, rapid pulse, and he was breathing heavily. All his strength had seeped away, he was tired and he thought it very possible he might vomit. This body was reacting as all bodies do when suffering from shock. He could see the goose bumps standing proud on his forearms and instinctively he pulled down the sleeves on the jumper he was wearing, to cover his icy skin as he sought warmth. Everything was different; a few minutes ago, he had been a spirit trapped in an alternative world, now he was apparently trapped in a body that belonged to someone else; in truth, a less than honourable man but a man nevertheless that he had tried to save; although it had been a battle he had lost.

The cosy kitchen had been the scene of the tragedy. Katie had tried so hard to save her former lover, but fight as they did for Mike, they were too late to save him. His light had burned out and when his life was extinguished, Louis had not been able to release himself from Mike's body.

Katie had helped him up from the floor, where Mike had died choking. Now, he sat in Mike's body at the kitchen table opposite the woman he loved, wondering if she would recognise him. Katie had only known him when he visited her in her dreams and when he took her to his world behind the wooden veil, beyond the Tree of Life. The carving on the headboard of her bed was not unlike the Garden of Eden with profiles of a woman and a man standing on either side of the tree. It depicted his sanctuary, where the sun shone and a meadow stretched out until it touched the purple blue hill on the horizon.

It was Katie's bed, but his carving, created over a hundred years ago and beyond the veil of wood, was a hidden kingdom. This was a world that had been created by him, but that had remained hidden until he died. He had brought Katie to his world and she had brought her imagination with her; she had brought new life to it. His world had become as much hers as his.

He looked at her tear-stained face and wondered what on earth she could be thinking, sitting across the table from him. Her face was a puzzled mask and her brows were knitted together.

She had heard him say, 'my darling girl' but still she was not quite sure that she had heard it right. Not only was Mike's voice softer, but his eyes looked different too. 'My darling girl', that's what he had said when she had saved him. Mike had never uttered anything like that in his entire life, but Louis had called her that and had written those words on her writing pad in her bedroom yesterday evening. He had taken her to his kingdom and they were near total intimacy until Mike and Debs had interrupted their lovemaking.

That feeling of anger returned for a moment at the thought of the disrespect Mike had shown her, bringing that woman back to her home. Using her home like a hotel, to make love to another woman, a woman with whom she worked, how could he? And then this happened.

The last half hour had been the worst of her life; she had just spent what seemed like an eternity trying to save Mike from choking on the salted nuts she had put out for him while she prepared the meal. He was her lodger and had been her lover but their relationship had broken down. She had been going to ask him to leave, to go back to his bedsit. At least that had been the plan, but fate had taken over. The offending bowl of nuts sat on the table in front of them. She averted her eyes. How small and insignificant they appeared. Yet their impact had brought her to this, whatever this was. What had happened?

The last months had been difficult, Mike had displayed behaviour that had become impossible to live with. When she wasn't angry with him, she was afraid of him. She had become worn-down with his attitude and his drinking. They had been a couple well before she had asked if he wanted to live with her and share the rent. It was all working out, until he started drinking and the bullying started. She had never seen that side of him until he came to live with her. He seemed to need to prove his manhood by constantly demanding favours from her, usually when he had been drinking.

And then, this evening, what had made him fill his mouth with so many nuts? She could still smell the whiskey on him. It all happened so fast; one minute he had been sitting at the table cramming his mouth with nuts and the next he had fumbled with the cup that seemed to leap out of his hands spilling scalding hot coffee over his legs. The sudden movement, jumping up in pain, caused him to gulp down the nuts. They blocked his gullet. She had watched him fight for breath; she had watched the colour of his face change from red to purple; she had watched his eyes bulge. It was horrifying. He fell to the floor where she tried to revive him. Very quickly, he lost his ability to breathe. She did what she could and punished his back with her fist trying to dislodge the offending blockage; and she thought she had saved him.

The last fisted blow on his back had cleared his throat; she had seen the nuts spew out of his mouth but Mike hadn't come back, at least not her Mike. They were not his eyes and the voice was not Mike's either.

But how could her ghost, her Louis, be there in front of her? It wasn't possible.

Louis was sitting on a chair that was less than comfortable, in a body that wasn't his and yet, here he was, with a beating heart and lungs pumping air, giving him life, and he was breathing.

By some strange magic, all the wishing and yearning he'd had over the years had been granted. He had longed to be mortal, to be given another

3

chance at life. He had longed to be living or dead but be spared of the limbo he was locked in. His head was in a spin, it was the craziest thing and he didn't know why or how it had happened but, somehow, he had become mortal again.

Now it had become a reality. He was alive.

He reminded himself of what it had been like, watching the years passing, when the pain of loneliness and of being disconnected from the human race had nearly driven him mad, if, of course, it was possible for a ghost to become insane.

At the turn of the last century, Marina had come into his unusual existence. She had bought the bed, not realising he came with it. She was recovering from a romantic betrayal, a condition he knew all too well.

In her grief, tossing and turning one night with the night terrors, he had touched her. By some magic they had blended and he entered her dreams. He became her guardian angel, saving her from despair. And, as luck would have it, one of the girls whom Marina had saved from the workhouse had second sight. Through Rosa he was able to communicate again. He was the secret that Marina and Rosa kept. They had made his existence bearable and worthwhile. After that, he had always blended with mortals when they were in danger and had left smoothly without damaging them. He had never had trouble in leaving their bodies; no one had ever died.

The last time Louis had blended with a mortal was almost sixty years ago when Marina's daughter, Lucy, had been in serious danger of being killed by a demon. Her boyfriend, Mark, had become possessed. Louis had come to her aid, and blended with her when she was at the edge of unconsciousness. His spiritual body and Lucy's mortal body became one. What she felt, he felt. Louis could feel the hands of Mark around her slender neck and he felt the pressure of those hands that were squeezing the life force from her.

Louis had given her his strength to fight the crazed boy who was trying to murder her. Jealousy, hate and anger had blinded Mark to the reality of his actions, his raw emotions had opened up a rift in the thin fabric that separated his dimension from the hellish world in which demons dwelt.

His hatred had called the demon and his soul had allowed the evil spectre to enter him to feed on his hate. Lucy's fear became an extra source of nourishment and the devil tried to harm the girl that Mark loved.

With Louis' help she fought off the demon until her family rescued her. But for Louis she would have died. Lucy and Mark had become the demon's victims. When Mark came to his senses, he couldn't understand what had happened to him and couldn't believe he had tried to kill her.

Louis had loved Marina right up to the time when she had passed into the next life. It was just a few hours after Rosa, his voice and friend, had also died, taken by influenza. His role in his nether-life had ended after that. He had forced his own self-exile in his netherworld, bound to his bed. But that was all in the past. It was the world in which he had slept until Katie found him. She roused him from his world behind the wooden veil of his bed and he found love again.

Now, his chest was rising and falling as his lungs filled with air. He touched his chest with the flat of his hand and he could feel the heart tapping out a regular beat under it. Should he shout with joy at his release from his constricted world he had lived in or cry at the knowledge that Mike had had to die for him to live?

It had not been his intention for this to happen, he had wanted to help Mike. He had just been too late when he merged with him; just too late to save him. As Mike passed, leaving his earthly shell behind, his body had somehow coupled with Louis before he could leave it; Louis had become trapped once again, this time in living flesh. He had become locked into Mike's body in Katie's world.

Was this a granted wish? Had God decided, after all this time, that he had suffered enough and deserved a new start? But he had never wanted life at the expense of someone else losing theirs. He shook his head, trying to make sense of it all.

But to no avail; it had happened so suddenly and he wasn't ready for it.

He had no idea whether the body he was in now would accept him or reject him. Would he ever be able to see his own world, that world he had carved and created behind the wooden curtain again?

He shivered: this body he was in was still coping with the shock. He wondered how permanent his stay in this complicated bag of bones would be. Was it temporary? If so, for how long? He had tried to expel himself from this living shroud, but couldn't. Would he be able to live a full measure of years, perhaps three score and ten and die an old man? Who knew?

He was trapped again, a prisoner. He shook his head sadly; would he be able to adapt to a life that was once again beyond his control?

Louis felt as though he was wearing six topcoats. This body weighed a ton; it was so heavy compared to the spiritual body he had had. For years he had moved easily. Now, he was carrying such a great weight around him, he felt overwhelmed. And this new feeling was not one he was sure he liked.

Along with coming to terms with the weightiness of his cocoon, he was painfully aware of new sensations erupting inside this new prison. His throat was raw; the surface of tender skin inside his mouth pained him each time he swallowed. Of course, it was tender, what else could he expect? He had watched the accident happen, had seen it all before he blended with Mike. The burning sensation in his groin, where the hot coffee had spilled on Mike's lap, stung him where the still wet trousers touched the skin. He saw on the table the small dish of nuts; they were sharp edged and abrasive, they must have cut into the delicate flesh of the throat and gullet, which he could now feel. The nuts must have had the effect of coarse sandpaper, rubbing and scraping on the delicate skin; and that was now something he had to cope with. Each swallow was a reminder to Louis of the fear that Mike must have felt in the last few minutes up to his death.

He looked across the table at Katie. Her brown eyes were open wide and troubled, staring back at him in a kind of trance. If only he could read her thoughts. He acknowledged that she must be in shock too; what had just happened was shocking indeed. It was not every day that a ghost changes place with a mortal. Shock then, not only at Mike's passing but also at the astonishing fact that she was sitting near a man who looked like him but whom she knew in her heart was Louis.

He shook his head very slightly again. His poor Katie must be struggling with this strange situation. She was still red-eyed from the tears she had shed while trying to save Mike's life; the strain of it all lay heavily on her and it showed.

He reached across the table, taking her hand. It was cold and stiff with the tension that she was holding. He squeezed it gently, offering comfort. Feeling the smoothness of her skin, he was aware of another new sensation but one he could not linger over, not now.

"My darling girl," he began, but he never finished the sentence because on hearing those his words, she gulped hard, trying to stop the dam of emotion from erupting from her heart. But it was no good; tears rolled uncontrollably down her face. She was confused, hurting and frightened. Those words, so old-fashioned in her world had been so right in her dreams; he had been so right in her dreams. It all seemed so out-of-place coming out of the mouth of this man who now sat at her kitchen table. Was it real and not a dream? Was she hallucinating?

The full impact of what had occurred was so shocking that she was finding it hard to take in. Her logic and emotions were at odds. She was still rejecting what her sixth sense was telling her.

The tenderness of his touch and the look of concern in his eyes could never be Mike's. She knew in her heart of hearts that this man with Mike's face who sat opposite her was Louis, her ghostly lover who belonged to her dreams not her reality.

Her whole body was gripped in deep, gulping sobs; her hands covered her face, her shoulders heaved with each breath, her head sank onto her arms onto the table. She cried, not knowing where all the tears were coming from, and she cried until the cistern emptied.

Louis had no choice but to wait patiently until the eruption of tears subsided; he sat uncomfortably, anxious, picking at his nails, unable to find any words of comfort to give to Katie.

After what seemed like an eternity, her body stilled and the sobbing stopped. She took a deep breath and steadied herself as she lifted her head and sat up ready to face him and the awfulness of the situation.

Her hands came slowly down from her face, revealing puffy eyes that looked red and sore. Her turned-up nose was damp and inflamed. Feeling totally out of his depth, all Louis could do was pass her a paper napkin from the table for her to wipe her face. She felt drained and completely exhausted.

The man looked back at her with tenderness as he waited for her to regain composure and she responded with half a smile and a nod of her head, acknowledging that she was ready to face whatever she must face.

She needed to think clearly; what was it she thought had happened? Could it be true? In denial, she shivered and looked into his eyes again, those eyes didn't belong to Mike.

At last, she found her tongue. Her first question was simple enough. "Are you, are you…?" She stopped trying to choose the right words. Awkwardly, she continued,

"Are you Louis…? What happened tonight?"

She suddenly felt huge sympathy for Louis. His face was grey and there was an unsteady tremor in his voice when he answered her question.

"I don't know what happened. I just knew I needed to assist him." He remembered sadly the events from yesteryear, and never expected to be trapped. Mike had left. When he did, it sealed Louis' spirit in the shroud that it left behind.

Once again, like so many years before, he found himself trapped in a situation over which that he had no control. Firstly, by his beautiful bed and now this.

She sat in silence as he recounted the story, listening intently as he continued.

"I hoped to clear the blockage in Mike's throat, that's why I blended with him. I only wanted to help. Once I was within his body, I saw that his light was moving on, it faded to a tiny spark, and then it was gone and I realised I couldn't help. I was too late." He continued.

"You were doing all you could on the outside, I knew that. You couldn't know it was all in vain; I felt an almighty thump on his back that reverberated through his body and into mine. Immediately, the peanuts that blocked his airway were dislodged and expelled, clearing his throat, but Mike was gone. His heart and lungs became mine, I struggled desperately to release myself from him but I couldn't escape his body. For the first time in many a year, I involuntarily took a breath of fresh air. It doesn't seem right, but it would appear I'm trapped here, in this."

He shrugged, raising his hands and pointed to himself. He couldn't hide the anxiety on his face, nor the smell of whiskey on his breath as he wriggled uncomfortably on the kitchen chair.

His mind was racing; this was everything he had wished for over the years. To live, to be mortal, to breathe once again. To feel, to touch. Now it had happened, in this most unforeseen and tragic way, he wasn't sure he was ready for all the complications that he faced. His darling girl would help he was sure of it. Thank goodness she was here. She was strong and kind. He would need help to adapt to life for the transition from spirit to mortal had been so sudden; if, indeed, this shroud that hugged his soul didn't reject him.

He didn't belong in the twentieth century, but here he was. She could help him adjust but that would only be a small part of the problems he would face.

Through the years of watching, observing people in all the different decades, he had learnt many things. But Katie's world changed so fast. He would be something like a filly in a race, blinkered to the other horses, charging on and on to some point in the future, not quite knowing the destination. It was fascination and frightening.

But knowing about it and living it… how was he to manage?

He was feeling strange.

"Could I have some water, please?" His soft voice croaked and he held his neck.

Katie could see his distress and brought him a glass immediately. His throat was horribly sore, his head ached and he was feeling light headed.

"God in heaven, what's happening to me?"

The kitchen was starting to swim. The body he was in was doing things that were out of his control and it was heavy and uncomfortable.

"Am I going to pass out?"

Fear started to tear into him, even with Katie by his side. Was he going to be able to cope in this landscape of an uncertainty? What was he to do?

He loved her so much and she had only just accepted who he was. Events had overtaken them again, and now his fear extended to her not being able to cope with his new identity. Would she be able to see beyond the skin and bone and the face that belonged to Mike? Would it stop her seeing him? He couldn't bear the thought of losing her.

The water seemed to have done the trick; he was less light-headed but something else was happening to him, something that he felt he should recognise but that he only had a vague, half-remembered memory of in the back of his mind. There was pain in his mid-section, and a grumbling sound from deep within his body was audible from behind the well-exercised six-pack of muscles that had belonged to Mike. His belly was hurting him. His hands had left his neck and were now placed over the noise that refused to quieten. Am I ill? Thought Louis. It was a new experience, another first and one he could do without.

The gurgling sounds of an empty stomach were not lost on Katie.

"Oh dear," she said, more to herself than Louis, "you must be famished."

She didn't wait for an answer; her practical side took over. She stood up and made herself busy at the kitchen counter. He watched her as she chopped onions and garlic, putting them in a small pan with a light olive oil, gently stirring as the heat took hold and the aroma of fried onions filled the air. Her back was to him; he couldn't see her face as she worked. She turned once to look at him; he thought maybe she was about to ask him something. The silence was eerie. While he sat there, she chopped fresh tomatoes and sprinkled dried basil over them before she slid them into the pan. Still stirring and talking to the wall, she asked in a subdued tone,

"What am I to call you?"

She half turned then, perhaps to see his reaction, before continuing. "I can't call you Mike and yet."

She stopped, fumbling for words. He knew it was difficult for her to see the face of Mike and yet know he was gone.

"Food first and then, well, we will see how we are going to sort this out, if," and as an afterthought, she added, "if we can."

His stomach growled loudly again, Hunger! That was it! That was the memory that had eluded him, the sensation of an empty belly. It had been decades since he needed to eat. He had almost forgotten mortal bodies needed food to survive.

Katie boiled the kettle and made him a hot milky tea, laced with plenty of sugar; that was sure to help with his shock and allay the shivering. She put the white mug of hot liquid in front of him and told him to drink up.

"It will do you good," she added in good measure, before turning back to her cooking. His hands gratefully slid around the ceramic container, enjoying the heat from it seeping into his hands. For a moment, he took pleasure from it before he brought the mug to his mouth, testing it on his lips before he tentatively sipped. It was good and, although his mouth was sore, the warm drink was comforting. He drank it eagerly; it temporarily stopped the grumbling in his stomach. The warmth hit the pit of his belly and radiated out into all the regions of his body. The shivering stopped.

Food and drink, so necessary for the living, had been unnecessary for him in spirit. He had been able to smell food throughout his bondage, and he fondly remembered Rosa's kitchen in Marina's home, fresh bread coming out of the oven, bacon for the girls' breakfasts. He had enjoyed all the aromas of it. Now the sizzling of the cooking sauce and the bubbling of the boiling foodstuff in the large pan made him eager for the experience of eating again. His growling belly moaned once more and his mouth was filling with watery substance; he was salivating in anticipation. He had forgotten that response as well!

Katie was finishing off the half-prepared meal, grating cheese, which she placed in a small dish with a spoon to sprinkle over the pasta and set it on the table. She stirred the saucepan one last time before readying a large colander in the sink to drain it. Louis watched her take two deep bowls from the cupboard and place them on the counter, ready to serve the meal. His eyes drifted up to the clock on the wall behind her: 8pm.

He could hardly believe that only an hour had passed since the accident; the accident that had changed everything. Their lives had altered forever. If only Mike had not passed, Louis would be back in his kingdom behind the carved headboard, still wishing for mortality; and waiting for the night to come and Katie's visit. He had never thought he would live again.

His kingdom was still there, hidden behind the carving he had made as a love token; it was the place he had shared love with Katie and it was she who had brought extra life to it. He wondered if he would he ever be able to go there again?

He was brought back from his thoughts, back to his new reality, when a steaming bowl of tomato sauce, red and hot sitting in a nest of pasta strings, was placed down in front of him. This was a dish that was entirely new to him, a dish his taste buds would experience for the first time. Hunger demanded that he devour it without any qualms.

"Would you like grated cheese?" she asked, offering him a small dish that contained fine shavings of creamy coloured cheese and a serving spoon. He took it and sprinkled a little of it over his meal.

As Katie took her first mouthful of food, she spotted the little bowl of nuts, half empty, set back on the table. Their impact now engulfed them both. Quickly, and silently, she snatched up the bowl and whisked it away, secreting it at the back of the cupboard. She would deal with it later, right now they didn't need it as a reminder while they ate.

The meal passed in silence, in part because of the event that had just taken place, in part because Louis was enjoying all the different flavours that were bursting on his tongue and exciting his taste buds. Even swallowing with a sore throat was temporarily forgotten.

It had been so long since he had tasted food or felt its texture that his senses were totally overwhelmed. Unable to curb his enthusiasm, he exclaimed with delight.

"Oh, Katie, this is wonderful. I had forgotten the simple pleasure of eating and this food is so good."

Smiling, Katie looked at him. She was pleased with the compliment, despite a sadness she was nursing. She hoped the food would help them think clearly. For, God only knew, this was an extraordinary situation.

"It's just a simple meal but I'm glad you like it."

"My darling girl, do you know how long it's been since I've tasted food? Just the act of eating, that essential part of living which you take for granted, is for me, who has spent years and years unable to experience it, pure magic."

The rest of the meal was eaten in equal silence, their bodies restored by each mouthful of hot food. Their strength was slowly returning, but when at last their bowls were empty, they found they were both at a loss to find the words to start the conversation they must have. The silence was heavy and awkward. When, Katie finally decided to speak, she sighed, it was almost deafening in the strained atmosphere but speak she must.

"What are we going to do now?"

It was a simple question with no obvious answer.

She tried to be logical, moving through the facts as she saw them.

"Mike's gone, but you have his body. There is no body to bury. If we assume that you are, as you say, trapped in that body, maybe you will have to be Mike, until," she stopped speaking, "until when, I'm not sure."

She was wringing her hands. Her hand went to her mouth; from behind it she whispered, "What are we going to do?" She looked desperately at Louis but he just shook his head slowly.

"I think for tonight we should not think too hard about it. Tomorrow, when we have had some rest, we may find some answers. And you, my darling girl, are still in shock and I don't know how long this body will allow me to use it."

Katie was not used to giving in at times of trouble. She responded fiercely.

"We should stay positive and think that you will be able to stay in Mike's body indefinitely. Mike can't come back to claim his body and you are breathing and speaking and moving like you own it. From that premise, I think we should make some plans, don't you? And tonight. We won't sleep, otherwise." she declared in a confident voice that hid her real fears.

He nodded in agreement; they would indeed have to have a plan. Some explanation would be required to account for what had happened. What was going to happen? he thought to himself. Right now, he was tired, and he may not have a body by morning. The body had recovered now that he had eaten, but to think of a future was impossible. He smiled at her, wanting to give her a reassurance that he didn't feel. He must try at least to act normally tonight; what came tomorrow would come, no matter how much he worried. Right now, he was with the woman he loved and he would treasure every moment with her as though it was his last, for it may be just that.

2

Clearing up after the evening meal was also done in silence. Neither had anything to say; neither was ready to face what must be faced. Katie swept up the dirty dishes and stood at the sink, running hot water into a bowl.

The foamy suds hid the dishes when she immersed them; the pans were waiting on the side to be cleaned next. She donned a pair of yellow, plastic gloves and was busily washing up when Louis came to her side, armed with a tea towel.

"I can do them," she said, a half-smile on her face, looking up at him through her dark-brown eyes. All the redness from crying had gone, her eyes were bright and shining again.

"I know," he responded, "This is my way of saying thank you."

She nodded in acceptance; it was good to be appreciated.

He was standing so close to her that he could smell the light floral perfume she was wearing. The fluorescent light cast a warm light that shone on her thick, chestnut hair. He had an urge to run his fingers through it, but knew how inappropriate that would be as she stood there with her hands deep in washing-up water. He felt comfortable beside her, despite the ordeal from earlier that evening, and he didn't want to spoil the moment with a hasty gesture. He knew he was in danger of being too forward. Right at that moment, he longed to touch her, he wanted to feel her smooth skin under his fingers, to kiss her, to feel her hair and kiss her neck, to hold her tight and never let her go.

His heart beat a little faster; it was so unlike the time they had spent in his sheltered world behind the wooded veil. In his kingdom he had felt in control; here, he had no control at all.

His thoughts in this man's body made it respond as only a man's body does, with a stiffness growing in his loins, an urge he must repress. Another memory stirred from the depths of his mind. It was another response he would have to get used to.

Would she allow him to get close? he wondered. Somehow, he had to break the ice and the silence. It seemed to be driving a wedge between them right now.

"Well, that's finished," she said with a committed voice, "shall we go and find a comfortable chair and try to make some sense of what has happened?"

He discarded the tea towel. The food had done the trick, his new body was free from shock; now fully fortified, his blood was coursing through his veins like that of any virile young man.

He had been about to encircle her waist with his arms and pull her towards him but instinctively he knew it wasn't the right moment, no matter how much he felt the need. He must bide his time.

He must gather himself and try to find a way forward in this new, scary world into which he had been propelled. When he touched her, it would be with a touch of warmth and sincere love.

She made them cups of hot, black coffee and topped the dark liquid with cold milk before ushering him along into the main living room. Coffee had been a luxury in his day and not a drink he was familiar with. The larger cities, like London, had coffee houses but for people of his station they were off limits. Now, he was to have his first taste of it.

They sat looking at each other over the coffee table with their hot drinks in front of them. Tentatively, he took a sip from the plain white mug, and was surprised. The smell and the taste were quite different in character. The aroma invited you to drink and taking a sip was an experience of a bitter, rich, satisfying liquid, that he could definitely get used to.

She watched his face. An expression of surprise and satisfaction registered as he drank. She realised that something she took for granted, like a simple cup of coffee, was a new experience for him. How many new experiences would he have before he was comfortable in this age that she lived in? she wondered.

How to begin? It was so awkward to start the conversation. Sitting before her was the human shell of Mike, her sometimes-lover and lodger. A man she knew well in every sense. But now he had different mannerisms. The way he moved his head, the body language was so different. His eyes were kind and he had a face that expressed care. The more she looked at him over the short time that they talked together, the more she could swear that even his face was changing to look more like Louis, the man of her dreams.

When it was coming up to midnight and several coffees later, they were exhausted and decided to call it a day. They had gone over and over what had happened and they had managed to agree on the obvious. Mike was dead and there was nothing they could do about it. They couldn't report his passing to the police because there was no body.

Mike didn't have any relatives that she knew of and he certainly had never talked about any uncles or aunts. He had been an only child of deceased parents that she assumed were only children too, though she didn't really know. At least, no relatives would miss him, now he was gone.

Unfortunately, that couldn't be said when it came to the workplace. There, Mike would be missed. Her colleagues would soon ask questions if he was absent from the office for too long.

Louis would find it difficult to find his way around the habits and customs of this mid-twentieth century. The written language had changed but he had adapted to the spoken word as he had travelled through time watching and listening to this world from his world around the bed.

Was it possible he could replace Mike at work? Katie felt that was hardly feasible. And it seemed so dishonest to think that way, disrespectful to Mike's spirit.

Oh my God, what are we to do? She thought.

It was time for bed, perhaps the morning would bring answers? A good night's sleep would revive them, but how was she to say goodnight to Louis? It was so strange; almost like being in the company of a stranger who wasn't a stranger. The familiar body-shape of Mike with the compassion of Louis joined together making a new person.

There was shyness in her approach when she suggested that it was time to go to bed.

She would go upstairs first. Louis would follow, but she would put him in Mike's bedroom. She felt she must get to know him all over again before she recommitted herself. She hoped he would understand, and maybe he would prefer that tonight as well.

Louis' heart dropped. He was disappointed when Katie pointedly said goodnight outside the door of Mike's bedroom, and although there was warmth about her, there was no kiss.

He needed reassurance and comfort from her, but acknowledged how she felt. The situation was new and uncomfortable for both of them, but understanding it did not subdue his sadness nor take away his anxiety. He didn't argue, but it was an awful feeling, being separated from her and from his own blessed kingdom, which was hidden away behind the wooden veil, empty and waiting for his return. He suddenly missed his creation. The Tree of Life abundant in fruits, the birds, and the babbling stream. The vast meadow and his purple mountain, which sat on the horizon of his world, the hidden cottage that he had never needed for shelter now, in a moment of grief, he longed to see again.

It was with a heavy heart that he climbed into bed wearing Mike's pyjamas and pulled the cotton duvet up over his body. This world of cold and heat, of life and death, the world he had missed so much, was losing its appeal without Katie beside him.

'I may be Louis,' he thought,' but I look like Mike.'

How else could he expect Katie to react to that fact? His logic, however sound, couldn't douse the anxiety in his heart, as he lay in that cold bed waiting for sleep. There it was again, another thing to get used to. Mortals needed to sleep. He hoped that when sleep enveloped him, he would at least forget the pain of the situation for a little while.

But sleep didn't come; too much coffee, perhaps, or the strangeness of a modern bed. Instead, memories of the past whirled around him like ghosts. The irony was not lost on him.

His history of over a hundred years stretched out behind him and brought back memories of the women he had loved: Sophia, Marina and now Katie. She had bought the bed, innocent to the fact that he came with it, and now she was asleep in it, all alone. His spirit and the bed had never been separated from the time he died, and now another death had split them up.

He remembered the laughter and giggling that Katie and he had heard when Mike brought Debs back to this room, this room that he lay in now. Katie was with him in his kingdom behind the wooden veil; they were finally about to make love when they were interrupted by the laughter from Debs. The laughter penetrated his secret world and in doing so brought Katie out of her dream, woke her and drew her back into her own reality. Was that the catalyst that had brought all these events to a head?

He sighed. 'If only' was such an obvious choice of words to describe some folly that might not have happened. If only Mike had been more discreet; if only Debs's laughter had not been so loud; if only they had made love before the drunken couple had arrived back; if only, if only, if only!

The bedside clock sat on the side table next to the bed, reminding him how late it was. One o'clock and the tick was a bother to his ear. He had lain for an hour now and sleep didn't seem to want to relieve his plight. It was the same clock he had elevated, the same clock he had used to frighten Mike a few weeks ago. Mike had been so boorish, rude, in a drunken state, and had frightened the life out of Katie with his threats and his sexual overtures. Mike didn't know it was Louis; he probably thought he was hallucinating with all the booze he had put away. He certainly had been no gentleman that night and Louis wasn't sorry for his actions. Mike had deserved to be scared and that was all there was to it.

There seemed to be no rest for him, either as a ghost or a mortal. He turned over yet again, his eyes away from the clock. Its ticking, in the middle of the night, was like a monotonous drum beat, deafening and reducing his chance to sleep. He reached for the quilt; the cold of the night had inched its way through his nightclothes and he was shivering again. He wrapped the soft quilt around his cold body feeling the warmth from the goose feathers. It spread from his head to toe.

After a few short minutes, he moaned as yet another new experience faced him; his bladder was full. A call of nature dragged him urgently up from his bed and along to the bathroom.

He trotted hastily onto the landing, passing Katie's door. He was just in time. He felt the relief and comfort of an empty bladder and promised himself he would not ignore what his body was telling him in future.

He was returning to his room, being as quiet as he could, mindful of Katie sleeping, when he thought he heard a stifled sob coming from behind her closed door. He moved nearer to listen, and a muffled sound confirmed that she was sobbing in her pillow and tears were falling freely.

Should he tap on her door or leave her alone? He thought that he should at least see if she was alright and put his hand on the handle ready to open it. But the sound of sobbing stopped. Perhaps she settled down to sleep? He paused; had he been wrong? But just as he was turning away, he heard another deep sob that encouraged him to tap lightly on the door.

"Can't you sleep either, my darling girl? Can I help?" For a minute there was silence then he heard the sound of muffled footsteps coming across the floor to the door, which opened just a few inches, revealing a strained-looking young woman. A teary-eyed Katie looked out at him, and the redness around her eyes told him she had been crying for some time.

"Oh, my dear girl, please don't cry. We will work it out somehow."

On that note, she flung the door fully open and threw herself into Louis' arms, grateful for his strength and concern.

At last, his arms tightened around Katie, his head nuzzling her hair as he did. Breathing in her unique scent, he whispered, "I'm here for you."

She clung to him, her distress ebbing away.

The sensation of touch was thrilling to him. He could feel the silkiness of her skin under the palms of his hands. There was an excitement, but it wasn't sexual. The excitement of feeling Katie in his arms, the smell of her skin and hair, feeling the warmth of her body, even the tear-stained face, was beautiful to him. Her slim frame was easily lifted in his arms. Gently, he lowered her onto the ruffled sheets of their bed. She was still clinging to him.

No words were needed; her hand held his, and a yearning look on her face said, 'Don't leave me alone.'

He kissed her forehead before slipping into the bed and laying down beside her.

How different this was from when they shared time in his kingdom. Gone was the dreamlike quality of touch; both bodies were now of real substance, lying together on the bed that had been made as a love token so long ago.

He knew now that it had become a token of his love for Katie.

He had not lain in the bed as a living, breathing person for over a century, but now it was wonderful to feel the solidness of the frame under his body.

He was a full-blooded male next to his darling girl. They lay together not speaking; words were not necessary. All they needed was to be with each other and share the comfort that they brought as their bodies entwined.

Katie's head fitted snugly onto his chest and under his chin; he held her body to himself in a protective gesture. They shared no kisses or passion that night, instead they allowed their bodies to touch tenderly and bond as they were locked together in the moment by their love, until, by some small miracle, they were both overcome by the blessing of sleep. It was two o'clock in the morning and Sunday was already here but there were a few hours left for sleep that night. They would rest until the light of morning. They would face the new day, whatever it brought, and they knew they would face it resolutely together.

The sunlight coming in from the window brought Louis up from the depths of sleep.

For a moment, he wondered where he was as he passed his tongue over his dry lips. His mouth felt parched, another new sensation for him to deal with; then opening his eyes he remembered the ordeal from the day before and the gravity of their situation.

He squinted at the brightness that shone on his face. The curtains hadn't been drawn the night before and the blue sky with a golden, low sun shone through the window and onto the bed. It brought a glow to the room. His eyes felt gritty from sleeping hard. Yawning, he stretched his back to release the stiffness from his shoulders. His hand touched his chin and felt the light stubble that had grown overnight, declaring softly under his breath, "God! I am alive." Not a dream, not a nightmare, a new reality.

Katie was still sleeping, lying on her stomach to his right. The duvet was pulled up high so that her face was half hidden from him under the crop of her chestnut hair; only the top of her head could be seen. He moved the hair that covered her forehead and kissed her tenderly. He was so grateful to have her beside him, whispering in her ear, "Are you awake, my darling girl?"

The words and the kiss brought her to the present. Here was her man beside her in the bed that she had not shared with anyone; his bed, their refuge. She reached up and kissed him on the lips.

The kiss that he returned was one of passion and longing. They had held back their true emotions the night before, tired and shocked with the rigours of the day and being more in need of solace than the needs of the body.

Nothing could dampen the feelings that they had for each other that morning and with passion pulsing through them, they embarked on a voyage to taste the fruits of love that only people truly in love can feel.

Still kissing her with ardour, his hand slid under the duvet and found her waiting for him. Her skin felt silky and warm under his touch; it sent a sensation like a mild electric shock through him. There was eagerness in her kiss and it urged him on. He kissed her neck, and she responded, her arms locked tightly around his shoulders drawing him closer. Her eagerness under his lips and hands brought a tightening to his loins like it had the night before; his manhood hardened, he had no control over this, his body was interpreting his desires whether he liked it or not. And right at that moment he desired no more than what was happening to the both of them.

Katie was wearing a cream, satin nightdress with narrow straps; they slipped off her shoulders when she sat up or moved about, it always annoyed her. But not this morning; sitting up, she knew that her soft skin would be revealed to him. This morning, she wanted him to love her and she wanted to enjoy the passion of the man she loved. As the straps slipped down, the view of her breasts was tantalising. Louis was being given an invitation to share lovemaking with her.

Somehow, she wriggled out of her silky nightdress while still enjoying the foreplay that was going on between them. Then, she took it upon herself to unbutton the pyjamas that Louis was wearing. He didn't need coaxing; and helped her to free him from the clothing.

For a moment, all petting stopped, as both of them took a long look at each other, drinking in the perfection they saw. In silent agreement, both were ready to commit their souls and bodies to their love.

The gentle petting and moist, full kisses became more passionate as the minutes passed. They allowed their love to flow between them; they sank deep into the bed, half-hidden under the duvet, in the semi-darkness they touched and found ways of pleasure that eventually led to a perfect union between them. His touch was unlike anything Katie had ever known before; it had her shivering with delight and passion, never wanting the petting to stop and yet there was a greater need for the climax that grew stronger with every kiss and caress. They were as one, each concerned to please the other; the love that flowed between them was flawless and when at last they reached their zenith they were spent. They had scaled to a higher spiritual plane that would join them forever.

Making love was all it should have been; tender, passionate and gifting each other a piece of their souls. They allowed themselves the luxury of lying together, enjoying the quiet of the morning while the embers of passion were still burning, knowing that the love they had shared had become even deeper.

It was after ten o' clock when Louis and Katie managed to pull themselves reluctantly apart from making love. It had been a time of renewal for them, a moment spent lost in a space where time didn't matter or exist. But like all good things, it came to an end. Whether it was the sound of the church bells ringing in the distance, calling its people to prayer, or the sudden realisation that half the morning had gone, neither knew. It might even have been hunger, their bodies calling for food after the activities of the morning. Whatever, they must leave the warm bed to get ready for the day.

Neither one of them wanted to break the spell between them but there was no getting away from the problems that they were facing. A way must be found to solve them, and today.

Louis was first to rise, kissing Katie lightly on her nose. He pulled himself up and rolled from the bed, patting the headboard as he did, thanking God that Katie had found him in that second-hand store all those months ago. He dressed in the discarded pyjamas that lay strewn on the carpet and strode over to the window gazing out into the garden. The sun was low, reminding him that winter was coming; but it looked fresh and sharp out there, the sky a cornflower blue. It was the start of autumn and the trees were changing colour of their leaves, turning to glorious reds, oranges and gold. The world somehow looked better to him this morning.

Making love had given her strength; it had been a good way to start the morning, just what she needed. Leaving Louis gazing out onto the garden, Katie silently slipped out of the room to get washed and dressed. It was odd, she thought to herself, that she had forgotten that the spirit of Louis and the shell of Mike were joined and that she had not seen Mike at all in that handsome face she had kissed, because it had subtly changed and the eyes were all Louis; strangely she had never realised how facially alike they had been until now.

3

The bathroom felt warm and cosy, and there was a feeling of satisfaction throughout her body that she had never felt before. That was how making love should be she told herself. Looking in the mirror that hung over the basin, she could see her reflection; it glowed, her face was flushed with life, smiling coyly at the precious thoughts that were popping into her head when she remembered the last few hours.

It was a miracle, however it had happened, she told herself before she washed her face and cleaned her teeth; how could she be so happy? A sudden thought invaded her happiness. The scene of Mike choking came back all too clearly; his bloated face and bulging eyes formed an image she was unlikely ever to forget. Her smile disappeared, a frown wrinkled her forehead, how could she be so callous? It was only yesterday that he had died. And yet, Mike had given her Louis, his sacrifice had brought Louis back into the mortal world. Her flashback brought sadness; she had never wanted Mike to die but her underlying feeling was gratitude.

Patting her face dry on the thick pile of the towelling, that question of Mike and how to deal with his passing had to be solved and solved today. She threw her shoulders back, straightened up, and the straps of her satin nightdress slipped off her shoulders. Again, she remembered that morning and smiled. Across the hall, her bedroom door was ajar, she pushed it open. It startled Louis and he turned to see Katie, half-in half-out, telling him that the bathroom was all his. She blew him a kiss, he pretended to catch it and blew one back just as she disappeared from view, the sound of her feet receding down the staircase.

His eyes went back to the garden; the grass, the trees, the shrubs; the multitude of autumn colours heightened his senses. A new world was out there, perhaps waiting for him. His thoughts were about this reality; his old reality was locked away out of reach. The garden, with its low morning sun, beckoned to him. His heart quickened, beating a little faster at the thought that now he would be able to go out, breathe in the cool autumn air and feel the warmth of a weak sun on his face. He would be able to take a walk, uncoupled from his bed, away from the house, something he had not been able to do since his own death. He was free.

He moved now, as he heard Katie downstairs; she hadn't come back into the room to dress, so he supposed she was making breakfast. The noise of a kettle on the boil and the sound of plates and cutlery being moved around drifted up from below; he imagined her still wearing her satin nightdress. It was his turn to smile; the memories of her wriggling out of it and helping him undress was a pleasing thought, almost too pleasing; this body responded.

Before using the bathroom, he went to get some clothes from Mike's bedroom. It felt strange walking down the hall in pyjamas that belonged to Mike. It was odd visiting the room, a room that didn't belong to him, but one he knew from when he was a ghost. Suddenly, it hit him, hard, like a punch to the stomach, the dreadful awkwardness of the situation that Katie and he were in. He almost felt winded. Dread visited him; the fear of not knowing how long he would be allowed to live was a terrible unknown. This borrowed body he was in, was now filled with a frightened guest. He had no way out until it released him; he was trapped there.

He moved his thoughts on, thinking of Katie and their love and was glad he was alive; however long he had, he would treasure the minutes, hours and, with some luck, days with her. He crossed the room; the quilt was still squashed and crumpled on the bed just as he had left it the night before. Yes! He was alive again. The white wardrobe beckoned him to open it, to select his clothes for the day. It pained him, pushing the clothes apart to view them; they hung so neatly, on their wooden hangers; he rummaged through them for trousers and a shirt. He felt like a grave robber, that he was soiling his hands with each brush of his palm against the fabrics of Mike's clothes. He knew it was no good thinking that way, but what choice was there? He needed to be clothed. In the end, he chose a blue shirt and denim jeans, carrying them along with the jumper he had worn the night before over his arm to the bathroom, his inner thoughts still rolling uncomfortably around in his head.

What an amazing age this twentieth century was. The magic of this century was all there in that small room where cold water and hot water came through with just with the turn of a tap. People no longer trekked outside in all weathers or in the middle of the night to visit the water closet; now they were right here in the house. The clay or ash toilets of yesteryear were gone. With a degree of nostalgia, he remembered the wooden plank to sit on with a hole in it and a bucket beneath. Oh yes, he remembered and the smell during hot summers; he wrinkled his nose in disgust.

Standing in the clean and fresh-smelling bathroom, he eyed the bath. A mirror on a cabinet above a green basin flashed in the light from the window. It was a shock; there he was. A version of Mike looked back at him. The eyes were his; 'mirrors of the soul,' that was what was said of them. He saw a shadow of himself in that face, Mike and he had been facially not so different; if he could see that, he hoped that Katie could see it too.

Ready to bathe, he turned on the taps, and felt the water run through his fingers. Both cold at first, then slowly the warmth came, quickly turning to hot. He dashed the plug into the plughole and waited, watching it fill. He stripped off the pyjamas and stepped into deepening swirling water. The water lifted around his body the heat from it tingling his skin as it washed over his naked body. It was marvellous.

Resting in a dish was a cake of soap, different in shape and texture from the soap in his day; it had a fresh smell that he couldn't put a name to. He enjoyed lathering up his body and then immersing himself in the water to rinse it off. Twenty minutes later he was clean and refreshed and lay enjoying the soak.

His thoughts suddenly flipped back in time, to the last occasion he had enjoyed the luxury of a warm water bath, the night he had died. Oh God! Why had he thought of that? He remembered he was bathing when Sophia decided to join him. He remembered pulling his feet up in the tin bath to make room for her. It had been a hot day and he had been exhausted; the bath that Sophia had prepared restored his energy and mood. They had eaten a light supper of cheese, salad and baked bread and they shared love in their bed before he had fallen into a deep sleep. He was asleep when she had killed him with the bread knife. He didn't remember any pain but the blood he shed had been caught and trapped in the wood. His spirit trapped with it, and it became his prison.

What had brought it about he didn't know, some foolish notion in her head. She was feisty and sometimes downright destructive. He guessed her anger and jealousy had surfaced again and taken her over in the night. It was all long ago. He shook his head, trying to rid himself of the memories, too far back in time to affect him now. Maybe the thoughts of yesteryear upset him, but the insecurity of his position crept back and threw questions at him. Would he be able to stay in this body? He had only had use of it for less than twenty-four hours, but in that time he had eaten and drunk, made love, and it seemed to work perfectly well.

He smiled involuntarily, casting his mind back again to that morning. Yes, it had!

He was no longer a ghost, no longer trapped in his bed but had been gifted a body to use. He was committed to his new love and as long as he could maintain a mortal life, he was happy. Should the time come when he was rejected, he would always have his kingdom to return to.

A large white bath towel hung on a rail that was within his reach. He stepped out of the bath, pulling the plug out as he did, so that the water was swallowed up, disappeared down into the hungry mouth of the drain. Dripping wet, he steadied himself, holding on to the rail that held the towel. No planks of stained wood for him to stand on, or clippie rugs. The floor was smooth and he was careful not to slip on the linoleum tiles, under his feet it. It was soft and warm and, was very comfortable. Another first.

Rubbing his face dry he realised he had to do something about the growth on his chin. What was he to use? Mike must have some razors and brushes somewhere; he half-dressed and went back to the bedroom. A man's toiletry bag ablaze with pictures of sportsmen sat on the dresser. When he opened it, he found a badger hair lather brush, a dish of shaving soap and a square-shaped razor that was so unlike the cutthroats he knew, but it, was sharp and would do the job. Back in the bathroom he quickly finished his ablutions. He was buttoning up the top button of his shirt when the smell of bacon reached him.

That rumbling in his stomach he knew from yesterday reminded him once again that mortals needed to eat and he was ready. He made his way down to the kitchen tapping on the doorframe before entering.

The kitchen was heavy with the smell of cooking, the table was laid and hot toast was popping up from a machine as he entered the door. Katie had her back to him but, half-turning when he said hello, she greeted him with the biggest smile ever.

She must have been back upstairs when he was in the bathroom as she was wearing a tee shirt and a pair of jeans.

"Can you grab the toast and butter it before it goes cold, please?" asked Katie. "I'm just finishing off the eggs, sunny side up?" She questioned, her head cocked to one side waiting for an answer.

"Sunny side up?" A question was in his voice.

"Oh, sorry, I mean just fried and not turned over,"

"Sounds just good, whatever way." He relieved the toaster of its wares and buttered the toast, placing it on a plate already on the table.

Katie opened the warming drawer on the cooker and pulled out two plates that were half-covered with pink, thick-cut bacon, then proceeded to lift the eggs out from the frying pan and place them onto the waiting plates.

"Let's eat while it's still hot," said Katie, placing a pale green dinner plate with bacon, two eggs and tomatoes in front of Louis, and putting down her own plate with rather less bacon and only one egg. She gathered up a glass container with a silver plunger containing hot dark liquid, and pushing it all the way down, released the heavenly aroma of black coffee.

The mixture of smells in the kitchen made Louis realise he was, in fact, very hungry.

It reminded him of Rosa's kitchen, her cooking and the breakfasts she had prepared for the girls at the beginning of this century. Only this time, instead of watching other people eat, he would be able enjoy his first breakfast as a mortal with Katie.

By twelve o'clock the meal was over and they had finished clearing up. Katie had gone up to bathe. He could hear the bath running upstairs while he sat at the table finishing his coffee. He was pensive; there was much to resolve and he wasn't sure whether it was possible to find solutions to all the problems.

When she returned, she was wearing blue jeans and a loose jumper that graced her slim shape; her hair was still damp but had been styled back into a bob. She had a look of determination on her face, and her shoulders were squared as though she was ready to go into battle. Whatever they had to do, they would do, they weren't quitters.

"We had better write a list of all the things we need sort out," Katie said taking up a writing pad and finding a pen in the bottom of her handbag.

They moved to the sitting room and, just as they had done the night before, carried the hot coffee in with them; it sat once again in front of them on the table. They were ready.

4

Question one: Who would miss Mike? Katie and Mike worked at the local paper, the Hertfordshire Echo. Mike had been the sports journalist and she headed up the advertising section, selling space on the paper to local businesses. Their work colleagues were obviously at the top of the list; his contacts in sport came second. In an open-plan office everyone saw everyone, all the comings and goings. It was generally a happy place where fellow employees got on with their colleagues at the next desk. Certainly, Mac and Charlotte would miss his company as his desk was next to theirs. It was a small company, intimate even.

Katie remembered first seeing Mike. He was a handsome rascal who loved the ladies, enjoyed having a good-looking woman on his arm. He was a man's man, more at home with the boys down at the pub swapping tales over a pint. A Peter Pan character that couldn't grow up. He was also charming and fun-loving; most people liked him, some even envied him. He had good qualities, was attentive and fit well into the sporting set.

Katie enjoyed work, lapping up its pressures; it gave her challenges, and she met them. She was friendly but not gossipy, someone that could be trusted with a confidence. Mike had flirted with her at the office Christmas party, he made her feel special and it had quickly blossomed into a full romance. She had dated Mike for a year before he moved in. What a pity that Janet, her close friend and journalist at the paper, had moved away to take up a new post in Leeds. They had shared so much; for nearly four years they had lived together. First, in student accommodation and then, working at the Echo. They had shared this house and all the commitments that it brought. And they had had fun, lots of it. When Janet left, Katie had to find someone to share the costs. Mike had been the obvious choice but if Janet hadn't gone, this would never have happened.

Katie had had her doubts about asking him to share but she hadn't listened to her fears. Instead, as the weeks passed and their relationship grew deeper, she had come to believe they would get on. When she broached the subject of sharing, he was delighted, only too pleased to get out of the bedsit he was in and to be with a woman he cared for. But once he had settled in with her something changed, and whiskey, his chosen tipple, made him aggressive. When he drank, she became the subject of his outbursts and bullying.

Whether he had deliberately hidden his drinking from her when they were dating, she could only guess. With hindsight, she thought that he probably indulged himself when she had left his accommodation to return home. Out of sight, out of mind.

Two nights ago, in a pique of jealousy and revenge, he had invited Debs, their co-worker from the Echo, out on a date. It was designed to embarrass Katie because she had rejected his lustful advances.

Louis had visited Katie in her sleep and taken her to his kingdom. She had heard nothing of the drunken couple arriving; only when their laughter invaded Louis' space beyond the bedroom had they disturbed her, awakening her and pulling her back to her own bed in a state of frustration and disorientation. She had been so close to making love with Louis. She had been brought back to reality by the sound of a laugh that she had only heard at the office. Katie was dismayed at Mike's callousness. Going downstairs to the kitchen, she decided to embarrass them, letting them know she could hear their love-making. She played the radio on full volume and waited. She was standing making tea and toast when she felt a draught from the front door, and realised that they had both crept down and out into the night. Katie could only suppose they had gone to Debs's bedsit to continue their evening of booze and sex. Mike had purposely embarrassed her in her own home; she was sure that had been his intention all along, and he had used Debs as a pawn in his game.

Living with Mike had become so disastrous that she had made up her mind to ask him to leave. There was no trust any more on her part and his behaviour had been appalling for weeks. She had concluded it would have to be sooner rather than later; things could not go on as they were. She had decided she would tell him that Saturday when he got back from work.

The accident had happened on Saturday evening in the kitchen when Katie was in the throes of speaking to him. The hot coffee she had made to sober him up had spilled over him, scalding him as he sat at the table eating handfuls of peanuts.

Sadly, she thought he had probably hoped they would absorb the whiskey he had drunk. Instead, they were stuffed solid in his mouth, causing him to choke to death.

And that was where, the two of them now found themselves searching for a plan.

Question two was not so much a question, more an impossible hurdle they needed to clear. It might be that Louis would have to take on the role of being Mike, go into the office if only to be seen. Would Debs see the difference in the man, if Louis turned up at the Echo? And what about Mac and Charlotte? Would they see beyond his face? Mac and Mike were friends, not really close but close enough to go to the local pub and share a half together occasionally. Could they risk Mac noticing a change?

Question three was more straightforward. Mike had sublet his flat to a fellow workmate, a young salesman in Katie's department. Katie knew he was keen to have the tenancy; all she had to do was tell him that Mike and she were settling down together, and it was his. The deal was practically done.

Katie had done most of the talking; a few scribbled lines were on the paper but a lot of her thoughts were internal.

He knew she was struggling with the whole business. While he was struggling to come to terms with the new life he had been thrust into, she was trying to work out how they could live together with the unreal situation they were in.

"I can't bear the thought of using Mike's money, Louis. What are we to do?"

It was question four, another difficult one to deal with. Mike's salary was paid into his bank account and Mike had a standing order that paid his part of the rent to her. That would carry on as long as there was money in the account. But both of them knew Louis couldn't pretend to be Mike indefinitely. It felt as though they were plotting to rob a dead man, and that hurt.

How could they explain that Mike's body was still in use but his soul had passed on? People would think them mad. How could they explain Louis? It wasn't feasible. Together they decided that, for a short time at least Louis would have to pretend he was Mike. Katie only had the rest of the day to school Louis in some of Mike's habits. It seemed impossible.

"Katie, I can try to mimic Mike. I saw him every day, every day since you brought me here, my dear girl. I knew him and feel I could copy him well enough in walk and gestures. The language has changed, but even that I have learned through the years. We are in this together, my sweet. I must play my part."

She was silent for a minute and then nodded.

"Together then."

She picked up the half-forgotten coffee as though, it was wine, held it high. "So be it." Smiling, she captured his eyes and said, "Cheers."

It was fortunate that it was October, when Mike was hardly in the office, what with the football and rugby seasons in full swing. Squash was also very popular and many new clubs had sprung up. Golf was still regarded as a toff's game but more men and women from middle-class backgrounds were starting to play. It all kept him busy.

First, they must find Mike's schedule for the week. It wouldn't be easy for Louis to turn up as Mike for interviews, but if he could watch the games and bring back some details, Katie would type up the copy for the paper and no-one would be any the wiser.

At least it was a plan.

The more they discussed the questions, the more they realised that observing and living in this modern world would be difficult for Louis.

"Oh, Louis, maybe it would be best if you handed in Mike's notice tomorrow and left immediately, taking his holiday leave instead of working his notice?"

Mike had often talked about leaving the paper when he was disgruntled; always stressing he could go to work for a larger newspaper where he would be really appreciated. It was all talk; he never had the courage to test his dream, but it would help to explain him leaving his job. Given the incident involving Debs a couple of nights ago, perhaps leaving would let Louis off the hook of trying to act as Mike.

Mike's spare keys were still on the sideboard, with his wallet. In the wallet they found his driving licence. Katie pushed the paper she held and a pen towards Louis.

"Perhaps it might be a good idea for you to try copying Mike's signature. We may need to sign a document at some stage, with witnesses. We must cover all eventualities."

It was a good job that Mike had always scrawled his signature with such a flourish it ended up looking like a wavy line. People had always teased him that he should have been a doctor because his signature was so bad. Louis picked up the pen. Writing now he was mortal again was easy, but having to copy the signature wasn't as easy as it looked. Deep in his heart he hoped he would never have to use it; it seemed so dishonest and yet necessity made its own rules. Louis must try to act like Mike and pretend to be him, however unpleasant that might be.

Tomorrow was Monday. Mike would be expected at work as usual.

Panic hit home. Suddenly, Katie was not so confident; in fact, she felt massive anxiety. How would Louis cope in the office, not knowing the staff and not knowing anything about sport? And Debs, what about Debs?

"Lord what a nightmare," gasped Katie. "You won't understand any of the rules of the games or know the players and Mike was as thick as thieves with most of them. Oh! Louis, it's not going to work."

There was panic in her voice and her eyes welled up with tears.

"Mike must turn up for work. What can we do?"

There was silence; their cold coffee was abandoned on the coffee table as they pondered where to go from here.

Katie got up, "I'll make more coffee, these are dead anyway." Taking the mugs away she strode out of the room. He heard her switch the kettle then rinse out the mugs and make fresh drinks. He called out to her from the living room.

"Could we use some of Mike's old reviews as samples to remake new stories?"

A ripple of relief passed through her. At least that way, the style of writing would be the same. They may just get through this nightmare in one piece.

"Louis, you're a genius, of course we can. We'll manage to put something together. It would only be for two weeks, after you give notice."

She rejoined him with a smile on her face, carrying a tray with fresh coffee and biscuits and a dish of brown sugar. After stirring a spoonful of sugar in both mugs, she handed one to Louis.

Louis was very still. He stared down into his mug; it was obvious he was worried.

"What's wrong, Louis?' asked Katie.

"I know so little of your time except what I've learned from watching you and seeing your television. I don't want to let you down. Do you really think that I will be able carry this off?"

"Well, yes, you can do it for a short time, I have confidence in you. We must make sure that you don't spend too much time in the office. You'll need to turn up with me for work, find Mike's diary, slip the list for the week to me and leave the office as though you were going out to a meeting. I will make some excuse to leave the office and join you; we'll do the interview together. We will work it out, day by day, don't worry." She sounded more confident than she felt.

The one thing that particular worried Katie was the Debs incident. The next morning would be the first time Mike /Louis would be at the office, after the disastrous evening. Knowing Debs as she did, Katie was sure she would be looking for some sort of apology or retribution. It could change everything they had planned. Mike had been wilful, and had used the impressionable young woman.

They drank the coffee slowly, with thoughts racing through their heads, trying to plan a course of action that would not compromise Louis, knowing full well they wouldn't be sitting here planning for an uncertain future, if Mike hadn't been such a womaniser who liked to drink.

Katie had to prepare Louis for the next morning. His first day in an unknown world, a world of technology that would be foreign to him but one he must pretend to know. She must also prepare him for his first meeting with Debs; had he seen her in his ghostly state? Perhaps not; it was she who had been brought back to reality, not Louis, at the sound of Debs's bawdy laughter. God, that awful sound, she could still hear it in her head. She prickled with resentment. Mike and Debs had interrupted a beautiful moment for her and Louis; but then her thoughts turned to that morning and the love they finally shared. The thought of his touch on her body brought a tingling up her spine, a smile touched on her lips, they had tonight to look forward to. What a wonderful thought.

Katie looked over at the man of her dreams who was now sitting drinking coffee, and she wondered how it all would work out. It had been obvious when Katie was at work that Debs was, not unreasonably, angry and put out by Mike's disgraceful behaviour. Katie guessed that she would want a very public apology.

"Louis," said Katie, her voice full of concern. "You must understand that Debs will be out for your blood, Mike's blood, tomorrow. And she will have her friends at work there to back her up. I just hope that they will not gang up on you. It's going to be really difficult."

Katie reached over and hugged him. She had thought that Louis would not understand Debs's anger and pain. Louis understood that sort of behaviour only too well; he had seen examples of bullying in his village. It only took one person to accuse another, for that person to become a target for people, to be whispered about and humiliated. Some people only needed a half-lie or a tall tale to believe the worst.

In Mike's case, however, it was apparent that his drinking and his cavalier attitude had caused real distress to Debs; and Louis in Mike's body would have to take the blame for his misdemeanours. Louis would have to deal with it best he could, he just hoped he was up for the challenge. He was afraid, yet it was necessary; he had to fit into this modern world as long as he wore this living shroud.

He looked at Katie, He trusted her and if she said he could do it, then he could. They were meant to be together and he wouldn't risk their future together. Breakfast had come and gone, and soup and sandwich had served for lunch. They seemed to have done nothing but eat and drink since getting up.

It was time to introduce Louis to a piece of equipment called a Dictaphone. The rectangle tablet of black and silver was small enough to fit into a hand. It was opened by Katie, who put small tubes she called batteries, into a cavity in the back of the machine. Louis watched, following every move, as she pressed a knob at the same time speaking to it, a count of 1,2,3. She looked at Louis and showed him how the same knob slid upwards and her voice came back from it as clear as a bell; 1,2,3.

This was a moment of magic, which, in his time, might have been called witchcraft, but this wasn't his age, it was Katie's and this was just another piece of modern equipment, like the telephone or television.

She handed it over to him Now if he needed to use it in an interview, he had a tool that didn't involve taking written notes, she hoped she had covered all the bases on her list.

Louis repeated Katie's example and heard his own voice coming back to him. Satisfied that he understood how to use it, he handed the magic tablet back to Katie. How strange it was hearing his voice, there was a hint of accent; he would have to be careful and measured when he spoke. Another challenge.

Another first. How many more would there be?

5

Debs was upset, bruised and angry; she had been used by the man she loved. Pain lay heavily in her breast, and her head could not believe that he had thought so little of her, that she was just part of a game he had played. All her longings and hopes were shattered; but he wasn't going to get away with it. A kind of hatred took over from the love, she loathed him, despised him and she was hell-bent on making Mike pay for the fear and indignity she had suffered.

On arriving at the office on Saturday morning, she had wasted no time in recounting the events of Friday night to her workmates; she didn't wrap it up, she laid it bare before the women who learned all about Mike's aggression to her. She felt such a fool, she had hoped for a night of romance that would lead to a real relationship. She had always had a soft spot for him. He was so handsome with his dark eyes and dark hair. He reflected his parent's heritage, part Italian, and part Irish. He was a dish.

The saying, 'be careful what you wish for,' popped into her head. She shivered, she felt even more foolish and her anger grew, how could he have treated her so badly? She had known the minute she had turned the key in the lock at her front door it had been a mistake.

Why had she invited him back? It had seemed like a good idea at the time she mused. Truthfully, she hadn't wanted the night to end!

But once in her room, Mike had become nothing more than a domineering, over-zealous drunk. He had demanded sex from her as though she was nothing more than a plaything; she felt he was asking for a payment because he had taken her out for a meal. It had been so humiliating. She felt a lump rise in her throat; tears were not far away. Not that she would let these women who were looking on see that she was upset.

She reflected that the evening had started out so well. She was flattered at being asked out. In her fantasy, she had secretly dreamed of making love with him many times before he had asked her out. She had rejoiced when she accepted his invitation; how envious her workmates would be, that Debs, the office girl, had caught him.

They had shared an intimate time that evening in the softly lit Chinese restaurant, hidden away in a small booth at the back of the room, little innuendoes being hinted at throughout the meal. It became apparent, an open secret, that both parties were assuming they would be sleeping together later. He had been so attentive, reaching across the table and touching her hand while listening to her conversation; he had seemed really interested in all she had to say. Sitting side by side in the half-light he gently stroked his fingers on her arm as he poured the wine and his fingers slid across her bare neck before he gave her a gentle hug. She had always felt invisible to him; she thought that he had never really seen her in the office, not like a real person, but that night was different, he seemed to really care. All the signals were there, he was really interested in her.

The meal had been excellent and the wine had flowed, more to Mike's glass than hers, she remembered, but she hadn't thought anything of it at the time, and they were merry but definitely not drunk. It had all gone wrong when they arrived Katie's house.

They had got a bit loud when they were making love in his room, that much she had to admit. It had all been a bit of a laugh, sneaking into the house carrying their shoes in their hands as they crept on tiptoe up the stairs, trying not to make a noise.

Closing the bedroom door, they had fallen on the bed and had been far too eager to gratify their needs. Their lovemaking had been rushed, neither of them emotionally satisfied. Suddenly, they were blasted by pop music coming up the stairs from the kitchen, nearly lifting the roof off the bedroom and they both knew they were in deep trouble for disturbing Katie.

He had been smashing, paying her compliments all evening.

She remembered that it was then when she had suggested going on to her bedsit. She regretted it now, but then, the evening had still been young and she hadn't wanted it to end.

Hastily dressing, they had slipped down the stairs and sneaked out of Katie's house. It had all been a bit of a giggle, until he insisted on going to an off-licence to buy some wine. Instead, he bought whiskey, as if not content with the whiskey he had drunk in his bedroom before they had left.

The taxi he had promised for them was forgotten, because her bedsit was only a few streets away, he said. He had suggested they walk there. She hadn't been happy about that and then it had started to rain. It was a real dampener to the evening.

She had been wearing new shoes; ones intended only to look good in, but walk they did, and by the time they reached her home, she had blisters on both heels that were weeping and hurt like hell. The rain had ruined her hair-do and her new coat was wet to the lining. By the time the two of them stood before her front door they were bedraggled and cold. The night had become a disaster.

She wasn't to blame, was she? Thoughts still tumbled through her head, while she tried to convince herself it was partly Katie's fault. If they hadn't been disturbed by Katie, they wouldn't have left and Mike wouldn't have gone off to buy another half bottle of Scotch. That was when he had become out of control; he stopped listening to her and wouldn't take no for an answer. She was shaking now at the memory; he might have raped her if it hadn't been for her landlady who had woken at the angry voices that seeped down through the ceiling into her bedroom below. Thank God she came knocking at Debs's door or who knows what would have happened? He had hurt her.

She had been so lost in her thoughts that she had forgotten where she was for the moment. No-one spoke, although she was encircled by mates that worked with her. She glanced around at the women who were looking at her with interest. It had been quite a story, though no-one looked shocked. Beyond them, the open-plan office looked empty, with nobody at their desks. Of course, they were empty; everyone was here beside her.

Well! She thought in triumph. She had told everyone in the office just what kind of pervert he was. The other women who worked at the Echo needed to be warned didn't they? That justified her actions. Debs's thoughts on the matter just kept going round and round in her head. He must be punished; there was no excuse for his behaviour. Yes, he must be punished. She nodded to herself, a slight smile hovering on her lips. She intended to make sure he got what he deserved.

On Monday morning at nine, she was back at her desk when Mike walked into the office. To her satisfaction, she could see he looked anxious. Well, why wouldn't he? He must be full of guilt now that he was sober. Strange though, he had a different air about him. What was it? She couldn't tell, but there was something. It was the way he walked, wasn't it? She thought to herself. That arrogant swagger, that told everyone how much he loved, himself, was gone. No, he had no swagger today and his haughty air had disappeared.

Just desserts, she sniggered, for his disgusting behaviour.

It had already been an exacting morning for Louis.

The journey by car through town in what Katie had called the rush hour had been difficult, and anything but a rush. The traffic was nose to tail and actually nothing moved very quickly; it had been a nightmare. The noise and smell from the cars that surrounded them seeped into the vehicle; the air they were breathing was tainted and unpleasant. Metal vehicles jockeyed for position, pushing and shoving for space, desperate to move forward, Louis could feel their frustration. Some drivers showed their impatience by honking their horns and mouthing words that he couldn't make out from behind the glass windows. It wasn't hard to guess what they might be.

All this was normal for Katie. How could she stay so calm as she negotiated the mayhem? Perhaps the music that played so softly from the radio against the hum of the engine helped her concentrate? He was only pleased he didn't have to do it.

Katie had dropped him in front of the office before heading for the car park. The sensation of knotting in his stomach almost hurt; his hands were sweating, as he reached for the doorknob to open the solid wood entrance. He had to get this right and be Mike for a few hours.

He pushed open the door. When he stepped into Mike's workspace, it seemed vast. He was exposed to a large open-plan office, where there were no walls nor screens to hide him from the onlookers. He felt everyone's eyes in the office fall on him as he walked forward into the heavy silence.

He felt like a condemned man walking to the gallows as he pushed his feet, one before the other, forward. The sound of his footsteps echoed on the tiled floor as he pressed on toward the desk that Katie had described as Mike's. Katie had done her best to explain the layout of the office work area and particularly his space or at least Mike's space, that he must head for.

Katie had described what she knew of the incident with Debs and Mike, as well as Debs's features as accurately as she could. As he walked to his desk further down the office, he could feel hostility coming from a rather attractive young woman sitting at a desk nearby.

How was he going to deal with this situation? Should he smile and acknowledge her with a greeting or pass with his head down and pretend she wasn't there? Taking a deep breath, he squared his shoulders and set a smile on his face, nodding to the faces that were looking at him. But there was no returned acknowledgement; everyone continued to watch him move down the office towards the desk that lay beyond the woman who was rising to her feet. Her face was like thunder and her body language was threatening as he moved nearer to her.

What had made him stop and say good morning and inquire how she was, he didn't know; it just seemed the right thing to do. What he expected to happen, he wasn't sure. The woman standing at her desk, ready for a fight, didn't respond. Debs seemed dumbfounded at his greeting and at his apparent attempt to normalise the situation between them. Staring at him with an open mouth and blushing, her face turned rather pink before becoming red. Her eyes, followed him as he passed by; she was filled with disdain at herself because she hadn't been able to utter a word and the anger she was holding was palpable.

Getting to Mike's desk unscathed under the threatening silence was a relief. The surface of the desk looked untidy, covered in papers sitting in small piles of organised chaos. At the centre of the desktop sat lists of fixtures for various local matches to be played that month, stapled to a large diary. At the back of the desk, pinned to the drawers, were a number of photos of young men and women wearing sports gear, faces that meant nothing to Louis but he registered that those face were probably friends of Mike's.

Pushed to the back of the desktop was a machine with keys, letters of the alphabet and numbers adorned them. He knew this machine from Katie's home. Katie had explained, it was a device to type letters and statements. Katie had called it was a typewriter, but this had a electricity to enhance its performance, though how to use it was a mystery and one he would not be trying to unravel today.

Their plan was that he would collect the diary with that week's assignments and leave the office as quickly as he could, as though *en route* to covering a story. Covering all eventualities, Katie had written a letter of resignation, which he had copied and signed in a Mike scrawl of a signature. It sat now tucked away in the inside pocket of the jacket he was wearing. Two weeks' notice the letter stated; he was to leave it on the desk of the editor before he left the office.

Somehow, he would have to pretend to be Mike for two weeks.

He was deep in thought when he heard the sound of heavy footsteps coming up quickly behind him. They were somehow threatening and they shook him out of his moment of concentration. He looked up to see Debs striding towards him, red-faced and clearly on the warpath. She no longer looked attractive; her face was twisted with loathing; he would have to be careful.

A tirade of foul language and hurtful comments tore through the air for all the office to hear as she vented the poison that had been locked up inside since her awful experience with Mike. It was all aimed at Mike, but heard by Louis who stood in mute shock not knowing how to react.

"You're not going to pretend that nothing really happened, are you? You can't wriggle out of it, you bloody pervert," she screamed.

She leaned on the desk and thrust her face into his, her fisted hands supporting her upper body, the anger clearly sapping her strength.

Louis could see the hurt in her eyes and knew that she felt used and betrayed.

He knew life could be like that. He thought of Sophia. He had loved her but she had cared more about herself than the love they shared, and it had destroyed a piece of his heart. Love was replaced by disappointment and bitterness. Sophia, his wife, had taken his life long ago. Her love had never been freely given; she only understood conditional love but he had believed that she loved him completely, just as he loved her.

Now, Louis faced the wrath of this young woman. All he could think of was not to hurt her anymore than she had been hurt already.

"Debora, I'm so sorry that you've been hurt," he said in a soft and humble voice. His hand reached out towards her to touch her arm in a gesture of sympathy.

She drew back from him, a puzzled look crossing her face. His voice and indeed his whole demeanour seemed totally out of character.

What's wrong with him? she thought to herself, who's he trying to kid? This was not the Mike she knew. Where had all his bravado and arrogance gone that he was so well-known for?

Was he trying to make a fool of her in front of her workmates? He had grasped her wrists when he tried to force himself on her on Friday. She hadn't imagined it; she tenderly rubbed her wrists, they still felt sore.

She wanted to take him down, hurt him like he had hurt her. For years she had wanted him to notice her; she had really liked him and he had abused her. She would never forget that.

He was obviously trying to play the innocent; well, he wasn't going to get away with it. She had expected an argument, one in which she would make sure everyone at the Echo would know what a dishonourable person he really was. She was acutely aware that the staff was watching them from their stations around the office. They were perhaps hoping or waiting for the scene to erupt into a full-scale row, like the climax of a television drama, but there would be no argument that day it would seem; it was turning out to be one-sided. It was obvious he was playing a game – one she wouldn't join.

He's turning the tables on me, she thought, trying to put me in the wrong,

God, he's trying to make me out to be a complete idiot. Once again, she felt her face was on fire, how could she rise above this and survive with some dignity? She turned around, and with her head held high, and walked back to her desk. All eyes were on her until she looked directly at her friends. Suddenly all the voyeurs found something more interesting to look at on their desks.

Katie, standing just inside the doorway to the office, witnessed everything. She felt sorry for Debs, now sitting at her desk, her face a mask of anger. How could she know that this was not Mike and that her anger was misplaced?

The atmosphere was filled with tension. Katie took a deep breath and marched towards her own station, ignoring the heavy silence and the eyes that followed her. As she passed Debs's desk, she stopped.

"Are you alright?" she inquired.

"Of course, I'm not alright, he tried to rape me," Debs said indignantly.

"But you were in his bedroom in my home last Friday night and seemed to be enjoying his advances. Are you sure that was his intention?"

"Well." Debs stuttered. "Well, we were okay at yours but just before we left, he swallowed half a bottle of Scotch. By the time we got to my place, he was well on the way to being drunk. Then he got pushy. Wouldn't take no for an answer, would he? He was all over me like a rash and I was telling him no."

Near to tears, she continued. "He hurt me, scared me. If it hadn't been for my landlady, who knows what he might have done?"

Debs's voice had dropped to a whisper and Katie had strained to hear her last sentence.

"Mike's impulsive but not bad, it's the whiskey," but Katie got no further.

It had been a word too far for Debs.

"Don't you put the blame on me," protested Debs. "He's the bloody pervert."

The two women hadn't heard Louis behind them. He had to intervene. He had been watching the unfolding scene and didn't want either woman to get so angry that it descended into a slanging match or worse.

He waved the white envelope that contained his notice to quit at both of them but spoke directly to Debs.

"I'm leaving, Debs. This is my letter of my notice. I'm on my way to the editor now to hand it in. In a couple of weeks, I will be gone."

"And good riddance to bad rubbish!" retorted Debs, her eyes lighting up at what she took to be a triumph on her side. He had lost after all. She could hardly contain her glee. In the end she hadn't needed to fight him, he was defeated and branded as a lecher and everyone would know it. It was everything she wanted.

When he knocked at the editor's door, he had a surprise waiting for him; fate had intervened. Instead of offering his notice to quit as he planned, the editor rounded on him. It had been rumoured that Mike would be sacked. The whisper had come from the editor's secretary who confided with the staff that her boss was less than pleased with Mike's bullish behaviour. Mike was already on his last warning and there would be no reprieve this time.

"It has been brought to my attention," said the editor in a raised voice, "that you are often under the influence of drink when out working." It was a subject the two men had spoken about before and although there was no mention of Debs, it was fairly obvious that he wanted to rid the office of a womaniser and a drunkard. He had been party to Debs's version of events with the rest of the staff on Saturday morning and was disgusted. Mike had had a good run at the Echo over the years and been given the benefit of the doubt several times, but this time he had overstepped the mark.

The furious editor told Mike to clear all his personal items from his desk and leave immediately; the farewell was courteous but cold. A white envelope with cash for the expenses due that had incurred over the last three months was pushed towards him over the editor's desk. The meeting was over, and there was no need for him to return to the office after that day.

There was a different atmosphere in the office as he retraced his steps; he was carrying two white envelopes, one containing cash and one his P45. When he pulled open the door to leave, he heard the sound of clapping coming from a single person behind him; he didn't need to look to see who was celebrating his departure. By 11.30 that morning, Mike no longer worked on the paper.

Louis was free to be himself and to get to know this body he was in. Now he could see if Mike's hands and his skill would come together, to create and carve like he had done so many years before.

He looked down at the piece of paper that he would need to get a new job. But the only job he wanted was to be back at his workbench, carving wood and finding in it, nature and the hidden spirits of animals. How he longed to tease them out from their imprisonment and free them from the wood, free them just like he had felt freedom that morning. Excitement ran through his veins.

He thought back to the night before and remembered that little machine that Katie had shown him that recorded speech. All the planning they had done was suddenly redundant. His heart leapt; the relief was overwhelming. Now, he really did have a new start.

6

Debs had a smirk on her face. She felt she had won a war. Mike had made her feel unclean, dirty, of no account and worthless in her own flat that night but now she felt vindicated and refreshed again. She couldn't help herself as she stood, watching him leave. Her hands came together and she clapped in time to his steps until he was out of the door.

Well, there's an end to it, she thought, the phrase, good riddance to bad rubbish, repeated in her brain. Her smirk became a smile, allowing the tension to melt away. With a huge sense of relief, she realised she would never have to see him again. The battle was over and she had won the war. Revenge was sweet.

She sat down at her desk, satisfied with the way things had turned out that morning and she turned on her electric typewriter. She was ready to work.

Katie, on the other hand, was so proud of Louis. He had taken the hostility, just like she knew he would, for their sake. It filled her with love and pride. There was no way in the world that she could ever disclose Mike's passing. But it was hard to watch Louis bearing the disgrace that belonged to Mike. Her neighbour Charlotte, who sat to her right, inquired in a low voice.

"Did she really visit your house and have sex with him?"

"I believe so, but I did disturb them and they left."

"Do you think he's capable of rape?" It was a leading question, a difficult one to answer. Katie had also met with Mike's over zealousness when he had been drinking. She too had fought him off a couple of times. He had been a Jekyll and Hyde character, Mr Hyde when he was drunk, a sweet man when sober. When she answered, she believed it to be the truth.

"Not deliberately, but he could be forceful after a few drinks. He just didn't think of the consequences of his actions. He was a schoolboy who wanted his own way," she said, remembering again her own struggle with him and sighed. Mike was gone. Louis was in his stead. "It's changed him, I think. This thing with Debs." Nodding in confidence to her workmate.

A voice from her left joined in. Mac, Mike's friend and the gardening guru of the Echo, had listened in and offered a friendly piece of advice.

"Don't get me wrong, I like him, always have, but leopards don't change their spots, Katie. I'd keep an eye on him if I were you, that is if he's still your lodger," he cocked his head on one side waiting for a response.

"Yes, Mac he is. This weekend has been very difficult for him. He's full of remorse and swears he's finished with drink," she thought of Louis, "I believe him."

"Nothing more to say then," Mac shrugged, women were a mystery to him, even his darling wife, Charlotte, who sat between them.

"Don't worry Mac, I'm really sure he's changed."

A wry smile broke out on his lips; he looked over to Charlotte and raised his eyebrows. Nothing else needed to be said.

7

They were turning the page on a new chapter in their lives, and as she contemplated the future with Louis, Katie felt a tingle of excitement run through her body; whatever came they would share it together. After all the stress of the previous two days, it was a blessing that he would no longer have to pretend to be Mike.

Louis was real, she could feel the power of life in his arms when he held her and felt the warmth of his breath when he kissed her. He was real, no longer the man in her dreams, no longer a spirit trapped in a different realm.

It was surprising how quickly Louis was adjusting to being mortal again. The body he was in felt less weighty and its messages, like hunger or thirst, were familiar again. As for this era in which he was living, he wasn't sure; the jury was still out on that.

The first few weeks together were heavenly, even though Katie was working during the day. Just waking next to each other in the mornings and sharing the comfort of each other's arms was a blessing; and that good morning kiss was as good as it gets. The evenings were filled with conversation and smiles, they talked about the Seventies, this age that he was living in, and the bond between the two of them grew even stronger.

In the scheme of things, Mike was largely forgotten, except when Louis looked in the mirror. Mike and he had been more alike than he realised and it was as if the two faces of the men had blended. Soon it was as though Mike had never existed. Even after such a short space of time, Louis' character had pushed through the skin of the living shroud he was in and it was his face that Katie saw when she looked at him.

Over the breakfast table, they talked of a future together, though in truth Louis was still unsure whether the body would eventually reject him. But it didn't matter for now; he could not eject himself from it. Even his kingdom had become off limits to him; when he had touched the carving on his headboard, the wooden veil, the doorway into his kingdom, had not given under his hand. He was stranded. There was no place of refuge now that he was mortal. His world wouldn't accept him, so there was no choice but to plan a future that included him working and earning a living.

But his future, was not looking great. His craft, so sought after in his time, was not really viable in Katie's world. Just as many inventions had been developed to serve generations, so had furniture; it was no longer made piece by piece by craftsman, except for the very rich. According to Katie, furniture was made in factories, mass-produced for working people. Real craftspeople were few and far between in this decade.

The sort of furniture Louis made, like the bed they slept in, was classed as art, and would be far too expensive for ordinary people to buy. Even if Katie sorted out some tools for him and they sourced the wood, he would still need a place to work and a list of wealthy clients.

He could, however, fall back on his training as a carpenter; people always wanted small jobs doing in their homes. They would advertise, have leaflets printed and post them through letterboxes in their neighbourhood. It would be a starting point, and later, when he had fully adjusted to this decade, he would try to join a company that built homes; he would never be out of work.

That was the plan. The expense money he had been given was still in the white envelope and resting on the dining room table. It was time to shop.

The tools he needed were expensive, but to start up he settled for second-hand ones that he found for sale in the local paper. After he collected the tools, he cleaned and oiled them. He had been taught to look after them; they would help him to provide food on the table and that was important to him.

Louis was good with people and when he found clients, he would make sure they were satisfied with his work. Satisfied customers were a sure way to build a business. He knew he could do it and 'Louis Parker' would be reborn.

The next few weeks were happy enough. He especially enjoyed the weekends, having two whole days with Katie. During the week on his own, he schooled himself and learnt all he could about the modern techniques in joinery and carpentry, staple guns, modern glues and varnish, aids that would make his job easier. That done, he waited.

At last, the phone started to ring, with offers of small jobs in and around the area where they lived. Louis was ready to give this new life a shot and build up a reputation just as he had all those years ago. With one solution in place, he had thought he could rest easy but no, another problem arose, that was life. How was he to transport himself from job to job?

Katie came to his aid and helped by fitting his work around what she needed to do at the paper; that way she could drive him to his clients. It was sometimes difficult, but somehow together they made it work. He could hardly use the driving licence in Mike's name, he had no skills in that direction; the nearest he got to driving was as a passenger. He really had no interest in driving on these roads with so much traffic; he marvelled at the way Katie managed them. He had not been raised to know this world and the mechanical car. He wondered if he would ever get used to the noise, the smell and the speed that these metal steeds got up to.

Weeks passed and October had come and gone. Everything had settled down at the Echo.

Debs more or less kept to herself and Katie made it a point not to engage with her in conversation. The odd nod in a morning was all that passed between them. A sort of truce was managed. Only when their eyes met could Katie see the animosity that was still there.

Office gossip about Mike had run its course, no one said anything to Katie about the event. But she did learn from one of her colleagues that Debs couldn't understand why Mike was still living with her and why Katie hadn't thrown the drunk out. That was something she could never explain.

In a few short weeks, Louis had gathered a number of customers. The small jobs were gradually being replaced by bigger and more skilled tasks and he loved it. His reputation grew; he was polite, friendly, and left the jobs as clean as a whistle. His clients put the word about; 'This new carpenter's very good, local too. And he doesn't charge the earth.' At least, that, was the word on the grapevine. Small local builders, who were always looking for skilled, reliable men, heard about him too. Suddenly he had more work than he could handle.

It was already the first of November. Shorter days and longer nights were the order of the day but the weather had stayed fine. It was warm for the time of year, the sort of weather that made you glad to be outside. Glorious colours enhanced the gardens in the neighbourhood; its many trees were clothed in their beautiful autumn finery. It was partly the sight of them that made Katie wonder, what it would be like to visit Louis' native Yorkshire. He had described the village where he had lived in detail. Bordered by hills, Ravensend was surrounded by trees, and, according to Louis, everywhere you looked the autumn leaves fluttered in a dance of red, yellow and gold.

But for how long? she wondered, surely no more than a couple of weeks? The heavy-laden trees would shed their leaves in the autumn winds. She mused; a riot of colour is what he had said. She suddenly had an urge to see them.

His new workload was heavy, working all hours for them. Katie was grateful that they had no need to worry about money, but as he was still not driving himself, she still had to ferry him to and from his clients.

Perhaps we could take a little weekend break? He'd been working so hard. It could be a special gift and a thank you, rolled into one, she thought. Never having been to the north, the idea of a break grew. She was curious, Louis talked of beautiful countryside; in her mind she only saw drab houses and rain, perhaps she had it all wrong?

Having decided on a weekend break, she needed to find a hotel near the village where he had lived. It would be a wonderful surprise for him and a treat for her. Fancy, a whole weekend being looked after in a hotel, no cleaning, no cooking or washing up, no work. Bliss.

As it happened, the Sunday paper had a whole page of holiday breaks in and around the counties. She spread the page out on the kitchen table and pored over it, sipping her coffee, eagerly reading; she must find the right hotel at the right price.

It must have been fate. She was amazed to see a rather splendid hotel advertising a short break on the edge of the north Yorkshire moors. Remembering a bookcase held a book of road maps, she decided to find out just where this hotel was. Eureka, it was only a couple of miles away from his village. Suddenly, she felt excited and circled the ad with a red pen; this looked like the right one for their visit. The Avondale Hotel.

The hotel looked very grand in the quarter-page advertisement. Its black and white image showed a fairly large manor house; it, had probably been the home of some wealthy member of the gentry long ago. Built in quarry stone, it was covered in thick ivy that clung to its walls around its entrance, framing and enhancing it somehow. The blurb boasted of formal gardens and a children's play area; well, they wouldn't need that, but it was always nice to walk in gardens even if they would not be at their best, being November.

It was near to Ravensend. Everything was falling into place. According to the map they could walk to his village from the hotel. That clinched it, her decision was made, and she phoned the hotel.

"Hello, Avondale Hotel, can I help you?" came a distant voice with a northern accent.

"I'm calling about the weekend offer in my newspaper. Do you have a double room from Friday to Monday this coming weekend, please?"

"I'll just check for you, Madam." The line went quiet. "Yes, Madam, I can book that for you now."

The very friendly receptionist, Jackie, quickly arranged it for them.

"Could you send a deposit to secure your booking? And we will see you this Friday."

"Yes, no problem." said Katie. "I'll get a cheque off to you today." She put the phone down feeling very satisfied; it had been so easy and they were going to Yorkshire.

What a wonderful surprise it would be for Louis to see his old haunts. Then she smiled, realising the irony of her thoughts. But how true it was, a lot must have changed during the passing of the years. No doubt, he would find it difficult, she hadn't thought about that, yet she knew by the way he talked that he longed to see his village again. In seven days, they would be on their way, travelling north together on the Friday and returning home Tuesday. The long weekend would be a chance to retrace his forgotten footsteps around his village.

Katie decided they would take the trip by car; she didn't mind driving and it would give them more flexibility, once they were there, to see Yorkshire. She wanted to spend time in the county he belonged to, where he had been born and lived so many years ago.

The trip would be an adventure for the two of them. The image she had received from television was one of drab stone buildings and people living a tough life. It was not a place she would have naturally wanted to visit, but Louis had painted a very different picture about his home county. When he spoke about Yorkshire, he spoke about breathtaking moors and rolling hills, of friendly people with warm hearts, of hardworking folk and home cooking. It sounded good, even though his memories were of a time over a hundred years ago.

8

What prompted Katie to plan this trip to Yorkshire, he didn't know but he was more than grateful for her thoughtful surprise. Thank God for the back of that dim and dusty room in the second-hand store where he had rested and thank God that fate had sent Katie to find a bed, the bed that kept him prisoner. He remembered the absolute surprise of seeing Katie, loving her on sight, so that his spirit reached out to her, willing her to buy the very object that was his jail and kingdom. Now, he was free from that yoke; that invisible chain that had kept him earthbound was gone. After all those years trapped in his nether world going only where the bed took him, he had at last a choice on his destination.

Come the weekend, he would be travelling back to his roots, back to his beloved home county and to the place where he had lived and worked. It was a strange mix of emotions, for he was excited and sad at the same time; all his friends and neighbours were dead and long gone. How was he going to feel walking down the village street in this age, all the while his memory still expecting to see old familiar faces that were no longer there? That was the sad part. No matter, time was relentless, and that was to be expected.

He longed to see the familiar shapes of his own hills and the countryside of his youth. Other memories would come tumbling back, he was sure of that, and he would deal with them one at a time.

When it came to packing for the mini break, Louis had a completely new wardrobe of clothes. Somehow, wearing Mike's clothes didn't feel right. They had fitted him well but it wasn't about the fit, it was much more; wearing the dead man's clothes felt like he was being disrespectful. And, although he had admired Mike's style and wanted to look like a modern man, Louis' fashion sense and colour choice were different. Katie had been incredible, taking him from shop to shop, until they had found clothes that suited his character.

Their clothes were packed into a green, chequered, small suitcase on Thursday evening and put in the boot of the car ready for the departure early next morning.

Perhaps it was the excitement that was burning inside him, or maybe anxiety about the journey that was ahead, but sleep did not come easily that night for Louis. He lay in the dark trying to find a comfortable position; the pillows lumpy as he restlessly tossed and turned waiting for sleep to come.

The full moon measured the hours as it travelled across the window. The pearly globe, high in the night sky, lit the bedroom as the ribbons of clouds parted revealing its powerful glow. Katie lay beside him, sleeping soundly. She looked like an angel in the light. He was tempted to kiss her but held back; it was bad enough that he couldn't sleep, without disturbing her rest.

It was 2.30 before his wish was granted and he fell into a deep sleep. He was ruefully woken at 7.30 by Mike's alarm clock, blasting in his ear with a high-pitched, relentless, ringing tone. He opened his eyes to the new day, though it was still dark outside. He fumbled as he half-raised himself up, he must turn the alarm off, before he realised that he was on his own. Katie was already up.

Louis was pleasantly surprised when the aroma of coffee hit his senses as he turned over to find a hot cup of the dark liquid on the bedside table. Katie must have just brought it; the timing had been impeccable. The half-hidden clock behind it was still ringing out. His hand reached over the cup and lifted it, squinting through sleepy eyes to find the off switch.

Not too gently, he killed the mechanism and breathed a sigh of relief now he was free of the noise.

The hot coffee was welcome, his throat was dry and he still felt groggy because of the lack of sleep. It had always been the same; when his brain was active, his thoughts spun out of control with no way of turning them off; it happened again last night. Now, he was on the back foot and he needed to get a move on to catch up. Katie must have been up some time. She, at least, was wide-awake, judging by the lyrics that floated through the air from the bathroom. It told him to drink up quickly for she was almost ready to start this grand adventure up what she called the Great North Road.

He remembered the London road. When she had showed it him on a map, he was amazed to see its 409 miles that stretched from London to Edinburgh, built by the Romans when they occupied Britain. Not that they were going that far, nor using it initially, because according to Katie it was now called the A1. They wouldn't join it until they got to Boro'bridge. Today, they would be using a new motorway that had recently been opened: the M1, a multi-lane road built for speed.

By 8.30, both of them were sitting in the bright blue Mini. An opened map lay on the dashboard for the journey, not that they would need it yet for a while. Hot strong coffee in a thermos flask with two plastic cups nestled in a wicker basket at Louis' feet. A Tupperware box containing egg and cress sandwiches and apples was placed on the back seat waiting for a time when they would stop to eat.

The car pulled away from the curb and onto the road leading north. Their adventure had started; they were off, and looking forward to a long weekend together. The first twenty minutes were spent travelling on local roads toward the town of Hemel Hempstead. Once a small village, it had grown into a town after the Second World War. Londoners, who had lost everything in the Blitz, moved out of the capital to find new lives. The terrible bombing of the city had lasted day and night from September 1940 to May 1941, 32,000 people died and almost three times as many were seriously injured over fifty percent of homes were destroyed, making so many people homeless and destitute.

The old village of Hemel Hempstead, dating back to 1086 had been surrounded by new buildings of houses, flats, new shops and a hospital, all on the orders of the government, according to Katie. Louis knew nothing about the wars; he had slept through the entire hostilities, hidden away behind the veil of wood in his kingdom. Since the time Marina had died, there was so much that had passed him by as he lay in his self-imposed exile. He wasn't sorry to have missed the world's madness with its wars, and millions of people slaughtered, cities destroyed and people displaced.

The only event he regretted missing was the moon landing, though he still couldn't quite believe that man had travelled there, stood on it, raised a flag on it, and come back.

It was either witchcraft, lies, a miracle or just another marvel of this age.

He settled down to the journey, only to be frightened out of his wits when they came to a series of circles called roundabouts marked in white on the road. It was called the New Plough roundabout and, it was the only one of its kind in the whole of the country. The locals called it the magic roundabout, so Katie told him. There was nothing magical about it, thought Louis, except, perhaps that no one was being killed. The roundabout had a number of arterial mini roundabouts at each entry and exit of roads that met, allowing vehicles to pass either left or right and helping the traffic to flow. Katie knew it, and it was no trouble to her; negotiating it with skill they were through the circus and now their Mini was travelling up the hill to where a sign pointed the way to the M1.

In a few short minutes, they were moving down the slip lane onto the motorway and into the throng of vehicles that were travelling at high speed. Katie manoeuvred them into the slow lane and positioned them, between the lorries, waiting until she could move out to the middle lane. Louis caught his breath; what sort of madness was this? He could hardly believe that vehicles could be travelling at such speeds and so close together. When Katie finally found a space to move out, Louis was almost traumatised by the noise and speed of it all. He shut his eyes tight for a moment. As if not travelling fast enough in their lane, cars whizzed passed to their right in the next lane; they seemed no more than a blur of colour and were gone. Did these people of this century have no fear? he asked himself. Lorries to his left were large and high and so long in length that he felt like a vulnerable bird waiting to be picked off by a larger aggressive variety of its species. His nerves were on edge and he wondered if he would survive the journey after all. Then he looked over at Katie who was in total control, or so it seemed. Once again, he recognised this was not his world but hers. She moved over yet again into the fast lane and he suddenly felt easier that they were away from the threatening lorries and the smaller cars that had surrounded them. It was with a sigh of relief he felt the little car leap forwards they were really on their way.

It took no more than fifteen minutes into the journey before he realised that his anxiety had passed, the tight knots in his belly had dissolved and he was actually enjoying the ride.

There was something exhilarating about the speed they were travelling at, a speed that only fifteen minutes ago he doubted he could have believed he would accept. It was very different from the carts pulled by horses, so slow and passive, so long ago. How the world had changed; a coach and six was the fastest transport for passengers in his era.

They were passing the larger trucks and lorries on their left and it made him feel in a strange way quite indestructible. He was in a solid vehicle with Katie who was totally in control of the drive. Feeling safe, he settled back in his seat his eyes moved over the landscape.

His serene and lovely Katie was busy concentrating on the traffic with only the occasional swear word escaping in low muttering under her breath, towards fellow drivers who appeared to be reckless or just plain thoughtless with regard to other drivers battling the traffic. It was going to be a long journey, but he would be seeing with eager eyes the countryside as he passed through the different counties. The world out there was larger, much larger, than it had been in 1790.

After an hour on the road, the basket that was between his feet, filled with coffee for the journey, was starting to get in the way; he should have put it in the back seat with the food. He lifted it onto his knee. Katie saw the movement from the corner of her eye.

"Are you hungry already or do you just need a drink?" she inquired.

"Neither, Katie, I just got a little uncomfortable," he nodded at the basket.

"Not to worry, there are service stations all the way up to Scotch Corner. We'll stop in a little while to give us both a bit of a stretch, you can rid yourself of it then."

He had never heard of service stations but he supposed they were like the post inns. When at last they pulled off the motorway down a slip road, he found, to his amazement, a huge area filled with cars. They passed row after row of cars of all different sizes, shapes and colours, all facing towards a two-storey building. Katie trundled on until she found a space and indicated her intention. She nosed the car into the space that looked way too narrow to fit but fit it did, and with plenty of room on either side to get out. She turned off the engine and pulled on the handbrake. She let out a deep sigh and visibly relaxed as she turned her attention to Louis who was still nursing the basket.

"Shall I pour some coffee for you?" asked Louis, picking up the flask.

"No." She replied, smiling warmly at him, before she leaned across to him and planted a kiss on his cheek.

"Let's save it for later. We can get a good coffee here and maybe a slice of cake to have with it."

She laughed as though she had cracked a joke. He loved her so much; she was a woman with a warm heart and a funny, cheeky side to her, as well being practical and full of common sense.

Dozens of people were coming and going through the glass doors of a substantial building with logos blazing from it, advertising the cafés and amenities within. The noise inside the building from the many people was a curious mixture of comfortable chatter. Although it appeared busy, people were good humoured and making the most of the facilities before restarting their journeys.

They found a table next to a window to sip their drinks while watching the cars and fellow travellers come and go. What a relief it was not to feel cramped. They gratefully stretched out their limbs for a few minutes, knowing there was still a long way to go.

New travellers came and sat near them, smoking. It fascinated Louis; no clay pipes for these people, they were smoking what appeared to him to be white paper tubes filled with tobacco that didn't quite smell like tobacco should. White wisps of smoke were expelled from their mouths with alternative movements of the cups of hot beverages that were reaching their lips in between the puffs. It smelled dreadful but the smokers were apparently unaware.

"Drink up," whispered Katie. "Let's go, I do hate sitting amongst all this smoke."

"It is unpleasant, isn't it," agreed Louis.

He was ready to breathe some fresh air before getting into the car and back on the road to continue the adventure up the Great North Road.

9

County after county rolled by; Northamptonshire, Leicestershire, and then Nottinghamshire. Three large, grey towers loomed on the horizon shaped like cotton reels. Katie had to explain they were storing gas, a vital energy that served most modern homes one way or another, used to heat and cook. A pall of white smoke was steadily spreading into the pure blue sky like an ominous expanse of malevolence from one of the towers.

"Doesn't that harm the people who live underneath it?" Louis asked with concern.

Katie didn't know the answer, but offered, "I don't think the government would allow it if it hurt the local residents." Louis watched it with misgivings; governments weren't always right. The plume stole across the sky, blotting out and destroying the vision of blue. It was disturbing. Another fifteen minutes and they were in the next county of Derbyshire. The shadow he had seen was behind them and the countryside was changing. It was becoming hillier, with houses built of grey stone just like the buildings in Ravensend. Louis took the map from the dashboard, peering at it closely, just a few more miles to the boundary that separated this county from his own.

Excitement, anxiety and fear were pulling at Louis' nerves when they finally reached Yorkshire, the largest county in England. Emblazoned on a large, white, metal, public notice-board was the white rose, its emblem.

In black capital letters the legend read, 'Welcome to the South Riding of Yorkshire.'

Sheffield was just a few miles away; it was a milestone marker for him, Sheffield had long been an industrial city, but surrounding it was the Peak District in all its moorland glory to the east, and the industrial Spen valleys to the north.

Stone walls divided up the fields as far as the eye could see, making a green patchwork pattern all the way to the horizon. More hills became visible as the Mini sped forward and valleys could be seen etched with dense wooded forests in the distance. This was what he knew. The lump in his throat was painful, it felt too large to swallow, as he held back the tears that wanted to be released from the deep well of his emotions. He was relieved to be back in the north of England, he was coming home. Even the autumn sun smiled on him through the windscreen, coming out from behind the clouds just as they crossed the county line. Here was Autumn at its best; the trees still clung onto their changed mantle, the reds and gold not ready to give way to the browns that conveyed the end of summer and death. How many miles to go? His hands held the map and once again he scrutinised it. How short the line looked on the map, the line that gave him a sense of the distance. It lied; they still had a way to go until they reached the North Wolds of Yorkshire.

He became impatient; wanting the car to go even faster to reach its goal. This part of the journey seemed tediously long. He was less interested in the landscape now. Once they left the outskirts of York where the M1 finally joined up to the A1, the signs became frequent for Ripon and Thirsk, places he knew. Louis started to feel more at home, more comfortable, the hills were suddenly familiar to him, he settled back and closed his eyes.

The sandwiches they had packed had been eaten en route, some time ago; only lukewarm coffee still lay in the thermos resting in the basket on the back seat. They had had a good run, but Katie was feeling tired. It had been a long drive, much longer than any she had undertaken in the past. It wasn't hunger or thirst that made her want to stop, she wanted to stretch out her limbs, her neck was feeling knotted. What she wouldn't have given right now for a neck and shoulder massage. The road and the traffic had taken their toll on her concentration. How many more miles were there still to go? The noise of the cars and lorries was making her head ache. Almost at the end of her tether, and just minutes later, a sign appeared, one she had been watching for, pointing the way to Topcliff and Thirsk. It was her turning, at long last.

When the car suddenly turned left off the dual carriageway, Louis woke up with start. Had he really dropped off to sleep? He couldn't believe it, it seemed just a moment ago that they were passing through the Vale of York. His eyes had felt heavy; the motion of the car had been hypnotic. As the car climbed the steep incline, he watched the junction coming closer until a large painted sign greeted them. An arrow pointing to the right exit was below the public sign that pointed to Thirsk and York. Signs advertising lodgings were scattered on the roundabout and a light green board with gold lettering advised that the four-star Avondale Hotel was fifteen miles down the road. Thank goodness, thought Katie, we are almost there.

Small settlements, villages and farms, dotted the vista through which they travelled, Louis was worried as they drove down the narrow roads; miles were passing but he was unable to recall any of the countryside he was seeing. Village names in the Yorkshire Wolds that stretched along the edge of the moors should have jogged his memory but nothing looked familiar. It was perhaps another half hour and a few miles further on when a sign for Newton turned up; perhaps that could be Newtown, the town near his village?

They came to a place where the moors stretched out on one side of the valley and the rich farmland on the other. A small white and black sign was set in a grassy verge that announced the approaching houses. At last, they were driving through his village of Ravensend. It was larger than he remembered and no longer a village.

He was drowning in emotions; his heart was racing and he wiped a small tear from his eye with the back of his hand. It was all familiar and yet changed.

"Katie, this is my village," he whispered, hardly daring to go on. "Can we stop?"

"Oh, Louis, I know you're eager to reacquaint yourself, but I'm tired. I want to get to the hotel. It will be dark soon. If you can bear it, let's get settled, have supper and a good night's sleep and visit tomorrow."

He looked at his darling girl. She had been driving since morning and she looked exhausted. He had had a little snooze, what was he thinking?

"Let's do that," he nodded, "we have until Monday to explore." Disappointed, he patted her on her shoulder, but at least they had a plan for tomorrow. The road stretched on and passed the hazel grove he knew; it was thicker and wilder of course. His heart, lurched as a memory flooded back. On a warm, summer night under the soft mellow light of full moon and the twinkling of stars, he experienced physical love there with Sophia, the woman he had married to his cost. He shuddered at the thought and pushed it to the back of his mind. He had half-expected the memories to come tumbling out, but still had not been ready for that.

The Mini sped on, half a mile down the road was the small village of Bagly, another name he remembered from the past. Katie indicated and they took a right turn at the T-junction and followed a narrow lane. He completely missed the sign for the hotel that was partly hidden by a large bush, but Katie seemed to know where she was heading. The tree-lined rough track lasted for about a mile. He thought it was familiar. Looking beyond the trees, he could see it coming to an abrupt end and opening up to reveal a gravel drive and a large gateway flanked by a pillar on either side of it.

Katie exclaimed in excitement. "Look, here we are."

Blood drained from his face he stared, open-mouthed. A house loomed large beyond the gateway.

What was he doing here? Memories that stretched back years flooded into his brain. This was where he met and fell in love with Sophia. This house represented that love, his fate, and his death all in one. She had wanted shutters for the south-facing sitting room. The commission had made his name famous and he had been sought-after for his skills. Sophia had become his lover, his wife and in a moment of madness and jealously his murderer, not in this house, but this was where it all started.

10

Eagles topped grey granite pillars that guarded the impressive driveway leading to the large house; a house that Louis knew all too well. Its name was chiselled in the granite – Avondale Hall was now the Avondale Hotel; why hadn't he guessed?

Slowing down, Katie indicated left to turn into the drive of the property.

"Oh my God! Katie, do you know where you have brought me?"

His voice was strained. She turned her head quickly to see him. The look on his face alarmed her. His forehead was furrowed with a deep frown of anxiety and he looked deathly pale.

"Louis, whatever is the matter?'

"This house," he answered through gritted teeth. "This house is the home, or rather was the home, of my father-in-law, Mr Pennock, and where I met my wife."

Katie was stunned. Of all the places she could have taken him to, fate had chosen this one! She was horrified, so much so, that she pulled over to the side of the drive and stopped the car.

"But, but," she spluttered, not quite knowing what to say. The lovely surprise she had planned for Louis was suddenly spoiled. "Louis, I'm so sorry. I booked here because it was near to the village that you lived in. I thought it would be just right, within easy reach of Ravensend and somewhere nice to stay." She stopped in mid-sentence not quite knowing what more she could say.

Things had gone horribly wrong, even before the weekend had started.

Taking his face in her hands, Katie looked into his eyes. "We can cancel and find somewhere else, don't worry." she reassured him with a smile on her tired but concerned face.

Louis was grateful for the offer; she was kind and considerate, but curiosity was urging him to take a look inside the house that had influenced his life and death. Time, after all, had moved on and changes were bound to have taken place, Sophia's home was an hotel now, what else had it been over the years after Mr Pennock had died? he wondered. It was his turn to look into Katie's eyes, and he reminded himself that Katie had driven for hours to bring him back to this part of England; his birthplace, his roots. He should be grateful and he was. He scolded himself and smiled.

"I was just shocked for a minute, my darling girl, of course we are staying here. Seeing the gates took me back to the time I first saw them; it was a surprise, that's all. Come on, let's park up and see what's happened to the old place." His voice was light-hearted, but in truth he was unsure of just what he felt.

There was visible relief on Katie's face as she moved the car into gear and continued to the car park. The journey had been a long one even though they had stopped a couple of times, and she was tired, desperately ready to freshen up, have a nice meal with a well-earned glass of wine.

She wanted this break to be special and only hoped that having started badly that things would improve.

As they carried their luggage to the front entrance, Louis could already see some of the changes around him. The flower garden had been considerably reduced in size; it had lost half of what it had been in his time. The sundial was still standing like an old friend on the same spot, and he remembered the image of Sophia standing there looking like a goddess in the sun. He could not still his rapid heartbeat at the memory, the memory that was tinged with sadness and a sense of loss. The small circular stone wall that had surrounded it had vanished, gone with the passing of time. It saddened him to see it missing. It had been a finishing touch to the flowerbed where he had first seen Sophia picking spring flowers all those years ago.

To the left of the sundial, in the shelter of the trees, he could see where a children's playground had been erected. A row of swings, a slide and a climbing frame painted in primary colours stood empty, save for one mother standing behind the small child on a swing. She dutifully pushed the excited girl who was squealing with delight and begging to be pushed higher each time the swing slowed down.

The kitchen vegetable plot, rich with home-grown food, had gone too. He seemed to be able to smell the herbs from it on the air, a figment of his imagination, a fleeting memory. It would now seem to be a staff car park, according to the large notice board that stood at its entrance.

He turned his attention back to the few steps that would take Katie and him up to the open black oak doors and a darkness that he couldn't see beyond. He suddenly feared the gap that looked like a large open mouth of some wild beast ready to swallow him. His nerves were getting the better of him. What on earth did he have to fear? It was 1972 not 1800.

These few steps he had to take were even worse than when he had had to walk through the Echo's office pretending to be Mike. Yet he wanted to see inside the building. He wanted to see for himself that the twentieth century had arrived in that house. He steeled himself as Katie walked up the steps before him and up to the glass partition that had a revolving glass door at its centre, separating the outside from the interior. Two people were coming out and passed them on the steps. Katie and Louis took position in the triangle of glass that the other couple had left and walked as it moved, spitting them out into what seemed like a dark reception after the daylight outside.

The glass-spinning doorway was another first for Louis. It took a few seconds for his eyes to adjust from the brightness of the car park to the half-light in the heavily panelled, dark hall he remembered, where he had once stood waiting to see the man that would change his life.

Katie was already at a long, wooden-panelled, high counter, and with great aplomb struck a domed bell to get the attention of the two receptionists who had their heads together poring over some papers whilst checking notes on a clipboard.

A blond young woman wearing the name tab Jackie looked up at the sound of the bell. She straightened up and came across to the counter bearing a smile showing her evenly shaped, whiter-than-white teeth.

"Good afternoon, can I help?" she asked in a singsong north Yorkshire accent.

Louis' heart leapt; it was good to hear that depth of warmth in a voice. His eyes had adjusted to the light and they searched the old hall; he saw the staircase that swept up to the first floor and its halfway landing and saw the image, a face that seemed to be looking down at him from the wall. The canvas hung against the stained wooden panelling. One could not mistake the beauty of Mrs Pennock, Sophia's mother. It looked darker than he remembered, as though it has lost some of its original colour, but it didn't detract from her good looks.

A hundred and seventy-two years had passed and she was still gazing down on all who entered her hall, strangers that now invaded what was her child's family home. He stared; he had to admit she was very beautiful in an old-fashioned way; there was something about the eyes.

A cold draught caught him at the back of his neck, and he shivered. The face seemed to overlay itself with another; it was only for a fleeting second but it seemed he saw the face of Sophia. A trick of the light? He heard rather than saw movement behind him. He turned; the revolving door was still moving as a new guest pushed their way out of it, struggling with a case.

That was the explanation of the cold on his neck and the light reflection from the glass must have glanced on the painting. It was just the past playing heavily on his mind. Sophia indeed!

"What nonsense!" he said out loud.

"What nonsense?" repeated Katie.

"Nothing, nothing at all, my imagination is running away with me." He pointed to the painting, "Tell me, what do you think of the portrait?"

"Do you know who that is?" Katie inquired.

"That, my love, is Mrs Pennock," he dropped his voice and whispered in her ear, "my mother in-law."

Before Katie could respond, Jackie broke into the conversation.

"Sorry, but did you say you know who that was? That painting I mean," she interjected. "Well, you see, it came with the property, and we had no idea who she is," she corrected herself, "was. Do you really know who she was?"

She stood behind the counter, holding a key for the room in one hand and the forms for Katie to fill out in the other, but she made no attempt to hand them to her.

Jackie's head was cocked to one side waiting for an answer, her face full of expectation.

"Well," replied Louis, "I do know a little of the history of this house."

But before he could go on, Jackie's smile widened. Words fell from her mouth as she informed them excitedly that the portrait had been found with some wonderful carved shutters that were wrapped and hidden in the attic.

"We had the painting hung there, it seemed the right place for it," she said, pointing at the wall. "You will see the shutters in the dining room this evening, if you're eating with us?" she added, the question hanging in the air. "We hung them in the sunniest room where they must have hung, originally, because they fitted perfectly. We couldn't understand why they had been abandoned. What's your story, what can you tell us?"

How much should he tell her? It couldn't do any harm could it? After all this time, he reckoned not.

"She was the wife of a rich merchant who lived here with their daughter. That is Mrs Pennock," he announced.

Jackie visibly brightened at the information.

"Do you know," she confided in low tones. "There's an old tale from around these parts about a Mr Peacock? His daughter was said to have been hanged for murder. Do you think they might be linked? The name is very similar. I know this place has been a school and hospital and he wasn't linked to those. It makes you think, doesn't it? Of course, that was before we, the company, took the house over and restored it to use as a four-star hotel."

Jackie had hardly paused for breath, but before she could go on Katie stopped her, asking, "Do you think we could have the key and go to our rooms? It's been a long day."

"Why, yes, of course what was I thinking? If I could just get you to sign this form?" She pointed to where a cross had been marked; Katie hurriedly signed her name, took the key, whispering under her breath to Louis as they walked away from the counter, "That woman could talk breathing in."

Louis was stunned. After all these years, part of his story was still being talked about, even if the names involved had somehow altered with time. He had not thought that coming back would be stressful, but his wife's crime, it would appear, had not been forgotten. It was a crime committed in the reign of George not Elizabeth the Second. There was no-one to remember him, no-one to point a finger and he must remember that now he was in Mike's body; a modern man.

11

SOPHIA

Because of all the changes that had happened in the house, she knew
that time had passed, had moved forward into a different century. This
was her home and yet strangers had come and gone, moving through the
house, changing it like they owned it, wearing different clothes from her
own century's fashions. In a strange way, she found it entertaining; the
compensation was that she had company.

She had woken up amongst her precious flowers by the sundial. She
couldn't remember going to sleep there, not that it mattered. She had
found her way indoors to search for her father but when she discovering
him, he didn't seem to see her or hear her.

She had tried to talk to him but he never answered.

She was different now; she knew that, but he had always loved her
dearly; surely, he could feel her nearness to him? She persisted in talking
to him for some time until it became apparent that he never heard her; in
the end she was just content to be near him. But she was concerned about
him, he was losing weight and tears were never far away. He would go into
the sitting room, that had once been his favourite room, to look at the
carved shutters; they had brought them together. He had ordered them
from Louis; she remembered the excitement when they were first hung.
It was that very afternoon that Louis asked for her hand in marriage. Her

father had agreed to it. She guessed that the pain of all the memories had became so great that he ordered his servants to remove the shutters, wrap them in thick woollen fabric. He also had her mother's portrait removed. Kneeling on the floor he had cried, tears streaming down his old, grey face as he wrapped the painting in blankets to protect its delicate surface.

"She looked so much like you, my darling wife," the words staggered between his sobs. "But she was selfish and jealous. Where was the kindness, the love? Where did I go wrong? I loved our daughter, indulged her. How could she kill Louis? Why? Why? Why?"

He could not gaze upon the painting without being constantly reminded of her terrible crime. She, stood next to him unable to understand why her father was taking Louis' side.

"Why?" screamed Sophia at him, but once again he didn't appear to hear.

"Why? Because he didn't want me anymore and I had given up everything for him."

In her anger, she caused the room temperature to plummet. There had been no sound for her father to hear; he wasn't aware of her closeness to him, all he felt was an icy coldness that swept around the room, making him shiver.

"What did I do?" he repeated in a half-whispered voice, sniffing in an attempt to stop the flow of his tears. He had a sore throat and a headache, and his remorse was painfully stabbing him in his chest.

"Nothing, nothing, you silly old man, it was Louis' fault, don't you see that?" was Sophia's reply. Why didn't her father understand that? Louis had all the fun; he got out and about with his work and everybody loved him while she had nothing and nobody. Her friends had let her down; they had felt she had married beneath her station and she paid the price. She was ostracised, not one friend turned out for her wedding. She was lonely and nobody cared.

The old man stayed with his labours, he never looked up as she shouted the words at him. He continued to busy himself, wrapping the canvas. Meanwhile, his servants worked to dismantle the carved shutters from the windows; they also wrapped them with great care in thick blankets before carrying them to attics. They would be hidden from the old man's eyes for the rest of his life. Out of sight, out of mind.

Dustsheets were placed over the items in the room; sofas, mirrors, tables and chairs. He closed the door and locked the room, hoping that the memories would stay behind the door and he might get some peace of mind

However, peace had been hard to find since he had brought her home after the execution. She had no place in the churchyard; her crime was too terrible to be buried in consecrated ground. There was no grave and no marker, and that pained him too. With the help of a trusted servant, he had laid her to rest in her flowerbed near the sundial, the place she had loved so much.

His short, evening walk after dinner had become something of an obsession. It always took him to her unmarked grave among the flowers; there he wept a little and tried to remember the good times with his daughter. In the early days, when she was small, there had been lots of happy times. He had doted on her, loved her too much, he accepted that now. How could she have turned out to be a murderer? He shuddered, as he always did, at the thought of it. He had held Louis in the highest regard: a skilled artist and a nice man. He had had such high hopes for the couple when they married. It was a love match, he had been sure of that, otherwise he would not have agreed to the marriage. What went wrong, he would never know. How could his daughter kill Louis in such a callous and horrific way? The emptiness in his heart grew daily. He couldn't fill the void that had been left by the heart-rending affair.

The months passed but the pain didn't ease for him, despite his friends reassuring him that it would get easier with the passage of time; it hadn't. A little piece of his heart was destroyed with each passing month. Food no longer interested him, and in the following months the servants saw him reduced to a frail old man who didn't want help from anyone.

She had wandered around the house following him. It was pointless trying to talk to him but she had wanted to comfort him and be comforted. If only he could hear her; but she knew that there was an invisible veil that separated her from her father. She could hear and see him but he was blind and deaf to her.

Sophia watched him when he took to his bed. A forlorn, grey figure lying under frighteningly white sheets that made his pallor look even greyer. She knew then he had given up the will to live. When death visited him, he was happy to be taken, to be away from the unhappiness of Avondale Hall.

Sophia had stayed by his side, watched as he died. Anger flooded into her, the whites of her eyes glowed red; Louis had done this, he had spurned her so that she had to kill him and now he had killed her father.

If only Louis had been more like her father, she thought, and made his money in international trade; then, she wouldn't have had to give up her social life, her parties, her style, her friends. It was Louis' fault.

She watched as the light came to guide the old man into the next existence, his spirit rising up out of the body, leaving the shell that he had used in life behind. She watched his spirit moving towards the circle of blinding white light, and she moved with it, keeping up with the spirit's shadow that was drawn like a moth to the light.

She badly wanted to go with him, realising that without him, she would be alone; he couldn't leave her. She thought if she kept up with him, they could pass through the circle together. It was a good plan, but as her father's soul stepped through the circular gateway, he disappeared. As she tried to step through it with him, the light closed down, denying her passage, separating her from the one person who had loved her completely. She had missed her father for a long time; he had gone to a place she couldn't go; she had tried but the light had refused her.

She knew she had committed murder and she wasn't sorry, there was no place for her where her father had gone. Her place here in this netherworld was all she had. It was all Louis' fault.

Her home had changed many times after her father had left her. The servants disappeared one by one until she was totally alone. The Hall was closed; curtains were drawn in all the rooms, shutting out the daylight and the outside world. Dustsheets were draped over all the furniture but over time she noticed that the furniture disappeared too, leaving the rooms empty and hollow. Her beautiful garden had grown wild, weeds overtaking the beds and killing her lovely flowers. When she found the gardeners, she would have something to say to them. She looked but she could not find them. Who would tend her flowerbeds? She had tried to take hold of a trowel to work on the beds herself but her hand could get no purchase on the handle. It was the same with the garden fork and she watched in distress as over time the wilderness grew. She had no one to vent her anger upon, no one to meet her orders, not that they would have heard her anyway, in the end she stopped going outside to visit her garden. It had been her joy; now it was her misery.

Mice and spiders had been her only company for so many years that she lost count. She watched as the curtains fell apart, dropping to the bare floors with the accumulation of dust and rot after being exposed to sunlight from the windows for years. Damp had crept like a disease spreading through all the rooms, and it continued to destroy her beautiful home.

Time was not relevant to her; days were not twenty-four hours long like they had been when she was mortal. A day to Sophia might have been a month or a year or even twenty years. She moved in and out of the Hall and saw the changing seasons; trees grew, shed their leaves before new growth sprouting in all the seasons that came and went. She saw them without recognising or counting the years that passed.

It was the workman that disturbed her solitude, her purgatory. The noise of the front oak doors being forced open was deafening and shook the building, waking her to a new age. It took her by surprise. She had only known silence up to that moment, but what followed pleased her. She watched as a team of men marched through the hall loaded down with pails, ladders and all manner of tools. A deep spring clean was about to take place. After the solitude she had endured, suddenly she was among men who were busy making her home habitable again. She enjoyed the noise, the laughter and even the swearing that went on between the men as they shouted and chatted to one another. Fires were lit in the grates to dry out the rooms, burning off the spiders' webs and years of dust that clung in the damp chimneys. The smell of wood smoke and coal was joyous to her soul. They were smells associated with her past memories of her father and happier times. The renovations took a long time, replacing the old wooden floors with new and renewing the plaster walls and ceilings. But it meant life; Avondale Hall was going to be lived in again and she would have company.

The Hall became a hospital. Apparently, there was a war going on somewhere; though not actually in Britain yet. Young men and women were involved in the theatre of fighting. The war office commandeered the Hall to use as a hospital to treat the soldiers who were wounded. Some were shot, burnt or had lost a limb, sometimes the men had all three conditions. Such was war!

It was hard watching death coming so often to the Hall, thought Sophia, taking men, handsome young men to the next world. It didn't seem fair but what had fair to do with anything? As always, she focused on her own pain.

She had died. Hanged. Hers was a crime of passion, an accident even; they had killed her, they didn't understand her plight, no one listened to her. They blamed her. Louis, Louis, Louis; all the sympathy was for him, but wasn't he the reason that all this pain had happened?

That bright light came so often, sometimes she could see it was shaped like a tunnel, drawing the souls into it. Grateful to be free of pain, glad to be free of the memories of the battlefield and the trenches where their brothers and friends had been blown to hell, those young men were pleased to go.

She heard them cry, scream with pain. She had accidently blended with a dying man, hoping to be taken with him into the light, but it was a dreadful mistake. She had felt his pain and seen the internal damage he had suffered and all because she had held his hands. He was already part spirit but still mortal; her touch had connected with him and some strange power had pulled her into his body. She would never know the exact moment his heart stopped. His soul hadn't given her passage. She was thrown from his body when he entered the tunnel, unwanted like an old rag doll for the rubbish bin. It was awful and she wouldn't make that mistake again. She had been rejected. It wasn't her fault.

Sometimes, she saw the spirits of people who had already passed, happy to greet the newcomers, to meet their brothers in arms and take them through the gateway to a life beyond this. She mused that her father had passed through such a light and she was happy for him, though she missed him dreadfully.

There were times when two or more young men would die within seconds of each other and it occurred to her she might be able to pass through within a group. If more than one soul was passing, she would just be another in the throng and would not be noticed. She had tried several times; she had even reached the circle edge with some souls but it was as though there was an invisible net over the entrance barring her way. Each time she pushed forwards, a force pushed her back.

She eventually gave up trying. Then the world inside her home changed again. The war was over. Fewer damaged servicemen came to be healed. Time moved on. From the windows, she could see that gardeners had been hired to tame the wilderness that hurt her eyes when she gazed on her once beautiful gardens. It pleased her to watch order come back into the borders, though flowers that perhaps she would not have chosen were now growing there. She had not wanted to go outside, to visit her sundial, but now the beds were in some sort of order, the garden beckoned her.

She watched as uniforms changed. The army no longer used her house but it was still a hospital. Civilians replaced the war casualties; the soldiers disappeared.

Doctors and nurses replaced the army medics. There was a new war going on with an infectious bacterial disease called tuberculosis. It was the new enemy, brought back from the trenches and caught by the unsuspecting public. It destroyed the lungs and killed indiscriminately. No one knew how to cure it; but with good food and fresh air some were saved.

Change came again, and death didn't visit so often. And then another war came to rob humanity of young lives.

Sophia heard the words 'baby home' when the nurses talked. More and more children came to the hall, some babies but mostly toddlers. She found out it was a home for war babies. These were children who had lost their parents in the Blitz or who were casualties of one-night stands, war babies in every sense. Life was hard for many women, their men never returning from the front lines. Most mothers were young and were required to work towards the war effort, and were therefore unable to cope on their own. It was a time of need for the children. Food was still scarce, but here they would be provided for, given shelter, food and a place of safety. Some were malnourished when they came, some neglected; all were cared for and brought back to good health by the staff.

For Sophia, it was a time to enjoy the energy that the children brought with them; she observed that children never seemed to walk if they could run, never stood still if they could hop. They spent their time playing and just being children.

She felt cheated; Louis had denied her the chance of being a mother, and she had wanted a child with him. A pretty little girl she could dress and shop with, sing together, sew together. He would have loved their child, he would never have left her, he would have been hers forever. He would have not needed to die.

She reflected that Louis had loved her energy and her boldness at first; she had been so beautiful and she still regarded herself to be so in spirit form. There were times when the trauma of her hanging came flooding back.

She didn't remember much about the lead up to her arrest. It had been early in the morning and she was outside in the street. She was still in her nightdress. Her nosy neighbour who was already up and hanging washing had seen her, she recalled that. Had she told the old crone what she had done? She supposed so. Creeping back into the workshop cottage, she entered the bedroom, not believing what she had done. Louis lay on their bed, the bread knife protruding from his back. She half-remembered getting dressed in a daze, not daring to look at the bed or Louis, before a number of men rushed in and dragged her to the constable.

Her trial had been over so quickly. After a while, she realised it hadn't been her fault, she had tried to tell them but they wouldn't listen. Where was her father? He always knew what to do when she was in trouble. Everyone was against her.

'Hanged by the neck until dead.' That's what the judge had said, wearing a silly black silk handkerchief on top of his wig. He had looked so ridiculous. But it hadn't been funny at all. Her clothes were taken from her, replaced by prison garb, and she had to stay in a cell that was poorly furnished and cold. The fact that she would die soon seemed too remote; it was as though it were happening to someone else and she was an onlooker, the reality of it evaded her.

For most of the time that she was incarcerated, she believed her father would come and rescue her from the hell she was in. But the weeks passed and nothing happened. She never heard from him. She guessed they were keeping him from her. The last time she had seen him had been on that final day in court, that dreadful day her future ended. Why hadn't her father come? He had always been there for her, got her out of scrapes and sorted out her problems.

Right up to the time the priest came for her last confession, she had believed she would be spared the hangman and go free. He father would come. But he didn't. Instead, the grey-haired old man with sad eyes, dressed in black robes, came to sit and pray with her. Her hope dissolved and as it disappeared it left a heavy hole in her heart. What did that old man know about life and passion? Of her life with Louis? She had played along with him, though her mind was not on prayer. She prayed because she needed some company and sympathy but, in her heart, she knew who was to blame for the position she was in, and it wasn't her.

Morning came on the day she would take her last walk; the walk to the room where she would die. It was early in the morning when they came for her, and the key sounded monstrously loud when it turned in the lock. The door squealed, as she did inside, when it opened, revealing the gaoler. The priest hardly lifted his head at the incomers; he had done this before.

They escorted her out of her cell, and the noise of their footsteps as they walked the stone-flagged corridor was so heightened by her fear that they seemed like deep drumbeats announcing her demise. How strange it was that she could hear the dawn chorus of birds; life continued beyond those bleak walls and she wouldn't be part of it again.

She remembered that and shivered at the old memory. She had not slept and was bitterly cold with tiredness. She remembered thinking that she would be sleeping for eternity soon enough, but she hadn't. The priest, with the prison head warden and a woman gaoler had brought her to her fate. She had nowhere to run. She fought the tears back. They were beneath her pride, so she stood tall and defiant while they tied her wrists and ankles.

The woman gaoler had made her stand on a white cross that was painted on a trap door.

It was the hood that broke her, that rough, smelly sacking that they forced over her head, putting her in semi-darkness. She closed her eyes, trying to force the tears back but they came anyway. When she felt the noose placed around her neck she was sobbing, but she was still aware of the priest chanting behind her, praying for her soul. Fear, tears and the smell of the hessian were choking her. God, she needed to pee and she was going to be sick. Somewhere behind her, the muttering of the priest continued until she heard the mechanics of the lever being pulled.

Her last thoughts as a mortal were why hadn't Louis loved her the way she needed to be loved? This was all Louis' fault!

She fell and then felt nothing until she woke in her garden.

The Avondale Hotel was where she lived now; her home, a place not unlike the upmarket hotels in Harrogate. The orphanage had closed and after the last of children had left, a large For Sale notice board had been set up on the lane near the old road to Newtown. It wasn't long before new voices and different men paced around the house, sizing it up. She heard the word hotel more than once. Workmen came into the building, knocking down walls, putting others up, changing her home so much. All the upstairs bedrooms now had bathrooms attached to them with water closets that they called toilets. She groaned when she saw them. How could people have water closets in their bedrooms? So unhygienic. The rooms were smaller, but they were still of a good size and they had been decorated with wallpaper. Of that, she approved.

These new people found the carved shutters her father had commissioned from Louis. They were back in the sitting room where they belonged, hanging at the windows as they once did, only now it was a dining hall, according to the sign. Her mother's portrait was also discovered, wrapped in blankets. It had no name on its frame, even the signature on the canvas was illegible; who she was they didn't know but it was a fine painting that belonged to the period of the house.

Without knowing, they hung it in the very place it had sat so many years previously. Just as it should, thought Sophia. A chair had been thoughtfully set under it. Sophia used it all the time; from there she could observe the comings and goings of the reception, as it was now called. She could watch the revolving door turn, it seemed to throw people into the hall from it. It was delicious. She observed that ladies' fashion had changed drastically since her home had been a hospital. The styles had become casual with women wearing unfeminine trousers and hairstyles where the hair was cropped. Very ugly.

She had been idly watching the door turn, as she was seated in the armchair under her mother's portrait, when she saw something that made her look twice. The revolving door released a couple who seemed rather dazed, or at least the man did. There was something odd about the man, he was different from the other men she had seen enter the hotel.

She moved quickly towards him and could see a double image, a shadow inside the man. How she knew what she was seeing, she wasn't sure, but she had been absorbed into a mortal body once herself and she was certain she was seeing a spirit within the shell of a body that didn't belong to that soul.

There was something familiar about the man; the way he was standing reminded her of someone. She moved towards the couple as they stood at the desk. She wanted to see this man up close, to look under the skin to see what, who was there? And there it was, there was something about the eyes. It was said that the eyes were the windows to the soul, and the soul she was looking at, was that of her dead husband, Louis.

It was a shock; how could it be him? Hadn't she killed him with the breadknife?

It was confusing. Louis was there just a few steps in front of her, wearing a living shroud that belonged to someone, a soul that had passed on. How could that have happened?

After all this time, was she really seeing her husband? How could he be alive?

How could he be able to live, breathe and function like a mortal when she could only exist? She had killed him, and they had killed her for it but she couldn't pass on to the next realm of existence. That's why she was here, walking the halls, haunting the rooms in the only place she could as a spirit. It wasn't fair.

The anger that she felt so many years ago was back and aimed at Louis. Searing heat filled her head and, her eyes burned a flame red; when she let out a scream, ice-cold air filtered around the reception area.

The cold of her icy scream hit the back of his neck and involuntary shivers shot down his back. What was that? He suddenly thought of Sophia. He looked at the portrait that hung above him. She had been so like her mother. A question hit him. He was afraid of what the answer might be; could the cold he felt be from her? Like him, was she an unsettled spirit haunting here right now.

He tried to dismiss the thought. A noise behind him made him turn and he saw the door revolving with its divided portals, having spewed yet another guest into the reception clutching a black-and-white checked overnight bag. He heaved a heavy sigh. It had been nothing more than the cold air that had been pushed into the reception from the door. That was it. Question answered. But why had he thought of Sophia?

Sophia stood, quivering, looking at the two of them. So, this small, chestnut-haired woman was his companion! Jealousy lay in her heart and anger in her passion; they fused together like smelted steel did before hardening when cooled, filling her with visceral hatred for Louis. She made a vow there and then that he would not have another woman in his life; they would not be together for long if she had anything to do with it.

Somehow, she would separate them and have her revenge. How she would achieve it she didn't yet know, but her cunning was awakened and she would get rid of this dowdy, insignificant woman and put him back in the netherworld that she and he belonged to.

How long were they here for? she wondered. Time was something she had plenty of, but not these two! She slid back to her place under the portrait of her mother; she would watch them closely while they were here. A plan would come; it always did when she put her mind to it.

She watched the key being lifted from its hook by the Jackie person, who in Sophia's opinion suffered from verbal diarrhoea. She was still talking as she handed the key to room ten to that small mousey woman who, by the looks of her, couldn't escape quickly enough from the lobby and the attack of words being flung at her.

She would visit them later, for now she must think of her next move. Purpose had returned to her; she would watch and wait.

12

A king-sized bed with a padded headboard of pale-blue velvet sat on the long wall of the pleasant room that was number ten.

It was blessed with two large windows overlooking what remained of the formal gardens. A weak, autumn sun still sent warmth and light into the room that afternoon when they opened the door, making long rectangles of shadows across the orange and blue floral quilted bedspread. The whole room looked as though it had just been decorated, a soft yellow paint graced the walls complementing the gold carpet that set off the blue striped chairs sitting on either side of the coffee table under the windows. A complimentary box of teas and coffees, sat by a plate of biscuits laid next to two cups, saucers and a kettle for the guests to make themselves a drink in the room.

Katie cast a discerning eye over the room; she was pleased with what she saw.

The bed, covered with the heavy bedspread looked cosy and warm. Just as long it is comfortable, thought Katie. The long drive had tired her; she needed a drink, a bath and a little snooze before dinner and in that order.

Louis had brought up the case and was hanging their clothes in the wardrobe as Katie clicked on the kettle and checked the small fridge for the fresh milk she had been assured would be there by the receptionist.

"Coffee or tea?" she called to Louis.

"Tea please."

Moments later they were sitting on the blue chairs by the windows, enjoying the view of the gardens and sipping tea.

"It's beautiful." And Louis agreed.

Katie found the bathroom and half-turned on the taps getting ready for the bath she longed for. Sipping tea, they could hear the water running slowly into the tub. Draining her cup, Katie checked the water level and turned the taps off, before coming back to have a second cup with Louis. She was longing to have a long soak but her throat was still as dry as a bone; she must quench her thirst. How good it tasted. After the refill, they both visibly relaxed. Louis and his memories were pushed to one side and Katie's stress from the drive was washed away along with the weariness of the long journey. They were at last ready to start their long weekend together.

The used and discarded teacups lay on the table, stacked and ready for the maid to clear later.

"While you're bathing, my darling girl, I think I'll take a turn around the grounds while there is still some light. It's been a long time since I was here and I'm curious to see the changes," announced Louis.

He was curious but there was more to it than that. His unease had started when he realised he was back at the house, and then cold air hit him in the lobby; it had been explained by the revolving door but couldn't shake off the uncomfortable feeling. He wasn't sure why, but something was niggling him. He needed sometime on his own to think about it.

Louis pulled on his topcoat ready to leave.

"I'm off now, Katie," he called out, opening the door. "See you shortly," Taking a key with him, he shut the door quietly as he left.

Katie was already up to her neck in the hot water. The bath was filled with a scented bubble bath, the white foam outlining her form as she laid there. He left her with her eyes closed enjoying the warmth of the water that surrounded her body, soothing and refreshing the parts that were stiff after the hours sitting behind the wheel of her blue Mini.

Louis walked down the hall landing. It was strange to be back inside this house. He had liked Mr Pennock; he had been a fair unpretentious man who had given Louis a step up in life when he needed it. If only Sophia hadn't been there. She had won him at first sight. She had been so captivating; a beautiful goddess. Things could have been so different but even, has the thoughts flashed through his mind, he knew he had loved her with all his heart. He had never understood why she had killed him?

This house was bringing all those memories back and he was filled with a hollow feeling of sadness. This wasn't what he wanted; he was in the here and now of 1972. He thought of his love for Marina and Katie; they had been worth dying for. He nodded, agreeing with his own thoughts as he walked down the hall to the stairs. He loved Katie and she loved him, and he wouldn't allow the past to interfere with what he had now.

He followed the passage to the stairs, passing the lift he had used earlier. He wanted to view the reception from the top of the staircase to observe the changes that had taken place inside the hall. The staircase was very grand; the banisters and spindles were fashioned in a dark ebony wood, the tall spindles stood like soldiers guarding the edges from the drop that would be a fatal fall without their protection. The stairs were split in two parts and halfway down there was a small square landing that held an armchair sitting under the portrait of Mrs Pennock. Louis stopped and stood, his eyes searching the canvas to reacquaint himself with the image and he saw what Mr Pennock had seen in the young woman that looked so full of life. She was so like the daughter she had given birth to, love shone in her face and for a moment he thought Sophia was looking back at him. It startled him. The portrait was so life-like. He could feel his emotions struggling inside him, he must not let the love and pain from the past overwhelm him. The hairs on the back of his neck were prickling and uncomfortable; in an automatic gesture he rubbed his neck with his hand, and he felt a cold chill pass around his body. Sadness filled him with the memories that were hard to ignore and so deeply upsetting. He must move on.

He shrugged his shoulders and fastened his coat, pulling it tightly around himself, continuing down the stairs when another cold draught seemed to rush at him.

There was another rush of cold air as he stepped forward. He lost his balance and seemed to trip over his own feet. He grabbed hold of the banister and one of the spindles with his two hands; only his quick reflexes stopped him toppling down the stairs, saving him from what could have been a nasty fall.

My God, that was close, how did that happen? thought Louis. Not exactly a good start to the weekend, only to die again in a fall.

He half laughed to himself but it wasn't funny. He would have to be more careful; he couldn't lose this body. Not now, he could not lose Katie, not his darling girl. He couldn't bear the thought of going back to the loneliness of his netherworld. The world he had carved for himself was waiting still and it was a beautiful place but he had got used to her touch; her presence made him feel whole; he didn't want to lose that.

The flight of ten steps took him down into the foyer and the revolving door took him out into the grounds he once knew so well.

Could it be warmer outside than indoors? It was touch and go as to which it was, he thought. Curious.

His unease increased. It was difficult to be back in these grounds and house without the past coming back to haunt him.

13

SOPHIA

Sophia had learnt she could move through solid objects. Doors and walls were not a problem, she slid through them with ease; she had no need to hide, sleep or rest. Following guests into their rooms – watching them, eat, sleep, make love, bothered her. She longed to be mortal like they were. Sophia judged the modern women; they didn't understand style or elegance like she did, they wore trousers like men, not a lace edge was to be seen, where were the silks and satins? Given the chance, she'd give those women a run for their money. If those men who accompanied the women could see her beauty, they'd love her. If only she wasn't invisible. She yearned for male company, it had been a long time since someone had touched her, embraced or kissed her. She missed a man's touch so much. She was a nobody, a nothing, wandering around her old home that had become a host to travellers. She knew she was a ghost, a spirit. Her father hadn't seen her or heard her, why then should these people?

However, she had noticed that her anger could generate a response. Shouting at these travellers tended to make them wrap their clothes tightly around them; she generated cold and they shivered until she moved away. There were times when her frustrations boiled over and she didn't want strangers around her and then she would remember the silence of the years when her home was empty, and she put those thoughts aside.

It was by accident that she found she could move through people; a silly woman had stopped on her landing and sat on the chair Sophia was occupying; sat on her, not that she had a lap. She knew that she was a spirit but she was still affronted by the indignity of it. The woman slipped off her one of her shoes and rubbed her toes. Infuriated, Sophia leapt up, passing through the woman without disturbing her. Sophia was surprised; she had expected a reaction, but only the drop in temperature annoyed the sitter.

"God it's freezing here," the shoeless person muttered. "It had better be warm in the bedroom or I'll be checking out."

Sophia had taken a dislike to the woman and once the toe rubbing had finished, had followed her to her room. It amused Sophia to shout abuse at the woman knowing it affected the temperature. The room became fridge-cold but instead of the woman leaving, like she said she would, she telephoned down to reception and demanded an engineer to come and sort out the radiators. Sophia left, though she hadn't finished with the woman yet. By the time the man came up the room had become toasty warm.

Ghosting the room was easy. She pushed her way through the wall throughout the night, leaving it icy after each visit. The lady slept very badly, waking cold and turning up the heat only to wake again too hot; she checked out the next day. Sophia had won that battle. Now, what else could she do?

The chair on the stair landing was the ideal place to sit and people watch, and it was Sophia's favourite place. Sitting under the portrait made Sophia feel close to her mother, a lady she had never really known.

She was sitting there when she saw the double image moving towards her. Louis was coming down the stairs to her landing.

He's handsome, she thought. There was even a small moment of remembered love for him as he stood before her mother's portrait, his thoughtful gaze absorbing the image. But her hate was stronger.

What was he thinking? she wondered, did he see her in that painting? Did he think about her at all?

Then she remembered the other woman in Room Ten. That chestnut-haired piece that had taken him.

'You're married to me,' she whispered in his ear, 'Me, me, only me,' her voice rising until she was yelling. His hand came up to protect his neck from the draught he could feel. He turned to see where it was coming from and saw the revolving door spin as someone had left. Fastening his coat up tight from the cold, he turned to go down to the ground floor and visit the gardens.

She followed his eyes. It's not that, you stupid man. I'm here beside you, your wife, why can't you see me? He was part-spirit just as she was, why couldn't he feel her presence? she thought.

Rage grew in her heart. Anger gave her the power to move objects, a vase here and lamp there. She confused the cleaning staff by moving small items in the rooms; it was peevish and childish but her frustration was too much to bear sometimes, and besides the staff blamed each other for the disorder in the rooms. That frustration was biting her now. She wanted to lash out at Louis, throw something at him, anything would do. But there was nothing on that landing to throw. He was turning to go down the stairs. As he did, she kicked out and hit him in the back of his knee. Her spirit-form passed through the living shell he was trapped in and connected with Louis' spirit. He fell forwards, stumbling as though he had tripped. His response was quick and he managed to save himself by grabbing the banister, steadying himself before carrying on down to the foyer and out into the late afternoon. She had never moved a mortal before, and she suddenly knew power. It was a new experience she liked it.

She thought she might follow him but then she remembered the woman in room number ten; perhaps it was time for a visit.

Sophia slipped through from the passage into the bright bedroom; it was nice enough, well-decorated, though not to Sophia's taste.

The furniture was white not at all like the stylish furniture she had chosen. She remembered the richness of the solid-dark wood in her own bedroom when she had lived here, all beautifully carved and every drawer and door had its own lock and key. It had been large furniture that fitting into large rooms unlike the cottage she lived in once she was married, but the new owners who claimed the Hall for themselves had reduced the room-size and created a small cubicle to hold a bath and water closet.

There was no sign of the woman. The only clue that she was there was a dress laid out on the bed. It looked new and was well-enough made but not of the fabrics Sophia had worn. The only trimming on the dress was a small amount of black lace around the neckline and on the sleeve edge. Could this woman be in mourning? The thought crossed her mind but she immediately rejected it. Sophia had seen lots of women wearing black, young and old alike, going down to eat in those widows' weeds, what were they thinking? How dull they were, it was all very boring, where were the rich colours like those she had worn to grace the dining room and impress the guests?

A sound from beyond the bedroom brought her back to the moment; it came from the small bathroom.

The swish of water moving in the tub and a small splash came to her ears, Sophia drifted over to its entrance, the door was slightly ajar, not that it mattered whether it was open or closed, no doors or walls ever barred her way now. Pushing forward into the steamy room, Sophia looked down on the figure that was up to her neck in warm, sudsy water. The woman had her eyes closed and looked totally at peace. The white of her shoulders protruded teasingly from the many bubbles that surrounded them and she looked as though she might be asleep.

The perfumes of the soaps and bath salts filtered through the air above Katie, bringing a sense of well-being to her as she relaxed in the softened, warm water. There was something special about a good soak in hot, scented water.

A chilling cold stirred in the bathroom as Sophia moved to the end of the sloping side of the bath that supported the head and shoulders of her husband's mistress. She looked down on the undesirable creature and felt a hate that had no space for pity.

How dare this slut of woman capture Louis' heart and then have the gall to come here to humiliate her? She wouldn't just sit back and let them have their way. No-one did that to her. As the red mist invaded her eyes, turning them into spheres, glowing like hot coals, her hands were already moving towards the pale delicate shoulders that were so provocatively just above the waterline. She was tempted to push. And push she did.

The body slid under the water so easily. All she had to do was to keep the pressure up for a few minutes and the trollop would drown: how sweet it was.

Fighting for air, the woman struggled to save herself. A smile stretched across Sophia's mouth. It only added to the pleasure; she had the power over life or death. The smile became a laugh of madness; it was all quite delicious.

The bath water was violently moving with the actions of the once passive body. Water flew into the air, splashing the wall tiles and spilling over the bath side, flooding the floor. Katie struggled, her arms and legs thrashing about as she willed herself to sit up; but as fear filled her, the huge weight on her shoulders that locked her underwater remained. Water filled her nose, and her eyes stung as they flew open with shock.

Sophia was laughing out loud when she heard the door open. She snatched her hands back from the struggling body, her laughter gone as the door shut behind Louis. It was time to go. She slipped through the wall into the hall passageway and made her way back to her chair. There would be time to try again.

"I'm back," Louis called out, as he shut the door. "It's getting dark and a wind's getting up. I'll visit first thing in the morning. Have you enjoyed your bath?"

The spluttering young woman surfaced, wide-eyed and shaking from the water, relieved to take a breath of air. God! What had happened? She pushed the soaking tendrils of her hair back from her face, reached for a towel to dry her stinging eyes. She had thought she was going to die. Her shoulders had felt a frozen mass under the water, so solid that she couldn't lift herself from where she had slipped. She actually felt as though invisible hands had held her down, she had struggled to breathe, fighting to live. Her arms and legs had thrashed about as she tried to save herself. She had nearly drowned. Had she dropped off to sleep?'

She had to admit to herself that she had been drifting on the edge of sleep. A nightmare then, part dream, part panic, until she was able to free herself from it. She had been overtired when she had stepped into the bath, the warm water and scented bath salts had seduced her, relaxing her weary body. Unwinding in the water had been sheer bliss until suddenly her shoulders felt icy above the water line. It passed through her mind to reach the tap to reheat the tub with more hot water, but she was so comfortable lying there, thinking warm thoughts about life and Louis. How lucky that by some strange miracle he had come into her life. Drifting in a daydream, her eyes had closed, wondering how the weekend would be, making plans for tomorrow and then she must have fallen asleep. There was no other explanation. She'd dozed off and nearly killed herself, that's what must have happened.

The bathroom was cosy and warm now, the excessive chill she had felt could only have been her poor body reacting to tiredness. Embarrassed, she admonished herself, what a fool she'd been.

"Are you okay?" Came a concerned voice from the other room.

"I'm fine," she called back, "Just washing my hair," she lied, not wanting to appear foolish. She was so angry with herself. It was a good idea, now her hair was wet, it would freshen her up, so it was only half a lie.

She left the bathroom wrapped in towels. One wrapped around her hair, the other a bath sheet tightly encasing her body, the overlapping ends tucked in at the top between her breasts. She sat in front of a large mirror that rested on the dressing table, her few cosmetics and her compact lined up ready to use. She opened the nearest drawer looking for the hotel's hairdryer and finally found it in the bottom one. By the time she had finished drying her hair she was feeling much better. The fear she had experienced was replaced with an annoying niggle somewhere in her mind, fretting as to what had really happened? Questions rolled; why had she been unable to lift her shoulders from the water? If she had fallen asleep, why couldn't she move when she woke? But there was no other explanation for her immobility. She was so quiet that Louis noticed that something was worrying her.

"Katie, darling, what's wrong?"

She looked up from brushing her hair and half smiled at him.

"Nothing, not really. It's," she hesitated, "I wasn't going to tell you, I feel such a silly fool. I nearly drowned." She laughed but it was not a good sound. "I must have dozed off in the bath. I woke up underwater, unable to move. It was weird! It was as though I was being held down. I heard you call out that you were back and then suddenly I was freed and able to sit up." Her voice was shaking by the time she had described her ordeal.

"Oh, love! You're shaking." Louis saw her distress and, recognising her need for support, he crossed to the stool. His arms slipped around her shoulders and he stooped over to kiss her. The first kiss was a peck really, but the warmth and love she felt from him brought her emotions to the surface, and a tear quietly escaped, running down her face, followed by another, then another.

"You had a bit of a nightmare, love, you must have been very tired after that long drive." He paused and kissed her again but this time on her lips, which tasted slightly salty from the tears that had escaped her eyes.

"Feeling any better?" he asked before kissing her again with rather more passion. It had been a long drive and it was a relief to think that his reasoning was correct. Nightmare or not, she felt safe now.

Standing up to kiss him back somehow loosened the bath sheet that covered her nakedness. As it fell to the floor, Louis scooped her up in his arms and carried her to the king-sized bed, stepping over the towel where it fell.

The warmth of the bedspread and of Louis' body near her, feeling his gentle touch as he explored her body under the covers, drove away all thoughts of the near-death experience. Indeed, their minds were focused on making love, and the next hour flew by.

14

Hunger reminded them that the journey with their homemade sandwiches had been several hours ago.

Katie had reserved an evening meal for them; it seemed sensible to take advantage of the special deal the hotel had offered when she booked.

At 7pm the two of them, dressed in smart new clothes, walked arm in arm down the staircase to the dinning room. Louis was mindful not to have another mishap and watched each step he took down to the ground floor.

Katie wore the little black dress that had been laid out on the bed. It hugged her figure in all the right places and with its low v back neckline was sexy without being overstated. She looked fabulous to Louis and he was proud to have her on his arm.

In the hall, the door to the dining room was open, but a notice clearly stated 'please wait to be seated'. They joined the grey-haired couple who were already waiting, nodded a 'good evening' and stood in line.

Through the open door, Louis could see the room he knew from over a century ago and glimpsed the elegant fireplace. It thrilled and saddened him, dressed as it was with mock modern oriental vases high up on its mantelpiece; the old china dogs he knew had disappeared. A large display of chrysanthemums was set in the central position, obscuring some of the mirror. The mirror was large and stretched the length of the mantelpiece, extending up, finishing just below the dado rail. Its frame was ornately carved and covered in gold leaf. Three chandeliers lit the room, their crystal glass twinkling like stars against a pale blue ceiling. It was modern-day elegance at its best. The reflection gave a feeling of extra space to the already large room. The orange and yellow flowers were beautifully reflected in the huge mirror, the decorations looking twice the size they really were.

An eager young man dressed in black hurried to greet the elderly couple, clutching menus in one hand and pen in his other. He asked their name and room number, and crossed them off his list. He smiled at Louis and Katie.

"Back in a moment," he said in a low voice before moving off with Mr and Mrs Greensmith, ushering them to the other side of the dining room.

Just as he promised, he was back, courtesy pouring out of him, introducing himself as Thomas. He nodded as Katie gave her name, crossing it off his list before taking them to a pleasant table for two by the windows. The gold-patterned curtains were not drawn and they framed the darkness of the gardens beyond the glass. There was a play of drama between the light and dark, a stage to show off a pair of hand-carved wooden shutters that stood as sentinels in the frame.

Here was Louis' first big commission, and maybe the very best carving he had ever done. They filled him with pride; and they looked every bit as beautiful today as they did when he had hung them all those years ago.

They were, in some way, the start of his long journey through time. Memories came flooding back. His passage had not been of his choosing but it had led him to being here with his darling girl.

Without thinking, he reached out to touch the images he had crafted. It was good to feel the warm, silky wood under his fingers. The day he had fitted them, he had asked Mr Pennock for the hand of his daughter in marriage. Tears were trying to escape from his eyes; swallowing hard he fought them back.

Not realising he was staring, he jumped when the young man said, "they're quite special, are they not?" Louis had been lost in thought; Thomas had brought him back to the present. Louis nodded and smiled in agreement.

Thomas called over a young waitress, who looked as though she was just out of school. 'Mavis will look after you tonight, anything you need, just ask.' He gave them the menus. Mavis nodded and said she would be back to take their order. With a broad beam on his face. Thomas left them, turning back towards the doorway to greet the new clients waiting patiently to be seated.

Katie's eyes lit on Louis' face. He was staring, not looking anywhere in particular but she could see his eyes were filled with moisture.

"Are you alright?" she asked in a concerned voice. "What is it?" Reaching over she took his hand.

"These shutters…" He reached out again his, fingers touching the grain of the wood. "Memories," he said in a voice just above a whisper.

She leaned forward over the table so that only Louis could hear.

"They are exquisite, Louis," she whispered back, unable to resist touching them herself. A pair of game birds was hanging down from the wicker basket the huntsman carried. Katie's finger traced over a hunting dog that was prancing excitedly at his master's feet. The sentiment of the carving was the joy of nature and the natural world. It was a feast for the eye.

"I love your work, Louis," Katie said, slightly squeezing his hand. "Just as I fell in love with our bed, this," she stopped, emphasising the sentence, "this is amazing!"

There was a cold blast of air that shot around the table where they sat. Katie shivered; it suddenly felt a topcoat colder in the dining room. Louis also felt an icy waft of air around his head and shoulders. He looked up into Katie's face and then saw the waitress standing behind her. Mavis' face was the colour of parchment; her eyes seemed devoid of life but, under his gaze, her face changed for a microsecond, and the face he saw froze him to the spot. Sophia stared back at him, then she was gone. He took a breath in and started to rise to his feet when Mavis startled him by apologising.

"Oh! Sorry, excuse me I was miles away, I came to tell you about the specials we have on tonight," she said, looking embarrassed. The colour had come back into her cheeks. She handed the Specials Menu to each of them.

Questions floated on the air, prodding and poking at him. Was his imagination playing tricks on him? The trip on the stairs; Katie's strange incidence in the bath; and now a shadow of Sophia on the waitress's face.

Was she a ghost?

Lord! He hoped he was wrong. Uncomfortable at the very thought, he didn't want to believe what he was thinking but he couldn't dismiss it altogether. He would keep his suspicions to himself, sitting in Sophia's old home, surrounded by so many memories; perhaps he was overreacting.

15

SOPHIA

She had followed them into the dining hall. It had been her favourite room when she had lived here with her father; she remembered it was the room in which Louis had asked for her hand in marriage, a marriage she came to regret. It was the same room with its south position, that had convinced her father to commission those decorative shutters that were now once again at windows. That was when she first met him. She shook her head in frustration; it was a bittersweet memory that had jarred in her mind.

She dogged their steps as they were ushered to a small table by the window.

Who did he think he was, acting so high and mighty, so well above his station? Parading with this bloody Jezebel dressed in black, thought Sophia, looking at Katie, resenting what she saw. Well! She should be more careful in her choice of men.

Meanness was building in Sophia's soul. She remembered her fears from the past and the jealousy she had endured, watching him with other women. Women loved being near him, and though she had never seen him act improperly, she hadn't trusted him. He was still her husband; this affair proved all her suspicions.

Maliciously she thought, I'll show him he's not free of me. A crooked smile played on her lips, once so beautiful, but there was no beauty in her face that evening. Her twisted soul betrayed her; her face was full of spite.

Standing next to the couple, her anger rose further when she saw them tenderly touching hands over the table. Shouting 'No' at their tenderness, she sent a mist of icy breath over Katie, making her shiver, Sophia smirked.

A young waitress stood with menus in her hand just behind her competition. Sophia sneered as she quickly melted into the body of the serving girl, blending with her, and stopping movement and speech in the poor woman. The laugh Sophia gave was terrible and sent out a further cold stream, directed at Louis who was inspecting his own creation of wood by the window. The cold blast connected with him and his concentration moved from the wood to Katie and then to the statuette figure that was in attendance. Attendance yes, but where was she?

Sophia peered out through Mavis's eyes at the man she once loved. Now it was the time to show herself. Without another passing second, she forced her face forward, overlaying herself on the face of the unfortunate Mavis. It was just for a second. But it was enough; she saw Louis' face change; he was shocked, he had recognised her but recovered himself quickly, and that silly Mavis girl found her voice, apologising and handing them the menus.

Louis would know now she was here, haunting her old home. She promised herself she would visit him again soon, in private. It had been a mistake for him to come back to Avondale Hall; she had been shocked to see him enter her home, albeit clothed in another man's skin. Here could be an opportunity to discover how he had found a donor body to live in. If her spirit couldn't move on, how wonderful it would be to live again, to feel, eat, dress and make love. She tingled at the thought of being touched, loved; a smile lingered on her face, she had enjoyed sex. Louis had been good at lovemaking, she remembered.

She nodded, sitting under the portrait of her mother watching these mortals. Yes, she would rather like to be alive again. She would never make the same mistakes she had made in her short life. No more jealousy, or temper, or at least not until she had got rid of Louis or the silly bitch. One of them would have to go. Her mind was set.

He had to be honest with himself; he had felt something as soon as he walked into the reception area. It was complicated by his memories of this old place, but it had been there; a feeling of Sophia in spirit. He thought it was all the memories that crowded in on him and hadn't wanted to believe it, but now, sitting with Katie and watching Mavis walking away, his concern was growing.

What talents had Sophia found on her long existence trapped in this house? He knew of Sophia's wrath, her temper and what she could mete out. Could she do more than haunt and blend? Could she use a donor body like a puppeteer pulling strings?

God forbid she could move objects and command people.

He must try to act normally and not spoil the evening or their stay for Katie. He felt sure he would feel Sophia's presence if she came near, now he was aware of her. He would be vigilant. If only he could work out what his dead wife's intentions were. He must think very seriously about it.

Mavis returned and took their order. They settled on a shrimp cocktail to start, followed by fish pie made with the harvest from the sea from Whitby.

When the dish was served, it was piled high with creamy mashed potatoes and a cheese sauce under which held layers of different fish, haddock, cod, and prawns. Buttered cabbage, carrots, and fresh garden peas accompanied it.

They toasted themselves with a German Riesling. It was a meal to remember. Strangely, once fed, Louis felt less worried about Sophia's restless spirit. Yes, she had shown herself to him, but for the rest, it could be his imagination and Katie had probably dropped off to sleep in the bath.

As they sipped the last of the wine, finishing off the cheese and biscuits, Katie could not help herself but relate the incident in the bath again. It was obviously worrying her.

"You're right, I must have dozed off," she said in an embarrassed tone, looking at her wine rather than have eye contact. "One minute I was resting in the warmth of the water, I felt a little cold so I slid down further in the bath, my eyes were closed." She nodded to herself at the memory of it. "Well, as I said, the next thing I remember was I was underwater. It was such a stupid thing to let happen, I suppose the drive took it out of me?" She offered it as a rational explanation, agreeing with Louis and his opinion. She took another sip of wine and suddenly smiled, remembering why she had chosen to bring Louis here.

"Anyway, we are here now. How do you like the place?" She leaned across to him, looking steadily into his eyes. "Has it changed much since your time?" She was looking at the shutters, admiring the elegance of them and how they suited the room.

"Those are definitely your work, as sensitive in skill as our, well my, bed," she teased, squeezing his hand as she finished her sentence.

Louis smiled back but he was troubled. The mention of the cold she had felt in a warm bathroom wasn't right. It could have been Sophia. He wasn't ready to share his fears with Katie, and he could be wrong. She had arranged this trip because she loved him, why should he bother her with his suspicions? He looked at Katie, wondering how he had become so fortunate to be loved by such a generous woman.

"I must make sure you don't go to sleep in the bath again. Perhaps we should have baths together?" he teased, in a light-hearted way, covering how he felt.

Coffee with mint chocolates finished off the meal. They had enjoyed each other's company. They discussed the world that Louis left behind and how the house had been the catalyst for his marriage and death. By the time they had finished the last dregs of wine, what with the journey and the meal inside them they both felt exhausted and ready to sleep.

As they climbed the stairs, Louis was already wondering where his ghost wife was lurking. At some stage, he would have to tell Katie what he had seen but not now. Not tonight.

The gentle pushing on his shoulder brought him out of his slumber. At first, he thought he might have been snoring and disturbing Katie. He moved to turn over. Wine somehow triggered him to snore. This wasn't the first time he had been woken from his sleep by an indignant Katie. He opened his eyes, wondering how long he'd slept. The room was very dark;

a narrow gap in-between the curtains allowed him to see the sky over the garden, where heavy rainclouds hid the moon, giving no light in the sky and none to the room. No light showed under the door from the hallway either; everything was in slumber and the dawn was still far away.

He been sleeping with his back to Katie; the wine and the food at dinner had been as good as a sleeping draught. With sleep still in his eyes, he rolled slightly forward to reach the light switch on the table lamp by his bedside. He felt her body close up to his as he stretched out to turn it on, and her hand came across him to catch his arm. "No, don't do that," her voice whispered in his ear. "Let's cosy up in the dark."

He felt her move even closer, curling up to the shape of his own body. She kissed his neck whilst stroking the arm she had caught, pushing her arm under his. Caressing his chest and entwining her leg over his she pulled him back to the mattress.

He hastily removed his nightwear. He could feel the softness of her skin next to his in the darkness and he realised she was also naked. Her hands were tenderly moving across his chest slowly making their way down towards his manhood. This was new; he was surprised but content at being the object of her love.

He lay there with his eyes closed, enjoying the foreplay of love from her. He couldn't think what had aroused her so, but perhaps this break was a tool to liberate her emotions, a way of getting over the Mike and Debs' incident back home.

Whatever it was, he settled down to making love with his darling girl. It was always special, not a game for those who didn't truly love each other; they understood the magic of sharing. Slowly the eagerness of their zeal grew until nothing in the world could have stopped them reaching a climax. It was then he felt the claw-like nails digging into his back as they rocked together in passion. His seed was spilt.

His back felt scratched. Katie had never done that before. She had always been gentle in her lovemaking. A memory from way back hit him like a thunderbolt. It couldn't be, could it? It was a truth he didn't want to face, but there had only been one woman he knew who used her nails when making love.

Almost in panic, he stretched out to the small side lamp, switching it on. Its light cast a soft, glow on the face of Sophia as she straddled him. A look of pure triumph lit her face as she stared down at him. Smiling like a cat that had got the cream, she was positively purring. His heart felt cold and heavy; like a rock it sank deep into his troubled soul. He hated what he saw.

"No! Not you." The words escaped from his mouth as he pushed the body of Katie off him. Sophia was laughing as she left the comatose body of Katie lying slumped next to Louis. She had no qualms about what she had done; she was enjoying herself. Louis had always made love well and it had been a long, long time since she had tasted the joy of making love. She was satisfied with the outcome of her little prank; he was still her husband after all. That common little bit she had used, deserved no less. It was a novel feeling being able to use a donor body; now she knew how to do it, it wouldn't be the last time. She'd enjoyed the experience.

Louis was shocked, Sophia had blended with Katie and used her body to have her way with him. He was suddenly ashamed of himself. He had been so sure he would sense Sophia if she was near. Like a fool he had not suspected that she would come while they were sleeping. He had been duped. He suddenly felt sick.

Sitting up, he covered himself and the prone body of Katie with the top sheet from the bed. Although he couldn't see her, he heard the voice of Sophia in his head as she circled the room laughing. He tried to stop the sound of her madness by pressing his hands against his ears; it suddenly faded when she passed through the wall into the hall and beyond. She had gone, but there remained an unpleasant smell of something he couldn't describe. Louis was horrified. What had he allowed to happen?

A startled Katie pushed her way up into a sitting position next to Louis. She looked dazed, still half asleep and in a confused voice asked, "What's happened?"

The top sheet dropped and she realised with a shock that she was naked. Where was her nightdress? She moved her legs and felt a distinct dampness between them. Reaching down she felt the thick moisture between her thighs.

The look on her face tore at Louis' heart.

"Louis, what happened, what's happened to me?" she repeated in a high voice, her face pleading for an answer.

How was he to answer? He'd let her down. He was there to protect her from harm and he had failed miserably. He was so choked with emotion he could hardly speak, and tears welled up in his eyes. What had Sophia made him do? How could he ever put this thing right?

His arms wrapped around her and he drew her close.

"Oh, Katie, I'm so sorry."

"Sorry for what Louis, what did you do?" Katie was trembling, her eyes filling with tears as she pulled back to look him in the face. He was sickened by Sophia's duplicity. His face showed his disgust and discomfort. What would Katie think when he told her?

"What do you mean; sorry?" The look of confusion on her face was being replaced with fear.

"What do you mean, Louis?" she demanded. She was frightened, where were her nightclothes? She had been dreaming a rather erotic dream of making love with Louis but she knew it was a dream. Or was it? Why did she think that? And where on earth was that smell coming from? It made her feel bilious.

Louis put his powerful arms about her and he pulled her towards him in a protective gesture. It did not help her fear; it proved rather to do the opposite. She was visibly shaking in his arms as he held her tight to him. His hand held her head gently into his shoulder like a father might do for a frightened child who had had a nightmare, but this was not a disturbed dream, this was an attack on his woman by an aggrieved spirit. His darling girl had had no power to fight back; somehow, he must find a way to protect her, and he must tell her the truth of what had happening that evening.

"It was Sophia, Katie, I should have told you." He stopped as she pulled her head from his shoulder. "I just didn't want to scare you." He searched her eyes.

"Look let's put our nightclothes on, make a drink and then I'll tell you what happened."

She nodded. She wanted to clothe herself. Feeling vulnerable in his arms was awful, she had never felt like this before and never wanted to feel this way again. A warm drink would help her stop shivering, she concluded, and quickly gathered up her nightdress before moving to the bathroom to tidy herself up.

Louis dressed in a hurry, putting the kettle on and waiting for it to boil.

The blue room with its gold carpet was pleasantly comforting with all the lights on. Even the offending stench had disappeared to Katie's relief; it had seemed so foul in the semi-darkness, it was a relief to breathe in clean air.

Soon they were back in bed together, propped up with the pillows and sipping hot tea. Katie appeared calm but her fear at that moment was only suppressed; anger also lingered but she wanted hear what Louis had to say.

Finishing his drink, Louis put down his empty cup on the side table, and once again drew Katie, who was still clinging to her cup, to him. He felt her resistance and stiffness in her body, but she came. Relieved, he supported her against the pillows and taking a deep breath, started talking.

"I sensed something when we arrived here, but I thought it was just the past flooding back in my mind. The cold should have been the clue. Why I didn't recognise it for what it was I'll never know." He rambled on, almost talking to himself. "After I left you to go out in the grounds I stopped on the little landing on the stairs. I was taking an extra long look at the portrait when I felt it, the cold I mean.

I assumed it was coming from the revolving door. Then I almost tripped down the lower stairs, catching myself just in time on the banister. I seem, to remember my knee going from under me, it could have been very nasty fall.

And that incident with you in the bath, I think that was Sophia. Whether she was intending to kill you or just frighten you I don't know, but tonight…" He paused and drew a deep breath, and felt her stiffen again beside him.

"At dinner I saw her, she'd blended with that waitress Mavis, much as I did with Mike, only I tried to help him." he said, with some irony in his voice. "It was just for a second, I saw her face transfigure on poor Mavis's face, and then she was gone. I still didn't really believe it. I didn't want to frighten you, I thought I would sense her if she came near to threaten us, but I didn't. God I'm so sorry."

"What happened tonight, Louis? Why didn't I wake when you…" Her voice faded away at the half-finished sentence.

"I only wish I knew," replied Louis. "I was woken by you, I thought it was you," he said earnestly. "It was your body and it was very dark. I…" he faltered. "I didn't put the light on, I thought it was you and you wanted me. It was only after…"

Again, he paused; using Katie's body that way appalled him. What had Sophia made him do? Katie could have interjected into the conversation but instinct told her that she must let him finish his confession. There would be time to talk later. He continued. "Her nails scratched deep into my back. You, you never did that, but I remembered that she did. I turned on the lamp and she…" He faltered again, never finishing the sentence.

"Sophia used your body; she looked at me with triumph written all over her face. She used me and she used you. Believe me I would never use you. You are my darling girl and I will love you for eternity." He tightened his arm around her shoulder embracing her with such force, he might have squeezed the breath out of her. Body to body she felt a tremendous sob pulse through him. Tears welled up within her, she was unable to fight them back and for the next minute or so they clung to each other sharing each other's tears and pain.

"I'm so sorry," he repeated, not knowing what else to say.

What else could he say? thought Katie. They dried their eyes and she made more tea. It was 4.30 in the morning and the hotel was as quiet as the grave. All staff and guests were sleeping soundly, except for them. What had happened seemed like a bad dream.

Katie felt violated and sick to her stomach but not by him. In her heart she knew he was kind and sensitive and would never hurt her.

This Sophia, whom he had described so many times, was responsible for this vile and godless act, a creature who only had her own interests at heart. Did she hate Louis that much that she intended to harm him still? The answer, obviously, was yes! And now she was in Sophia's sights too.

What were they facing? It had been such an exciting idea of having a little weekend away, taking Louis back to his roots, but fate had taken a hand in bringing them to this hotel. She could not have known, of course not. She was shaking her head, unable to believe that a ghost could blight their break and possibly kill one of them.

"More tea?" she wasn't really asking. She needed to be busy.

The kettle sang as Louis got up to join her by the coffee table.

"I think we should have sugar in our tea," she said, having already spooned two heaped measures into the cups and stirring them briskly. She looked across the table at Louis, who, still in pyjamas, was watching her warily from the blue striped chair.

"It's good for shock," she added with a smile. "I know it wasn't you," she said, passing over the hot brew to him. Relief flooded his face. He mouthed silently, "I love you." It brought an even broader smile on her lips. It felt so uncomfortable and weird knowing that she had slept through what amounted to an attack; the dream she had of making love with Louis was real but only half-remembered; she hated she'd been used like a living doll for Sophia's pleasure.

Sophia was a danger to them as long as they stayed here. They had to find a way of protecting themselves, for God only knew what she would try to do next. It was after five by the time they had finished their beverage. Talking together, they soon recognised that if they slept, they would be vulnerable from the acerbic spirit who meant them harm. Resigned to staying awake, they talked to keep themselves going until the dawn chorus was audible from the trees outside. They were both exhausted when at last a watery sun made its appearance and dawn broke.

"We can't stay here. We need to revise our plans, Katie," a solemn-voiced Louis stated.

Katie agreed and they decided that it would be best to leave the hotel after breakfast; they would check out and find a Bed and Breakfast in Ravensend for the following two nights. They showered; it refreshed them a little standing under the warm water stimulating their skin. The tired couple, wearily, went down for breakfast having already packed. Only their toiletries were left out in the bathroom; toothpaste and brushes and Katie's make-up were waiting for their return from breakfast.

The dining room served an English breakfast of bacon and eggs, toast and marmalade. Tea or coffee. His shutters graced the room in the morning light, but they only reminded him of Sophia and her spiteful appetite to hurt. He asked for a table away from the windows. The waiter serving them looked surprised but said nothing. They both ate, but not heartily, the meal was partaken for the strength it would give them and not the pleasure of the food.

An hour later, back in their room, Louis shaved, while Katie decided to apply her make-up. She was shocked to see how pale she looked in the bathroom mirror. Rooting in, her toilet bag, she rummaged for eye shadow and mascara and brought out the powder compact her mother had bought for her birthday three years ago. It looked expensive, with a circular picture of a white rose designed in the Art Deco style dressed in rolled gold. It was actually of a modest price but treasured by Katie. Opening the compact, she used the pressed powder, patting it around her eyes where dark circles had appeared from nowhere overnight.

Half an hour later, carrying their luggage, they descended to the reception.

Asking for the bill they explained they had been invited to stay in Ravensend by old friends, a white lie but one that was less embarrassing than admitting that they were chased out of the hotel by a ghost. It was a huge relief driving the car down the drive from Avondale Hotel and pointing the car in the direction of his old home. He wondered what he would find there. Changes were guaranteed.

16

As they passed the grey stone-terraced houses on the outskirts of Ravensend, Louis realised that the large village had grown substantially from when he had lived there but not so much to have changed the character of the place. The watery sun had given way to a white-grey blanket of cloud that stretched out like a lid across the sky.

The village he had loved had grown into a small town. It was not looking its best in the dull light as they travelled down the hill leading to the centre. The cobbles had gone from the main roads, tarmac had replaced them, but he was pleased to see the cobbled square survived just as he remembered it. It had served as the market place in his time. Wistfully he wondered if market was still held on a Friday as it had been in his time. A new tall stone monument topped with a Celtic cross stood like a sentinel at the centre of it; he would like to inspect it more closely once they had parked the car. It was somewhat of a surprise when he saw that his old haunt, The Royal Oak pub, still had pride of place in the middle of the row of shops. It had hardly changed.

A sign ahead of them announced that there was car parking available in the next side street, so they turned and followed the road. A Community Centre and toilets were visible as they turned into the parking area, finding an available space next to a sign that stated that parking was free, but no caravans could stay overnight. They had arrived, tired but rather excited too.

"Ready to explore?" Katie's voice had a light ring to it. Still sitting behind the wheel, she took his hand in hers. "As awful as last night was, we can try to forget it. I know you would have been loving and gentle, thinking it was me you were making love to. Yes, it was frightening and I'm glad we are away from that place but I'm determined to enjoy the rest of our break. Although, I think it might be a good idea to find a place to sleep tonight; we can't sleep in the car." She nodded to the sign.

Louis was feeling a mixture of excitement and fear; he squeezed her hand, smiled and kissed her.

"You're right, first things first, and of course I'm ready, let's go. Let's visit the pub first; the barmaid is sure to know who can put us up for a couple of nights."

They walked back to The Royal Oak and discovered that it had become a bed and breakfast inn and restaurant; it served 'Good Pub Food' according to the large sign screwed to the wall by the entrance. Inside the porch, a second door with a leaded glass window and brassware beckoned. It needed only a slight push to enter the pub properly; it clearly had retained many of the features that belonged to another century. As he stood at the bar, a shiver went down Louis' back. Old tankards hung as decoration around the overhead frame. The saloon bar had retained its rustic look and the floor was still of stained wood, sporting marks from the many feet and spills it had endured over its life in this spot. As for the rest of the pub's décor, it had been chosen to look old but was in fact modern. Louis felt he was back at home.

Now they had left the Avondale Hotel, Katie felt safe. She would not allow Sophia to drive them apart or damage her love for Louis, if that had been her intention. Standing in front of the bar with Louis she could see he was happy to be in familiar surroundings.

"Let's stay here, if they have room," she whispered, breaking into his thoughts and bringing him back to her. As she spoke, a woman bustled into the bar carrying a two boxes of potato crisps that looked almost half the size of her.

"Oh, there you are, can I help you?" Her cheery face and sincere blue eyes greeted the couple.

"Do you have room to put us up for a couple of nights?"

"Bless you, of course. I have a nice, quiet, double, back room, away from the noise of the bar. Let me show you. If you like it, we can discuss terms."

Still talking, the woman emerged from behind the bar. Her stocky form suited her face wonderfully, her bright eyes were intelligent and inquiring. Her plump cheeks and rosy lips were emphasised by her short dark hair, stylishly feathered around her face. She wore a loud, floral blouse and black, loose trousers, and she insisted they called her Doris.

Breakfast was between 8am and 10am and they served a full Yorkshire breakfast with all the products sourced from local farmers. She smiled at the couple, asking them to follow her, taking a key from a panel that held three other keys. They supposed The Royal Oak had four guest bedrooms to let.

She chattered on. "I've lived here all my life," she told them as she guided them up the stairs to show them the room. "My family go way back. We've always lived in the village before it was a town." It was said with pride. "And where are you two from? I can just detect a Yorkshire accent in you, Sir."

What were they to say? They looked at each other waiting for each other to answer her. Finally, Louis said "My roots are from around here but I've been living in the south for some time." Katie nodded "That's where we met," she smiled at Doris, knowing they hadn't lied, but wary of not revealing too much about them. "We are visiting the north for Louis."

"Goodness, this is not the north! Now Northumberland is; it gets really cold there." Doris replied.

The long corridor led them to a light oak door fitted with a mortice lock. The key Doris held was firmly pushed into the keyhole and turned, if a little stiffly. The door opened to reveal an old-fashioned bedroom that looked warm and cosy. Curtains with a large rose print hung at the windows, and a quilted bedspread in pinks was laid out on a double bed that faced it. The furniture was old but loved, looking at the shine and by the smell of polish that hit them as they stood in the doorway.

Following Katie into the room, Louis gasped and stopped in his tracks when he saw an old rocking chair with its carved back sharing the morning light under the window. He crossed over to it. A new cushion graced its seat but apart from that it looked exactly like it did on the day he had made it.

"I see you like the old rocking chair," said Doris approvingly. "It's a bit of an heirloom actually. It's been in the family for a few generations, I can tell you. Bought by my great-great-great-great-grandfather. There's a bit of a story if you would like to hear it?"

Doris paused for breath, not waiting for an answer, before she rattled on. "It was made by a carver who lived right here in the village long ago." In a whisper she added. "He was killed by his wife." She looked at the two of them with satisfaction written all over her face. "Well, the way it was told to me, passed down by the family, like, she was gentry and he was only a craftsman. At any rate they got married but on their fifth wedding anniversary, she stabbed him while he slept. She was said to be very beautiful but wild and jealous. Why she did it, who knows?"

Louis was taken aback that after all this time his story was still being told.

"It's said, though can't say whether its true or not, but it's reckoned his troubled spirit hung around for a long time. She, the wife, was hanged." Doris said in a matter-of-fact tone. Then, almost as an afterthought, she said. "Well, what do you think of the room?"

"It's lovely, Doris, we would like to book it for two nights, please."

"Of course, love, here's the key, I'll be downstairs if you need anything. You can pay me when you leave. I'll need your name and address when you come down." Doris judged the couple to be honest and would pay the going rate, she was a good judge of character.

After the door closed behind her, Louis and Katie looked at each other knowingly and then at the chair. It was Louis who broke the silence.

"I made it for my dad." His voice was no more than a whisper, his emotion flowing over and he was choking back a lump that seemed to be stuck in his gullet.

"It's wonderful, Louis," Katie had crossed the room and was looking at the detailed carving in the wood. March hares with long ears were among the poppy heads and dormice were climbing up the grasses to peer at the hares. No wonder it had become a precious heirloom; no-one would ever want to get rid of such a splendid piece of history. Louis could even smell the wood he had held at that time; he remembered carving the scene, loving making each mark, each chip. Making an image that his father, Massie, would relate to. The countryside and the land were part of his father, and Louis felt as he carved it that he was echoing his dad's love of the land in wood.

At that moment he could see in his mind's eye the old man sitting there smoking his clay pipe in front of the fireplace. It warmed his heart. He felt totally reconnected with his roots, and he had a deep urge tugging at his heart to seek out his old dwelling, his cottage and workshop.

When Doris asked them to sign the register, she assumed that they were married. Louis didn't disillusion her and signed it has Mr. Louis Parker and Katie Parker. He was free at last to be himself again, and it was a partnership he hoped would come about in the future.

"Let's have a cup of coffee now we're booked in and then explore the village and collect our cases," suggested Katie.

Louis slowly nodded, He had been away for a very long time and a few more minutes would make no difference to what they would discover today.

Doris was happy to make them coffee. When it came, it was hot, strong and milky and accompanied by homemade shortbread, made, according to her, with fresh butter, it crumbled in the mouth and melted on the tongue.

Louis felt he had come home.

17

Louis peered through a small window. He shielded his eyes with his hands pressed to the windowpane, shutting out the daylight to see the interior better. It allowed him to see into the living room of his old home. His heart was racing; this had been his home and workshop for over ten years and was the place he had died in. How strange it was looking at a different era through a single pane of glass. His workshop was gone, giving way to a smart living area of the twentieth century, and it all looked clean, light and inviting.

Katie wandered around the outside of the building. It was the end cottage of a terrace and the adjoining street stretched back with much larger Victorian houses.

The gap between them and cottage was filled with a modern studio, set back and partially hidden from the main road. There was a To Let sign posted near the outbuilding that was obviously part of the property.

Excitedly, she called to Louis. "There's a notice, the Studio Cottage is vacant, it's up for rent." She wasn't sure what was going through her mind, but the cottage had certainly piqued her curiosity. Maybe they could get the keys and look around inside?

Together they went to read the details on the notice.

"I would love to see inside." He had a wistful look on his face. "Look, it says here that there is a there is a workshop/studio attached to the rear of the property. One would work from here, be independent, working for oneself."

She could hear the longing in his voice. In this modern world it was doubtful he could make a living unless he sold his work in London. Who would have the funds to pay the high prices he would have to charge?

She pushed her thoughts to one side. Deal with the now, Katie, the rest are merely daydreams, she scolded herself.

The two of them had a yearning to see inside the cottage. She sympathised with him. If only she could make it happen, it would be a perfect way to end the weekend. If they were quick off the mark, they might be able to view it Monday morning. They would have to get in touch with the estate agent today.

Seeking direction from a local man, the two of them were put them on the right path to Ruskins and Browns, and after a ten-minute walk they stood in front of the shop. Its two bay windows had a great many photographs of local houses displayed with detail and prices. Katie was astounded how reasonable these properties were compared with the equivalent in the south.

The bell sounded as they pushed open the door. A tall, friendly man seemed to pounce, almost hugging them as they walked through the door. He ushered them to the cream leatherette chairs near his desk and bade them sit down. It had obviously been a quiet morning and he was glad to have some company. He introduced himself as Derek.

Saturday could be a slow day for real viewers. To Derek, it seemed that people liked to spend the weekend looking at other people's homes without any intention of moving. Was this such a couple? He took their particulars, anyway.

After chatting for a few minutes trying to weigh them up and hearing familiar tones in the man's voice, Derek decided that they sounded as though they might even be really interested in a property.

"Can I offer coffee or tea?" he asked, beaming at the two of them. When they declined his offer, he sat down behind the desk and shuffled some papers, bringing the one he needed to the top.

They explained that they were only here for a few days but rather liked the look of the Studio Cottage and they would love to view it. Derek checked his diary. As it transpired, he had a slot free and could meet them on Monday morning; it couldn't be done today as he was manning the shop on his own. He had keys and yes, the cottage was fully furnished. He hoped they were serious punters. Perhaps they were planning to move north? That would be unusual and not very likely. In his experience, people tended to move south, not north. Maybe it was to be a holiday home; those people in the south had pots of money, and it wasn't unheard of for people investing in homes to sub-let.

On that thought, he pointed out that they could not sub-let this property if they went ahead and rented.

By the vigorous shaking of their heads, he was reassured that their interest was only for themselves. Shaking Derek's hand as they left, they confirmed that they would meet on Monday morning at 9.30 outside the cottage.

With that meeting booked, the couple decided to spend the rest of the day reacquainting Louis with his roots and exploring the surrounding countryside. As they left the office, the sun had slipped out through a crack in the clouds, sending a flood of warmth and light on the small town; a light wind had pushed the grey lid of clouds away while they were in with Derek. They took it to be a sign; it lifted their spirits, and the small town suddenly looked rather smart in an old-worldly way. It pleased them both.

They headed out on the A19 towards Thirsk, another old market town that sat on the edge of the Yorkshire Wolds. The North Riding of Yorkshire was full of character, Katie discovered. They passed through village after village, each attractive in a strange, austere way. 'Built to last' was a phrase that passed through Katie's mind. The gardens they passed were neat; a riot of colour, from the mixture of flowers and vegetables growing there, showed that pride had gone into the tending of them.

Dusk started to creep quickly over the fields; darkness was near. It was a countryside that Katie didn't know and with no lights on the quiet roads she was happy to turn the car around and return to Ravensend. They had at least seen a little of this area. Sadly, for Louis, he didn't recognise much of what they were seeing; time had clouded his memories. By late afternoon they were back at The Royal Oak, sharing hot tea and scones, which they devoured in front of a log fire in the comfortable sitting room that was reserved for paying guests. They had it all to themselves. Autumn was the off-season for the B&B.

Doris popped in through the open door to see if they wanted a refill of tea.

"Did you have a nice day?" she enquired, her head cocked on one side with interest.

"It's been lovely, thank you," Katie responded. "I thought of the north like a Lowry painting, interesting but full of mills. But it was wonderful to see the countryside stretching out forever in front of you. Tomorrow we are going to Helmsley to see the castle and river and I want to see Bylands Abbey. I know it's just a ruin sacked from the time of Henry the Eighth, I saw a painting of it by John Piper, It's so powerful."

"The weather report is good for Sunday. Helmsley is a lovely place to visit."

Doris sat herself down on an empty chair. "Just needed to take the weight off for the moment." She discarded her shoes and wiggled her feet. "It's been a long day and more to come." She sighed "Do love the job, though," she added. "Will you be eating with us, tonight?" she asked, "We have Steak and Ale pie with cabbage, carrots and mashed potato or Chicken, same vegetables," she smiled, "or in the bar we serve Breaded Scampi and chips in a basket. We serve until nine."

It was much later when they finally climbed the stairs to bed. They were full of good pub food and had shared a bottle of wine. They were slightly tipsy and very tired from the trauma of the previous night. The excitement of knowing that on Monday they would visit Louis' ex-home had been put to one side. The double bed was beckoning as soon as they opened the door. In the space of a few minutes, they changed and snuggled down under the blankets. Sleep was not far away, and tonight they could sleep without any fear. Louis could not help but look over at the rocking chair and once again felt close to his father, his image fixed in his mind. He even imagined he could smell pipe tobacco and Dad in the chair, rocking it gently. It gifted him with a feeling of love and it was a comfort.

When they kissed goodnight and turned over to sleep, it was wonderful to feel safe.

18

THE DREAM

Louis was back in his cottage workshop, tooling the back of a dining room chair. His father had been sitting in his familiar space by the fire when he came up beside him.

'You can't stay here, Son, it's not safe. She's been on the prowl for many a year since the old house became a hotel. You don't think you're the first to be driven out by her haunting. I knew you would return when you could. I saw you wander without purpose, trapped. I couldn't speak to you when you were so angry. You need to leave, Son. Go back and take your lady with you.'

'What do you mean, Dad?'

'Listen, Son, don't tarry here, leave.' Massie started to fade in front of Louis' eyes, but his voice lingered. 'The spirits know what the spirits know.' Then he was gone.

Louis woke with a start. It was five in the morning, he had slept heavily for seven hours, his mouth was dry. The room was still and dark but the moon shed just enough light through the curtains to give it an eerie glow and he saw movement out of the corner of his eye.

He could have sworn that his dad's chair was rocking. He shut his eyes tight and when he looked again, the chair was still. Sleepy eyes playing tricks, perhaps? Then he remembered the dream. A tiny involuntary shudder activated across his shoulders. What did it mean? He sat up. Clearly, the episode with Sophia had disturbed him and he was feeling anxious. He felt in his bones that he belonged here; fear of going back to the south with an uncertain future was niggling him. He imagined he could restart his business making and carving here, given the chance.

Looking at the sleeping figure beside him he worried. He must never put Katie in danger again. He promised himself that. He couldn't bear the thought of being without her, but was he being selfish with his dreams? Could she uproot herself for him? More questions, the kind that came in the middle of the night. They needed answers. Perhaps by morning things would be clearer?

This body felt like his now. As each day passed, he felt more confident that it wouldn't let him down. He had a future, but he knew he was a drain on Katie's finances and he couldn't live with that indefinitely. He had his pride.

Anxiety had woken him. It had been a full-on twenty-four hours since the drama with Sophia, but it was of little wonder that he felt shaken. It was 5.30 in the morning, time to put it behind him and think about his dream, his wish and hope.

"Are you alright?" came a sleepy voice from next to him.

"Perfectly," he answered, as he slipped back down under the blankets, patting her shoulder. "Never better."

Sunday morning light crawled over the windowsill, making its way along the carpet and onto the bed. It found two sleepy heads that were content to stay undercover in the warmth of blanket and quilt. But the light would not have it and grew stronger and brighter until it forced an eye to open. It was 8am and time to meet the day and the adventure it promised. There was little noise from downstairs. Having washed and dressed, they followed their noses to where the bacon was being served. The private lounge had become a dining room and a round table was set for two. Sounds were echoing from a kitchen, and then some movement from the other doorway. Doris greeted them.

"Sit down, then, that table's for you. Did you sleep well? It's a nice room, isn't it?" They were questions that she didn't expect answers to, but offered with a friendly smile.

"When I heard you finish in the bathroom, I put the bacon on. It's crisping up now. Scrambled eggs or fried? Coffee or tea. Oh! And there's orange juice if you want it. Julie will bring it in, now." She waited, expecting an answer; they agreed on fried eggs and breakfast tea.

The short autumn day went so very quickly. Plump cotton wool clouds floated like elegant swans across the cerulean sky on their way to Helmsley. The weather had been kind to them. Enjoying the drive through the well-groomed countryside they saw that farmers had been busy, fields were ploughed ready for next year's plantings. The sun lit the landscape, enhancing the hills and fields, showing it at its best.

Helmsley was all that they expected and more. A solid market town in the North Yorkshire Wolds, sitting as it was near the moors, it attracted walkers, artists, antique dealers, shoppers for farm foods and visitors to the medieval castle. So many interests to suit many people. The cobbled square, used as a car park today, had a dominant black and grey stone cenotaph at its centre. The square was bustling with people enjoying a day out under the fine autumn sun. Some sat on the steps around the monument, eating bought hot pasties and sandwiches, from one of the many cafés that served food around the square. The cenotaph was a larger version of the one in Ravensend, raised as a memorial to the fallen in the two great world wars.

Louis was reminded of the many years he had lost in his netherworld, not connected with reality of what was happening in the wider world. He promised himself he would pay homage and read the list of names when they got back; there might be names there that he would recognise, from the families that had lived there in his time. They joined the throng eating meat pasties for lunch, sitting on the steps, listening to the chatter and even joining in with the general consensus that the food was delicious.

By the end of the day, they had seen the castle, looked in the antique shops and admired the gentlemen's clothes shops that sold smart outdoor outfits, although the prices were out of reach of most people who were milling around the town. They had tea at a café so they could people watch before they set off to visit Bylands Abbey on their return journey. They had ticked all the boxes.

19

Monday morning came like every other morning. From the black of the night, a small glow showed faint on the horizon. It grew, bringing light over the houses until it filled the cosy bedroom. Katie was standing at the window, looking out but not really seeing anything; how long she had stood there she didn't know. She had got up when the bedroom lightened with the dawn and she couldn't sleep anymore. The water gurgled in the radiator, and she was grateful for the warmth it gave her. She turned to look at the sleeping figure of Louis, lying there peacefully. She hadn't slept well; small niggling voices had swirled around in her head all through the night. The finely carved rocking chair reminded her of Louis' skill; lazily she gave the high back a gentle push, watching it move with a certain rhythm, she watch it until it settled back upright and was still. Louis had been so enthusiastic about returning to Ravensend to set up business.

It was a sign, that his old home with workshop was up to let. That's what he had said. He was so sure that he would be able to earn a good living from his craft; he didn't seem to understand the implications that went with his dream. He was eager to feel wood under his hands and to create again.

Today was going to be tough. At 9.30 they would be meeting Derek. Why on earth had she encouraged Louis to see the studio cottage? Well, curiosity had got the better of her. On top of that, she discovered she had lost her compact. The last time she remembered using it was in the bathroom in the Avondale Hotel. She would have to go back there and retrieve it. She hoped it had been handed in. It was definitely going to be a difficult day.

In half an hour, the alarm would ring and bring her slumbering love into the new day. She decided to creep back into the double bed and keep him company until the cock crowed or the bell rang. She must have disturbed him getting into bed, though she hadn't meant to. He was stretching out his stiff limbs and rubbing the stubble on his chin.

"Morning, my darling," he said, peering at her with one eye still closed. "Come and have a cuddle before we get up." Her smile was all he needed to confirm her acquiescence.

He caught her up in his arms and pulled her to his chest. He could smell the scent of her hair and naturally he kissed her. Starting with her hair, then her forehead, before finally kissing her with passion on her lips. Then nature took over. The kisses become more passionate as their bodies responded to love. Katie's fears were forgotten, lost to the world, spending their desires of the moment together, until the noise of the alarm crashed into their privacy. Its ringing surprised and shocked them back to realising they were still in the bedroom of The Royal Oak. Lying in each other's arms they both burst out laughing, seeing the funny side of the situation. Killing the noise, they kissed once more before agreeing to get up.

The smell of bacon cooking drifted up from the kitchen. It was still early, only 7.30am, but their stomachs were grumbling. The sound of distant singing broke through the comparative silence of the bedroom; it was Doris singing along with a morning radio show, down below them. The smell of bacon and the singing reminded Louis of his past, at the turn of the century when he was an unseen guest of Marina and his first meeting with her extraordinary family. It warmed his heart; it was a good memory.

"I'm going to get dressed, I'm hungry." Katie wriggled in his arms. He released her, and she pulled herself from the bed, gathering up her clothes as she went, snatching up her wash bag. She was heading to the door to go to the bathroom when he called out.

"Hang on, wait for me." cried Louis, still wrapped in the blankets. "I'm hungry too."

With a good-natured laugh he threw the bedding back, leaped out of the bed and chased Katie to the bathroom where laughing she escaped, closing the door hard against him.

"Make it quick," his voice came through the door. "I'm next."

His footsteps could be heard walking back to their room.

In the silence of the small room, she suddenly felt nervous again. She washed, thinking about Louis and his talent. Did he really want to stay in the north? Was that the reason they were viewing the cottage that morning? She wondered how this all was going to work out for them. She knew in her heart of hearts he wanted to come back to his roots but how would they survive? She was the main breadwinner and did she want to leave the Home Counties? She left that thought hanging, knowing how much she loved Louis. She could find a job in the north, couldn't she? Janet had; her university and best friend, now worked in Leeds. Katie hadn't contacted Janet earlier, because the trip was decided on suddenly and was all about Louis and him coming back to his roots. Now she would telephone Janet, for some advice.

Would she have to start her career path all over again if they moved here? Could she help him start up again in the trade he was obviously a master at?

Looking at her reflection, she shrugged her shoulders and stuck out her tongue at the Katie in the mirror. "Stop being so negative, you silly woman," she said, scolding her other self that stared back at her. "Get ready and seize the day." Her tummy rumbled again and reminded her she was hungry.

Doris greeted the couple and led them to their table and recommended a full Yorkshire for both of them.

"Breakfast is the most important meal of the day. It'll set you up a treat." She beamed as she asked whether they would have coffee or tea this morning. "I prefer a good drop of black tea, that's good and strong," she confided, 'but we have coffee if you prefer." In a matter-of-fact tone she added "I hope our friendly ghost didn't disturb you last night. He's no bother. I could smell the pipe tobacco when I came up to bed. It lets you know he's around. I think he came with the rocking chair, personally, because it's only that bedroom where we get the smell. I've never seen him but one or two guests have, although, as I say, he's no bother." She left to place their order.

Louis was astounded with Doris's statement. It meant the dream and the chair's movement were more than a product of his anxious state. Katie looked at Louis, opened-mouthed. "I noticed that smell, but thought it had come up from the bar. Can it be true?"

Louis was quiet and patted her hand. "Yes, me too." But he didn't tell her about his father's warning.

Monday morning started well, despite Katie's apprehension about the future. Now that she was fortified with bacon and eggs, sausage, tomatoes, mushrooms and fried bread, she was feeling more confident and surprisingly ready to start a new chapter in her life. Her phone call to Janet had been brief, with a promise to call and stay the night on their way home. A separate call to the hotel confirmed that a maid had found her compact and she could collect it from reception anytime that day. Katie was as pleased as Punch.

It was Louis' turn to feel nervous. He was excited about viewing his old home, he had no qualms about that, but returning to Avondale Hotel, knowing that the ghost of Sophia would be lurking there, worried him. The compact meant a lot to Katie and she must collect it but if Sophia saw them would she try something? Yet he feared Katie going in on her own. They discussed the situation over breakfast and decided to go and collect it when guests were checking out. Katie would just be another body in the reception; the more people around the better. They must they get there between eleven and twelve, then all would be well.

It was more than annoying that Derek was late turning up at the cottage. "Traffic," he said, full of apologies when he finally arrived with the key, dangling from his hand. Fitting it in the lock, he opened the door, stepping to one side to let Katie and Louis into the living room. It was surprisingly spacious for a cottage; it felt homely and comfortable to Katie. She looked across to Louis who was standing stock still, staring at the room. His face was a mask, empty of emotion. It was as though he was in a trance.

In his mind's eye he was back in time, seeing his father sitting by the fireplace rocking back and forth in his carved chair pulling on his pipe. A full bowl of tobacco was lit and enjoyed by Massie, as a nightly habit. Louis watched the smoke escape from his mouth, as the old man relaxed before retiring. In his next thoughts he pictured Sophia in the tin bath in front of the fire where they bathed together before making love in the bedroom that was just beyond this room.

"Louis."

Calling his name brought him back to the moment; he turned and smiled at Katie who had a concerned look across her face. He nodded to reassure her, then observed his old room, now in a 1972 style. Whoever decorated had made it seriously modern. No candles were needed here to light the space; smart wall lights were installed. The rough finish on the walls had gone. They were smooth and painted a delicate shade of buttercup gold, making the room glow in the sunlight that was streaming through the windows. The furniture matched the room. There was a long teak sideboard standing on four spindly legs, a racing green three-seater leather sofa facing the fire place, two matching upright chairs against the other wall with a drop-sided table. Modern Scandinavian designs and influence were all around them. It somehow suited the room. He liked it. He nodded approval to Katie and gave her a dazzling smile.

Derek took them through to the main bedroom. A white padded headboard decorated the bed that was set against the back wall. It was odd not to see his own bed there, but that was in Katie's home 199 miles to the south.

Next, Derek showed them the small box room that had once been Louis' father's room. A lump came into his throat; he swallowed it away. The next bedroom had originally been his workshop; a bathroom and toilet had been cannibalised out of its space, new additions to the property.

"Derek, where's the workshop?" asked Louis abruptly.

"Oh! Just through here." He pointed to the small kitchenette that led to a back door. They pushed their way through the narrow space between the counters to open the door that revealed a yard. The purpose-built outhouse, with access to the road, was just two steps away. Louis could not wait to view it.

In his time, this yard had belonged to the coalman; it had been where the horse and cart was housed. Now this space apparently belonged to the cottage.

Inside the workshop, a long wooden bench stretched out with strong fluorescent lights overhead. A gas heater was tucked away at the far end under a large window. Fitted to the wall was a series of metal shelves; all empty, they sported a thick layer of dust on them. No-one had used this space for a long time, and it smelled rather musty. Musty or not, Louis' wish-list had this workshop right at the top of it.

Derek was giving it his best sales talk. He could not know that Louis knew this place back, front and sideways and that Louis wanted nothing more than be back in his old home. If only, Louis was thinking, if only he hadn't been shipped off south, if he had met Katie here in the north. Wild thoughts continued. If Katie would come to live in Yorkshire, perhaps he could start his business again. Was it a pipe dream? A dream that couldn't come true? No! he needed to work again and the only craft he knew was with wood.

Perhaps the excitement of the trip was colouring his thought processes? He couldn't go on being Mike Develin. He needed the feel of wood under his hand again, to make beautiful objects, to release the trapped spirits of nature hidden in the wood.

Yes, that's what he needed.

He looked across at Katie, he couldn't read her face but he knew she was holding back her emotions.

What was she thinking? he wondered. Had she guessed how he felt, now he was standing in what could be his workplace?

Katie worked so hard and had achieved so much, how could he ask her to give it up? He suddenly felt deflated. He wasn't being practical.

Derek was still talking. They could have it on a yearly rolling contract, if that suited them. The owner lived locally on a large farm, not that he was a farmer, he employed a manager to run that. Having given them all the important information, he smiled and asked. "Any questions? what do you think?" He could see one eager client but the woman seemed less keen.

Katie stepped in. "I think we will have to go away and mull it over. We'll get back to you. Thank you so much for showing us around this lovely cottage. It is delightful. But we will have to work a few things out before we can commit to anything right now."

Derek looked crestfallen. He had been sure the man would go for it. Still, perhaps he could talk his missus round.

"If you want to view it again, let me know." Derek gave them his card and ushered them through the door and out onto the street.

It was 10.30; the viewing had taken longer than they expected. Right now, they had to go back to The Royal Oak, collect their things and say goodbye to Doris. Getting to Avondale Hotel for eleven would be touch and go.

20

They hadn't shared much conversation walking back to the car and the journey to Avondale Hotel was spent mainly in silence.

Now, they were sitting in the car park. The house was a few hundred yards away, its revolving door like a gaping mouth was inviting them in. An uncomfortable tension filled the car; unspoken worries about the viewing and the threat that might be waiting for them under that roof. On top of that, they had obviously missed the time slot they were aiming for and were sitting in an almost empty car park. Not many, if any, people would be in lobby now. But the powder compact, that precious gift loved by Katie, must be retrieved. There was a risk that Sophia would spot them if they went in together, but Katie on her own?

Words were clipped, but somehow it was agreed that Katie would go in on by herself. It seemed to make sense.

"I'll wear sunglasses and that pull-on old winter hat that's lying on the back seat. With my hair tucked up inside it, Sophia won't recognise me," she hoped.

Louis watched through the window, with a worried look on his face as Katie walked up to the entrance and disappeared through the revolving door as though house had swallowed her. He shuddered.

Coming in from the sunlight to a darkened lobby she paused waiting for her eyes to adjust. It seemed unnaturally cold. The portrait of Sophia's mother stared down at her ominously as she walked across to the reception desk.

She was very beautiful. If Sophia looked like that, it was little wonder that Louis had been locked under her spell. What a pity her beauty was only skin deep, Katie thought ruefully.

She marched up to the counter, with a confident smile on her face, but behind the sunglasses her eyes would have let her down.

Jackie was standing behind the desk. She had an indifferent look on her face but greeted her as she came forward to inquire about her lost compact.

"Hello, Jackie," Katie said in a whisper, dropping her head slightly. Her nerves were in a tangle and she was feeling rather odd. "I'm here to collect my lost compact. I phoned earlier and was told it would be here waiting for me in reception?"

The question hung in the air for a moment, as though Jackie was collecting her thoughts before answering.

Katie suddenly experienced a pulsing in her head and felt rather sick; was it a migraine coming on? Then, feeling faint, she gasped for breath. There was no air in the lobby and she struggled to breathe. A chair was close by; she half staggered to it and sat, grateful for the support it gave her.

"Are you alright?" came Jackie's voice from the counter. "Can I get you some water?" It was a question that had already been answered, as Jackie handed Katie a tumbler.

"Thank you," she responded, looking up into the receptionist's face. Jackie reached out and took hold of Katie's free hand to give reassurance.

"Just sit there, my dear, you'll be okay in a minute or so." The words were comforting but Jackie's eyes looked strangely hard and uncaring. The lobby had become uncomfortably chilly, and a draught was swirling all round Katie's chair.

Jackie's hand was cold too. Her fingers closed over Katie's hand, holding her firmly.

"You're so cold," said Katie involuntarily. She tried to pull her hand away but Jackie held on.

"You know what they say, love," Jackie responded. "Cold hands, warm heart." She smiled but Katie sensed it was artificial and Jackie's eyes were without humour.

Katie felt her hand tingling with cold and she was aware of a chill seeping into her body. It crept up her arm into her shoulders and flowed down to her toes. Panic held her for a moment at the sensation, then, as quickly as the cold had overwhelmed her, it was gone. She was relieved and felt normal again, if a little cold.

Jackie was patting her hand. The icy grip had gone, concern was in her voice and her face was animated.

"Here, are you alright love? You've had a bit of a turn, I thought you might faint a second ago. But the colour's coming back in your cheeks."

Despite feeling back to her old self, Katie was still very cold and had a yearning to get out of the hotel and into the sunshine.

"I'm fine now," Katie said in a faltering voice, repeating her request. "I've come to pick up my compact. I left it in Room Ten when I stayed here on Friday."

"Oh yes, I remember," said Jackie. "I spoke to your husband about the portrait. I remember." She nodding as she spoke. "I have your property back here under the desk. I'll get for you right away."

Having her mum's special gift back in her hands relieved Katie. Clutching the precious property, she marched to the exit, and pushed herself through the revolving door into the daylight. The warmth lifted her spirits as the sun shone on her face. A few yards on she was in the car park. She waved to Louis and gave him the thumbs up sign. All was well.

21

SOPHIA

From her chair under the portrait, Sophia watched the young woman stride through the reception from the revolving door. The woman was strangely dressed, wearing sunglasses and a woollen winter hat pulled down over her ears. It was unusual for guests to wear sunglasses indoors; it seemed very odd. The figure reminded Sophia of someone; maybe it was the way she walked. Then suddenly Sophia connected her memories together and realised it was Katie, the strumpet whom she was watching. Immediately, she was beside her, matching her stride toward the counter.

Where was Louis? Sophia wondered. Was he hiding from her? And why was this woman in disguise in her lobby?

Sophia had searched for them, going back to their room only to find it empty. She'd gone back several times but on her last visit, a different couple was bedded down in it.

She had searched for them in other bedrooms, in the dining room, the lounges, and the gardens. Disappointed, she had decided to wait and watch from her landing. They would pass sooner or later. But they hadn't, it would seem, until now.

Empowered by tricking Louis into making love to her, she planned to humiliate him further. She hadn't finished with him or the woman. One way or another, she would destroy them.

Now, here was that interloper she had nearly drowned. What a pity she hadn't had more time; just a few more minutes would have done it, she mused, remembering the struggling figure underwater, a smirk twisted on her lips. If only Louis hadn't come back. Was this her opportunity to have a second chance?

Sophia buzzed around Katie's head, unsure of just what she wanted to do. Perhaps she could kill her? That would hurt him, but would that help her to find Louis? Where was he hiding? She had to find him.

She put her ghostly hands over Katie's mouth and nose. Sophia watched Katie's bewilderment. Struggling to breathe, Katie seemed to be on the edge of collapse. Was that what she wanted, to kill her now? Sophia felt like a cat playing with a mouse before the kill; should she, shouldn't she? She needed time to think. Perhaps if she blended with her again, she would take her to Louis. Sophia removed her hands from Katie's face and watched as she staggered from the counter, watched her blunder towards a chair and sit down heavily. Katie was floppy and very pale. The receptionist suddenly took notice of the woman in sunglasses, and started to come to help her, so Sophia took the opportunity to blend with Jackie who had already got a glass of water to give to the fainting woman.

Through the eyes of Jackie, Sophia saw a weakened Katie, half-lying, limp on the chair, and pale. Using Jackie's body and voice, she gave Katie false sympathy as she came from behind the counter, water in her hand, taking it over to Katie and holding her hand with concern in her voice.

After a sip of water, Katie visibly relaxed. Sophia held her hand making soothing sounds and Katie's breathing returned to normal. The time was right for Sophia to slide her spirit into the unsuspecting woman. Passing through Katie's hand, Sophia stole into her.

Katie's face registered puzzlement and then panic to Jackie who was now herself, again. Jackie, still holding Katie's hand, was reassuring her that she was recovering from her faint.

Sophia heard it all. Contented, she settled in the body, which she intended to share, very much as Louis was sharing someone else's. Sophia told herself could bide her time, be quiet, watch and wait, and soon she would see her husband again.

Katie was up on her feet and standing at the counter, receiving some trinket from Jackie, which she put deep in her pocket.

It was with deep joy that Sophia felt herself being carried out of the lobby and into the sunlight. Peering through Katie's eyes, she saw she was moving towards a car in the car park. Katie was giving the man a sign. He got out of the car and nodded to her with a small wave of his hand.

And there he was, the man who had caused all her sorrow; a sorrow she intended to return to him a hundred-fold.

For now, Sophia would dwell in complete silence, be totally invisible. She had no intention of revealing herself; not yet.

22

Some of the tension lifted between Katie and Louis as they travelled towards Leeds. It was obvious that Katie was looking forward to seeing Janet, but Louis was uncomfortable at the thought of the visit. He would have to pretend to be Mike again; Janet had worked with the man and knew that he had become Katie's lodger and lover. She didn't know, nor could she know, about the swap that had taken place. Would Janet see through his act? He hardly dared think about it. It was only going to be an overnight visit, so with a little luck he could stay in the background and leave the ladies to their catching up.

In less than an hour, they were on the outskirts of the large city. The directions were clear on the paper that Louis held in his hand. Katie had written them all out and he was going to navigate.

It had been over a year since the girls had seen each other. Now here she was, just a few miles away, and soon she would see her dearest friend again: her friend with whom she had shared so much since meeting at University. Katie hadn't told Janet that she was coming to Yorkshire. The complication of Louis in Mike's body had made her hold back. She had decided that the trip should be about Louis and his memories. But things had changed. Katie wanted Janet's opinion on what life was like working and living in the north. It had suddenly become important to know.

She came back to the moment, on hearing instructions coming from her passenger.

"Follow the A58 into the city centre," advised Louis.

Katie manoeuvred the car into a left lane and followed the traffic that was heading into the city. She had been thinking about the trip and how coming to the north had changed her perspective of it. She had found that the countryside held a certain kind of beauty and that she had fallen in love with it. The idea of living anywhere north of Watford Gap would previously have been dispatched to the waste bin, but not now. She knew how the landscape changed every few miles from lush fertile fields, to rough, rugged windswept moorlands, as wild as the animals that lived there, to small hidden towns nestling in the valleys between the moorlands, filled with a culture of neighbourliness.

Yes, she decided; she could live in Yorkshire, just as her friend Janet did, and it would be good to live near her. If she found a job on a local newspaper, that could use her skills. Louis could come home.

It was a good thought; one she wouldn't dismiss.

Sophia could hear the noise of the traffic, rather like a baby in the womb can hear its mother's voice and music and noise beyond the wall of skin. She was inquisitive to know what the noise meant. She would just take a peek...

She saw a moving car, coming towards a pole with flashing light. What did it mean? Then Louis shouted and she returned to hide within her host.

"Watch out," cried Louis. Katie applied the brakes quickly. God! The traffic lights had turned red and she hadn't noticed really noticed them; she had nearly run into the back of a white van. She really must concentrate on the road ahead. Leeds was a large city, so vast that even with written instructions she was afraid that they might lose their way and end up in God knows where?

They followed the road, past Leeds University. Katie was amused to see a sign for Little London, which was definitely not on her route. The classic architecture of the Town Hall, the Library and Art Gallery was very impressive as she drove past them and it meant they were going the right way, so, not long now to Janet's place.

"We need to take the A61 towards Wakefield, just after the Corn Exchange," Louis reminded her. "It will take us over the River Aire. The turning is just after that for Crown Point Road."

"Thank goodness, we are nearly there. I lost my concentration moments ago; we might have had an accident if it hadn't been for you. I do love you, Louis"

All tensions between them dissolved.

"I love you too, my darling girl. I didn't mean to put pressure on you back in Ravensend, I had an impossible dream, the cottage being vacant, I suppose it was just being back there. Roots and all."

"I understand, darling, and in many ways going back there to live would solve the problem of your identity, you could be yourself. Let's talk more about it later."

She saw her turning off to the right. A row of stone terraced houses with grey slate roofs and tiny front gardens appeared before her; all she needed to do now was find number 61.

The emerald green door of number 61 was flung open directly the car stopped at the kerb in front of the house. Janet appeared with a beaming smile on her face.

"You got here, then." She almost ran down the short path to the passenger door and yanked it open. "There you are," she said, bending down to see them both of them more clearly. "I was standing at the window watching for you. You found me alright?"

Katie smile broke into a laugh, "Lord, Janet, I've missed you and your enthusiasm."

With that, she leapt out of the car and dashed around it to her friend and hugged her. Louis sat with the instructions still in his hand. He looked quite bemused; it was as if he was invisible to them. 'Long may it last!' he thought, heaving himself up out of the car and collecting their overnight bags from the boot.

"Mike, it's good to see you," called Janet as she ushered Katie towards the open door.

"You too," replied Louis, "I'll be in, in a minute."

They gathered in the kitchen and waited for the kettle to boil.

"Well! I must say, you both look well, if not a little different," said Janet as she inspected them, looking them up and down. "What have you been doing with yourself, Mike? lost a bit of weight, or is it a different hair style?"

"Maybe a bit of both," came the reply.

"You must be good for each other. You look happy, Katie."

The kettle snapped itself off.

"You go in the front room, there's cake and biscuits in there. Make yourselves comfortable while I make the tea."

They sat down on the sofa and looked at each other. Janet had noticed something, but she could never guess what the real situation was. They agreed they just needed to act naturally and all would be well.

After eating cake and drinking tea, Louis offered to clear and wash up.

Janet looked up at him. "Are you feeling all right?" she asked with a snigger.

"I just think you girls should have some time together. Three's a crowd, isn't it?"

"Thanks, then." said a subdued Janet.

"And I think I'll walk up to the centre, it's not too far, and visit the Art Gallery. I noticed it on the way in." added Louis, as he picked up the tray that held the dirty cups and plates. "That will give you plenty of time to gossip."

He winked at Katie before leaving them to talk. They heard the door shut ten minutes later as Louis went on his way to the Gallery.

Janet was even more surprised he had actually gone out. She leaned into Katie and spoke in low tones. "What have you done to him? The Mike I knew would be looking for a sports field or the nearest pub. I'm gobsmacked."

Katie smiled a knowing smile. What could she say?

"Oh, Mike's a changed man since he left the paper."

"What do you mean, left the paper? Reporting on sport was his life, well, that and socialising with the sportsmen."

"He's given all that up, Janet. Honestly, he wants to become an artist, carving wood."

Janet covered her mouth with her hand as she tried to hold her laughter in.

"You're kidding me?"

"No really, he's surprised himself and he has a real gift."

Janet was not convinced. Though she had left the Echo she had heard on the grapevine that there had been woman trouble that involved Debs. But she didn't know he had left his job. The Mike she knew was a womaniser and liked his drink. But this man, who was he?

He looked like Mike, only his voice seemed softer, his eyes were gentler too, and he had no arrogance in him. Had love done that? She supposed it must have.

They had always been able to talk, but Janet felt Katie was holding back. The ease they once knew was gone.

"You haven't told me why you were visiting the North Riding. Now Mike's gone out we can chat."

Katie flinched. She hadn't thought she would be questioned like this by her friend. What was she going to say?'

"By accident. I saw a special offer for a hotel near Thirsk and I had never been north of Bedford. You had said how much you liked living here, so I just thought we would have a trip and see a bit of England."

Even to her ears it sounded true. Janet seemed satisfied and changed the subject to shopping and men in general. She was still looking for Mr Right.

Louis had returned from the town very disappointed. Monday was closing day for the Gallery, but he had enjoyed the walk. Seeing the centre of Leeds for the first time – its buildings, the people in the market, its hustle and bustle of life – had been exhilarating, and it had given the girls an hour or two just to chat and be girls.

When he arrived back at Janet's house, they were sitting in the kitchen peeling potatoes and carrots, just two of the vegetables that would accompany the chicken that was roasting in the oven and would be served up at 7pm with a dessert of lemon sponge and custard. The walk had given him a healthy appetite.

The meal had been excellent and the three of them were feeling extremely mellow, having drunk a bottle and a half of wine with the chicken dinner. The plates were pushed to one side; they would clear up later. Right now, they were enjoying small talk and Janet realised that she really liked this Mike. Katie was very lucky. Janet had warmed to his charm and was amazed how love had apparently changed him.

Sophia, hidden within the depths of Katie, was reacting to the noise and laughter that she could hear. It must be a party. She didn't like to think that Louis might be having a good time while she had to hide away. She just couldn't resist but take a look through Katie's eyes to see who was with them. Despite the noise, it was not a party, just Louis with his woman and a rather attractive brunette who was sitting next to him and hanging on his arm. The laughter and the nudging of arms that was being displayed between them annoyed her. Anger at the injustice of the position she was in was boiling up. She was almost ready to reveal herself; she knew she must stay in control. The time for that was not now.

Katie had stopped talking in mid-sentence and had a vacant look in her eyes.

"Katie are you okay? You were telling us about your first boyfriend and how embarrassed you were when he kissed you."

Louis had put his arm around her shoulders. It took a few seconds for her to respond to him. Blinking her eyes, she slowly turned to him. "I just drifted off somewhere, sorry. Now where was I?" she smiled and then shivered. "It's very cold in here, isn't it?"

"The central heating is on full," Janet responded to the question. "I hope you're not coming down with a cold."

Louis felt Katie's cheek. She was cold to touch.

"I've actually been cold all afternoon," she said, nodding her head as though agreeing with herself. "Perhaps a cup of tea will warm me up."

"Good idea," said Janet, "Louis can help me to clear the table and get straight.

Tea will be five minutes, love. You stay there."

Katie watched the two of them carry out the remains of the meal, and watched Janet pour the last of the wine out for Louis and herself. Janet was chuckling and could still be heard in the kitchen down the hall. "Kettle's on, back in two ticks."

More laughter, Katie wondered what was so funny.

A small voice in her head broke into her thoughts. He doesn't love you, look how he's acting with Janet.

Katie hugged herself; the cold was icy in her bones.

Her friend laid the tea tray on the table in front of Katie, with a cup, teapot and milk. Louis and Janet sat with her and sipped their wine while Katie poured the strong hot tea. She cupped her hands round the cup and felt the warmth from it seep up her arm. The cold was subsiding; the shivering stopped. She looked at Louis and then at Janet. Janet was her friend; she wouldn't betray her, surely? and she was certain that Louis loved her. But wasn't it always the best friend, who cheated with husbands or boyfriends?

The voice was whispering again. He'll leave you for her. He doesn't love you.

"No." The word was out of her mouth before she realised it. She had shouted it out in response to the voice. She was suddenly embarrassed, sitting at the table her friends staring at her in amazement. What had caused that outburst?

"What is it, Katie?" they said in unison.

"I must be coming down with something."

Seeds of doubt had been planted and she looked at Janet with suspicion for the first time. Hadn't she said she hadn't found Mr Right? Well, she wasn't going to take Louis from her.

The friendship seemed to have cooled and the fun atmosphere had disappeared from the room, it was time to drink up and go to bed.

Sophia left the body of Katie as she slept. She was glad of the release from her chosen prison. Leaving the bedroom with the couple sleeping soundly, she explored the strange little house with only three bedrooms and two reception rooms. It was so tiny compared to the Hall where she had been brought up. But she remembered the cottage she had shared with Louis after they had wed. It was about the same size. She passed through the walls without difficulty until she found Janet spread out across a double bed, dead to the world. She gave a little snort now and then as she breathed under the influence of sleep.

Mischief was written all over Sophia's face. It would be fun to play a trick on this sleeping beauty, but what and how? Searching through Janet's things she wondered what she could find to tease her. No-one must know she had been here. In the end she decided on the lip rouge laid on a white dressing table. She picked it up, and glided down the stairs and scouted around looking into the drawers and cupboards for a place to hide it. In the end, she decided to leave it in the cupboard that had a light in it and was as cold as ice. She left it there next to the butter. She giggled at the thought of Janet finding it in the morning. She would wonder how it got there, and she would never know. Back up the stairs, the brunette was now laid on her back, her hair splayed out over the pillow. Sophia lay next to her, touching her warm body when she moved her hair from around her ear. Why did Janet have life and not her?

She moved her face close to Janet's ear. "Katie doesn't like you, you know that really, don't you, deep down. She's using you, just like she always has, can't you see that you are being a stupid fool? You like him, don't you? You could have him if you wanted. Can't you imagine his arms around you, laid beside you in your bed, keeping you warm instead of Katie?"

The whispering words disturbed Janet's sleep; she turned over, rolling onto Sophia and through her. It was time for Sophia's exit and she removed herself quickly, back to her host.

Janet opened her eyes to the dark room. She felt strangely, disturbed somehow. She had had a dream and she remembered words, uncomfortable words that she would rather not recall. Lord, what a thought, it must have been the wine. Now she was awake, she might as well get up and spend a penny. The cold of the room hit her when she threw the bedding back to get out of her bed. 'God, it's freezing,' she shivered. Even her breath hung in the air in a white fog. Had the central heating failed?

It was all go the next morning, Janet was embarrassed when she opened the fridge and found her lipstick in it. "God, how much wine did I consume last night?" But there was no hangover; she felt fine and had to get to work. Katie and Louis had to find their way back to Little Bourne.

Janet didn't understand why Katie seemed so distant. She hoped it was because she was unwell; she couldn't bear the thought that she might be angry with her. When she hugged Katie before she left, Katie was still cold to touch and more reserved than usual. They had been friends for so long that Janet didn't want to lose that friendship. Louis was amiable and hugged her, thanking her for her hospitality.

But in truth Janet was glad when they set out after breakfast that morning. To her mind, neither Katie, nor Mike were quite themselves.

23

Katie hadn't felt quite herself since arriving back in the small town of Little Bourne. She felt cold all the time, even in her centrally heated home and although it was autumn moving into winter, she couldn't understand it. She had the strangest feeling of being watched or rather a brooding shadow, hanging over her, and she feared something bad was going to happen.

The room was dark when Sophia emerged from hiding. So, this was where Louis had come to. She wondered how he had got here? It was so far away from their roots.

She looked down on the sleeping couple. God, that made her angry. They were lying in *her* bed; Katie, that dowdy bit, was sleeping with her husband, in the bed he had carved for her. She looked at the headboard. Wasn't that her profile that stood along beside him next to the Tree of Life? He had loved her when he had carved it and look at him now. If only she had a knife! But that would mean history would repeat itself. That would never do. She had never thought when she laid eyes on them at the Hall that she would be whisked away to this neck of the woods when she blended with Katie. They were only 29 miles from London. She had visited the capital once with her father but that was long ago.

She had listened in to their conversation as they travelled back to this pokey house, discussing the possibility of moving to Ravensend and Louis starting a workshop. If she caused their deaths now, she would never be able to get back home. Killing them would have to wait. Had she made a mistake using Katie as a host? She'd thought it would be exciting to see out of Katie's eyes, to see the world as it was now, but up to now all she had been was bored. Every day the dreary woman went to work; there were no parties or excursions and she didn't shop; She really ought to; the clothes she wore were as dull as she was.

Katie had returned to work nearly a month ago on the Tuesday, but it wasn't the same. She was uncomfortable in her own skin. Concentration was difficult; the more she tried to be in control, the more lapses she seemed to have. Was she going senile? Losing small pieces of time, seconds really, and surfacing with a start when it happened was very disconcerting. And why was she always cold these days, living with tight knots of tension in her stomach? She couldn't answer either of her questions.

The job, that she had once enjoyed so much, was a trial most days; it hadn't been convivial working there since Debs had turned so many of the staff against her. But since she got back from their trip everything had got far worse. Although not ill, she didn't feel quite herself. Her condition was made worst by working with Debs who had become quite insufferable.

Debs never let up, with snide remarks directed at Katie because of Mike. She had poisoned the minds of their work colleagues, destroying his reputation and, by association, Katie herself. Only Mac and Charlotte had remained genuinely friendly and gave her the moral support when she needed it. It was good to have them on her side.

Debs was still focused on settling the score with Mike and somehow Katie was included in that target. He was dead, but there was no way that Katie could share that fact with Debs. Debs thought Mike still lived with Katie and she wouldn't let it go. The destructive language she used was hateful; Mike had been a chauvinist and definitely not a gentleman when he drank. But Louis was a kind and sensitive man.

"How can you live with a man who abuses women?" was the latest taunt. How could Katie answer "I'm not."?

For months now Debs had been deliberately passing Katie's desk so that she could throw out damaging remarks. They were whispered at first, but as the days passed, she didn't care who heard. It wasn't long before she deliberately raised her voice so that all the office could hear. "What's it like living with a pervert?" Katie was ready to strike her but kept her cool.

Sophia was enjoying the dialogue that went on between the Debs woman and Katie.

It was good to feel Katie squirm under the malicious tongue from her and although she didn't understand the history, she understood hatred when she heard and saw it and it was written all over Debs' face.

Katie had never risen to the taunts until now. Her blood was boiling. For the first time in her life, she was experiencing real hatred for a fellow human being and she didn't like it. She never really had a temper, but now she was ready to explode at the slightest provocation. Not even Louis could dispel the gloom she was carrying when she got home at night. Since returning to Hertfordshire, Louis watched the worrying changes that were taking place in Katie's character; her breezy and bubbly personality had been replaced by an edginess that was getting worse. She wasn't sleeping well, that he did know. He had been woken by her cries in the middle of the night, begging to be spared. When he questioned her about it, it was a dream that frightened her about drowning in the bath. The experience at the hotel was playing on her mind. His poor darling girl was haunted by the incident. He wrapped his arm about her shoulders and told her she was safe; he tried to convince her that she was in no danger, Sophia was miles away in Avondale Hotel. From his own experience, he knew that she wouldn't be able to move far; perhaps to the gardens but no further unless she had a vessel to carry her. That wasn't possible. The only reason he was here was because of the bed he died on; it had been shipped here from the north and he was shipped with it. Katie was safe, it was just a bad dream. If they ever decided to return to Yorkshire to live, providing they stayed away from the hotel, they could live without hindrance or fear. Yet, for all his comforting words to Katie, he was worried about her.

Sophia struggled to stop her laughter, as she heard Louis explain that she was still in Yorkshire. That stupid man. She was so much cleverer than him. But she mustn't get over-confident. She still needed to a ride to get home. It was only at night that she could escape from her chosen prison. To be free for a little while, free to enjoy a little mischief.

She was able to evoke in Katie's mind the memories of when she had almost drowned. To make it seem real she covered Katie's mouth with the blanket and pinned her shoulders down, she pushed her face up to Katie's, whispering death threats in her ear. But it had not quite worked the way she'd wanted. How was she to know that Katie would cry out and wake Louis? She had had to scuttle back to her prison within Katie rather quickly. She half felt Louis' arms as he hugged Katie until she calmed down and settled back to sleep. He used to hold her like that, she thought miserably. Her prank was over, and the mischief was finished until another night. Now, she had to be quiet once more. She had enjoyed frightening Katie in the night. It was so easy to do and if it gave her immense pleasure and gave Katie pain, then she was all for it.

The day had started well after the bad night. Katie was feeling quite her old self, apart from her cold hands and feet. Louis and she shared a cooked breakfast, hot porridge with sugar and milk and a boiled egg with toast soldiers. There was nothing like it for setting you up for the day to come.

"Are you feeling better this morning?"

She could hear the concern in his voice; his eyes were on her trying to read her thoughts.

"Yes, thank you, I'm not sure what I'd do without you."

"You would do just fine, but I don't intend to go anywhere soon, except perhaps to work?" He winked, his good-natured face breaking out into a smile. "Life is good living with you, I don't intend to lose that."

Their hands met across the table and with a squeeze of love, they finished their meal and went to work.

Debs didn't know when to leave Katie alone. The mornings were an endless repeat of the previous day. Katie had hardly sat down behind her desk before Debs sidled up spitting out her usual poison. "Got a bit rough last night, did it? You look a wreck," she sneered.

"Before you pass judgement on me, I think it's time for you to look at yourself, you malicious bitch." Katie retorted standing up to make her presence felt. The gloves were off.

Debs was stopped in her tracks. She hadn't expected a response from Katie. She had never come back with so much as a word before, in all the weeks this had been going on.

"What do you mean? You're the one who's sleeping with a man that uses women, not me," she added defiantly and loudly so that her friends and colleagues could hear all around the office.

Equally loudly, Katie hit back. "For your information, Mike is a changed man." At least that much was true, she told herself. "He's working hard and he's stopped drinking. You're not blameless in what happened to you," she went on. "Did you tell everybody how you sneaked into my house and into his bed while I was sleeping, when you knew how it was between Mike and me? You were rude and noisy and I think you wanted to humiliate me. You were going to show me that you were going out with Mike at last, because, Debs," she said in lower tone, "you always wanted him." She paused and took a breath before ploughing on.

"What happened later, after you left my home, I don't know, but I do know that the blame is not all Mike's. If he was so vile, why didn't you go to the police with your story? Was it because you had already tasted the forbidden fruit in my house? Well?" She waited for an answer but none came.

The office had become as quiet as the grave. People had stopped working and some had stood up to get a better view of the women rowing. Debs was ashen as she made a beeline back to her desk. Mac and Charlotte almost applauded from their adjacent desks. They had long thought that Debs was going too far with her attacks and it was about time Katie fought back. They looked at each other and then at Katie who had sat down with a bump; she had surprised herself and even found herself smiling when Mac gave her the thumbs up sign. It would seem that not all the staff were on Debs side after all, though sometimes it felt like it.

Another day at the office had proved difficult for Katie. Her nerves were on edge and she was ready to quit. The thought of seeing Debs on the morrow was eating at her as soon has she got home. Things had to change. That evening over dinner, the two of them came to a decision.

"I can't go on, Louis, Debs is driving me insane at work. It's hell, sheer hell. Day after day she pokes and prods me with awful taunts about Mike. She thinks you are him and I can't tell her otherwise. I think we need to think about moving on. Going back to Ravensend and starting again. I know you would like that."

"Do you really mean it?'

"Yes, I do. We need a new start. You need a new identity or at least a chance to be yourself, I can get a job locally and besides we can live much more cheaply in the north. The rents and rates are so much more reasonable in Ravensend. We will be able to manage quite well until you get your workshop up and running."

Louis couldn't believe what he had heard. It was like a prayer being answered. "My darling girl, I'm so happy."

"I'll have to work my notice, but that will give us time to organise ourselves. Tomorrow I'll call Derek to see if the cottage is still on the market. If it is I'll set a date, and start our preparations."

A load had been taken off her shoulders, now the decision had been made. She wouldn't have to put up with Debs and keep pretending that the man she was living with was Mike.

So that was the plan; well, not before time. This place wasn't where Sophia wanted to stay either. She was missing the comings and goings that belonged to the Hotel. How she was going to get back there, she didn't know; but going home to Yorkshire was the first step and Ravensend was only a hop, skip and a jump away from Avondale Hall. She would think of something.

That night, when she escaped from the restrictions of Katie's body, she decided to inspect the headboard. Touching the wood and seeing how beautiful she looked in the carved profile, she was filled with sadness. This had been his gift, his love token to her. Allowing her fingers to trace her own form next to the tree, she was surprised how soft the wood seemed under her touch. How odd, she thought and pressed a little harder.

She watched her fingers disappear through the headboard followed by her hand and wrist. She pulled back in sheer surprise; what was happening? She knew the headboard had been carved out of solid wood, she had watched it grow under Louis' hands. Was it some sort of magic? She had never been afraid, except when she had gone to the gallows and the hood had been put over her head but this unexpected occurrence made her feel more than anxious, but curious too. Using the flat of her hands she pushed against the wood and fell headlong into Louis' kingdom.

It was beautiful. The sun was shining and the tree that she fell under was heavy with all kinds of fruit, the mirror image of the carved one in the bedroom she had just left. The meadow grasses were moving in the warm breeze and she could hear insects buzzing over the wildflowers. Somewhere nearby, she heard water bubbling over stones in a brook or a stream. The purple hills in the distant were lit by the sun, with a backdrop of a pure blue azure sky.

As her eyes searched the land, they lighted on a white-walled cottage that was half hidden in a dip of the land under the hills. Was this paradise? Everything was perfect. A rough stony path led the way to the hills and she had a yen to pick up her skirts and run towards the horizon. It had been such a long time since she had run anywhere. She ran as she had never run before, enjoying the perfect nature about her, the space and the sense of peace that the kingdom gave her. She arrived in the small valley, exhilarated. It had been good to feel young again and race without being breathless, but she stopped in her tracks when she recognised the building. It was Louis' cottage workshop, the one that had been her home for five years.

Her mood changed as she remembered the knife, the blood and the bed. Well, that was then, she thought defiantly. She couldn't change it. If only he hadn't changed towards her; but she wasn't going to allow herself to be discarded by him. That's why she had done what she had done. And hadn't she paid she for it, her life for his?

She had watched her father die, she had been left with nothing but emptiness, and had been trapped on her own for years, watching her home crumble in foul, squalid decay. She felt the heaviness in her heart and then the anger. Louis, however, had been living in this, a Garden of Eden, full of light and nature.

It wasn't fair and now he had a new life. She wondered how many lives he had lived while she was lost in a netherworld of hell. She could taste the hatred in her mouth. She went back to the point where she had entered this kingdom, pushing the space with her body she returned to the bedroom. The couple were still sleeping. They would pay one way or another, but not yet. She still had a use for Katie. She would bide her time.

Debs never learnt her lesson. Not even after yesterday, when Katie had retaliated letting the whole office know that Debs had willingly had sex with Mike. It was almost like she was looking for trouble the next morning when Katie arrived at work.

Katie had been to the kitchen area and was taking her drink back to her desk when Debs' voice piped up behind her.

"I thought you were a better person, I did. Fancy living with a perv and letting it into your bed." she sneered, coming round Katie and pushing her face into hers. "Feeling his grubby paws moving all over you, it's sickening."

Katie made to sidestep her but Debs mirrored her step, not letting her pass.

"What do you want, Debs, what do you really want? Haven't you done enough, getting him sacked and trying to ruin my reputation?"

"Touched on a raw nerve, have I?" she said cockily, looking around at her audience, though in truth she was disappointed to see many of the staff still working, ignoring her stand against Katie.

"Go away, you foul stupid woman." Once again Katie tried to sidestep Debs and the hatred that was coming from the woman in front of her.

"You know nothing about him, not now he's changed. Take your vicious tongue and lock your mouth up. You only ever think about yourself. Get real, look in a mirror and see the person you have become. I was quite sorry for you at first, but all you have done, playing on the sympathy of the staff and poisoning my name so you can be the centre of attraction, it won't do."

Debs had pulled back, and her face was turning red with rage and embarrassment.

"Who are you calling foul and stupid?" Spitting the words out from her mouth.

"You need a mirror not me. It's not me sleeping with a rapist!" she said, pushing Katie on her shoulder and spilling her hot coffee, missing her blouse and trousers but catching her shoes and watching the spread of the liquid over the floor.

"Blast you, Debs," she said, turning and hastily putting the cup down on a nearby desk. "Who do you think you're pushing?"

"You, you bitch."

At which Katie pushed back.

You could hear the mugs of morning coffee being put down; the office had become so silent you could hear a pin drop. Faces watched the two women. Was there going to be a catfight?

Debs was not going to be outwitted or shown up in front of her mates; they had all been on her side up to yesterday. Katie had changed all that. Debs badly needed to be seen to be in the right and to gain sympathy and she could see it all slipping away.

More indignant than ever, she pushed Katie even harder, making her lose her footing on the wet floor and fall into the desk behind her. Mac, who was sitting there trying to be invisible, stood up, appealing for calm in his Scots accent.

"Now, now, ladies, think about what you're doing."

"Stay out of it, Mac, I've had enough of her slander," retorted Katie.

He put his hands up in mock submission and stepped back. Debs chose that moment to slap Katie hard across her face, knocking her half way across Mac's desk, to his horror. He came forward to help Katie just as Debs appeared to be going for Katie's hair with both hands. Katie started to straighten up from the desk, turning around to face Debs.

Debs was stopped in her tracks, paralysed in the moment, when she saw the strange vacant look on Katie's face and saw eyeballs that were no longer human staring at back at her. The whites looked bloody and the pupils were black circles.

"Oh! My God," uttered Debs, as a hand from Katie reached out and grabbed her by neck. The other hand followed, finding the target and the hands squeezed.

Mac was unable to see Katie's face, but was shocked at what he was witnessing, this was so out of character from his colleague. He grabbed Katie instantly and pulled her towards him, trying to stop the assault, but the hands were still tight on Deb's neck and she came towards him too. Katie's body was sturdy and rigid, the hold powerful and strong. Then he felt a shudder move through her body, it slackened, and it was all over. When Katie's hands sprang off Debs' neck, he was deeply relieved. Katie had removed her hands as though she had burnt her fingers on hot coal, recoiling from the woman she had been attacking; half turning to Mac who released her from his grip, she looked disorientated but managed to say 'sorry, Mac' although she was not sure what she was sorry for.

Debs, who had witnessed those devilish eyes was relieved, but still afraid.

She was rubbing her neck. "Bloody hell, you should be in a straitjacket." She spat the words out at the woman who was now supporting herself by leaning against Mac's desk.

Looking now at Katie, she wondered what she had seen? Blooded eyes! That was impossible. Her own eyes must have tricked her and the heat of the moment had befuddled her. She had been frightened, but now anger raged in her belly and more than ever she wanted to have her moment of triumph over the woman who was still with the man she had once wanted. The one she had set out to destroy. Life was so unfair.

Sophia, like all spirits, drifted in and out of her netherworld existence. It was as though she rested unconscious in the ether, in an unknown place hidden from mortals.

Even though she had blended with Katie, she was able to rest within her. She didn't need to worry where she was, she was content to know that neither Katie or Louis actually knew she was in hiding within the dowdy woman's body. That, was how she thought of Katie; a dull person with no personality.

She had been awakened and rocked back into her kind of reality when her host body was jolted by crashing against some kind of solid object. When the next blow came, shaking the body even more violently, she had taken it over instinctively. Her eyes had become Katie's and her hands had closed around the neck of the woman who had disturbed her sleep.

She felt her host body slacking and sensed a new power in the shoulders and arms that they shared. It was a new experience; one she would have enjoyed but almost as soon she had committed herself, she realised she had made the mistake of showing herself to the Debs woman. Somehow, she had got away with it. When the man had pulled Katie off, restraining her from harming Debs, she had withdrawn. The assault had only been for a few seconds but it had been a huge mistake. It made her realise that she must find another vessel to hide in and it couldn't be in Louis. She thought about the place behind the bed head façade, that beautiful countryside she had discovered just a day ago. That was the place she would go to. She could hide there until the time was right to show herself.

It was part hers anyway, she thought grimly. She had more right to it than anyone, didn't she?

She accepted that her adventures would have to be curtailed until such a time when she would be returned to Ravensend, back to the house where Louis had carved the love token. She wanted nothing more than to return to her roots. The cottage behind the headboard was calling to her.

Debs had her wish. She had become the victim again and was threatening loudly to call the police. "You need to be locked up, you mad bitch. I'm going to have you arrested."

"Do you really want to do that?" interceded Mac as he stepped in to defend Katie and end Debs's rant.

He pointed out that the whole office had witnessed her starting the fight, that she had thrown the first blow by hitting Katie across her face and knocking her over his desk as well as causing Katie weeks of torment by her taunts. So, today, Katie had fought back. He didn't actually say Debs deserved what had happened but it was implied. Debs was speechless.

Katie wasn't sure what happened. Had she really tried to strangle Debs? It had been in her thoughts for days, crazy imaginings whirling around her brain but she would have never acted on it. How wrong she had been. Now, she had attacked Debs, but it had happened during another lapse in her memory and she couldn't actually remember doing it. There had been another slip of time and it frightened her; was she going mad? She was ashamed and she couldn't tell anyone about the time slips, certainly not Louis, at least not now.

The shame of it and the fear that somehow she was not in charge of herself was terrifying. What if it happened again, God forbid? Mac was there this time, but what about the next time? She logically put it all down to stress. It was time to move on; she had spoken to Derek that morning and the cottage was still available. What she needed was a new job and a new start, miles away from this place. Despite her recent promotion, it was time to leave the Echo, the paper that had given her her first job after university. She would always be grateful for that, but the combination of visiting Yorkshire with Louis and the terrible atmosphere at work it made it impossible for her to continue. The physicality of attacking Debs meant she would have to leave right away. She felt some guilt, but her assistant was more than capable of taking over and with that thought ringing in her head Katie marched off to visit the editor.

The editor was not without sympathy for Katie. The atmosphere created by Debs had been poisonous for weeks. He enjoyed Katie's bubbly personality and her can-do attitude but even he knew that the tension in the main office was so bad that it would explode, as it had done today. In his heart of hearts, he had hoped it would be Debs standing before him when that day came, but it was not to be. It was however a solution, and sadly he agreed that Katie should leave with immediate effect. Her papers and pay would be sent on to her.

As she walked through the office for the last time, she saw Debs' cronies crowding around her as she soaked up the outpouring sympathy. Mac and Charlotte were standing waiting for her. When she told them that she was leaving, Charlotte rushed around her desk to hug her. "You will be missed," was all she could say, because tears welled up in her eyes and her throat closed on her. Katie, who was being so brave, could feel her own eyes sting as she tried to lock back her own tears. She squeezed her friend goodbye. Mac just held out his hand and wished her good luck. It was all too much; she grabbed her handbag, gave her friends one final hug, with a promise to stay in touch, and walked out the main door with her head held high. It was December 14th; not exactly how she had intended Christmas to start that year.

24

Louis was surprised how quickly the last four weeks had passed since returning to Little Bourne. Now that Katie had admitted that she wanted a change of job and a change of scenery, a move to Yorkshire could become a real option. A month ago, he had resigned himself to staying in Little Bourne indefinitely.

How four short weeks could change one's destiny; it was remarkable. He genuinely believed that it would be good for them to concentrate on their futures in Ravensend where his roots were. This false identity irked him; it was hard living a lie. Watching every word he spoke in case he said something that would betray them.

Louis' love for Katie increased daily. It made him sad to think his lovely girl was having to endure a hate campaign from Debs each day in the office, a place where for years she had happily enjoyed the work and her companionship.

He knew only too well how unsettling fear could be. He still harboured his own; how much time did he have in this body? He didn't know, couldn't know; that was his deep worry. He was only part mortal. His soul would sooner or later be expelled from the living shroud he was trapped in and he hoped his sanctuary would welcome him back. But his kingdom had been a lonely place for the many years after his death until he found Marina.

The headboard was the doorway to his kingdom. His place of retreat was tantalisingly near, but now he was carried in a mortal skin it refused him entry. If and when the time came and he was returned to spirit, the dread of the loneliness overwhelmed him. He remembered well how desolate he had been through the years when he had not been able to connect with anyone.

There was nothing like anxiety to make the wheels of the mind turn, and that morning he made up his mind to find a place somewhere on the headboard and carve an image of man's best friend. Any kind of dog would do; a four-legged friend to keep him company, insurance against the many years he might have to spend alone in the future.

His fear of losing the body was always there in the back of his mind and he would be foolish to think it couldn't happen. Unexpected things happened all the time, as he knew only too well.

After breakfast, he stripped the bed, removed the mattress, and laid a dustsheet over the slats. He would have to sit cross-legged on them to carve; it would be awkward but doable. By mid-morning, he faced the carved scene on his headboard and selected a spot that would house the new figure. There was a small mound next to his image by the tree; with his tools laid out beside him he selected a small chisel and made his first light cut into the wood. The inspiration came from his heart and the skill came flooding back through his fingers; a shape of a dog soon developed. It was curled up sleeping under the tree, its long tail tucked close to its back legs. What breed of dog it was didn't matter, and he hid part of its face between the large front paws as it nestled on the grassy bank. Only the muzzle protruded; its ears were like a Labrador's, soft and droopy. His dog was laid near his master's feet. He liked what he had done and carefully he sanded the rough wooden edges until they sat as well on the picture as the rest of the carving. All it needed now was a light coat of varnish or two; it would be dry by the evening and the bed would be returned to normal.

He hadn't expected the relief and the lightening in his heart, knowing his fear of loneliness had been considerably reduced. Louis was content that he would have a dog waiting for him on the other side but he hoped he wouldn't be meeting it for a considerable time.

He was standing in the kitchen making a late lunch sandwich, when he heard the key in the front door, and the door opening gently. He wasn't expecting Katie back until after six. He had just finished varnishing his headboard and was about to put his tools away before eating. He was feeling rather pleased with himself. It had been a good morning's work.

"Katie, is that you?"

Her voice came back to him, "Where are you?"

"In the kitchen, love, just making a sandwich, would you like one?"

"No thanks, not hungry." She hung her coat in the hall and walked through to the kitchen and sat down rather heavily on a chair.

"Are you sure you don't want a bite to eat?" he said, turning back to his ham and tomato sandwich, cutting it in half with a knife. He looked across at the table where Katie was sitting. He could see something was troubling her.

"Are you okay?"

"Yes, well, no not really, you wouldn't believe what happened this morning."

She got up and walked over to the cupboard, reached in until she found a mug, and she was still talking as she took a tea bag from a jar and dropped it in it.

"It was awful, I had to give notice, I won't be going back."

Her voice was unsteady, filled with emotion. She moved as though on autopilot, checking the water in the kettle, finding it was half full and switched it on. She was deciding how much to tell Louis; was it enough to tell him that they were free to move? Did she need to tell him about the fight? It felt so wrong keeping things from him, but how could she tell him about her problem of blanking out, and the moment of madness during which she had attacked Debs?

The kettle clicked off and she proceeded to scald the bag with boiling water, pushing it down with a spoon waiting for it to brew. Louis was moving towards her and put his arm around her.

"What is it, tell me?"

She had to tell him something; she was flushed with embarrassment and she was glad her face was hidden from him as he held her close. She pulled away after a minute and her words spilled out in a rush.

"All that unpleasantness at work came to a head today. Debs attacked me. It could have been nasty if Mac hadn't stepped in." At least that was the truth.

"The editor let me go; well, actually, I invited him to do it. It couldn't go on, could it?" she quizzed, looking him straight in the eye.

He was listening as he opened the fridge door, taking out the milk for Katie's tea.

"No, of course not, your stress levels have been going through the roof this last month."

Leaving his sandwich on the table, he took Katie by the hand, and guided her to the other room where he placed her tea on the coffee table, sat her down before it and waited. She stared at the mug for about a minute, gathering her thoughts.

"Okay, this is what happened." She told him of her shame and responding to anger and her hands on Debs's neck. The only thing she omitted to tell him was her loss of those seconds when her body blocked time.

This was not the Katie he knew; she was far too intelligent to resort to physical violence. Regardless of the pressure, he couldn't believe she would resort to this; she was normally a strong, passive woman. Louis could hardly believe what he was hearing. She had been unsettled for weeks but he had thought she was torn between living here and the possibility of living in the north. This was her home; then he had come along and changed the balance of her life. His dear Katie was not happy in her skin, he knew that.

She settled down, sipping her tea with her eyes fixed squarely on the liquid in the mug front of her. He sat beside her, putting his arm around her, brushing his hand on her chestnut hair, stroking it to give comfort. She looked up at him. She was close to tears.

"It was good to escape," she confided in him, "With bad dreams, little sleep and hateful jibes from Debs, my life had become intolerable. Thank goodness I had Mac and Charlotte to stand up for me against the onslaught from Debs." She was embarrassed and became edgy when she thought about her hands clutching Debs's neck. With a great sigh of relief, reflecting on the knowledge that she was now safe and sitting next to Louis, she continued.

"I can't wait to get away, to rid myself of the memories of this place and make new ones. Happy ones, that only you and I can make together."

Love shone out of her eyes but there was something else there. She was holding something back; he hoped she trusted him enough to know she could share anything with him. He loved her unconditionally; he would tease it out, the secret that could come between them given time. It was time to hold her close and reassure her. The kiss that was comforting to begin with became longer, harder and more passionate.

The day drifted as days do. The eager kisses in the afternoon had left a small fire of passion smouldering in their hearts, and the dark nights of December were an excuse for early bedtimes. Louis hadn't mentioned the new bit of carving. He wanted to surprise her. He slipped up to the bedroom to make up the bed and checked on the image. He was pleased with it; it needed another coat of varnish to match the rest but if you weren't looking for it you couldn't see a difference. Would she notice the dog? he wondered.

They lay side by side in the double bed. Passion was taking hold of them; he would show her the carving later, much later, after they had shared love.

Absorbed as they were, Katie noticed that her body temperature had become normal she was no longer cold. Whether it was making love with Louis or relief because she wasn't going back to the paper, Katie didn't know. Wrapped in each other's arms, the world and its troubles were lost outside their bedroom in another time and place, and lying there after making love with Louis she noticed she felt physically different. She was warm again; the cold coat she had seemed to be wearing recently was gone. She had become quite her old self again. Louis was glad to have his bubbly, kind and patient, darling girl back.

Still wrapped in each other's arms, Louis told her about the new image on headboard, and she turned onto her belly to look at it. He told her about the dog and his thoughts; he could not decide what breed to carve, so that come the day when he met the mutt he would be in for a surprise, apart from the long tail and droopy ears. Would it be male or female? He would find out one day but not today; the body had not rejected him yet.

Sophia knew it was time to leave Katie. When the lovemaking started that evening, she took the opportunity of leaving her host's body and drifted into the kingdom beyond the wood. She would be going home soon and this would be her new residence until then. She stood in the sun and surveyed the view. On reflection she thought Louis' kingdom was a much better place to hide than in Katie. She had beauty all around her, she could walk, run and this time she would find the stream that was babbling nearby. How long had it been since she had paddled in a stream, a century or more? She half-squinted in the brightness and decided to find shade under the tree. Walking up the grassy mound to the shade of its branches, she almost stepped on a furry shape half-hidden in the base of the tree. An ear cocked up on hearing the footsteps coming towards it, followed by its raising of its head and opening its eyes. A wet black nose sniffed the air and a pink tongue licked its muzzle. Sophia half bent, stretching out her hand to it but the dog gave a warning growl in its throat, and shuffled back behind the tree trunk. The dog, with its extra sensitivity, was wary of this spirit that held so much hate in its soul. Sophia moved towards it again but the dog responded as before. Anger was not far away.

"Come here, you silly mutt."

The growl became deeper and louder; it sounded even more threatening when her hand came to touch the dog's fur and it snapped at her. Without a thought she kicked out at it, but the dog moved quickly and her foot missed its target; in her eagerness she slipped over, landing in a heap on the earth. Some loose pebbles were responsible for her fall; they were at her feet and within her reach. Taking a handful, she aimed them at the dog who was standing his ground. The wave of small stones hit the dog sideways on. It yelped once and then ran for the hills beyond the white cottage. That would be the last time she saw him. He would keep his distance from the spirit that was tainted with evil.

25

With Christmas nearly upon them, it was not the ideal time to be planning a move and, to add to the frustration, when she rang Derek she found they now weren't the only people interested in renting the cottage workshop. It was going to be a race between the new interested party and herself to find the six months' deposit. It was another complication she could do without.

Six months' money was a hefty amount and she didn't want to take out a loan. Dad would help out, she was sure of it. It would be a short-term loan, perhaps no more than three months; she only needed help to tide her over. Having made the decision to make a new life in Ravensend they wanted to secure the tenancy and sign up quickly.

Katie still had three months of lease to run on her home in Little Bourne. It was enough time to give notice to her landlord and sort the out the move, and with a bit of luck they could look forward to spending their first night in the cottage workshop on March 1st 1973.

She would need a couple of months to put all the pieces in place. It was exciting, but a lot to organise. The utilities, telephone, doctors, dentist and post would have to be changed and things she hadn't thought of yet. And they would need a moving van, though in truth she had only a few pieces of furniture that were hers, apart from the bed. The house had been fully furnished when Janet and she had rented it, which had been beauty of it. She would miss her home, but it was time to move on.

When she rang her parents, her mother answered.

"I'm so glad you rang, darling, you are coming for Christmas this year, aren't you?"

"Yes, Mum, but I really want to bring my boyfriend with me, I hope that's okay? You'll love him," she said with enthusiasm. "Can we stay for a few days? I know you'll like him and I have some news for you."

There was a pause on the line before her mother replied.

"Katie, whatever is it?"

"Well, apart from finding the perfect man, – he's called Louis by the way, we have decided to start a new life in Yorkshire."

The line went deathly quiet.

"Mum, Mum it's alright, really it is. Work wasn't working out for me, not after Mike left the paper."

A concerned response was whispered, voice down the line.

"Mike left the paper? but he was your lodger – and you are moving to Yorkshire? Are you quite sure about this, Katie?"

"Positive, Mum. Let me tell you about what happened."

They talked for an hour. Katie hoped she had convinced and calmed her mother's fears. It was a huge step, she knew that, but she and Louis believed the move was right for them.

Finally, Katie spoke to her father and was able to ask him for help. Like his wife he wasn't a hundred percent sure she was doing the right thing but, in the end, she convinced him she knew exactly what she was doing. He agreed to a three-month loan and they would talk more about it when she came to visit for Christmas.

The journey was under an hour. Katie felt a lump come up in her throat as she pulled up in front of the semi with its neat garden that belonged to her parents. Christmas lights decorated the front window, flashing in a colourful rhythm. Dad would insist on decorating the outside of the house and every year her mum would say it was too much, but Dad always won. Her eyes scanned the street and saw many of the houses had followed Dad's example; Santas, snowmen and reindeer all heralded the coming of Christmas. It made her smile.

The red door of the semi opened and her mother came out; she must have been watching out for them. The petite brunette waved a greeting, with a wide smile on her face. Louis could see the family resemblance. His Katie was a younger version of the mother.

"That's Mum," Katie mouthed to Louis, and he nodded back, "You'll like her."

Katie had told him many times that her mother, Lori, was a kind and generous lady. Someone who never had a bad word to say about anyone, and as he looked at this smiling woman, he could see a peaceful aura about her and he believed it. A man followed her out from the hall to greet the couple.

"That's my dad, you'll like him too, he has a rare sense of humour." What she meant by that was lost on Louis but at least the man who was striding down the path was smiling too.

Even though Katie was smiling back her heart strings were pulling at her. What if they didn't like Louis?

That long conversation they had had over a week ago was still uppermost in her mind. Her mother had been very understanding; of course, Katie must find her own destiny, but her mum's concern had come through while they talked. "Are you sure?" was said more than once, and then finally. "Well, if you are really sure, of course you have our blessing and we will be pleased to meet Louis." It was like an endorsement; her mum was saying she trusted her daughter's judgement. All she knew was that she was bonded by love to Louis and she simply must be with him.

Now she was to spend Christmas here, she recognised she would miss her parents terribly. The New Year and a new beginning would bring new challenging adventures. Thankfully, her mum had promised to visit, especially when Katie described how lovely the countryside was in the north.

There had also been the conversation as to when and where Katie had met Louis. Truthfully Katie related that they had met in a furniture store when she was looking for a bed and the attraction grew between them. That he was a carpenter and a carver with extraordinary gifts, and that he had been born in Yorkshire. The rest was history.

Like Katie, Louis was wary of this meeting. It must go well with her parents; they had to be confident that he would care for their daughter. When he got out of the car and stood by Katie's side and saw her mother's smile, he somehow knew everything would be all right. He was greeted with a kiss on his cheek and the word welcome. Joe, Katie's dad, ambled up to him with outstretched hand, shaking Louis' hand with bone-crunching force before slapping him on his back and saying,

"Nice to meet you, son, Katie's told us all about you."

Louis smiled and greeted Joe in similar style, thinking that half a truth was better than the whole truth in his case, and Katie was right; he liked Lori and Joe immediately.

It was the best Christmas Louis had ever had, even though it was a quiet affair with only the four of them. Katie's brother was spending Christmas with his wife's family.

Tinsel and holly decorated the house; an imitation evergreen spiky fir tree, dressed in glass baubles and gold bells, sat in a corner by the window and small candles in brackets clung to some of the branches. They were never lit, Lori explained, but one must have candles or it wouldn't be Christmas. A lively selection of Christmas cards was dotted around, resting on every available ledge, shelf, mantelpiece and sideboard throughout the rooms and in the hall. The festive feel was everywhere Louis looked. It was obvious that Katie's parents were popular and had many friends. The home was warm, comfortable and it had a genuine light-hearted feel through it.

Christmas Day came all too quickly. The bluest of blue skies accompanied the crisp winter morning; there had been a sharp frost that made the plants shimmer when the weak sun shone on the trees and grasses. It was as good as having snow.

They got to the church for the ten o'clock service. Sitting together and singing carols made him feel totally connected to Katie's family. And after the service they spent some time mixing with the congregation, greeting and wishing everyone a Happy Christmas. The turkey had gone into the oven at breakfast time; they were going back to share preparing the vegetables, have a sherry or two and put the wine in the fridge. It was going to be a late lunch, but the table had been set with Christmas roses as a centrepiece and expensive crackers, at each setting; the best wine glasses stood waiting for the fruit of the vine. The four of them helped with the preparations and at three o'clock they all sat down to a turkey dinner, followed by rich black plum pudding with brandy sauce and sherry trifle. They told each other the awful jokes they found in the crackers, wore the paper hats and abandoned the small trinkets on the dinner table. The wine made them feel mellow, but all things come to an end, and they left the table very full and satisfied.

They moved into the sitting room and sat around the small coffee table in front of a living fire. Small parcels wrapped in colourful paper and tied in red ribbon were stacked on the table waiting to be opened, coffee and port were served and presents exchanged. The whole day had been a celebration of the birth of Christ and the celebration of family. The value of family was not lost on Louis; it reinforced his commitment to Katie, and he promised himself that soon he would buy her a ring.

Katie's mum had taken her to one side and had given her their approval of the man who sat chatting to Joe like old friends. Louis was easy to be with; he had no airs about him, you got what you saw and it was comforting to know he was a man to be trusted. Could he start a new business and be a success? Would they be able to live on their income? These were still Lori's fears, but Katie seemed sure they could.

It had been a perfect few days, getting to know Lori and Joe. He had learned about them and in turn Lori and Joe got to know Louis, and approved of him. At the end of the visit, Joe and Lori came out to wave the couple off; they watched the Mini pull away, move down the street and turn out of sight. Lori's eyes filled with tears; she missed her daughter already. Joe put his arm around his wife.

"Cheer up, love, she's in good hands."

"I know, Joe, He's a good man and you can see how much they love each other."

"He's a gentleman in an old-fashioned sense. He will be loyal and he will look after her, that I'm sure of. We can't ask more than that, and we will visit often."

"You're right, and she must find her own way in this world. With Louis beside her, she'll be happy."

Lori looked up at her husband. "Just like we are." He smiled and hugged her, before guiding her back into their life behind the red door.

26

SOPHIA

Sophia was content most of the time behind the veil in Louis' kingdom. It was a peaceful and beautiful place, but even in paradise there were moments when it wasn't easy being alone.

When she heard them lying in the bed, the intimate conversations of pillow talk drifting through the veil to her, their laughter and the sounds of lovemaking, her temper would rise up. She had reckless thoughts; she had a great urge to reveal herself to them, to prove to the fools that they were not alone, that they had not been alone for months. She had out-manoeuvred them and she almost laughed at their presumption that she was in Yorkshire. The urge was powerful but up to now she had managed to control it.

Her desire to go home grew as the days passed. She badly wanted to wander the rooms in her own house, to see the guests come and go from her special place under the portrait of her mother, to see her own garden even though it was winter. The pull was ever present and getting stronger.

For almost a week, things had been silent on the other side of the veil. She hadn't heard any voices coming across the divide for a while, so she took a peek in the dead of the night and the lovers weren't there; the bed was empty.

Then she remembered that they had talked about seeing the woman's parents for Christmas. When did that conversation happen? She couldn't remember. So that must be where they were. She drifted off into the living room and then the kitchen, where she found the calendar pinned to the wall next to the fridge, it had a red ring drawn around December 23rd to 27th and the words Mum and Dad written across the dates. She was right. That was where they were; they would come back soon and then perhaps the plans to move back home might start to happen. She must be patient.

Time passed. Back in the kingdom, she was dozing under the tree when she heard the key turn in the lock of the front door. Footsteps were climbing the stairs and the sound of voices heralded their return. She heard rather than saw suitcases being set on the floor of the bedroom; she heard the wardrobe doors being opened, and the clatter of hangers being removed and replaced with their clothes on them. They were back.

"It was lovely, wasn't it? I do love them so, but it's nice to be back here on our own, isn't it?"

Louis nodded in agreement, placing the empty suitcases on top of the wardrobe.

"Your parents are very special, my love. They went a long way to make me welcome. It was great to have such a wonderful time over Christmas. I felt part of your family."

"But you are, darling. Mum gave me her approval, so that's it."

"Come here and show me," he invited, his arms held out in supplication. A large smile crossed Katie's face as she abandoned what she was doing and moved towards him.

"Well, sir," she said, in a coquettish voice. "And just what do you want from me?"

"Come nearer and I'll show you," he said, grabbing her hand and pulling her to him; searching for her lips and finding them willing, they embraced. It wasn't long before the double bed had the amorous couple spread out on it, enjoying an interlude of love.

Sophia was not amused. Her back was propped against the tree trunk, resting under the sun-dappled branches, and she had been reminiscing, lost in the thoughts of her childhood of so long ago with her father, of happy days in her garden. She was given her own special plot that she made into a rose garden; it was all hers and she remembered the perfume that came from the roses.

Sitting there daydreaming it all seemed so real, until the voices floated over to her. When she heard Louis and Katie making love, she was incensed; the urge was upon her to peer out that them, to confront them, but somehow good sense prevailed. She got up and walked towards the cottage. Once inside, she couldn't hear them.

She felt as though her heart was being pulled through a sieve and was in a thousand pieces. If she could have cried tears, she would have done; instead hate, jealously, sorrow and the need for revenge were choking her.

January was the first real month of winter; the cold, dark days stretched out before them. It could have been depressing but this particular January the days were the prelude to a new start and plans needed to be laid down. Katie was already registering with employment agencies in the north. Any doubts about the future were gone; it was full steam ahead.

The urgency to get the deposit money together to beat the other prospective tenant had had disappeared too. When Katie had last spoken to Derek, her competitor had backed out so the way was clear for them. It was an omen; they were doing the right thing.

March 1st was now in the diary for their move and it was only a few weeks away.

In early February, they would take a quick trip up to Yorkshire to sign the lease and meet the landlord. In the meantime, they requested through Derek that the bed in the double bedroom be removed to accommodate their own carved masterpiece. Their bed would grace that room, just as it had over one hundred years ago. It was only right that it be brought back to the place where it had been made. Its proper home.

The cottage/workshop was partly furnished, which was just as well, seeing that they were moving from the same set-up. Katie only owned two armchairs and the coffee table to take with her. She did have table lamps, some good pans and cutlery, and a toaster, a couple of bedroom rugs, and her own wardrobe and that was about it. She would only hire a small van to move them which would keep the cost down, and that was a relief. They did have money, but Katie didn't know how long it would take her to find a new position, so their money would have to be eked out carefully until she found a job. Louis was still working locally and that helped the coffers.

It was a rather damp day, early in February, when the two of them travelled up the M1 again to Ravensend. They set off at 6.30am. It was dark and cold when Katie started the engine of the Mini. Their plan would give them plenty of time to reach Derek's office by 11am. As the sun came up, they watched the wet grass verges change to a covering of white powder, to the crisp and stiffness of a sparking frost.

The road was fairly quiet for the first half of the journey but by the time they had reached Nottingham, cars and lorries seemed to appear from nowhere. They had allowed for traffic and even managed some breakfast at a service station and still had enough spare time, arriving early with 30 minutes to spare, to meet their new landlord and sign the lease.

By the time they reached the estate agents, the weak sun climbed up into the pale blue sky, the dry, cold, crisp morning had turned into a perfect winter day. Frost still hung about on the windowsills, fences and ground sparkling like glitter on a Christmas card in the sunlight.

Derek saw them coming and opened the door, greeting them like old friends. Standing with him was a handsome man in his forties, dressed more like a gentleman farmer than a landlord. Derek introduced Mr Ramshaw and Louis quite forgot himself, for the man that stood before him was a face from the past. Without thinking, he greeted the man with a friendly slap on his shoulder.

"Harry, it's so good to see you."

There was an awkward moment, a raised eyebrow and a frown, and an odd look covered the man's face. "Do I know you?"

Louis was brought back to the present, shocked by making such a mistake. This Mr Ramshaw was so like Harry.

"Sorry, no, for a minute there I thought you were someone else."

"Well, you got the Harry right, a someone else with my name, then." He laughed and shrugged; the moment lightened and there was warmth in his laugh and eyes. "So, there's a doppelganger out there pretending to be me, is there?"

"Apparently so." Louis responded, rather embarrassed. How stupid could he be? His friend must be the four times removed grandfather of this Harry Ramshaw.

Louis offered his hand to him and their eyes met as Harry offered his in return. There was friendliness there and as the two men chatted there was a charge of chemistry between them. It was agreed that once Louis had moved into the cottage they would meet up and have a drink.

This new development convinced him that moving here was the right thing to do. All doubts he had were washed away in that moment.

Katie could see an immediate bond between Louis and Harry. It was obvious that the men had hit it off and she liked what she saw. It was good that Louis had made a friend here in the north, the first male friend he had made in a very long time.

All signed up, done and dusted, the pair, walked towards The Royal Oak.

"Happy?"

It was a question Louis posed but what he really wanted was confirmation from Katie that she was with him all the way, so to speak.

"I am, and I'm looking forward to learning about life here." The pace of life was less frantic and peacefulness was all around; the few local people she had met were friendly. She had Janet, in Leeds, not too far away, and she already knew Doris from the pub to be a good sort. She would make friends and she would be happy with Louis. The thought of her parents passed through her mind; a small spot of sadness invaded the moment, but only for a moment. She would visit them and they would come here; she might even see them more than she did when living in the south. She was content.

They were almost at Doris' when Louis stopped and caught her arm mid stride. She looked puzzled. "What is it?"

He had rehearsed it a hundred times, but the speech was forgotten, as the words rushed from his mouth.

"Katie, darling, I wondered if you would do me the great honour, of wearing my ring when we move here? I would love to marry you in church if I could, but with another man's papers, that's impossible. The ring, would be an outward visible sign of my undying love for you," he paused and looked into her eyes, they were shining.

"What do you think?"

"Yes, please." She came close to him and kissed him.

When they pushed open the door of The Royal Oak, Doris was behind the bar. She looked up from cleaning the glasses with a pot towel and a big smile crossed her face.

"Well, I never, so you're back to see us, are you? I understand you're going to be living here in the not-too-distant future?" Doris had a knowing look on her face.

"The drum beats loud around these parts; you can hardly do something before the whole town knows about it."

Almost in the same breath she said. "Will you be staying with us overnight?" She was never one to overlook business.

"No, not this time, but we would like to book March 1st for just one night, That will be our moving day, Doris. Is that okay?"

Doris nodded. "The end of the winter and just before spring, time of the snowdrops and daffodils, a good time to move. I'll pop you in the diary and reserve the back room for you. You liked that one, didn't you?"

"You have a good memory, Doris. Thank you, that would suit us just fine," responded Katie.

"We have just signed the lease for the cottage and workshop and met a lovely man called Harry Ramshaw."

"Oh yes, Harry is the salt of the earth; he'll play fair with you and that's a fact. Will it be dinner then before you set off back?"

Louis and Katie nodded, smiling. Doris never missed a trick.

"Good idea," said Louis. "I'm starving."

27

With only a couple of weeks to go before they moved, Katie decided to use the time to say goodbye to her friends from the paper. In truth, she was missing going to work, missing her colleagues and missing the interaction of her clients. The one thing she didn't miss was Debs and her bullying. The phone call to Charlotte and Max that Friday morning inviting them to tea on Saturday afternoon delighted them, and they accepted without hesitation. They knew that in a week's time Katie would be saying goodbye to Little Bourne, leaving friends and acquaintances behind for a new life in the north.

She hadn't made a cake for ages, but she pulled out all the stops and baked a Victoria sponge plus scones on the Saturday morning, and as an extra treat she bought clotted cream and strawberry jam to top her newly baked scones. Cups, saucers and plates were set out on the coffee table with floral patterned paper napkins. Satisfied with the look, she decided to leave the food in the kitchen until her guests arrived. All Katie had to do was to wait for the doorbell to ring and at precisely 3pm it did.

It was February but the season didn't seem to know that. The March winds had come early to Little Bourne, and it had been blowing a gale for a couple of days. It was sneaking into the house, rattling the windows, coming under the door and causing a cold draught around her ankles.

Bypassing the draught-excluders, the wind found a way into the house from who knows where?

Opening the door, she found her married friends, on the step, looking cold and windswept. Their cheeks and noses were ruddy from the chafing wind, and they were wrapped up in thick overcoats to keep out the chill that was blowing all around them.

Katie ushered them indoors, and the house seemed to wrap around them, hugging them in its warmth. Charlotte was holding a large bouquet of flowers in one hand and a bag that looked suspiciously as though it might hold a bottle. Smiles and kisses were exchanged in the hall before they hung their coats, on the waiting pegs. Katie pointed the way into the sitting room. She had lit a fire in the cosy room that welcomed them like a warming tonic. Charlotte handed the flowers to Katie, before sitting down.

"I hope you like chrysanthemums, I just love them, I always think yellow is such a cheerful colour, don't you?" Not waiting for an answer, she continued. "Mac bought some plonk for Mike, and you, of course."

Katie gestured to Mac, who was still nervously stood in the doorway, holding the package of wine that Charlotte had handed to him when she was hanging up her coat.

"Come in and sit, Mac," urged Katie. Responding to her invitation he moved to join his wife on the sofa opposite the open fire. The orange and red flames were dancing and flickering making shapes in the blackened space of the fire grate; a gust of wind rushed down the chimney, causing sparks to shower back up the dark shaft. It was like fireworks on Bonfire Night. Mac flopped down, welcoming the heat after the cold from outside.

Sheepishly, he passed the bag over to Katie. "I wasn't sure whether it was a good idea or not, but I thought what the hell, a bottle of bubbly was something you could toast to your new home with when you get there. But you could hide it and have it all to yourself if Mike's on the wagon." He looked uncomfortable. He hadn't meant to be so blunt, but everyone knew Mike had a drink problem and the words just sort of blurted out. He hadn't meant to offend anyone. Now he was embarrassed.

"Sorry, Katie, that came out wrong,"

"It's okay, Mac, he did have a problem, and I know you meant well. Let's not dwell on it."

She smiled, the awkwardness in the room disappeared, and Mac visibly relaxed.

"The office is deadly quiet without you."

"Don't be silly, Mac, the last weeks there were hell."

"Yes, I know. Debs is still obnoxious but in a different way. Now she has no-one to torment, she's just unpleasant to everyone. Even her gang seem to steer clear of her. No, what I meant was you always rose above her nastiness, and kept your dignity until, well, you know. Whatever else, you always cared about the job and us."

"That's quite enough, Mac, you'll have me in tears. I loved my job and I miss it a little but it's time to move on. I'll miss you and Charlotte but I'm looking forward to a new start."

"Are you sure you're doing the right thing, Katie?" Mac took her hand, his eyes searching hers. "Mike could be a Jack the Lad at times, even though I always liked him. But he was unreliable when he had a drop too much, and your move will take you away from your friends and family, the safety net of support."

She could see that Mac was genuinely concerned about her. It warmed her heart. He was a good man and now she must put his mind at rest if she could.

"Mike's not the same man he was, believe me, Mac. I wouldn't consider moving with a man I couldn't trust. He's sorry not to have been here to see you this afternoon but he's out working."

"Working? Has he joined another paper?"

"No, not exactly, in fact he's doing something completely different." In a low voice she said. "Carpentry."

Mac was stunned; he had never seen Mike as practical man. He almost laughed. Mike was a keen sportsman. He had almost been too attached to the sports fields and the athletes. He remembered his chauvinist attitude when it came to women's athletics. Mike had regarded women as accessories on his arm, and never as dedicated athletes. Carpentry! Was she joking?

Katie wanted to move the conversation on. She should have thought of this; what a fool to think they would come here and not bring up Mike's sacking, or her leaving, for that matter. It was impossible to explain the complication of the Mike situation; he really wasn't the same man.

In the silence and looking at the surprised expressions on her friends' faces, she took the initiative.

"Make yourselves comfortable, I'll just put these in water." She left for the kitchen in a hurry, leaving the couple with questions still ready to ask hanging in the air. Flowers in her hand, she was still talking, "And let's eat, would you prefer coffee or tea?"

Tea was just fine by them; thank goodness she would have a minute or two to herself in the kitchen. It gave her space to gather her thoughts. How could she guide the conversation away from Mike? She was on automatic pilot for the next few minutes; after filling a vase with water and immersing the flowers in a pleasing arrangement, she put the kettle on and waited as it boiled. She warmed the teapot before putting spooning leaf tea into it. Scalding it with boiling water, she set it to one side to brew. She reached into a cupboard to take out a tea strainer and saw the little bowl hiding behind it. It was still half-filled with peanuts, the same peanuts that had killed Mike, and her blood ran cold. She had forgotten all about putting them there. Why hadn't she thrown them away and why did she have to see them today? She closed the cupboard door on them. She was shivering, though not with cold, rather with the memory that came flooding back.

For a few moments she relived the horror of Mike's death on her kitchen floor. Her eyes involuntarily looked over at the spot by the table. She could see him lying there, his bloated face turning red and then purple, his hands flailing at his throat as he choked, his life slowly leaving him. She saw it all over again.

Somehow, she forced a smile back on her face when she returned to the sitting room with a tray carrying the cake and scones, along with the teapot, filled to the brim with Assam tea.

"Scones first, I think. Help yourselves to cream and jam," she said cheerily, her emotions at odds with her smile. She set the tea down and poured the hot liquid into the waiting china cups; milk came last.

Mac and Charlotte were not slow in helping themselves. At least while they were eating, they weren't talking, and the subject of Mike was forgotten for now. Katie took a mouthful of the hot tea and felt the pleasure of it as it warmed and steadied her, taking away some of her fears. She was revived and by the time she had emptied her cup she felt her old self again. The conversation was renewed but it was more about booking holidays, where she was moving to, and had she found a job yet? It was politely inquisitive and not too intrusive. She was glad to be with her old friends, for God only knew when or if she would see them again.

Saturday afternoon eating cake and sharing old times with old friends was idyllic, and, it was well after five when the front door opened and Louis walked in. He had been fitting shelves for two brothers who lived just down the road.

Katie's heart sank. Was he back early or had she forgotten the time? The one thing she hadn't wanted was for Mac and Charlotte to be still here when he came home. She looked at her wristwatch; time had gone so quickly. The sun was going down; dusk and darkness was fast approaching.

Louis appeared at the doorway of the sitting room still in his dark blue overcoat and checked scarf, tied at his neck. All the faces in the room turned to look at him.

He was cold through to his bones, pleased to be finally home and out of the wind that cut through him, and looking forward to having a hot drink and a warm by the fire with Katie. He was stopped in his tracks as he untied his scarf. Two new faces were staring back at him.

"Oh, hello there, I got finished sooner than expected," he explained looking at Katie, his voice trailing off to almost a whisper as he mouthed 'sorry'.

Charlotte and Mac looked at Katie and then each other before Mac said in a raised voice. "Good to see you, Mike, how have you been?"

Mac was up on his feet to greet his old colleague, grabbing his hand and pumping it like one might a water pump. Louis was at a complete disadvantage; was he supposed to know who this man was that gripped his hand so tightly? When Katie said that her friends from the paper were coming to tea, it had not occurred to him that they would still be here when he got back from work. They would know him as Mike, but he didn't have a notion who these people were.

"Mac was just telling me about his and Charlotte's holiday," informed Katie, to make Louis aware who her guests were.

He knew the names, and that Mac had helped Katie after Debs assaulted her at the office but apart from that, these two people were strangers. He had no history with them but they surely would have a long history with Mike; years, in fact. He wondered how he was going to deal with this bizarre meeting. Mac released his hand and Louis moved uncomfortably into the room, discarding his coat and scarf on a chair and taking a seat next to Katie.

There was a slightly unreal feeling in the room. Katie forced a smile and the pair on the sofa were looking expectedly at the now seated Louis, waiting for him to speak.

Katie broke in. "There's cake or scone, Mike, what would you like? While you make your mind up, I'll make a fresh pot of tea." She half-rose, reaching for the teapot but Louis beat her to it. "No, let me, I'll have a slice of cake please." He was up and into the kitchen before anyone could ask him a question that he couldn't answer.

Sophia had heard voices that she didn't know. It piqued her curiosity and the more she heard the more she wanted to see these faceless people, especially the one with a Scottish accent. She reasoned that it wouldn't hurt to take a peek. They were so busy talking that she could mingle and they would never be aware of her joining them. She slipped out of Louis' kingdom, through the walls and down the stairs, and stood behind the sofa. She was enjoying the small talk when the front door opened and her husband joined them. The wind came through the front door with him, whipping up the newspaper that was on the sideboard. She knew that she brought a chill with her when she roamed but today, with the wind's intrusive force coming in from outdoors no one would feel her presence, she felt safe. The draughts that circulated the room would hide her; Louis would never guess she was there watching.

Mac and Charlotte glanced at each other; Mike was making tea! He had taken over from Katie, relieving her of the teapot and had dashed into the kitchen. It was odd. Not a word was said between them but the raised eyebrow from Mac and a slight nod from his wife was a kind of code; the married couple often thought as one.

Louis re-emerged carrying a tray with clean cups and a fresh brew. Katie had cut his slice of cake and it was waiting for him on a spare white china plate on the coffee table.

"Shall I pour you fresh tea?" Louis asked the couple, who were watching him intensely. He was already in mid-act when Mac spoke.

"Who are you and what have you done with Mike?" Mac was smiling. He found his wife's hand, squeezing it lightly, sharing the joke with her. His face turned to Katie, expecting her to understand his humour but his smile faded when he saw disbelief on Katie's face. She was motionless and open-mouthed, though no sound came forth and as for Louis, missing the cup entirely, he poured tea onto the tray. He too looked across at Mac, with a shocked expression and alarm on his face.

This time it was Katie who jumped up. "Whatever do you mean?" she spluttered, as she engaged herself in mopping up the tray with the patterned paper napkins. She almost forgot herself and was about to call Louis by name; she got as far as 'Lou' before she changed it to 'Look what you're doing darling, be careful, what's the matter with you?' She scolded lightly, but underneath she was scared. Was Louis so different? She answered her own question; she supposed he was. Not just in actions but she knew his eyes were gentler and his voice kinder.

"What did I say?" Mac was understandably at a loss at the reaction to his little joke. Had he offended in some way? Surely not.

"I only meant." he said, looking directly at Louis. "You! Playing mother, that's not the Mike I knew. He would have left it to the little woman. It must the love," he said. "It changes people."

Charlotte giggled like a schoolgirl and snuggled up to Mac. "I always said there was a nice man under his skin, didn't I, Mac?"

"You did that, my love. Here's to the two of you," and Mac toasted them with a fresh cup of tea.

A ripple of relief passed around the room; the embarrassing moment fizzled away, more cake was passed around, received and eaten with the fresh brew.

Louis felt a draught but he barely noticed it. Pouring himself a hot tea, he settled down in the chair to enjoy the cake. He decided that the best thing to do was to listen to the guests, not to make conversation but simply to nod and agree with them, be amiable and rely on Katie to steer him in the right direction. And that's just what he did. The chat continued with Mac doing most of the talking, laughing at his own jokes and reminiscing about the time he had spent working at the paper with Mike. Louis laughed with him and nodded in all the right places, drinking in the enormous amount of good will that was coming from the likable Scot.

Mac and Charlotte were finishing off a yet another cup of tea when they announced it was time to leave. It had been a good visit, and before saying their goodbyes and wishing them all the best in their new home, they invited Katie and Louis to come and stay with them the next time they came to Hertfordshire. Katie was gratified. They really had been true friends and she was going to miss them. She nodded and accepted their offer, knowing that she could never actually visit them. She could not put Louis under a spotlight; that would be wrong and the more they saw of Louis the more likely it was that they would realise that he was a different man.

Katie wrapped her arms around Louis; Mac was telling them that if they were as happy as he and Charlotte were, Katie would never need to complain.

"You make a perfect couple."

"Oh, Mac, you'll make me blush in a minute."

"He always had a smooth tongue," said Charlotte, laughing, pushing Mac towards the front door and grabbing their coats on the way. "Thank you for the afternoon tea, it was lovely. We hadn't meant to stay so long. I hope we didn't overstay the welcome."

The wind had dropped but it was dark and cold when they opened the door to leave. Katie gave them a final hug and waved them on their way. Though she had enjoyed their visit, it was somewhat of a relief to close the door behind them. She felt she had concluded a chapter in her life and it gave her a satisfying end.

She nearly jumped out of her skin when an unexpected noise came from the sitting room; the sound of crockery breaking and a loud voice exclaiming. "Oh hell, damn and blast it, how did that happen?"

She hurriedly returned to see Louis standing with tea stains down his trousers, his cup and saucer lying on the carpet and one of her best china plates smashed into several pieces with the cake scattered around his feet.

"What happened?"

"I don't rightly know, one minute it was on my knee and the next," he was looking puzzled, "the next it jumped out of my hands." The stain was spreading on his trousers. "It was a good job the tea had cooled or it could have burnt me. Sorry about the plate, I hope it wasn't a good one." He was looking down on the mess. A draught passed around the room and he thought he could smell something that was faintly unpleasant... then it was gone. The fire flared, with the flow of air making the fire spark for a second.

Katie was standing in the doorway, not sure of what to say to Louis. The mess didn't matter but the plate belonged to a set that had been her grandmother's; she couldn't replace it. "Accidents happen." The refrain flashed through her mind; the plate was only a thing and Louis hadn't been hurt. Somehow the bowl of peanuts came into her thoughts; but hot tea not coffee had caused the accident, and this time no one was hurt. She felt she should be grateful for that. But her grandma's plate couldn't be replaced and she felt sad.

Sophia had waited until the couple from the paper had left. Louis was sitting cradling a cup and saucer on his knee and a plate of Victoria sponge was balanced on the arm of the chair. He had his eyes closed and was obviously relaxing after a day's work; he was enjoying the heat from the fire and the fact that he was no longer under the scrutiny of Mac and Charlotte.

Simultaneously, she pushed the cup, saucer and the plate off the arm and from his hands; the sound of the crashing crockery was music to her ears. What fun. She laughed out loud, knowing no one could hear her.

But she wouldn't push her luck. Dashing out of the room, she left a ripple of air, behind her, an imprint of her spirit, a faint odour that she took with her, back to the bedroom and into Louis' kingdom.

What a pity the tea wasn't scalding; it would have been only fair to hurt him after all the hurt she had suffered because of him. It was his own fault she had killed him, she thought sulkily, her elation fading. He had killed her indirectly. He had no idea the pain she suffered walking to the gallows, and she could still smell the odour from the hood they placed over her head. Damn him. Had she missed an opportunity when they had gone to sign the lease in Ravensend? she thought not, it was better to wait to move with them, she couldn't risk being stranded with no bed or home to hid in. Soon, they all would be back in Yorkshire, then his woman would be fair game. He would hurt, really hurt when she took Katie away from him. The thought brought a twisted smile to her face. Soon, very soon, they both would be her prey.

Katie sent Louis upstairs to change his trousers. To get rid of the stain they must be washed immediately. Katie was clearing up the mess when Louis reappeared, but she said nothing about the plate. He was looking rather shamefaced, sensing that she was upset and he didn't know how to put things right. Katie gave up a silent prayer of thanks; the cup had not been chipped and the saucer was still whole. While she was on her hands and knees cleaning the carpet, she could smell a faint odour and wondered if the spitting coal had given off the sulphuric smell that still lingered. It was faint but unpleasant and she was rather glad it hadn't happened while her friends were here.

Louis felt like a spare part, watching her clean up his mess. "Sorry, Katie." He helped her up from the floor and took the cleaning equipment from her. He quickly whisked them away and stored them in the kitchen before putting the kettle on.

"I'll make us some more tea, shall I?" He called the half question, but she didn't answer. Coming back into the sitting room he saw the sadness on her face; she looked so vulnerable. He caught her into his arms, kissing her forehead.

"You're upset with me, I can tell." She lowered her head so he couldn't read her eyes, but he gently took her chin and lifted her face up to once again to look into her eyes.

"It's all right, Louis, it's just a plate but it was my grandmother's. It's just an object."

He pulled her nearer and whispered "Sorry" into her ear, nuzzling her hair with the words "I love you."

"I love you, too."

The warmth of their bodies kindled their affection, rousing a passion between them. The kettle sang, letting them know it had boiled, but tea was the last thing on their minds at that moment. The carved bed was their destination as they climbed the stairs still wrapped in each other's arms.

The love-talk, and sounds of passion drifted though the wooden veil to where Sophia tried in vain to shut them out of her hearing. Her anger was rising; this was not a good ending to her day. She swallowed hard. Revenge was a dish best served cold and she had all the time in the world.

28

It had rained for a full week leading up to when they were due to move.

"Anyone would think it was April instead of March, and only just March at that," Katie grumbled in disgust as she looked up at the leaden sky that morning.

It was a wet and damp Thursday when March 1st finally arrived. She was disappointed at what she saw through the window, but come rain or shine they would move today.

The grey-purple clouds were gathered layer upon layer as far as the eye could see; there would be no let up in the deluge anytime soon. Her usually cheery disposition was as damp as her surroundings.

Tonight, they would be sleeping at The Royal Oak, back in the room that held Louis' father's rocking chair and its memories. Doris, would welcome them in her own direct way, and Katie was sure they would become great friends given time. Her heart lifted at the thought. The weather didn't matter. Tomorrow, Friday 2nd would be the first day of the rest of their lives; a new chapter, living in the cottage that had been Louis' workshop in his previous life, and where they would make new memories and new friendships. Sod the rain.

She looked at her watch for the fifth time that morning, willing the time to pass more quickly. The brothers with their van would be here in twenty minutes. Some of the tension she was holding in her shoulders released; they would soon be on their way. Some possessions were already waiting in the hall. Two cardboard boxes were marked in red marker pen. One read 'kitchen' and another was marked 'bathroom'. Her coffee table and armchairs were waiting in the hall beside her, and she could hear Louis upstairs. He had been dismantling the bed. It was just about ready to be brought down before the moving men came. As he wrapped the finely carved headboard in an old blanket, he stopped to touch his new piece of carving. A smile lit up his face seeing the tail of the dog and its floppy ears he had carved in the wood. He had no doubt they would be good friends when they finally met. It was only a matter of time, but, please God, not in the near future. The fear of loneliness was less; the dog was his insurance, a safety net that gave him peace of mind. The bed was ready to be tied up and labelled; he would haul the pieces downstairs as soon as Larry arrived with the hired van.

Downstairs, bedside lamps and vases were packed in an old tea chest that sat in the kitchen. They were protected, wrapped in old newspapers with scrunched-up paper stuffed around them. Rugs were rolled up and pushed to one side and the dismantled wardrobe was propped against the hall wall wrapped in blankets. Three suitcases that held their clothes would go into the Mini when they left for the north later that afternoon.

Had she forgotten anything? Katie held a feeling of sadness in her heart, it would be strange saying goodbye to the house; it held good memories… and some not so good.

Her thoughts floated back, swirling around her head as she watched the rainfall. Janet had found the house when she had started with the Hertfordshire Echo. Katie was still looking for work so, that when Janet told her that there was a job available on the Echo, she applied for it. It was Katie's first job after university. The friends were living together again; it · had been like old times. They had lived first in halls and then rented while studying at university. They were still the best of friends. For a year, they had worked alongside each other, enjoyed each other's company without living in each other's pocket.

Life was great – she made a small sound of amusement, a half laugh and a shrug of her shoulders – with one exception; Janet had grabbed the best room with the double bed, and Katie had had to sleep on a fold up Z-bed that was narrow and uncomfortable. She nodded to herself as she relived the memory. She had saved up to buy a double bed, not knowing what it would bring to her. She had visiting the second-hand store in the nearby town, searching for a bed she could afford and not knowing fate had taken a hand in selecting one for her.

Louis' bed, she remembered, was in the dingy showroom that was half lit and filled with run-of-the-mill beds. Louis' bed was half hidden at the back of the room, with a cover thrown over the headboard hiding the carving. It seemed to draw her to it like a magnet attracting metal. When she had lifted the dusty cover, she had been surprised to find a work of art.

She smiled; for a moment she was back there, standing next to the carved headboard and looking at the price tag. It was expensive, too expensive for her but, somehow, she knew she had to buy it. After making a bargain with the store owner, she arranged to pay for it over a six-month period until it was hers.

Shortly after it was delivered, the dreams had started. Louis had woven stories like dreams while she was sleeping; he told her his history and that he was trapped in a netherworld. In her dreams he took her to a kingdom that was truly beautiful, a world she shared with him but not knowing him as she did now. She never suspected at the time that the dreams were his true history; she thought they were just flights of fantasy. And then came the shock of Janet leaving for a new job in Leeds.

Then, the problems came. If she was being truthful to herself, she hadn't really been sure about Mike coming to live with her, but she had thought she loved him and they got on well on both sides of the sheets. She had had to share the house with someone; she couldn't afford the rent otherwise.

A horn blared from outside the house. It brought Katie back from her daydreams with a start. This was it; this was the removal men.

Looking out of the window she could see the medium-sized, navy-blue, van with, 'WE WILL MOVE YOU REMOVALS.' The logo was printed in yellow on the side and written underneath in small letters was, 'No Job Too Small' One man was getting down from the cab while another was opening up the back doors. Both were getting wet.

Larry and John were brothers who lived and worked together. The forty-year-olds had never married, though both had girlfriends. Louis had been working for them for a few weeks, building new units in their kitchen and putting up shelving for books and a music centre in their sitting room, finishing just days ago. It was over a coffee in their kitchen, when they were having a bit of a chinwag, that Louis had told them about his forthcoming move to Yorkshire. It turned out both the men had been born in Doncaster but came to live in the south when they were teenagers. They still had family in the north, but it had been a while since they had visited there.

"We do removals if you're interested, we could give you a quote." They mostly did deliveries for stores, sometime for charities, taking furniture here and there. Louis was relieved. This offer was a godsend. Katie had been thinking about hiring U-Drive Van Hire, which had all the complications that went with it; only she could drive.

John was knocking at the door, and the rain was coming down like stair-rods. He tried in vain to shelter under a folded newspaper that he held over his head. It was limp and soggy by the time Larry had shut the back doors of the van, having collected a wheeled cart for carrying furniture, and joined him at the door. Louis was carrying pieces of the bed down the stairs into the cluttered hall, but responded to John's knock.

"Come on in, you too Larry, get out of the rain."

The men acknowledged Louis and, wiping their feet, crowded into the already cluttered hall.

"It's brightening up," said John, shaking the soggy newspaper on the welcome mat, much to Katie's disbelief at what she was seeing. "I reckon give it half an hour and we'll have a dry spell." He sounded so sure of himself. "Trust me."

Louis and Katie liked the brothers. They had enjoyed a glass together when the men came to give them a quote on carting Katie's few bits up to Ravensend. An overnight stay was included but the quote was reasonable, and they had booked them.

John was convinced if they waited half an hour before loading up the van the torrential rain would peter out. "I'll make a cuppa, shall I? asked Katie. Half an hour was neither here nor there. There was no rush; they had planned to get the keys for the cottage tomorrow morning.

"Just enough time to have a last pot of tea," said Katie with good humour, putting the kettle on. She had deliberately left it unpacked, just in case they wanted a drink before they left.

"Is everything here ready to go?" asked Larry, as he came into the hall.

"Just our bed to come down and we are there."

"A cup of tea then, watch the rain for thirty minutes, then we'll get at it."

Katie was in the kitchen when the three men joined her; she was putting a few biscuits on a plate to have with their brew. The four sat around the kitchen table. John was telling Louis that the brothers were looking in on some family relatives, seeing that they were passing their doorstep, so to speak. The plan was to drive up there, stay overnight in Doncaster and finish the journey the next morning to arrived, at Ravensend about 11am to unload at the cottage.

Just as John predicted, almost as soon as they finished their tea, the grey clouds cleared and a pale-yellow sun crept out, peering though the thin veil of cloud that was left.

"Well! Imagine that," Katie mused, looking out from kitchen window and up at the sun. John had been right. She collected the mugs from the kitchen table and moved to the sink to give them a final wash. They belonged to the house. Drying them, she went to the cupboard to put them away. Everything must be in order when she left. The small bowl of peanuts was still there; she'd forgotten them. She took them out. Walking to the bin, she pressed the pedal, and when the lid popped up, she threw the salted nuts in with the rest of the rubbish. She should have got rid of them sooner. As the peanuts left the dish Katie felt sadness and sense of closure. Her eyes were filled with tears, and she wiped them away. She couldn't bring Mike back; she must put the past behind her. At last, it really was time to move on.

The men were heaving Katie's belongings into the waiting van. It was loaded very quickly. Almost before she knew it, the van had left on its journey and Louis and Katie stood in the empty hall with the suitcases at their feet.

But for Louis, there was one last task to perform. He had kept the box deep in his pocket until this moment.

"Give me your hand." He opened the black velvet lid to reveal a gold band. "As promised, my darling girl, together we will embrace our new life."

'Yes, we will.' She said, her eyes were smiling and filled with love, as she slipped it on her finger.

It was the moment to lock the door one last time and head off to the leasing agent to hand in her keys and to say goodbye to Hertfordshire and hello to Yorkshire.

29

SOPHIA

Sophia was excited. She was going home. She heard Louis dismantling the bed and knew that today was the day she'd been waiting for.

John and Larry were busy talking in the van when Sophia decided to see where she was. She knew she was in a vehicle and moving fast, faster than she liked. There were no horses or carriages in this age; where had all the elegance gone? She remembered that on a fine day, she would take the open carriage and ride through the villages. She probably impressed the locals; she must have looked like a princess to them, dressed in her finery, sitting there with her best silk parasol protecting her skin from the sun. A tan would have made her look like a field worker and that would never do. How she missed the simple pleasures.

The distant rumble of traffic was seeping through the wooden veil and into her space. Curiosity overcame her again, but when she tried to step out from the kingdom a thick obstruction was barring her way. Determined she wasn't going to be locked in, she pushed her way through it. Once she emerged, she saw the barrier was nothing more than a thick old grey woollen blanket, which was wrapped around the headboard to protect it from damage. She was standing in a very small space in an odd-smelling vehicle with furniture stacked all round her. Wall straps anchored the pieces to stop them moving about on the journey. The noise inside the space she was standing in was overwhelming; so much noisier than in the kingdom; it seemed to be coming at her from all directions. The van was a huge echo chamber. Magnifying the sound from the vehicles that travelled alongside it as they all sped up the road. At that moment she most appreciated the relative peace she had back in the kingdom.

What was that smell, she wondered? It seemed to be a mixture of wood, woollen fabric and something that offended her nose, something she couldn't put a name to. She remembered it from when she had been in Katie's car. It permeated all around her. The smell and the noise had almost driven her back into the sanctuary of the headboard when she spied a small oblong window with light coming through it. The view from the small window allowed her to look into a space where she could see two men. Neither were young or very interesting. The bald one appeared to be controlling the transport; the other was reading a newspaper.

John was concentrating on the road. He had been driving for an hour and the weather had turned again, the conditions were awful. He was driving at what he considered a safe speed and distance from the other travellers. Lorries were speeding by them, even though the rain had become torrential.

His hand stroked his bald head in concentration when he was suddenly aware of an odour that wafted up from under his seat. He gurned his face. Had some food rolled under it some time and was rotting there? he wondered

"Here Larry, can you smell that? It's just crept into the cab. Boy! What a pong."

"Could be coming from outside, you know how the heater draws in the smells, all those fumes coming out of the exhaust pipes from those big brutes of lorries. God knows what we're breathing in."

Yet another large vehicle sped by, lifting water from the road on its tyres and spraying the van's windscreen. A wash of dirty water ran down the glass, obscuring John's view for a second.

"Bloody Hell, those wipers are only just managing, John."

"You're right, I guess we'll be okay, though we need the bloody rain to ease up. I'm taking it steady until we get to Doncaster." Another lorry crossed lane and moved in front of them. Visibility was almost nil with the spray it produced and the height of the vehicle blocked the view of the road.

"It's no good, Larry. I'm going in the slow lane. Someone's going to have a shunt and it's not going to be me."

"Right you are, better safe than sorry," Larry responded, before going back to read the newspaper.

Sophia was watching and listening; she wondered how far they had travelled. She knew that they were still a long way from Yorkshire, but why were they going to Doncaster? In her day the journey would probably have taken four days to complete.

Hidden away inside Katie, coming south, she had heard nothing but muffled sounds from the outside world. Here she was free, travelling in a metal vehicle so unlike any coaches she had known. She had expected to be home that day, but now she wasn't so sure.

The view of the road was partly obscured from where she was in the back, but if she was sitting next to the men, she would be able to see much more. Her concern was that she had never passed through a metal wall before. Would she be able to do it? Brick or stone walls had never been a problem; would this? She put her hand flat against the cab divider and pushed gently. It moved under her pressure.

A space on the long leather seat waited for her, and she was soon sitting between the two men, staring out of the glass screen at the moving cars. It was quite hypnotic at first and exhilarating to be travelling at such a speed. She had never seen such movement before. Being close to so many vehicles that were making their way up the wide road, she wondered where they were all going? Out of the blue, she suddenly felt very small and insignificant; it wasn't a feeling she enjoyed. All these people were rushing about. They reminded her of an army of ants, going to God knows where, for God knows why? What a strange age this was.

"God, it's cold in here, turn the bloody heater up, will you?"

"You're right, must be the damp coming in." John leaned forward and pressed a knob on the dashboard to high.

Sophia giggled; she knew her presence had changed the temperature. It amused her to think that she was invisible to them, that she could do what ever she wanted and they wouldn't understand what was happening. Amusement was quickly dispersed when John mentioned the odour that was still hanging heavily in the air. The magic of invisibility faded away. Were they speaking about her?

"It's a f...ing evil smell. We'll have to stop at the next services to find out where it's coming from, it's vaguely like sulphur and it just got worse." John nodded as he glanced over at Larry.

"It's not you, is it?" He was patting the seat and pointing a finger.

"Not me, mate, I thought it was you and your smelly feet, you can clear a room instantly when you take your shoes off."

"Cheeky beggar." said John, laughing, as he rolled down the window an inch to let in some fresh air. Driving rain attacked him, wetting him, but somehow that was better than the breathing in the foul stench that filled the small cabin.

Sophia was affronted; were they talking about her? Both the men had looked at and through her. John had even patted her ghostly body. What did they mean? Was it her? Could the odour of her decomposition still be around her? She had never smelled anything, not on herself anyway. Hadn't she always prided herself of smelling of rosewater or lavender? How dare these scruffy workmen accuse her of causing an odour?

They were of-no-account workers while she was almost gentry, she sniffed; wasn't her father an important man? Oh God, what was she thinking? that was long ago before she was hanged. Her mood changed, her anger rising and her power growing. Was it coming from somewhere beyond her, outside herself? From where didn't matter; it was making her feel omnipotent. She sucked in the air from the cab. When she exhaled, it became steam and a grey mist formed, gathering around her, covering her like a shroud before creeping over and around the two men. Her ghostly breath shimmered and moved. Once more she drew in the cold air, turning it into ice particles. Filled, she finally let go of her breath, spitting the grains out at full force onto the window screen in front of her. It froze on the glass.

"Bloody hell what's happening? Is the heater on the blink, blowing cold instead of hot?" John was shouting. "God, I hope it's not going to catch fire."

"Pull over onto the hard shoulder," suggested his brother. John took his advice; it was hard to see through the mist.

John parked the van on the hard shoulder, relieved to be safe for the moment. The noise from the passing vehicles was frightening; the van rocked as each lorry passed, pulling as though it was in a wind tunnel.

Even when the brothers opened the doors to allow the mist to disperse it didn't escape; instead, it sat between the men. It was moving as though it was breathing. For one second Larry thought he saw the indistinct outline of a body. Fear gripped him. It was something beyond normal; supernatural might be a better word to describe it.

The chill in the cabin grew colder and the men watched in astonishment as the window screen suddenly frosted over again, making icy, fern-like patterns grow from the centre of dashboard to the top of the glass.

Larry, always the sensitive one, started praying.

The windscreen wipers were still working, moving backwards and forwards at speed, sliding over the glass and removing the rain that fell like a tempest. The ice was obviously on the inside of the glass. The brothers flapped their arms and hands about, trying to encourage the grey mist to leave the cabin; trying with no real success. They couldn't ignore the manifestation that had happened in front of their eyes. Frightened, mystified, neither knew what the hell was happening.

They were dithering. They couldn't make up their minds whether they should get out of the van into the rain or stay with what they thought was a faulty heater.

What if the heater broke out into flames? John had to shout to be heard over the traffic noise. "Bloody hell, what are we going to do? Should we drive on Larry?" But not waiting for an answer, he continued in a weary voice. "We've got to check it out and that's a fact. We may have to turn around and go home. It's a shorter journey to go back than carrying on. What a bugger."

Larry agreed, and was getting out of the cab into the rain using his newspaper to shelter under as he did. Still flapping at the mist, he hoped to clear the cabin for them. Just when he thought that things couldn't get any stranger, the mist moved. It appeared to be sucked into the back of the van through the metal partition. It took his breath away. Were his eyes playing tricks? He had heard that faulty heaters could affect the brain; he'd read it in the Mail. John was still fiddling with the heater and didn't seem to notice.

Larry climbed back into the cabin, shutting the door, and was shaking his ruined newspaper when the heat hit him. The heater, was set on maximum. The ice on the window screen melted, dripping down onto the dashboard and running onto the John's knees and soaking his trousers. John snapped off the heat. He was flabbergasted, beyond words. What just happened?

"The heater must be faulty," he said, switching it off. "When we get to the next service station, I'll give it a look over."

Both men were nervous when John engaged the first gear. Indicating, he pulled the van out and rejoined the moving traffic.

"What was that ice thing all about?" asked Larry, drying himself off with a duster he found in the door well. "I know it's colder in the north, but hell's bells, that's unreal!" Things did not add up. What caused that mist in the cab? It was a worrying puzzle.

There were no more incidents after they took to the road and they stopped gratefully at Leicester Services to check things out. Under the hood, John inspected the wiring on the heater and found the wires were all intact; no burning smell or any other smell came from it. He couldn't find anything wrong with it; not that he was an electrician, but he could tell if something was loose. One thing was sure; whatever had happened to the heater back there, he wouldn't risk it happening again. The heater would be scrapped rather than risk the van that was essential for their living, and for the rest of the journey the two brothers sat in the cold. A new heater would be ordered as soon as John found a phone. It was all a mystery.

Sophia had bolted back into the noisy space in the back of the van before retreating into the kingdom. She had nearly ruined it all for herself.

She'd always had difficulty controlling her temper; it wasn't her fault though, things and people got in her way. The men had been rude, intimating that she smelled; she couldn't and wouldn't stand for that. It was little wonder she reacted; anyone would. Still, she had probably gone too far.

When John said he would return to Hertfordshire, her anger was replaced by anxiety. That was the last place she wanted to go. It was sensible to go back to the kingdom and wait. She must return home. She must remember that that was her aim and she mustn't let her anger change that. Once back there, it would be payback time. She smiled at the thought.

She lay under the tree and listened to the faint noise, that like a buzzing insect that came from the other side of the wooden veil. Then, she ignored it and focused on the sound of the stream. That was much better and she fell asleep.

30

Well! We are on our way, thought Katie, pleased to be moving on. The door closed on her old home and the key was returned to the agency. Their time in Little Bourne was behind them; the Mini was making its way to the motorway, driving through yet another cloudburst. The weather was not being kind. In fact, it was acting in a horrid fashion. Katie had been lured into thinking that the lull in the rain earlier meant they were free of the wet stuff for the day. How wrong she was. The sky was filled with black, purple and grey shapes, which by the looks of them were ready to discharge the weight of their load on the already soaked ground.

The little blue car wove valiantly through the traffic; its windscreen wipers were working at top speed, sweeping away the rain to give Katie a clear view of the road ahead; the road that was leading them to a new life. It was going to be a slow and difficult drive if the rain continued as it was, but it wouldn't dampen their spirits. They had waited for this special day, when Louis could finally discard the persona of Mike forever.

The sportsman image would be left behind in Hertfordshire and the creative woodcarver/carpenter would be reborn in Yorkshire.

Katie put the radio on, basically to drown out the noise of the rain and traffic. Elton John's hit, *Crocodile Rock* rang out from the speakers. The sound immediately surrounded them and the catchy toe-tapping tune got into their heads; the refrain would stay in their brains for most of the journey even if they would rather it didn't.

Ed Steward's voice, with his usual repartee, introduced more pop songs as they travelled through the counties. The squally rain came and went, sometimes heavy sometimes light, but didn't stop. Inside the Mini, the two people who were very much in love sat back and enjoyed the music. It helped to pass the time as they drove to a new chapter in their lives.

When they saw the sign announcing South Yorkshire, the skies changed, the waterlogged clouds became sparse and the rain began to peter out. The dark clouds were being replaced by a scattering of white ones playing hide and seek with the blue sky, while a pushy sun was trying to break through into their game.

It was just what they needed, sunshine for the last bit of their journey; an altogether better proposition than driving in a deluge. They were looking forward to arriving at The Royal Oak. One and a half hours later they parked up in the small car park behind the pub. What a relief, thought Katie, pulling on the handbrake and turning off the engine. Taking the key from the steering column, she dangled it provocatively, turning in her seat to Louis, and announced. "We're here."

She was taken aback to see his eyes were moist; he looked close to tears, yet he was smiling. He was obviously overwhelmed and his emotions filled the car. He reached over, taking her face gently in his hands and kissed her.

"Thank you, my darling. You've brought me home."

And then, in hushed tones, he whispered. "How am I ever going to repay your sacrifice and kindness in what you have done for me?" His eyes were pleading for an answer.

"For us, my love, for us. And anyway, fate took a hand in all this," she said, almost dismissively. She was in serious danger of being overwhelmed and crying herself. "It seems that this was preordained for us; we are meant to be here." Earnestly, she kissed him back to reassure him that she meant what she said. In a much lighter tone she said, "Tomorrow, we'll settle in the cottage and then I'll look for a job. You will start to plan work in the workshop and together we'll carve out a new life and we'll be happy."

He squeezed her tightly. She nudged her head into the v of his neck; fighting back her own tears. She allowed them a few precious minutes to accept the moment and then in harmony they uncoupled, and gathering themselves, collected their overnight bags from the car, and walked to The Royal Oak.

"Welcome back." said Doris, standing behind the bar, not pausing for breath she asked. "Did you have a good trip? It's good to see you. We had terrible rain earlier. I hope it didn't affect your journey, but I see you've brought the sun with you. That's good." Smiling, Doris came round and over to Katie, giving her a big hug as though they were old friends. "Your room's ready when you are. How about a cup of tea, the both of you?"

"That would be very welcome," said Katie, giving Doris a hug back. They were going to be good friends; Katie just knew it.

Doris gave Louis the key to the back bedroom. "You know the way. Why not get rid of the bags and by the time you come back, tea will be ready. I might even find a bit of cake to go with it." She winked at him before walking away, taking Katie with her to the dining room.

Doris was quite a case, but so likeable. Louis was laughing to himself as he climbed the stairs, following her orders. He dropped the bags next to his dad's old rocking chair. He gently pushed the high back and watched it rock backwards and forwards. It brought back warm memories. He was back home and tea was waiting downstairs.

The ladies were already sipping tea in the dining room when he joined them; a homemade cherry cake had been sliced and three plates held the single portions.

"We were waiting for you," said Doris, pushing a plate in front of him.

"You'll never guess," said Katie leaning forward excitedly with a big smile on her face. "Doris has offered me a job, working here with her in the inn."

She looked expectantly at Louis, waiting for him to say something, but he kept his counsel, so she went on. "I was telling her I was looking for work and that I had studied business studies at Uni." Katie looked at

Doris who was nodding. "And she said, 'isn't that a coincidence?' because she was just about to advertise for a manager. Isn't that good? Here less than an hour and I have a job," she said, with satisfaction in her voice.

Louis was astounded; he hadn't been away for more than five minutes. Had Katie just grabbed the offer because she was afraid to be without a job or was this a genuine opportunity for her? Had she already accepted the position? They needed to talk.

Doris must have read his mind, or his face. She spoke up. "I've been looking for someone for some time to organise and help me expand my business. I can get bar staff easily. They come and go, but I need someone that can overlook the running and advertising of the B&B side, someone able to see the bigger picture, and I want to upgrade the restaurant. I want this place of mine to be the very best in the district and give better service and food than they serve at the fancy restaurant at the Avondale Hotel." It was quite an eye opener.

Louis stared at Doris. This neat, straightforward, northern woman had made a grand statement. He knew she was a keen businesswoman but hadn't recognised her raw ambition.

Doris continued, "We'll have to work out the details, but we can do that when you have settled in."

Suddenly she changed hats; the businesswoman became the landlady again. "You'll be staying for dinner tonight, will you? Though why you southerners call supper dinner and dinner lunch, I don't know, but whatever you call it, I'll get you the menu for this evening's meal." She was beaming at them. "Enjoy your tea and cake, I'll see you later."

At that she rose and was swiftly striding away back to the bar. The cake was good and the tea refreshing, but Katie could see that things needed to be talked over.

"When you've finished your tea, let's go to the room."

Louis didn't smile. Katie felt the tension as, hand in hand, they climbed the stairs to their room. It was not just the weariness on his face but that slight droop in his shoulders, that made her realise he was unhappy about her accepting a job from Doris. Behind the door in the cosy bedroom Louis opened up to her. There was real concern and passion in his voice.

"Is this something that you really want, Katie, or are you taking it because you believe we cannot manage without you working? I couldn't bear to think that after you have given up your life in the south, you would sacrifice your future prospects by taking the first offer that comes your way, even if it is from Doris."

Her voice was soft and almost pleading as she answered. "Louis, I only took the job on the Echo because I couldn't get my desired job. I trained to manage, not to sell advertising space. Believe me, I want nothing more than to find out what I can do, to use my training. It's going to be fabulous. This is part of our new beginning and if it doesn't work out, I'll find something else, and having a job in management would look good on my C.V."

Katie looked so happy; she obviously felt she had fallen on her feet. His fears were unfounded. It was a great relief.

After dinner they were sitting in the lounge having coffee when Doris came to join them. "It's going to be a big day tomorrow for you, so if there is anything I can do to help, let me know."

"You're so kind, I think we'll be fine. You must pop in once we have furniture."

"I'll do that. See you at breakfast then, goodnight."

Key in hand he turned the lock and opened the door. Katie slipped though catching his hand, half dragging him in behind her. She seemed elated, on cloud nine.

"What a day this has been, everything is going our way, Louis. It's all going to be fine," she declared.

The door closed behind them and he locked it.

She was already kissing him, encouraging him by drawing him close. What Louis had on his mind then for the two of them was something that didn't include being disturbed. He struggled out of her clutches, dashing back to the door to hang the Do Not Disturb sign.

Katie was pulling off her top when he stopped her. "No, let me," he said, kissing her on her neck just below her ear. A shiver of a thrill ran down her back, urgency and anticipation were building between them.

Slowly and deliberately, they undressed each other, petting as they went. Finally, throwing the blankets back on the bed, they rolled onto the crisp, white cotton sheets. Katie grabbed the top sheet to cover them and for a magical moment they locked themselves in a tight embrace, enjoying a small moment of calm, drinking in their love.

She always smelled so good and her skin was soft. It felt like silk. Following the outline of her body, he stroked her from her shoulders until his hand stopped at the roundness of her bottom. Her breasts were crushed against him and he could feel her heart beating against his own. The full depth of his love hit him.

"God, I'm so lucky to have you, my darling girl. May this moment go on forever I love you."

Although nobody would hear, Katie whispered back in hushed tones. Somehow the intensity of the moment required it.

"I'll never leave you, I love you too."

The kiss that they shared was soft but it was a kiss that came from the bottom of their souls. The moment was over, passion overwhelmed them and they were lost to everything, locked in their private world.

The dream was so real that Louis really thought he was back in the cottage in 1790, with his father sitting in his usual position by the fire, rocking in the chair that Louis had carved for him.

"You came back then, lad, I knew you would. It's the pull of your roots."

Massie was smoking his pipe and watching the smoke curl and twist in the air before it was sucked up by the draft into the chimney. "She's a bonny girl, that you've brought with you." After a slight pause, he continued. "You should have never married that other lass. Stuck up and out of your league. I knew it wasn't right but I never thought she'd kill you."

"You saw that?"

"I did, but I was gone and couldn't help. I was waiting in the light for you but you didn't come through. You never crossed over, and look, where you are now?

How long do you think that body will let you use it? Then what will your lady do?"

"Do you know how long I have, Dad? Tell me."

"It's not up to me. There are laws on this side as well as on yours. You will be given as much time as the angels can give you. Make good use of it."

Angels, what angels? Louis didn't understand. And what laws?

He hadn't spoken but still his father answered his questions.

"There are angels everywhere, if you have a mind to look. They can respond to your needs if you ask but they can't interfere otherwise. For a long time, your anger shut them out and so you remained trapped in your netherworld. Your kingdom was created in response to your needs. Marina was a gift from them, a soul so similar to yours that if you had both been mortal you would have had your soul mate for life. They could not interfere when she became ill. When she died you shut yourself off, but even in your misery you longed to be rescued, so they sent Katie. That universal power gift of carving came from the heavens; it only comes to the chosen."

"Why are you here, Dad? Or 'why am I here' might be a better question?"

"It's in hand, son but if in doubt ask Doris about the tools.?"

His father's voice had grown faint with the last sentence and now he was gone. Only the rocking of the chair remained.

Louis woke in disbelief; it had been a dream, hadn't it? In the pitch dark it had felt so real. He stretched out his arm reaching for the bedside lamp and clicked it on. The soft light gave him comfort for a millisecond while waiting for his eyes to adjust. He sat up to check the room. His hand cramped across his mouth in astonishment. The chair, his father's chair, was rocking gently, making no sound, and there was a faint but real scent of pipe tobacco in the air.

Was he still dreaming? The smell of smoke lingered. Katie hadn't woken; should he tell her about the dream? Was his father really trying to give him a message? It took him some time to settle down and sleep.

In the clear light of day, he wasn't sure if he could explain the dream. A spirit visiting another spirit to give advice? It was hard to retell. For now, he would keep it to himself. But it bothered him. What did his father mean when he said 'ask Doris about the tools'?

Breakfast was served with a song from Doris. It reminded Louis so much of Rosa, his friend with second sight, who had recognised him in spirit in the Victorian era. She was his saviour and first contact after he died; she saw him and she heard him after a hundred years of loneliness and silence. Most importantly, she introduced him to Marina, and through Rosa he had became a member of that unusual household. Rosa was the songbird that sang making breakfast, and, coming home to Yorkshire, he had found another one.

He wasn't quite sure what Doris was humming when she placed the plates of full Yorkshire breakfast in front of them, but she was certainly in a good mood and more animated than usual. Two other tables were occupied, and one was waiting to be cleared; an early bird had come and gone. Doris was hovering and saw his searching gaze, and she was quite happy to inform him that the two men drinking tea were long distance lorry drivers, two of her regulars. And after a bit of craic, one would be off to Scotland, the other down to Dorset. Sharp-eyed as ever Doris could see the puzzled look on Katie's face. "Sorry love, I should explain. A bit of craic just means a good gossip, it's a northern thing. The other couple are walking the Yorkshire Wolds; I hope the weather stays fine for them. After the rain yesterday they came back like drowned rats. It's a good job they have lots of kit." She rolled her eyes to heaven before stepping back to clear the empty table.

A young woman with a small child was just coming into the room as Doris returned to served Katie and Louis fresh tea and toast. 'Oh, Mrs Brown. Just over here love.' She pointing to the table she had cleared. "I'll be with you in a sec."

The toast server was stacked with hot toast. "I always think toast should be brought out hot so the butter can melt in it, don't you?" Doris said looking at Katie.

"I'm sure you're right, Doris. I see I have a few things to learn." It had never occurred to Katie, whether toast should be eaten hot or cold.

At Little Bourne it had been grab and go when she was working. She remembered it was usually cold and brittle and snapped into bits when you bit into it. Hot toast doesn't do that, she thought, feeling the warm butter running down her chin. It was delicious.

It was barely 9am when they finished. Louis decided to see what the weather was doing and popping his nose outside, he was encouraged to see blue skies and no clouds.

His home county seemed to be welcoming him back with the sun and a warm breeze. He walked a little; his dream still bothered him but with the sunlight on his face and stretching his legs around the block, his mood was lighter when he returned to collect Katie. The dining room had emptied of all its clients, including her; he'd been longer than he thought. He went into the bar, which had towels draped over the pumps. It was closed, but he had expected to see someone working in readiness for the day.

Perhaps the sound of his footsteps had been recognised on the slab floor. Katie called out "Louis, we are in here."

Louis followed the voice, which came from the private room just beyond the bar. The door was open and Katie was standing there waiting for him. The room was small, a woman's room, cosy, and painted in duck-egg blue. Cream-coloured curtains gave the room a larger feel and a two-seater sofa in dark blue cord faced an art deco fireplace. The image was only slightly spoiled by a three-bar electric fire in its hearth; it looked so out of place. A leather-topped desk of dark wood was tucked in the corner; it had orderly piles of papers on it and a reproduction Victorian lamp standing in for a paperweight on one pile.

Doris was sitting in a large red plush armchair. In front of her a coffee pot was placed on a wooden chest that acted as a coffee table, draped with an elaborate embroidered cover. Two cups were filled with black liquid, steam rising from them, and a third cup was there waiting for him.

"There you are, come and sit." She indicated the sofa. "Coffee or tea?"

"No thanks, Doris, I couldn't manage another thing. I'm positively bursting. Breakfast was terrific and I've drunk enough tea to last all day."

He obediently sat down next to Katie; it would seem that Doris was holding court.

"As you wish." She looked small sitting in the large chair but also rather regal, someone with authority. "We've been talking about you Katie tells me you're quite a handyman with a talent for carving. You must have loved the rocking chair in the back bedroom." He was nodding in agreement as she spoke.

"Well, if you liked that, you'll like this." She pointed to where the coffee pot was standing with the crockery. "Here, give us a hand."

A tray appeared in her hand from the side of her chair; the coffee and bits were removed and carried on the tray to the desk by Louis. When he turned round, he took an extra hard look at the wooden chest.

"Move the cloth, Louis, and have a good look." Her face was a picture of expectancy.

But Louis didn't need to move anything. He suddenly recognised the shape and size of the chest that was partly hidden by the cloth. His hands became clammy and his heart was beating a little faster. He moved across the room and touched the embroidered cloth with shaking hands, then, he knelt to remove it.

When it was uncovered, he saw he was correct; the chest with the carved lid was indeed his. He had never believed he would see this earliest test of his skill again. It was his apprenticeship piece, the first complete piece of furniture he had built and carved, when he was still a boy.

His hands tenderly ran over the lid. The hare with its huge hind legs sat upright, alert in the meadow, listening, ready to run at the first sign of danger. Daisies, poppies and cowslips with the odd butterfly surrounded it, and a ladybird sat among the blades of grass. Later, the butterfly became his signature on his work. Emotion was overtaking him; he must not let Doris see.

Doris's voice broke into his moment. It pushed the past away and brought him back into her private space in The Royal Oak. His face was flushed when he looked at her, and she could see a kind of excitement there.

"I thought you'd like it." She looked pleased with herself. "I'm only guessing, mind you, but I think it came into the family the same time as that rocking chair upstairs. I believe that my great grandfather, several times removed, bought it with that chair, 'cos if you look carefully the carving it has the same kind of touch about it. If you open the lid, you'll find some ancient tools wrapped in sacking in the bottom. I couldn't get rid of them. They seemed to belong to the chest, so I just left them there for a day like today." Her laugh sounded like the tinkering of glass, it was so light. Louis did as he was bid. When he removed the cloth, his tools looked back at him like old friends.

Doris was still in full throttle and was obviously enjoying the reaction she was getting.

"I don't know whether they are good enough to use now but if you think they might be useful, you can borrow them," she said, hoping to be helpful.

His tools looked tired and dull but other than that, they were not in a bad shape. A little oil and a sharpening stone would soon bring them back to life and he longed to feel them in his hands again. He yearned for the moment when he could shape wood again, to find the hidden spirits within, the ones that needed to be set free.

"Thank you, Doris." He was genuinely pleased but also saddened that he couldn't claim them from her. "I will take up your invitation once we are in the cottage." He rewrapped them gently in the sackcloth and placed them back in the box.

"I have got to get the workshop up and running. Find clients. Starting from scratch is not going to be easy." Hearing his own words, they became a salient fact to him at that moment. Had his longing to return and find himself overtaken logic?

He knew he would have to take any job that came along. The dream of carving would only happen given time. Building a reputation would be slow; he couldn't be choosy, and his creative side might well have to wait. The people of this age, this generation, cared more about price than quality. He would have to adjust to this mindset. He hoped and prayed he hadn't bitten off more than he could chew.

Katie set down her cup after finishing off the last drop of coffee.

"We'll be off now." Getting up she headed for the door. "Thanks for everything, Doris."

Louis followed her.

"I'll have a walk up later to see how you are getting on. I'll bring you a sandwich."

"That's very sweet of you, thanks again."

31

They were standing in the cold March sunshine, waiting impatiently for Derek to arrive with the key to their new home. Their short walk here, linked arm in arm, had freshened them up and walked off some of the breakfast they had eaten. As they walked, they talked.

Louis told Katie eagerly about the chest that Doris was using as a coffee table in her snug. "It was my first piece. I remember my master was so impressed with it that he gave me his blessing to carry on carving, although he warned me to be practical; that carpentry would feed my belly. The carving might give me meat occasionally but my woodwork would be my bread and butter. Carving became my passion and, in a way, my downfall."

Katie couldn't argue with his assessment.

"Time to put the past behind us now love, and think of all the new pieces you will make with your clever hands." She squeezed his arm. She felt good; all their plans were in place and she was looking forward to taking the key and opening up the cottage and a new chapter in their lives.

She was stamping her feet on the flagged stone pavement. The cold was starting to seep through her shoes and affect her feet. It had been a poor choice of shoe that morning. She had underestimated how cold it was, deceived by the sun and not judging its lack of strength. On reflection, a winter boot would have been better, but it was too late now. Where was Derek?

The man striding towards them wasn't Derek, Louis could tell even from this distance. As the figure got nearer Louis recognised it to be their new landlord, Harry.

"Well, here I am, sorry if I kept you waiting. It's a bit parky this morning, isn't it?" A wide smile opened across his handsome face. He pulled an envelope from the pocket of his topcoat. "Who wants this?"

His blue eyes danced from one to the other. Katie and Louis both stepped forward at the same time, but Harry placed the envelope in Katie's hand.

"Ladies first," he joked, slapping Louis on his shoulder. He had another set of keys in his hand. "Come on, let's open up the old cottage and I'll give you another tour and perhaps stay for a cuppa."

"You'll be lucky. We haven't got any groceries yet." Louis scoffed.

"I thought as much, I came in yesterday and left a small food parcel to welcome you. Milk, tea and coffee all provided."

He shrugged; his smile even broader. "You're welcome."

Katie and Louis followed Harry into the property. "I took the liberty of putting the heating on the timer. It should be at least warm inside now."

This sort of greeting was unusual. Certainly, in all the rented accommodation she had leased the landlord had never turned up to welcome her. She wondered if there was something more behind it. Harry led them into the kitchen and put the kettle on. A small cardboard box sat on the table; his gift. A small jar of coffee, some PG Tips tea bags and two packets of biscuits were inside it. Three mugs were already sitting on the worktop and when Harry opened the fridge, it held milk.

"Don't worry I'm not taking over." Harry laughed. "I'm interested in my tenants and I like to get to know them."

The gentleman farmer with his tanned face and easy manner lifted the milk from the fridge to cream the coffee that was now waiting to be drunk at the table.

"So, Louis, what job do you do?" The question was asked without any aggression; it was more like a friend inquiring after another friend. "We didn't get time to talk last time we met, and I hope we can get to know each other and have that promised drink together now you're here."

Louis couldn't help liking his new landlord.

"I'm going to set up a carpentry business in the workshop. I shall get cards and leaflets printed by next week, with all my information, and I'll be hoping the word will get round about me. I'm a good carpenter and I carve a little too," he said modestly.

"This is my dream, but a brand-new venture for me. With no clients in this neck of the woods it's going to be a slow start," he said with a slight sigh, "and, until I get established, Katie will support us." He paused; there was a long moment before he said "She has just accepted a job with Doris at the Royal Oak."

"Wow, that was quick you've only been here two minutes. I like Doris, she's got a lot of get up and go and she's been talking about expanding for a year now. What will you be doing?"

"Not quite sure yet. But I have a degree in Business Studies and she wants me to overlook the business and put a plan in place."

"So, I'll know where to come if I need advice. Our paths are bound to cross again." He paused as though he was thinking of something else. Then he seemed to make up his mind. "So, Louis, you need work? I might be able to put some your way. I own twenty or so properties and my own carpenter has gone off sick and could be unfit for a couple of months. I'll give you a try-out. If I like what you do, I might, just might, talk to my friend on the council. They always want good men to work on their council properties. That will at least get you started. Are you up for it?" The smile on Louis' face said it all.

He held out his hand and the men shook on it. "It's agreed then."

For the next few minutes, they chatted like old friends. Louis was reminded of this man's relative whom he had known in the past. Harry was so like him and Louis felt that he had known this man forever. Before he got up to go, Harry gave his card to Louis, with his contact numbers on it.

Their telephone was due to be connected in a couple of day's time, and then Louis would call him to get instructions on the jobs Harry wanted doing.

Fate had smiled on them again. It would seem that someone was looking after them; perhaps a guardian angel that they couldn't see was working for them behind the scenes. He remembered his father's message about angels. So, it wasn't fate after all; it had been requested and delivered. What a privilege. Both of them had found work even before the removals van had turned up.

It was eleven forty-five when the dark blue van finally pulled up and parked on the single yellow line on the road outside the cottage. The door of the cab opened and John climbed out. He was looking rattled and slammed the door, leaving his brother inside. A man was just leaving the cottage and in the process of closing the door, they almost collided with each other. "Sorry, mate, I nearly got you then. I was just about to knock at the door, you can leave it open." Harry turned to the man, assessing him before smiling at John.

"You'll be the movers. They'll be glad you're here." At which, he opened the door and shouted through. "The van's here, Katie. I'll send him in, see you later."

Disappearing down the street he left the door open, for John and Larry to start unloading the boxes and furniture.

Katie was just about to clean the kitchen cupboards ready for her crockery with cloths she found under the sink when she heard Harry call to her. She called back "Thank you," and heard new footsteps coming towards the kitchen.

When John appeared at the kitchen door, Katie greeted him with a smile. At last, they were here, and with a little luck they could get the place straight before bedtime.

"John, there you are, I'm glad you're here. I was getting worried. You're late."

Louis had gone with the vacuum to check the bedroom carpet and was about to plug into the electricity to ready it for the arrival of their bed when he heard Katie and went to greet John.

"Sorry, Katie, we had a problem with the van yesterday and needed to check it out this morning before we set off. I'll tell you about it later once we've got your bits in. Just you tell us where you want us to put everything, it shouldn't take long."

Larry was already carrying in the box that was marked Kitchen. He stood it on the table, shuffling up three empty mugs to one end, before he left to fetch another box in. Louis was already digging into the box to relieve it of its contents, unwrapping the newspaper from the crockery and piling it on the counter. It would be washed clean before it was found a new home in the cupboards.

It must have been about 1.30 when the men carried in the last pieces of the wrapped bed into the double bedroom. They unwrapped the parts quickly, setting the headboard to stand on the main wall opposite the window. The carved piece was waiting to be assembled; it stood in the sunlight looking superb. Louis felt proud seeing it back in the place where it had originally stood and belonged.

John and Larry were impressed. "Cor! That's a bit of alright, Louis, where did that come from?"

Louis just smiled John wasn't expecting an answer, and Louis couldn't have told him anyway.

Larry, who rarely spoke, was touching the wood sensitively. "Is it Adam and Eve? It looks like the Tree of Life. Look at all that fruit on it, and the sun with its rays touching the edges of its world. It's terrific."

"Must have cost a bob or two, that must." John was nodding his head in agreement.

"Some things can't be measured in money," said Larry in a hushed voice, folding the wrapping up and putting it by the door. God, he thought, if we'd had a fire in the van. It might have been lost forever. His thoughts stopped abruptly. It was too awful to think about it. Yesterday had shaken him up and he still had no explanation for what had happened.

The garage had given John the green light on his van; nothing was amiss but Larry knew something had happened, something he couldn't explain.

He was startled when Katie called them from the kitchen, "I've put the kettle on, boys, are you ready for a drink?"

"Not half," replied John for the three of them.

The voices of the men had seeped through the wood and into the kingdom. They brought her out of her slumber. So, they'd arrived. She was back where she had lived with Louis, back in the cottage where she killed him, back to the beginning. It was almost a full circle.

Sophia peered out from the kingdom and saw the room she was in. It was her old bedroom. Though it was different from how she remembered it, she knew she was home, back in Yorkshire. How she was to get to her father's house she didn't know, but it was only a few miles away. But she couldn't go back until she had separated Louis and his new woman. She was sure an opportunity would present itself given time. And she had plenty of that.

The kettle was already singing when there was a knock on the door. Doris was standing on the doorstep clutching a large paper bag. She raised it up for Katie to see. "I've brought sandwiches, I said I would. How are you doing?"

She stepped inside as Katie moved to one side to allow her through. "Go into the kitchen, Doris, I've just boiled the kettle."

The men were just coming out of the bedroom.

"Did I hear the word sandwiches?" Louis was hungry, breakfast was only a memory; they'd eaten nearly six hours ago. Katie made the tea and put plates out on the table that was now clear of the boxes. John and Larry had food in the van and John disappeared to collect it.

"I've eaten," said Doris "but I'd love a cuppa." The four of them sat around the table; Doris found a kitchen stool to perch on, and introductions were made. As they sat small talk came naturally.

"Once we've got that bed of yours built, we'll be off. It'll take a good few hours to get back," said John, who was the talkative one. "Yeah, sorry we were late this morning; we had van trouble yesterday. We were almost halfway here when the heater started playing up. Well! We thought it was the heater 'cos smoke was coming from it and there was a funny smell. The weather was foul, it was pelting down with rain, visibility wasn't good inside the cab or out." He half laughed at his little joke, but the memory was still sharp from the day before.

"We pulled over, to check out the wiring and then again at the service area but couldn't find any loose wires. We stayed over with our aunt in

Doncaster like we arranged and she asked her friend Bill from the local garage to take a look at the engine, just to make sure like, it was safe for us to drive. We wouldn't have wanted your lovely bits going up in flames, would we?" He laughed nervously, knowing it wasn't really a joke.

"Poor you. Is it okay now?" asked Katie.

"Yes, the garage couldn't find a damn thing wrong with it. It's all a bit of a mystery."

"The main thing is you're all right," nodded Katie

"Yeah, but having just seen that bed of yours, whew, what if?"

"Yeah, that carving's bloody lovely." Larry agreed.

"Carving?" Doris was suddenly interested in the conversation.

"Yes, the headboard's a rare beauty, and that's a fact," confirmed John. "A piece of art, not that I'm an exper,t but I know what I like."

Doris put the teacup down. "I'd love to have look at it some time, I have two pieces I value myself back home."

She looked over at the table and the empty plates. "You enjoyed them, then? Cheese and tomato chutney are the best sandwiches, don't you think?" She had a good-humoured smile on her face and a look of satisfaction that said that she was pleased to have helped them.

"Doris, they were delicious, many thanks for bringing them." Louis was on his feet and, in a second, he was standing with his arm around her shoulders and had placed a kiss on her cheek.

"You've made us feel so welcome, thank you. And if you want to have a peek at the carving, be our guest. Come on, I'll show you." He took her by her elbow and guided her to the bedroom, leaving the group at the kitchen table. Louis looked over his shoulder. "Back in a minute, love." He nodded to Katie. "We'll be there in a minute, Louis," called out John. "We'll just finish our tea. Get that bed together and be off."

The daylight from the window fell across the headboard making the grooves in the wood dark in shadows, showing the picture of the Garden of Eden with the silhouettes of the man and woman standing either side of the tree, joined by their hands as they reached out across it. The sun that never set was high in the sky with its beams reaching out, touching the hills and kissing the meadow with its light.

Doris's mouth dropped open when she saw it. She was stopped in her tracks at the power that was coming from it. It was beautiful.

"You like it then?" said Louis, breaking into her silence.

"I'm amazed, Louis, there is something so familiar about it. The same hand could have made my pieces as well. You've seen them, what do you think?" She moved nearer and bent down to inspect it close up. "Look at this portrait of the man's face." She looked up and her eyes lighted on Louis' face in profile. "Louis, it could be you."

He couldn't believe what she had just said. After all, he was in Mike's body but she had seen him in the carving. He was at a loss as to what to say to her. In the end he agreed with her. "Well, I suppose it's a profile that could fit many men, but I can see what you mean."

Not wanting to engage in more questions he excused himself and left her alone to gaze on the scene.

Her hand brushed the top of the headboard while her finger on the other hand traced the outline of the woman. "You're very elegant, aren't you?" She could smell the faint perfume of rose water in the room and wondered where it was coming from.Her finger suddenly felt cold, and the cold travelling up her arm made her body chilled through and through. Her logic told her that the house had been empty for some time and it wasn't surprising that she felt cold. It was time to get back to The Royal Oak anyway; at least it would be warm there and her staff would be waiting for her."

She found her way back to the kitchen and said her goodbyes to Katie and Louis asking them to call at The Royal Oak the next day. Wishing Larry and John a good journey home she quickly donned her coat and was out of the door and away down the road to the B&B glad to be going back home to get warm.

Sophia totally agreed with the woman inspecting her wedding gift. Louis had done a good job; the silhouette did look like him. And the woman was right; Sophia was very elegant. This woman had taste when it came to art. Sophia had been very beautiful and the headboard was beautiful too; she was glad this woman recognised it.

It was then that Sophia made a decision; it would be good to see the world outside this bed and beyond this room. To see how the village had grown. She heard Doris invite Louis and Katie to The Royal Oak tomorrow. If she hitched a ride with this woman, she could be there before them and she could have a whole twenty-four hours of freedom to roam with Doris.

It was all too easy to slide out of the kingdom. Her spirit entered Doris's finger as it probed the carving and climbed up her arm and into her body. Sophia blended with her so easily that the woman didn't notice any change, except a cooling of her body. She wasn't sure why she had taken that action; perhaps it was plain curiosity, a need to see what had happened to Ravensend, the village in which her happiness had changed to loneliness and anger after she had married.

Had she been foolish and headstrong joining with this woman? Perhaps, but she was back in her own county and wanted to see it. This woman would be the start of her adventures. Tomorrow, she could take a ride back with Katie but for now she would have some fun.

Doris pulled her coat around her. Funny she hadn't felt that cold walking up to the cottage, and she would have expected the day to have become warmer now that she was walking back but it hadn't. She shrugged and hurried on; it was only the beginning of March. What else should she expect?

The sun had fooled her into thinking the day was warmer than it was. She would be glad to get indoors. Pushing the door open she was met by her barman, Barry, on the way in. He was halfway through cleaning the counter when Doris arrived.

"Oh, you're back then." He nodded an acknowledgement. "What's wrong with you, you look frozen"

"Lord, love us, it's cold out there Barry. It's brass-monkey weather alright. I could do with a whisky toddy just to warm up. I don't understand how the temperature could drop so much in the hour I was out visiting the cottage."

"It's warm enough in here, you'll soon thaw through," he replied, but she was already past him making her way to a heater in the lounge bar.

It was quiet in the lounge with only two couples sitting talking and sharing a drink. There were never many punters this early in the afternoon. Her two regular guests, the fishermen as she thought of them, were sitting heads together, with their trilby hats, covered with hooks of homemade flies in feathers of many colours, still perched on their heads. Why it reminded her of Morris dancers and the fool, she wasn't quite sure. They had left with the dawn chorus that morning to fish in the river. As always, they were back for a late lunch and then chatted fishermen's tales until the evening. A young couple that worked for her occupied the other table. All eyes turned to look at the newcomer coming in. The young man, who was one of her chefs, gave her a half-wave of recognition before turning back to the private conversation he was having with his girl.

A ginger and white feline came walking purposely towards Doris. Suddenly its tail was held high, its ears flicking and twitching, and the hairs on the back of his neck were standing proud. The cat could sense a presence; he suddenly stopped in its tracks, hissed and spat at Doris before turning and bounding to the other side of the room.

"What's wrong, Mouser?" said Doris, shocked at her cat's behaviour. Her eyes followed his passage across the room before he found a hiding place under a table. Mouser huddled down watching the room from his half-hidden position, his tail flicking like a small whip that had released a spinning top.

"Something's upset him," said Doris to herself. He could be a little unpredictable at times but this was unusual, she thought, before focusing back on her cold body and her need for hot tea.

"I'll make a cup of tea for you," said Barry, who had followed Doris, concerned that his boss was shivering so badly.

"Thanks, love, I'll have it over here by the radiator," she said, moving to a chair next to the white heater hugging the wall. Heat was belching out from it but, because her hands felt like ice blocks, when she touched it, it almost seared her skin.

"How did I get so cold?" She shivered, waiting for the heat to absorb into her skin and warm her through. She was still huddled over the heat when Barry brought her the hot beverage.

"Get that down your neck," Barry told her. "It'll put some warmth in them there veins of yours and maybe you might find a small drop of the hard stuff in there too."

She smiled in grateful acceptance and he winked at her before turning and walking back to the bar. Doris called after him. "I'll be with you in a minute or two." She was already downing the hot liquid with relish, enjoying the feeling of the tea and the little extra creeping, spreading through her and reaching all the extremities of her body.

"That feels better," she confirmed, looking at Barry who was standing behind the bar and giving him a thumbs up sign. Doris never realised that the uninvited guest who had hitched a ride to her home had at that exact moment, chosen to exit her body.

32

SOPHIA

Sophia had achieved her goal. She was not only back home, but she'd been freed. However comfortable the kingdom had been, it was still a prison, but Doris had carried her here and now it was time to explore, to reacquaint herself with the old place.

The Royal Oak had changed; well, of course it had. Change was all around her. Her heart warmed when she saw the inglenook fireplace was still there, standing proud, but looking like an empty carriage with its two seats on either side of the grate devoid of life. A fire had been laid in the grate but was waiting to be lit. A large copper jug with a cluster of tall dried flowers that were looking a little dusty, stood in front, half-hiding the space. It was a nice enough decoration, but Sophia thought it was a strange place for flowers to be put to decorate the room.

The black coated wooden mantel was adorned with horse brasses; they were pinned along the front of the beam like a showy row of medals given to long lost heroes; and perhaps they were, thought Sophia. On top of the mantel stood an array of miners' lamps that had been polished until they shone a bright brassy yellow, bringing back memories of a past and present time when other heroes worked in the deep mines and pits; bringing the black gold to the surface for the industries and the mills that brought jobs to the villages. Some lamps were elegantly thin and tall with glass-fronted windows; a candle would have shone its dim light out in the dark, hot and claustrophobic underworld as the miners made their way to the coalface. Other shaped lamps stood in line, sporting a brass name badge noting which colliery they had come from. She counted eight.

She smiled as her eyes lighted on the odd sight, beyond the miners' lamps. At the far end of the mantel was a small bottle of water with a sliver of wood floating in it. So plain and ordinary and totally out of place next to the fancy brasses, it was as though it had been stranded there by some unknown hand, put down in an absent-minded moment and forgotten. Perhaps it had, but Sophia remembered what it was. The papists that lived in the village displayed them in their homes on mantels or shelves; it was a little piece of their Saviour's cross that had found its way to England from Jerusalem and the Place of Skulls. She scoffed at their foolishness; if every Catholic in the country had such a prize in their homes, then Christ must have died on several crosses.

The room that she stood in was a good size. It was clean and light in the bar and lounge; white walls reflected the daylight from the windows. The polished wooden tables were laid out to give privacy to those who used them. Some were marked with white rings, stained from the wet bottoms of glasses that missed the cardboard coasters advertising the brewery. Red and gold upholstered chairs in a diamond fabric were pushed under the tables awaiting guests. Two tables were occupied.

Two men were deep in conversation discussing fishing, and a young couple appeared to be whispering sweet nothings to each other. Some black-coloured fizzy liquid called Tab according to the label, was left untouched at their elbows that afternoon. Sophia assessed the room. It was quite comfortable, cosier than in her day when hard cold stone flags had covered the floor. A plain red carpet had replaced them but her sharp eye noticed marks; what a pity it had been soiled by spilt drinks. Then the walls caught her eye.

That's odd she thought; there were no streaks of black on the walls or ceiling, which almost shimmered in their dazzling white paint. There should have been soot marks from the candles that were fixed in their ornamental black painted sconces. Curious, she drifted over to have a good look at them, only to discover that they weren't candles at all but shaped glass dome cases with an outer cover, made to look like melted candle wax. They called it electricity; it was the same source of light that they used at the Hall, and she felt foolish that she hadn't recognised it. It was yet another change. How many more would she see, now she was free to explore?

She drifted over to where a young couple sat chatting. They were so involved with themselves that they were completely unaware of the inquiring spirit hovering there, eavesdropping on their conversation.

The troubled spirit brought cold with her, forcing the temperature down around the table where she hovered. The young woman with red hair pulled her cardigan close across her body and buttoned it up as she shivered. Her young male friend felt a cold draught touch his body and wondered where the cold was coming from. There was no apparent reason for the draught as all the windows were closed. He saw Doris, his employer huddled over a radiator over by the bar and called out to her.

"Hey, Doris, has the heating gone off? It's suddenly gone cold in here." The couple turned their attention to her. Doris had warmed up nicely; her body was enjoying the heat that was bursting from the wall heater. She responded with a thumbs up sign and pretending to touch the heater and burning her finger. "It's fine, hot," but she decided she would check the other radiators once her tea was finished. Doris's body had returned to normal now her uninvited guest had left her.

Sophia hovered before sitting down with the young man and woman. They were engaged in whispering endearments to each other, when Sophia heard him promise to love his woman forever. It was a phrase that turned her heart upside-down. She had heard it so many times in her lifetime. Men were such liars. This modern woman wouldn't be fooled by him. She remembered Louis had made the same promise to her, but in the end, he hadn't really meant it. Forever: what a promising word. How he had abused it. She felt the anger rising. Sitting next to the redhead, she saw the young woman lean forward to return the words of love to the man she called Nick.

"Forever, Julia." He said the word so beautifully, with passion.

Sophia didn't believe a word the man spoke; what a good actor. Surely, this Julia could see through him; if not she must show her. Making a decision, Sophia blended with Julia. It was so immediate that the girl was already in mid-sentence when her warm personality changed to an angry cold persona. Sophia looked out through the girl's eyes into Nick's, she smiled the girl's smile, and with Julia's voice she ended her sentence for her; "You're such a wonderful, … liar." There was a look of total disbelief on Nick's face. His forehead creased, frowning, but his mouth dropped open as though he wanted to say something but couldn't find the words. He reached for Julia's hand but Sophia snatched it away. "Don't lie to me, Nick, I know what you are really like. A womaniser, a heart-breaker, but you won't break my heart." She blew a kiss in his face. He was shocked; the breath was cold and laden with ice particles that stung his eyes. His hand came up to protect his face. Nick jumped up; the chair rocked and rolled back, crashing to the floor with a thump.

He was bewildered. What had just happened? One minute they were talking as lovers. The next…

The noise was softened by the carpet but the cat, shocked at the disturbance, shot out of its hiding place as though it had been stung by a wasp. He whipped across the room to Doris and wrapped itself around her ankles, where she welcomed him with a friendly hand scratching around his ears.

Doris flinched with surprise when the chair landed with a thud in the middle of a lounge bar. What was going on with Nick and Julia, she wondered. They were good kids; a match for each other, she thought. But looking at their faces something was definitely wrong. Should she go over and see what was going on? They might resent an interfering woman trying to help, and she contented herself by putting Mouser on her knee and stroking him. He settled down and was soon purring contentedly on her lap.

She would give them a minute or two.

When Doris heard Nick, she was shocked.

"It was only a fling, it didn't mean anything." He was standing next to Julia, bending down to her level. His face had a desperate look as he said earnestly, "I love you!"

The words poured from his mouth while his brain ran like a runaway train, bringing back visions of his secret. The secret of that night when he succumbed to a pretty face and his male ego. How could she know? He was shocked; his face showed disbelief and yet it was his sin, his indiscretion with her best friend. Barbara was a beautiful girl and it had only happened the once.

Sophia discharged herself from Julia feeling rather pleased with herself. She had known somehow that this man had roamed, that his intentions were less than honourable. But she hadn't thought about the girl who, through no fault of her own, had heard Sophia's one word 'Liar' coming from her mouth, with no idea where it had come from. It had changed her life.

Julia's soulmate was standing in front of her, confessing that he had been unfaithful, that he wasn't trustworthy and that all their plans for a future together were now in doubt. The pain in her chest ached as though an invisible club had struck her between her breasts. Her stomach was in knots, and tears much like drops of rain fell from her eyes becoming a cloudburst. She had nowhere to run and no one to run to. She felt under a spotlight sitting in the middle of the room. What had this man done to her? She slumped forward. Her head felt so heavy that she couldn't keep it upright, and she allowed it to fall onto her arms resting on the table. It was something of a relief to rest it there, shielding herself from the faces that were turned to look at her; she hid, in the semi-dark safe place her arms gave her and let the tears flow.

Nick had always enjoyed female company before he met Julia and, if he was truthful, loved the chase but once he had gained the prize, he lost interest. He was a handsome young man with intense blue eyes, the kind of eyes that looked into a person's soul and melted the coldest heart. He had a crop of coppery brown hair and despite having fair skin he had gained a light tan from the long walks he enjoyed. He was proud of his physique and exercised to keep himself fit. Until he met Julia, there was always another girl to chase and win. He never gave much thought about what happened to the girls after he had bedded them. That was not his concern nor on his conscience; he had enjoyed their company and he assumed they had enjoyed his and that was the end of it, a game in which both parties won.

It had been different with Barbara. He was driving, on his way home after having a row with Julia. He was cross with her; she had been so unreasonable, but for the life of him he couldn't remember now what the row had been about. A persistent drizzle and grey leaden skies hung like a heavy burden over the town, taking his mood down even further, and then he saw Barbara standing at a bus stop. She was looking wet and miserable. What choice did he have? He had to offer her a lift.

It was her smile that lifted his mood. Even though she was wearing damp clothes and her drenched hair was straggling her face, she still looked good. Her perfume was discreet, unassuming really; it wafted gently towards him when she gathered herself onto the passenger seat. A look of relief passed over her face having got out of the rain and in a warm car. She obviously admired him, and he felt it.

It was good to be wanted and suddenly he wanted her. Both of them had been thoroughly fed up but somehow this chance meeting had allowed them to escape the mood.

He had been a fool to mess about with a girl who was a close friend of Julia.

Barbara lived in a bedsit above a shoe shop at the other end of the town. The faint smell of leather hung in the air but the flat was just what a single person needed. One main bedroom, a box room, kitchenette and a lounge/diner. He envied her. He was still living with his parents and his mum stayed up until he was home after a night out. What chance did he have with a girl, nowhere to take her, his parents vetting his every move. She asked him in for a coffee when he pulled up outside her home. He wasn't going anywhere, and a cup of coffee wouldn't hurt, would it? What a fool he had been, sitting so close together, something had happened. They fell into each other arms. How foolish was that?

The sheets smelled of her scent. He was lying in the crumpled linen, his seed still wet and staining the sheet. Beside him, Barbara looked flushed and even more beautiful. Sex had been good, but now the enormity of what he had done was hitting home. The exciting adventure was over, and he was left with regret and that shocked him. What the hell had he been thinking? He screwed up his face; disgust for himself showed and Barbara saw it. Subconsciously, she tried to push the feeling of being used away but couldn't. Shame, guilt and regret overtook them and they promised never to breathe a word to Julia about that night. Barbara had been a beautiful prize and he had enjoyed the time with her, but he hadn't loved her. They both realised that they had betrayed Julia through their selfishness.

Back in The Royal Oak in this moment, for the first time in his life he realised he couldn't bear to lose Julia. She was sitting with her head in her hands, crumpled with pain and with tears streaming from her eyes. He had broken her heart. How in God's name was he going to mend it? The regret and distain he had for himself was palpable. His gut hurt like hell; a physical pain he hadn't expected. He had never felt it before and never wanted to feel it again.

He found himself on his knees in front of her, begging her to forgive him.

It was a funny thing, and peculiar that until this awful moment he hadn't realised just how much Julia meant to him. He was desolate at the thought he might lose her and he was a fool. He had let his male ego take over and look where that had got him. If she forgave him, he swore to himself that he would never fall into that trap again and would never take Julia for granted.

Looking at the girl he loved from his kneeling position and watching her sob was breaking his heart. He couldn't see her face that was hidden in the crook of her arms, but he heard the sobs, the little sounds of pain that left her mouth with each breath.

How in the world was he ever going to put this right? he thought. How would she ever trust him with her heart again, if indeed there was going to be a future for them?

He touched her arm gently, his fingers wrapping around her wrist and easing it to one side, trying to release her beautiful face from the shelter of her arms. When she did raise her head, he saw the wet reddened face and eyes that accused him with pain and bewilderment. Tears rolled down her cheeks, tears he had caused, pain he had inflicted on her.

He moved her soft red hair from her face; instinctively she turned away from him, unable to look him in his eyes. He took her chin and moved her face to look directly at him. Her accusing eyes burned into his.

"How could you? Who was she?" The words whipped into his heart.

Should he tell her? If he did, she would never come back to him, and she would lose her best friend too.' It was not easy seeing Barbara when Julia and her were altogether, their heads together sharing girly things. His fear rose inside of himself, along with his guilt. Would Barbara tell her. He would have to learn how to live with his sorry secret. He still liked Barbara. It was going to be difficult; would Julia guess in the end and feel betrayed by both of them? God, he hoped not.

All this caused by a moment of madness, flattered by the attention Julia's friend gave him. There it was again, his blasted ego.

Should he be honest with her? Or let sleeping dogs lie? He looked into her eyes; her cheeks were still puffy with crying, but the tears had stopped as she waited for an answer.

He saw the distrust, the anger, in one look. He decided in that moment that he would do the latter, hadn't he caused her enough pain without inflicting more?

"She was a one-night stand, honestly, love. A big mistake, one I'll never make again."

But in the back of his mind, he wondered if he was making yet another mistake in not being truthful. Time would tell. He prayed he had made the right decision this time.

Julia saw the regret on Nick's face and the remorse in his eyes, and her heart softened. She did love him. All he had to do was to walk into the room and she was smitten all over again; he was her soulmate whether she liked it or not. She was tied to him by love.

He moved to kiss her but she wasn't ready to respond to his affection. She wanted him, but she knew that a kiss meant he was forgiven and he wasn't. Her shaky voice, low and husky, asked, "Can I trust you?" She held a hand up for him to keep his distance before going on. "How do I know you'll not do this again? I couldn't bear it."

Tears filled her eyes again.

Something happened to Nick, something he never thought would happen. He found himself wishing that he had Julia all to himself, body and soul. His forever. He was already on his knees in front of her begging her forgiveness, and he was ready for the next step.

He was ready to propose.

Almost as the thought ran through his head, the words were out and he believed every word he spoke because they came from his heart and soul.

"Will you marry me, please? I promise that with you by my side I'll never stray from you again."

Julia's eyes that had been so full of doubt and apprehension were suddenly changed in that magical moment when she heard those words. Words she had longed to hear from him from the first moment she had met him. The sun stopped in its cycle in the sky; there was silence as time stopped too. Her heart held the moment and the broken piece that floated nearby magically rejoined to the whole. Her puffy face, still red from her tears, became calm and untroubled; she looked beautiful and serene. Her eyes glowed as she looked down at her man's face imploring her for an answer.

"Do you mean it, Nick, really mean it?"

"Every word, Julia, every word. Marry me."

The bad karma that was leaping around the room, zapping all the corners like super-charged electricity rod vanished on his last word. It was replaced by a hopeful excitement and it surrounded the two lovers.

Pain and love had visited them both all in a few minutes and it would reshape their lives forever.

Doris watched the drama act out from her chair with her cat still curled on her knee. She'd been tempted to help the crying girl. Julia

worked for her as a general help, waiting on and upstairs maid; she
didn't want to lose her. Nick was her second chef; the couple met
under her roof just a few months ago. For the last ten minutes, Doris
had wondered what was going on with the two of them. Now, seeing
the couple embracing, smiles replacing the tears she had witnessed,
she was glad she had held back. Nick was not a bad lad; young and
rather full of himself, a bit of a flirt if she was honest, but on the whole
a good boy. She could only guess what had happened between them.
A falling out, that was obvious. Was it about another woman? She
had seen the way he looked at Barbara when she came in to the bar to
meet Julia. Whatever it was, it was over now she hoped. Men could be
so childish at times.

His voice was full of emotion when he called out with a large smile
on his face.

"Doris, we've got some good news, we're going to get wed. What do
you think of that?"

She could swear his chest grew in inches as he said it. Doris swept across
the room to the couple and gave them both a hug; her eyes were moist,
emotion erupting from her as she held them to her. 'Young and foolish'
flashed through her mind before she said, with feeling. "Congratulations
and think on, you two, be kind to each other, and never, never go to bed
on an argument."

Julia, who thought she had cried herself out, managed to find a tear.
It slid down her face while she was smiling and laughing, hardly daring to
believe she was going to be his wife.

Sophia couldn't believe was she was witnessing. Hadn't she just tried to
save this girl from a fate worse than death? It had been all in vain; her help
had been completely lost on Julia. Well, she better get on with it but Julia
would rue the day she married him, Sophia was sure of it.

She turned tail and sought to investigate the other rooms in the house,
leaving a draught so cold that Doris was quite sure that someone had left
the main door ajar.

She shouted to Barry to close it, only to be told that it wasn't open.

It was a mystery where the cold had come from? All in all, it had been an odd afternoon with the temperature dropping like it had. Doris was used to the cold; she lived in the north of England after all, but there was something different about this, something that made her feel uneasy although she didn't know why.

33

SOPHIA

Leaving Doris and the couple behind her, Sophia passed by the fishermen who were still discussing the finer points of making flies with hooks and feathers. They had hardly been disturbed by the wailing girl and the boy on his knees, so intense was their conversation. They looked up, mildly interested, when Doris jumped up from her seat and leapt down the room to embrace the couple. Just a few minutes before, they had observed a tiff of some sort. Then the boy had announced they were going to wed. The two men looked at each other knowingly; had the young blighter knocked the girl up? was that the reason for her tears? Whatever it was, it was nothing to do with them, they were only here for the fishing.

The room beyond the bar was next to the kitchen. Sophia could hear the clanging of pan lids and smell onions cooking. Someone was singing in a loud but off-key voice. Another voice interrupted the melody; a rather annoyed person was shouting loudly at the vocalist: "Put a sock in it, will you?" What did it mean? Sophia speculated, but couldn't find a reasonable answer. It could not be a serious suggestion, but perhaps the word 'sock' meant something else in this century.

Puzzled, she turned away from the singing and stole through the closed door into the next room, which was small and cramped. A woman's room, thought Sophia, as she eyed the decorations and soft furnishings.

There was little to take her attention as she perused the room, until she saw the small chest that was half-hidden under a white embroidered tablecloth. It was the colours of the threads that caught her eyes; they danced in such a lively way, gracing the floral pattern along the edges of the cloth.

It guided her eyes to the chest that was hidden under the flattering cover. She could hardly believe her eyes. Could it be – she had quite forgotten about it – could it really be the chest that had once held her fine linen bodices? Those that were waiting to be decorated with her silken embroidery threads. Was that really it, sitting on Doris's carpet? Embroidery had been her only pleasure living at the cottage; she had stitched samplers, pillowcases, handkerchiefs, everything she could. It had saved her from madness when she no longer had a garden to tend. How she had missed it. The planting, the trimming, watching nature grow in front of her eyes, the outdoors, fresh air and warm sun. She even liked the rain. Then, when she married, the garden was gone.

Her eyes fell on the chest again. She must know. Somehow, with great resolve, her hands took purchased on the edge of the cloth and she pulled the cover to one side. If she could, she would have taken a great breath of relief, as it revealed the hare, butterflies and ladybirds. This was Louis' special, precious piece. Louis let her use it; she kept it by their bed, the bed that rested in the cottage which she had just left with Doris; the bed that had hidden her and carried her back to her Yorkshire home.

Why was the chest here and how did Doris come by it? Were there more treasures tucked away in this large roomy building?

It was time to explore further and she passed through the ceiling onto the first floor to visit the bedrooms. It was all much as she expected the bedrooms to be: clean and bright but rather uninteresting, until she went into the back bedroom. Sophia was stopped in her tracks. The carved rocking chair with the folded quilted throw on its seat was well-known to her. The March sunlight that was coming through the window sharpened the relief on the carving and the depth between the tooled marks of darks and lights helped to tell the story. The chair had stood by the fireplace in the cottage. Louis made it for his father, Massie, who had died before she came to the house as Louis' wife. On cold nights, Sophia sought its comfort by the fire, enjoying the soothing rocking movement, wrapped in a woollen shawl, waiting for Louis to finish his work before they took their evening meal.

She reached out to touch the back of the chair to set it rocking. The movement had almost started on its own, and she watched the rocker move with a silent smooth action, but rather than naturally slowing down, the rocking speeded up.

Not much surprised her – she'd been around too long and had seen too much for that – but she knew that this was beyond the laws of gravity. Mesmerised, she stepped back, watching it speed up until the chair was in danger of toppling over with the extreme motion. Suddenly, it stopped dead, as though some strong arms had caught it mid movement, and she watched as faint particles, like fine grains of sand glittering with light, filled the air around her; then, in one graceful movement, they moved to the window, forming the translucent shape of a man of small stature. The window behind the figure began to fog up until the coating of mist obliterated the scene beyond it; an arm resolved itself from the form, and a hand with a pointing finger pressed itself against the coating and wrote. The first letter was M and it continued until the full word Murderer stood out in capital letters, followed by, 'You killed my son.'

So! Massie was in the room with her.

She knew from the light that was still glistering around her that his spirit was not trapped like hers. He had passed and was just visiting the places or things that meant something to him in life. Even now the form was dissipating in front of her eyes; he was leaving. She cried out as he disappeared, "You don't understand! Louis made me; he didn't want me any more. I couldn't let him leave me." The words, so pitiful, were left hanging in the air. No one heard her, either in the dwelling or on the other side where Massie rested. There was no one to respond to her and the anger that was never far away began to rise to a rage inside her again.

She wanted to bawl, to roar; the hatred and bile trapped within her had built up and she needed to scream, to let it out. Opening her mouth wide she let rip. It was loud and long when it came, causing a rift between the heavens, the earth and the underworld. A lightning rod erupted in the space in front of her, and the fabric that held the worlds apart ruptured. A fissure opened up, allowing her in those few seconds to glimpse the other worlds. The heavens shone with an overpowering vista of golden light, so great that it almost blinded her. Through the split she saw multiple planets, orbs stretching back one after the other. Were the souls of the departed reborn on these perfect worlds? Were these the many mansions in God's house?

The rift widened, allowing the faint smell of sulphur to drift into the bedroom. Sophia crinkled her nose up, but couldn't take her eyes off the black gaping hole as it grew until the golden light from heaven was obscured. It allowed shimmering shapes of black chiffon to emerge from it. They glided around her, creating an odd sort of dance as they moved in rhythm together. She couldn't see any bodies under the floppy, smoke-like cloaks, but she could see skulls. Empty eye sockets stared at her from the decapitated grey-white and yellow helmets that once had been the faces of mortals. They circled her, as many as fifteen of them, encased in their black veils of ectoplasm. Sophia was not worried; beguiled, she only wondered why they had surrounded her, dancing like girls around a maypole. She was the maypole.

She flinched as one of the grotesque masks of a skull moved towards her. She felt defiance ripple through her body. What could they do? She was already dead, even though she hadn't passed on. Could these creatures cause her more hurt, more pain? She doubted it.

Anger was bubbling up. Perhaps the spectre that was moving towards her felt her resentment. The skull stopped a few inches from her face, the gaping mouth open wide, moving. Waxy teeth, blackened with age, arrested her gaze. They were unearthly creatures. There were no sounds, no words and yet she could have sworn she heard 'Let us help you.'

There it was; a connection was made between the ghostly spectres and herself, and they filled her with anticipation.

The skull came even closer. There was no threat, although she felt she might fall through the large eye sockets and down into a well, to a place unknown but to which she might belong.

"Who are you?" she called out, but there was no immediate answer and then two words came into her head. Always and Forever. What did it mean?

The socket grew larger, drawing her further into its cavern; a picture was forming as she stared into the black, empty space until she saw a huge battle going on. No, she was wrong; not one battle but a kaleidoscope of many battles from down the ages. Bows and arrows, spears and swords, battle-axes and clubs, knives and guns.

Warriors, soldiers, and clansmen, fighting their bloody fight. Swords were slashing, leaving bodies headless and limbless figures lying on the battleground. Men were knee high in bloody mud; the stink of death was all around, and the cries of the dying and injured were ignored. The warriors, unable to think or walk away from the madness that had called them, stood in a hell of their own making.

Unseen ghosts in their black capes hung around in the deadly throng, goading the soldiers on, and collecting recruits for their army. Always and Forever suddenly made sense; these were the spirits of chaos.

Men had fallen, their spirits leaving them, and quickly dissolving into a tunnel of light. Others fell; their spirits lingered on the earthly plain not knowing where to go but they soon started to evolve. Sophia saw the familiar black mist cloak their souls, adorning them; flesh evaporated from their bodies leaving only their white skulls gleaming under the veil. They were absorbed into the army of chaos, never leaving the war zone. Their task was to urge the madness on.

Exhausted from the battlefield in the madness of war, victory was declared; there were no winners, only losers. The vanquished were in chains, and the booty was gathered to pay for the next war, more death, and more chaos.

'Strength overcomes weakness. Honour and revenge come as a delicacy to the bold.' The words spun in her head.

So, she was being introduced to a demonic army. What good was that to her? Why would she join them? She withdrew from the cavern.

Another spectre was pushing its way through the throng, 'Your father died a broken man, what are you going to do about it?'

'What indeed?' It was a question she asked herself continually, but why would these creatures they want to help her?

'Many of your thoughts are as one with ours. You have been chosen,' the voice went on, the empty eye sockets staring into her spiritual soul. 'Wasn't Louis really responsible for your death, which in turn caused your father to die of a broken heart? Two deaths to avenge, Sophia. Think about it?'

Sophia saw the group around her, nodding their dismembered skulls in agreement. "Yes." She knew they were right.

As she thought more of it, the skull staring at her transformed. A young woman with blue eyes was staring back at her. An ugly scar ran down the side of her face. It was raw and angry. 'My husband did this to me, and killed my only love. I was betrayed too. You are one of us and we claim you. Come into our fold and rejoice in our strength.'

Sophia hesitated.

'We can make the strong stronger and the bold bolder. Promise yourself to us and we will help you claim your goal.'

Sophia looked into the blue eyes of the demon. 'Eyes I can trust,' she thought calmly.

"I promise."

The whispered words reverberated around the room through the wispy veils of black. Mouths opened on the yellowing skulls. The sound of only one word was heard.

"Yes"

The souls that surrounded her backed away, rejoining a frantic dance around the bedroom, the hems of their misty skirts flying out and touching Sophia as they moved towards the rift, the split of the dimensions that separated their time from hers. One by one they returned to the void to which they belonged, disappearing into the cavern of darkness.

The very last demon with the blue eyes turned to her before she left. 'He will touch you and give you a gift.' Laughter ended the sentence as she took leave of Sophia's world.

They had given her something she wanted and needed; a feeling of being loved and belonging.

A gift, what sort of a gift and who was 'he'? Sophia stood in the empty room.

The split was growing and a smell of burning came from the other side of it. She watched with a fascination, mixed with fear. A trickle of a thick black substance was pushing against the opening. It bubbled out of the narrow slit, forcing itself into the earthly plane where she stood. It was changing shape and texture as it moved towards her; suddenly a hand thrust itself from the black material, and a finger of fire flared up, trying to touch her. Fear gripped her. She screamed, but it was too late. It leaped forward, touching her ghostly body on her hand. There was no heat from it. It was not what she expected. The molten mass changed again into the black mist she already knew, reshaping itself from the hand and forming itself into a man, a handsome man with green eyes.

She could feel the power in him.

A second later, a blinding light forced its way out of the split dimensions and into the room. The spectre of black fled back into the world it had left.

The light she felt had tried to blind her; she shouted the word 'No' and it bounced around the room, hitting the thin fabric of the split, closing it as quickly as when it opened it up. It sucked all black particles and sulphur back into its bosom. The blinding light was choked off and she could see. Only the slight aroma of woodsmoke was left in the air, Sophia was no longer angry. She felt lighter, refreshed and strangely more powerful than she had ever felt before.

34

It was almost 9pm when Katie and Louis were finally straight and tidy. The cottage was spick and span, everywhere had been deep cleaned, and even the workshop was spider-free. All the boxes were emptied, their contents washed, sorted and put away.

It was warm and cosy inside the cottage and the armchairs they had brought from Little Bourne sat proudly on each side of the open fire. The flames were licking the fire back, playing chase and dodge as they disappeared up the chimney. They were ready to spend their first night together in the cottage. The bed, dressed in new cream-coloured linen with a new duck-down eiderdown of greens finishing off its look, was in its old setting waiting to share its comfort with its maker and his woman.

For the last half hour, Louis and Katie enjoyed the quiet of the room in the new atmosphere they'd created. The chairs wrapped around them as if welcoming them into the heart of the cottage.

Louis was home at last with his beautiful darling girl. His heart was lifted and light, but his body was heavy and tired after the spring-clean they had given the place. When they had sunk into the old armchairs in front of the roaring fire, he had had to fight against falling asleep. Katie was tired too but her head was still buzzing from what had turned out to have been a hectic day. Tomorrow they were going to see Doris and she wondered what she wanted from them?

She wriggled in her chair, moving it away from the heat for fear of burning her legs. It was nice to have a roaring fire, but as it was getting late, she thought it was time to dampen it down before they retired.

She looked over at Louis, who was slumped in the chair. His eyes kept closing and his head fell forward in sleep. It jogged him awake each time it happened and he shuddered in wakening himself up. She was happy watching at him; they could be themselves at last, no more pretending and no more white lies, and it was almost time to go to bed. With the poker in her hand, she rattled and raked through the coals until the ash dropped through into the grate, then she closed the flue, reducing the draught to the flames. In seconds, the red and orange curls among the cinders died down until they were no more than flicking a chorus of dancing light.

The sound of her raking the fire brought Louis back from the edge of sleep; he yawned and stretched, apologising for dropping off.

"No need to apologise. If my brain would stop spinning, I'd probably be asleep too."

Louis yawned again, rather loudly, and laughed at the strange noise he had managed to make. He was warm, content and ready for bed.

Almost before he had finished the thought, he realised that he wasn't ready to go to bed after all.

A chill swept through his body.', the last time I slept in this house, in that bed, Sophia killed me.

Where had the thought come from? He shuddered.

He just hadn't thought about it up to now and he wasn't prepared to dwell on it, but it was there like a spectre hanging in the front of his mind. The excitement of coming home with Katie by his side had pushed the past away into a corner he seldom visited, except perhaps to wonder how long he had with her. Now the past had crept up on him, leapt into his head, and he remembered the moments from long ago when he thought he awakened from a nightmare. Beads of sweat gathered on his forehead, his mouth and lips became dry, his tongue traced his lips as he tried to moisten them.

He felt sick, remembering the fear all over again.

It had been a hot day and he had been exhausted but, after a bath and supper, Sophia and he had made love. She was so lovely that night, understanding and loving. For weeks they had been at loggerheads, with her demanding more and more attention even when he was working. He had been at his wits' end wondering how it was all going to turn out, then suddenly she had become the sweet girl he had married. He had gone to sleep quickly, contented and feeling good with Sophia laid by his side.

Then a terrible pain had started high up on his back, spreading out like barbed spikes into his neck and down to his waist. It woke him from his slumbers, but far from feeling awake he felt trapped in some sort of strange nightmare. Lying on his side, he tried in vain to reach the spot that was hurting but couldn't manage it; then suddenly the pain dissolved away and he felt lighter. He sat up, relieved to be free of pain.

A small pinprick of light had opened up on the wall opposite him. He watched it grow, expanding like a flower bursting into full bloom. The circle it created erupted with sharper and stronger light, until the rays coming from it were blinding. He could feel a small tug on his body, a pull that grew in strength enticing him into the light. He hadn't understood; he had still thought it was a dream, a vivid nightmare and instead of accepting the gift of paradise, he had resisted. At that moment he had become trapped between worlds.

It was that enormous fear that made his heart pound and his head spin; he never wanted to be trapped in the netherworld again. That thought frightened him the most. Fear was a powerful thing.

Nodding by the fire his mind in his semi-sleep state had wandered; his subconscious had prodded him in his heart, throwing up unpleasant memories of long ago.

The crackling of the dying embers in the grate brought him back into the sitting room and a concerned Katie was on her knees beside him.

"Louis what's wrong?" Her concerned voice was pleading with him. "You've lost all the colour in your face, you look ill."

"I'm fine, honestly." He smiled back at her. "Honestly, darling, for some strange reason my mind visited the past, back to the time of my death when I refused to cross over. For a moment, I was locked in there but I'm back now."

His smile grew broader, trying to reassure her further. It was a relief that his memories were over a century old and he was here with Katie in 1973, living a new life in a borrowed body. He was determined to make the most of it, whatever this life gave him. His distressing thoughts of just a few minutes ago were being chased away by new desires that were taking over as he looked down on Katie's face.

"What we need is a good night's sleep, what do you think?"

He didn't answer for a minute, drinking in her lovely face, and her kind eyes as they searched his face.

"I think you, my love, look good enough to eat." He leant forward and pretended to take a bite out of her nose and then instead landed a wet kiss on its tip.

"I'll tell you what. Why don't we celebrate our first night here with a glass of wine before we retire? Mac gave us a bottle. Let's crack it open?"

"Sounds good to me. I put it in the fridge earlier, it will be good and chilled by now. I'll get it."

Her eyes were shining.

She could see that Louis was all right now; whatever his thoughts, they had been dealt with. His brown eyes burned into hers, sending her a message of love. The fear when she saw the grey pallor had passed. Like Louis, she often wondered how much time they had, but colour had returned to his face and she saw the love in his eyes.

It didn't take them long to share half a bottle of Blue Nun as they cuddled up together in front of the dying fire. They watched it until the last of the hot embers darkened and died as the heat left them. When at last all that was left was black cinders, Louis took the wine glasses; moving quickly into the kitchen he deposited them on the counter saying as he went. "Time for bed I think, I'd better lock up."

He stood by the door, key in his hand and turned it in the lock, and heard the click when the movement dropped in place. They were secure for the night.

"Shall I escort Madam to the bedroom?"

He held out a hand, using his other to touch his forelock in mock servitude.

"Madam would like that, Sir," she replied and giggled. Her mood had mellowed with the wine; she felt happy but perhaps she was just a little unsteady when she got to her feet. By the time they reached the bedroom, she felt elated. Louis opened the door revealing the neat room and the rather smart bed waiting for them.

Katie slipped through the open door. The room looked totally inviting; she couldn't wait to slide into the bed.

"What a day this has been. We're here and everything is going to be fine," she declared as she turned, closing the door and resting her back against it. She reached out and pulled Louis towards her, promptly kissing him. She was trying to unbutton her blouse when he stopped her.

"No Madam, allow me, practice makes perfect," he said, before kissing her again focusing on his new task of undressing her. Once the blouse had been dropped on the floor, he started to undo her skirt. She giggled again and wriggled to help him find his way to her skin. Not to be outdone, she decided it was time to undress Louis and help him to shed his garments. A thrill ran down her back; anticipation was building up in her body and, in between kisses and giggles and moans of delight, the two of them were naked before they made it to the bed. Lying in fresh clean sheets they enjoyed the pleasures that only true love can bring.

35

SOPHIA

Sophia felt empowered after being touched by the demonic disembodied hand. It came from what she could only describe as 'the gates of Hell' and it had changed her.

She'd been fearful when she saw the rift in the fabric of time; the black image that presented itself as a man was one she couldn't get out of her head. The power had pulsed out of that fiery hand and fused with her.

Her darkest thoughts became visions in her head, but how to get even with Louis still escaped her. She was no nearer to her goal but given time, the opportunity would raise its head and give her a solution.

She punched the air in a silent salute to the demon. In her imagination she could see his soul standing beside her. He was beautiful; his flesh was bronzed and shone as though his skin had been oiled, his dark wavy hair curled up at the base of his immense neck. His eyes were translucent, a bluish green that shimmered and seemed to move like small waves on the sea. He had a smile that would have encouraged the most alarmed soul to place their total trust in him and there was strength in his square jaw-line.

Black suited him. His silk satin shirt was opened to just above his waist, showing off his broad chest, and rippling muscles were suggested under the fabric that covered them. His trousers were made of some sort of animal skin and were cropped and slightly baggy to accommodate his powerfully formed legs. His feet were strange; they were covered in leather but she was struggling to see what kind of shape they were; not feet as she knew them. What then? Unknown.

She brought her eyes back to his face, which was alight with mischief. A thought danced into her mind; she nodded in agreement. Yes, it would be fun to frighten the guests and Doris that night, and she remembered the fun she had back at the Avondale, spooking the people there, who never knew it was her. A giggle started in her throat; it grew until the room she was in was filled with hideous laughter. The people downstairs couldn't hear her but tonight she promised herself they would see her. She looked towards her beautiful man but he had vanished. No matter. She didn't need him; she could manage a haunting perfectly well on her own.

A wind was whipping up outside. She could hear the cries of the rooks in the trees behind The Royal Oak and the crackling of twigs on the weak branches that bent and strained under the strength of the gale that was upon them. She moved to the window. It was going to be a wild night; even now the old window was complaining, rattling and groaning under her gaze. Nature was providing the sounds; it was a perfect time to haunt but perhaps it would be all the better when night fell and the patrons were ready to sleep.

She had time to practise a little routine before she showed herself; practice makes perfect was what her father had told her and she wanted to scare the living daylights out of those mortals downstairs. Envy, jealousy and resentfulness bubbled up inside her. They were downstairs enjoying each other's company without a care in the world. She couldn't talk to anyone; nobody heard her, nobody cared. Well, they would know she was around tonight. She would be centre stage, in the limelight and she was going to make it as theatrical as possible. She looked around the room for possible props. Could her spirit support material things if she really tried? Well, now was the time to try. The corded tiebacks on the curtains looked interesting. They reminded her of the noose.

She shuddered and then laughed, "It didn't kill me, *it didn't kill me,*" she shouted at the top of her voice to no one in particular. It was just a little madness and if old man Massie heard her, well, so be it, he was only a shadow. No one else would be disturbed, not yet.

With difficulty she removed the tieback and placed it around her neck, but it sat there for only a moment before falling through her body to the floor.

She must think of something else. Was that the answer? Could her thoughts play a part in her plan? She stood in front of the mirror and thought about a noose around her neck… a shadow and a outline appeared around her neck at first and then it was there. Clearly, her beautiful man had given her more power than she knew; she was a powerful spirit, and one not to be messed with. Come the night she would test her gifts and have some fun.

Tomorrow, she must hitch a ride back to the cottage with that wench Katie. Who knew what opportunity might start there?

36

Doris was puzzled. A strange air had settled in her property, and some of the rooms had developed cold spots even though the heating was on. She couldn't explain it. She would walk into a room and it would be warm and then, without warning, it would quite chilly as though a waft of arctic air had somehow blasted its way into her home.

It was a mystery. The drop in temperature didn't last long, but it had been going on ever since she got back from Katie's yesterday. At first, she thought the heating was on the blink but no, she checked the radiators and they were fine. No windows or doors had been left open; it was an anomaly for which she could find no explanation.

She had slept badly and wasn't her usual self that morning. What with the day before with its mysteries and the wild winds that had pitched themselves on the town through the night, she was feeling distinctly prickly. The howling winds had disturbed her guests and Doris felt the elements had picked on her deliberately.

She was sitting talking to Harry and telling him how the wind had disturbed her sleep over a cup of coffee when Katie and Louis arrived. They came in looking thoroughly windswept, and red-faced with windburn. The wind had reached scary speeds as the day ended and night fell; and it hadn't finished with them yet. It had been loud as it careered around the buildings, butting its force against the walls. Light sleepers tucked up in their beds were kept awake with its sighs and groans, like the sounds of ghosts who had been set free from the underworld, their bony hands rattling the windows outside and in.

The storm had torn at the trees and more than a few branches were scattered on the pavements around the town. The couple had practically been blown from the cottage, dodging the debris in their path as they walked down to The Royal Oak.

"Lord, it's mad out there, I've heard of March winds but wow, this is more than bracing." Louis declared.

The aroma of coffee hit them when they pushed open the door at the entrance to the lounge/diner and they were surprised to see Harry there with Doris.

"Come and sit yourselves down," called out Doris, waving them over to the table.

Doris ordered fresh hot coffee. It was appreciated when it came, rich and dark in a china mug. The couple wrapped their cold hands around it, enjoying the warmth before drinking the delicious beverage that Barry had served them.

Katie could see that Doris was not herself. She looked weary, with dark circles around her eyes. Her elbows were on the table and her hands were supporting her chin. She looked as though she hadn't slept much that night.

Katie thought she understood; the weather had upset her too. It was 3am when she was awakened by the strength of winds around the cottage. The groans as it passed through the bushes and trees sounded like the cries of unsettled spirits from the darkest corners of hell. It was disturbing and frightening but Louis, bless him, had slept through it all. So, when she looked at Doris, Katie naturally thought that was what had upset her as well.

"You don't look too good."

"Thanks, pet," Doris retorted sarcastically. "I had a bad night, what with the wind and all. I couldn't get warm in my own bedroom. Hot water bottles, and extra blankets made no difference. I didn't get a wink of sleep all night. Well, that's not quite true. I had a hell of a nightmare and it felt so real, as nightmares do. I can't think what caused it, but I dreamt of a woman emerging from the wall, her head hung to one side and a noose around her neck. Her eyes were bulging and her tongue was flicking in and out of her mouth like a lizard. She disappeared through the walls on the other side of the bedroom before returning, only this time without the noose and bulging eyes. In fact, she would have looked quite pretty if her eyes had not been blood red. She was holding flowers in one hand and a knife in the other and her nails were dripping blood. She came and stood by my bed before disappearing. I woke up then, I think. God, it gave me a fright."

Doris was too grounded and sensible to think that anything supernatural could have visited her, but she had been terrified. It wasn't like her to have a dream as vivid has that. She was reluctant to admit that she believed in a spirit world. Although she couldn't dismiss the smell of pipe tobacco, that lingered in the back bedroom sometimes. She had put it down initially to cigarette smoke that had found its way upstairs. Or, maybe, one of her guests had had a crafty smoke in a bedroom, although her policy was, 'for smoke free bedrooms'. But the punters didn't always follow the rules. Her unhappy and tired state culminated in her blurting out without thinking, "could it have been a ghost?"

Harry broke the silence by laughing out loud. He tapped her arm. "A ghost? really, it's an interesting thought. Perhaps, we could let it be known the pub has a ghost or two; let's not forget the old man and the rocking chair. We'd better change the name to The Royal Ghosts' Hotel and sell tickets"

"Oh, trust you to scoff. Well, I've never seen him, smelled his tobacco on occasion." said Doris defensively. "And I've lived here twenty years.

"Maybe you haven't, but you can't deny that others have."

"So they say, but I reckon they either had a drink too many or have an over-active imagination. I don't know what made me say that. A crazy dream, but a bad spirit, all nonsense."

Harry shrugged. "Have it your own way." He was smiling. "You always do."

Katie and Louis glanced at each other, Doris saw the shared look and nodded to Harry.

"Harry here is going to join me as a partner of The Royal Oak. We are going to extend, six more bedrooms and a proper restaurant; we'll give the Avondale a run for their money. That's why I need your help, Katie. Over the next six months there will be a lot to do."

Harry nodded, "We can't put all our eggs in one basket, if we are going to survive these days. Life's changing all the time. The old jobs like going down the pits will soon be over. Farming is changing too. We have to tap in to new businesses and give people what they want."

Katie was delighted with the news. It meant her new job was secure and she was ready to immerse herself totally, but who did she answer to?

"I'll be a silent partner," said Harry, reading her mind. Katie gave a quiet nod in acquiescence. They called for more coffee and settled down in conversation; they had to consider how they could continue running the B&B and bar while the builders were in.

A loud screech stopped them in mid-conversation, Mouser shot across the room from the direction of the kitchen like a bullet from a gun. A blur of ginger and white fur flashed before their eyes as it hurled itself to the farthest corner of the room, making the smallest target it could make while still being able to view the room from under the chair. A blast of cold air followed him in. It filled the room with such a chill they might as well have been out doors.

"Oh no, not again," bleated Doris, as the draught wound its path around the feet of the four of them, leaving them astonished by the cold.

The behaviour of Mouser was uncanny. The tomcat started spitting at them from its hiding place, its ears twitching like a clockwork toy, backwards and forwards, backwards and forwards, using all its senses against the terror that stalked it.

The four observers were taken aback at the antics; the cat was obviously rattled and possibly afraid of something, but of what? There was no-one in the lounge but them.

And then they heard the front door close with a loud bang.

"I'm back," shouted Barry. "I just popped out for a paper. God, it's cold outside. Sorry about the door clashing; the wind got it."

"Well, that explains the cold," said Doris. "But what in the world's got into him?" Looking at the cat, she added. "Something spooked him."

"Back to ghosts?" Harry muttered but nobody laughed.

The cat suddenly started creeping forward, its nose pushed out from the protection of the underside of the chair. It held it high as though it could taste the air it was breathing in. Cautiously one paw came out of hiding then another. Slowly but surely, Mouser emerged, his back slightly arched, his tail stiff; his whiskers twitched and a little pink tongue protruded from his mouth as it tested the air. Whatever the scare, it was over, and the cat walked as though it owned the building, proud and straight, and headed for Doris.

Everything seemed to be normal again until Mouser stopped in midstride in the middle of the room. He sniffed the air again; his tail was stiff but it flicked like a lash in small tight movements, unable to make up his mind whether to carry on to the group or not. The next minute he turned and bounded off back towards the kitchens.

"Bloody hell, what's going on with that cat? He's been acting odd since yesterday." Doris scolded.

The table was quiet. It was all really odd. The group just looked at one another. What was the blighter up to? was he on the prowl, hunting? The cat had disappeared to who knows where? No-one had an answer.

Katie was not feeling quite herself; the cold had gone from around her feet but some of it seemed to have visited her bones. Well, it had been a very cold walk here this morning and she was not yet used to the northern climate, she thought. I hope I haven't caught a chill with the move. Sleeping here and then at the cottage, changing beds can sometimes do that. If she were coming down with a cold, two paracetamol when she got home would take care of it.

The conversation returned to the table and she was distracted from thinking about her ills; they had to plan dates for the alterations and builders, for advertising, for the electricians and dates for Louis. Harry had included him in the list of tradesmen they would use.

Louis would always be grateful for the man's kindness.

It would seem that Doris and Harry had formed a partnership, although Katie wondered if there was a more personal relationship there already. Harry would help with the finances to enable the expansion of the business, but he was positive that he would stay a silent partner. He would not be involved in the everyday running of the place. That would be down to Doris and Katie.

Louis and Katie would both benefit from this new venture. The kind hearts of their new friends would make their future here secure, and life was looking rosy.

37

SOPHIA

Sophia blended with Katie as she sat at the table. Soon she would be back in the kingdom. There she would wait patiently for opportunity to come knocking. She understood waiting. She could play a long game.

Louis and Katie still thought she was a few miles away, haunting the guests at the Avondale Hotel. She hitched a ride just as she had planned. It was so easy; they never suspected she was sharing their lives, despite her little indiscretions and distractions over the months. And the army of souls she connected with were there if she needed them. She no longer felt completely alone. It was largely because of that, since arriving back in the kingdom, that she was content. A mighty throng was out there; friends that she could call on, when the time and circumstances were right for her promised payback on Louis and that woman.

She was changing; since being touched by her beautiful man she felt different. An extra something coursed through her. Now she understood his gift. Like a genie in a bottle, he granted her wishes, her thoughts were made whole. In The Royal Oak he had helped her with the haunting of Doris and now back in the kingdom it was the same.

Her first wish was to have a garden and the tools to tend it, bulbs and seeds to plant. Water she could get from the stream. She walked down to the cottage. The hill behind the building was a sheltered space, pleasant but too shady for her garden. She needed the full sun for her precious plants to grow. Striding around an area in front of the cottage that faced the meadow and the tree, she marked out her plot. Her tools would be kept in the shelter of the porch's front door.

For a long time, she quite forgot her longing for revenge on Louis. She was happy planting and tending her new garden; even carrying water from the stream was not too much trouble for her. Her plants flourished under her green fingers. Her roses bloomed and sent out the most fragrant of perfumes. The kingdom had no seasons and she was able to grow roses, daffodils, tulips and peonies all at the same time; she was in her homemade heaven.

The plants had grown, been picked and grown again at least three times before the courtship with the garden lost some of its gloss. With no seasons to worry about and no weeds to threaten her blooms, gardening was less of a challenge and she needed more. She was sitting under the tree, thinking that perhaps she should introduce weeds and more insects, when a small breeze caught the leaves above her, making them rustle loudly. The sound reminded her of the satin dresses she'd worn to balls, how the fabric gave off a similar sound when one moved or sat down.

The tree, abundant with all kinds of fruit, teased her, what a pity she didn't need to eat. A lovely red apple hung over her head tempting her, the apple she remembered from the story of the Garden of Eden. That garden was here. It was just as Louis had imagined and planned it, and she thought of herself as Eve. Imagining taking a bite out of it, she felt her mouth salivating as she remembered the taste and it excited her. Louis used the story as a template for his carving; her image as Eve by the tree adorned the headboard and here, in the kingdom, she was Eve again, sitting under the Tree of Life. The thought of the serpent pushed into her head, offering her the rosy apple, begging her to taste it. The scene became so clear in her mind that when she heard the sound of rustling above her head she was not surprised when she saw through the sunlit leaves on the heavily laden branches high above her, that there nestled a huge snake.

Feeling no fear, she wondered where on earth it had that come from? It moved with such grace, smoothly lowering itself down on the lower branches. With its green and gold scales sparkling in the sun, it was beautiful as it wrapped itself around the lowest branch so that its wide head raised itself up to look into her eyes. The eyes that met hers were not what she expected to see. Those eyes were not reptilian; they were liquid blue and moved like the restless waters in the oceans. The snake's tail unfurled itself until it was trailing on the grassy bank beside her. Its broad head was at her head height; a small forked tongue displayed itself but its eyes were locked on hers in a hypnotic stare, so that she couldn't divert her eyes away from them.

The breath from the snake was soft on her cheek and it smelled of mint. This was no ordinary reptile. Out of the corner of her eye she could make out a change taking place; the tail was standing on the ground and the body had become rigid, but more than that, it was filling out and the skin was starting to split; the head was transforming at the same time and before her eyes her beautiful man stepped forward from the scales and the skin of the snake disappeared.

'Hello, again.' His mouth hadn't moved but she had heard the words quite clearly. 'You called me?'

"I did?" She was surprised; she hadn't intended to do that, but she was very glad to see him.

With one small movement, her beautiful man slipped down to sit next to her on the grass under the tree. His blue-green eyes never left hers; in the warm dappled light her eyes searched his face, and she could see gentleness there. His deep tan made his eyes look even bluer and his shock of thick black hair shone with glowing health. He was handsome.

I wonder if he likes me?

A smile crossed his handsome face. "Of course, I do." No thought transference this time; his voice was deep and mellow, like a musical note from a church bell, and the sound of it seemed to stroke her whole body. She shivered with pleasure. Those eyes pierced once again into hers, seeking to reach the depths of her soul. She wanted him to see her good side. She tried to use her old charm; Sophia the little tease, flirting in hope of a conquest.

'Really, Sophia, I think you are more than that.' This time no words were spoken but the smile widened on his face and his eyes were suddenly flecked with red. Shame-faced, her eyes dropped from his. What was she thinking? His mellow voice whispered in her ear. "You can't hide yourself from me. I know you, you're a tender woman who needs love and attention. Without it you would go mad with frustration. You were driven by an aching heart to do the unthinkable. Louis never understood you. But I do."

His touch was cold when he took her face in his hands. Whether she shivered from it or from the excitement of being so close to her beautiful man she couldn't be sure. His lips tasted of honey when he kissed her, yet they too were without warmth. But they were soft and she had forgotten how good it was to be touched and shown affection. The sweet lips of this man stirred a passion in her and she reached up, locking her arms around his neck, binding them even closer. The kiss lingered and, although she was swept up in the moment, she couldn't ignore an icy wave travelling through her body until it reached her toes. It numbed her senses and her thoughts were no longer concerned with the weeds and insects she needed in her garden.

Would this man stay awhile? There was a nagging in her breast. Louis had to be taught a lesson but she pushed the thought to one side. Right now, all that mattered was being with this…What was he? An angel?

She opened her eyes from the kiss and looked into his. They had changed. They no longer reflected liquid pools of water but were as black as obsidian stone that shone like a mirror. She looked into them and saw an image staring back at her, a young woman with a twisted broken neck, huge staring bloodshot eyes and skin the colour of alabaster; the dead face of herself. She pulled back from him, horrified at the reflection she saw, averting her eyes from the painful sight. He held her tight, shaking her gently, forcing her to look again into his eyes. The image that had shocked her had vanished. Instead, she saw the Sophia she knew. It was a face full of beauty and life and then she realised that his eyes had returned to liquid blue. She heard his voice.

'Life was so unfair to you, wasn't it? to die because of love.'

That old feeling of resentment rose in her belly. Her life had been so full before had been reduced to that of a tradesman's wife, becoming a nobody in a village of peasants. Her beautiful man understood. Her reward for marrying and loving a man beneath her was to be hanged. Resentment grew; her thoughts of Louis, his smile and easy manner that made him a friend to all the villagers (especially the young women) goaded her. He had never admitted to seeing other women, but she knew better; she could feel it. She should have been his star, his one and only love. Where did she go wrong? Wasn't she special? He used to say so all the time and then he stopped. A deep sadness hit her like a blow to her chest.

Louis deserved it. He did, didn't he? she questioned herself. That night he'd made love to her but she felt used; she had to punish him, though she only recalled what she had done after the event, remembering the bloody knife deep in his back. Her thought transferred to her angel who was still holding her. She knew he could hear her thoughts. No message came from him, only a sense of emptiness and a sad half smile was set on his lips. Once again, the thought flooded into her mind; he understands.

He kissed her again with passion and the kiss washed the thoughts away. All she knew was that she wanted this angel to stay with her; she wanted to be held, to be loved. Her flower garden that had occupied her so much of late, was no longer of any interest to her. When the kiss ended, she was still clinging to him.

Her beautiful man had no choice but to hold her; she was clinging to him like a lost child. No matter. A small forked tongue protruded from his generous soft lips, flicking in and out as though tasting the air. All gentleness had disappeared from his face. Scales of green and gold could be seen just under the top layer of skin, ready to reassert themselves when this was over. There was movement in his hair, the thick black curls waved and swayed like hundreds of wire worms looking for a meal and his eyes were like red coals; no irises, no pupils. He had been on the verge of leaving; now that he planted discord in her heart, he must give it time to grow. Soon, she would be fully turned and become part of his great kingdom. She pulled away from his chest to seek out his face, to confirm from his eyes that he cared. Changed again, his blue eyes looked at her tenderly and a pink tongue moistened his lips. There was trust in her eyes and a yearning. She needed him. All to the good; her soul was almost his.

38

It had been six months since the meeting at The Royal Oak. The plans had been submitted, and everything was moving forward but very slowly. The feeling of urgency was frustrated by the slowness of the architects in getting the plans drawn up. For the first three months, everyone in the town hall seemed to be dragging their feet – all that red tape, – and the plans were going backwards and forwards. It all cost money to the annoyance of Doris, who was ready to go down to the council offices and give the bureaucrats a piece of her mind. Harry talked her out of it; he had friends in the Town Hall and he didn't need her upsetting things for the both of them. For Katie, however, the delay was a bit of a blessing because it allowed her to get to know the workings of the pub, the people and this new county she was living in.

Barry, the barman, was amazing. A Geordie from Newcastle, he was everybody's friend. Balding but good-looking, he had blue eyes that laughed when he told a joke; he was never rude or crude, never swore. He said he left the swearing to Doris. His natural charm was a real asset and he made everyone who came through the door welcome. He was an asset that Katie intended to hang on to, for even when customers got awkward, he had a way of taking the heat out of the situation.

Katie soon got to know all the regulars, what they liked, who belonged to whom, all their family stories and what was expected of her on a daily basis. The life of the business depended on the long-distance lorry drivers and the fisherman, along with the travellers who came to visit the Northern Wolds, Whitby, and Scarborough.

The chef, Nick, was a cheeky young man who was rather full of himself, and who sometimes forgot his place. Occasionally, Katie found him flirting with young female guests when he should have been working. Doris had a soft spot for him and an even softer spot for Julia, his fiancée. They had been with her for years and were due to marry in the spring. Doris had related to Katie, in confidence, the story of his confession of a one-night stand before proposing to Julia.

Katie felt sorry for Julia. People seldom changed. Working under the same roof might help to keep him on the straight and narrow for a time, but men with wandering eyes usually strayed. Katie could see trouble ahead. The stupid lad had even tried it on with her, just after she joined the team, patting her bottom as she passed him in the kitchens. Just being friendly, he said. It was far too friendly for her. She didn't trust him, so she kept a close eye on him. His card was marked and he knew it. Whether Julia had heard the warning Katie had given him, Katie didn't know, but she noticed that the couple seemed to have regular spats that were becoming quite public. It might just end with one of them leaving and at the moment that would not be helpful at all. She needed both of them at The Royal Oak. Katie, believed that all the workforce had to work as a team; that that was one of the secrets of building a successful business.

Harry popped in and out all the time; watching his investment, he said. He was very likeable and always had a smile on his face. Katie often wondered if he ever felt low; she never saw it. He was always upbeat; it seemed his glass, at least, was always half full. Lunchtime most days would see him at the bar, holding a pint and eating a bar snack that he called dinner, chatting with the regulars. Sometimes, he invited Katie to join him but she never did; she didn't believe in mixing business with pleasure. He only ever drank one pint though, she'd noticed that; even when offered another by some patron, he would just smile and say, "I'm driving," and that was the end of it. He was back out working, once he had eaten.

Harry was a clever businessman. He seemed to have a finger in every pie and business in Ravensend and beyond. That said, he was popular; no-one had a bad thing to say against him. Doris said he was a bit like a chocolate, dark and hard on the outside but soft on the inside. Katie didn't how Doris knew and didn't ask; it was none of her business. He was handsome. Katie had to admit that she also had a tender spot for him and he was in and out of their lives all the time. If she didn't see him at The Royal Oak, she would see him at home. He would pop in to see Louis; there always seemed to be something to discuss about the next job that Louis was to do for him. Sometimes, the way he looked at her, she wondered if he had a little crush on her too, but she couldn't be sure. It never went beyond a look or perhaps a squeeze of her hand in a conversation. Harry was a good friend to both of them. And besides, he treated Doris in the same way. It was a comfortable life that she and Louis had slipped into in Ravensend.

It was September. The months passed quickly once the plans had been passed and there was only a little disruption in The Royal Oak during the building work. The extension was built at the back of the property. The knocking through to join the main part would be any day now. The refurbished restaurant had been open a week; everything was going well. Doris had taken on a new head chef, Maurice, and that night a few personal friends would gather at 7.30pm, invited to experience a new taster menu that he had put together. Katie hadn't taken to him. She saw him as old-school, the kind of man that thought women's roles shouldn't extend into men's territory. Hairdressers, nurses and receptionists, and of course housewives, were the designation for a woman; at least that was what Katie felt as she stood in front of him on their first meeting. While he spoke courteously to Doris and Harry, he had looked her up and down with an air of superiority about him, and given short curt answers to her inquiries. His attitude was the same to her staff, and Katie didn't like feeling like a second-class citizen.

Doris thought he was the perfect chef. A small man, rather round in every way, he had a mean look and was quite vain. He was one of those men who grows their hair longer on one side to comb it over to hide the balding part on their head, and he had tiny eyes that looked at you through slits. Although she had only known him for ten days, Katie didn't like him. But then, as Doris said, you can never trust a skinny cook, and you can't judge a book by its cover; and she had to give him a chance. Doris usually knew what she was doing, and Maurice did come with excellent references although Katie reserved the right to have her own views. She thought he was a pompous man with a huge ego.

The extension was almost finished; six double bedrooms with en suite bathrooms, all looking very grand, with their tiled floors and walls. Luxury had come to Ravensend, and in less than a fortnight the new furniture would arrive. They would be up and running. But, tonight would be a taster of what was to come in the restaurant and, hopefully, it was all going to be delicious.

39

Life couldn't be better. Six months ago, Louis had found his tools, wrapped with a note, on the kitchen table the day after the big meeting. Katie had brought them back from The Royal Oak on Doris's insistence. The note was short. 'You should use these. I think they'll bring you luck. Doris.'

Bring me luck! He smiled at the thought. My own tools back in my hands, yes, I believe they will. Had his father influenced this? Was it another prayer answered by the angels? Whatever had brought them to him, he was grateful. He had spent the day cleaning, sharpening and laying them out in his new workshop, ready for the day he could carve again.

Life never worked out exactly as you expected it would, thought Louis. It was cold comfort when he realised that his dream wasn't likely to materialise for a long time yet. He had underestimated the political and financial position of the people living in this age. It was a time of uncertainty; there was not much extra cash available for luxuries, and his furniture and carvings certainly fell into that category.

However, it didn't stop him thinking about his future, planning and drinking in the nature around him. He walked the hills, listening to the birds, touching the trees. He saw more than most people did, but that was the nature of being an artist. He saw the tree bark as a raised relief full of texture made by nature itself. Beautiful to see and touch, but how many hikers or picnickers really saw the beauty he saw?

Surrounded by sycamore, cherry, and oak trees that grew on the hills, he walked the paths, looking at them with affection. These trees would give him his material when the right time came to make his sculptures. Until then, he had to work on other men's projects.

He worked long hours with other carpenters, electricians, plasterers, and decorators; there wasn't a lot of spare time in the day. Harry had been as good as his word, and Louis soon had six months of work in front of him, and the promise of more to come if he wanted it. Katie and he had settled in Ravensend, busy and confident in building a foundation for their future. His problem was finding time for his other love, carving.

A routine developed as the weeks passed and he managed to set some time aside for himself each day in the long summer evenings, or even in the mornings before work. Sunrise woke him early, often by 5.30. He didn't disturb Katie, he just slipped out of the house to his own space to work on teasing an image out of the wood. He would work in perfect isolation until he heard Katie call him in for breakfast.

To begin with, he managed to source some lime, a beginner's wood, about two foot six in length. With no practice for over a century, and his confidence at an all time low, it seemed more like a million years since he produced high relief work. The tools felt awkward in his hands; and the first cut when he made it was terrifying… and then he connected with the wood.

Gently, he stroked it with his scalpel, peeling back the first layer slowly.

After the first few cuts his tools seemed to be more balanced, an extension of his hands. His thoughts galvanised him; find the grain and follow it, feel it, seek the hidden spirit.

After fifteen minutes he was lost in its world.

His eyes looked into the depths and saw an angel, a dormouse and a key. The angel was in flight, carrying a key, holding it aloft in her hand, and the mouse protected in her cupped hand was pressed to her bosom. He realised it was a symbolic image, a piece of his history. The angel held the key to his kingdom – hadn't his father said so? – and the mouse, the smallest rodent in the meadows, was being protected by a spirit of the heavenly host. Was he the mouse? Were the angels pleased that he used his gift to portray nature and the natural world, knowing he cared about all living creatures, even the smallest. He certainly felt small in this world, and in the scheme of things. His passing and his journey to 1973 had been blessed; absolutely remarkable, when he thought about it. He set to work to find the image within. Thoughts from his past rattled around in his head; the days of his apprenticeship came flooding back. He could even smell the old workshop and all the woods that were stored there. The voice of his master was there in his head, a patient man who helped him to grow his skills. When the master had seen that Louis had a special gift with wood and could carve, he had told Louis of a genius carver called Grinling Gibbons that worked in the cities of London and Oxford. Gibbons was the man who carved the choir stalls for Christopher Wren's St Paul's, who had worked for the royal family in London, and who died in 1721. His reputation had spread because of his fine carving. But Louis' master had warned him North Yorkshire was neither of those cities, and it was important to be grounded in the craft of carpentry. Louis had seen drawings of Gibbons' work and he marvelled at them, not that he aspired to compete with that man's greatness, but he too loved high relief carving, for which Gibbons was especially noted. Louis smiled to himself as he pushed the memories away, and came back to the present.

The wood felt good under his hands, this would be a test piece and, after this first carving in lime, he intended to be more ambitious. Gibbons had been an inspiration to the young Louis. Gibbons could read a piece of wood like no other. The movement of nature spilled out from his carvings; layer upon layer, growing and twisting, in and out, animals peeking from the depths of flora and fruits. Schools, colleges and stately homes would attest to that.

Louis quite forgot who he was or where he was; the only thing that mattered was his work. He was lost to time, busy now in his new workshop. It was dinnertime when a concerned Katie appeared at his door.

"Do you know what time it is?"

He hardly raised his head. "I'll just be a few minutes."

"Darling, it's late and dinner is ready to serve. You have been out here four hours. And it's Sunday, our day, do you remember?"

He was reluctant to put his tools down. The angel had started to appear.

Her garments were swept up around her feet as though she was flying high in the heavens. Her wide wing-span hinted at feathers. Her face was already serene; rough shapes were laid where her arms, the key and mouse would come to life. The white wood of lime was working magic in the light.

"Six o'clock, Louis, time to eat."

Katie smiled to herself at the look of utter contentment on Louis' face.

"Come and have a look," invited Louis, "I hadn't intended to stay out here this long but this little lady," he nodded to his work, "this angel just wanted to be found."

Katie accepted his invitation and went over to see the new piece.

"Oh, Louis, her face is so gentle, and the wings... I can almost see the feathers."

Louis could smell Katie's perfume; it took him by surprise, back to when Sophia had stood close to him to admire the shutters, he had carved a century ago. He looked at this dark-haired woman, so very different from Sophia. This girl was so generous and giving. He pushed the thoughts away of the past they didn't belong here.

"Why an angel?" she asked.

"I don't decide what to carve, the wood tells me. I only release it."

"You do more than that, my love, you really do. Come eat. Tonight, I'll excuse you if you want to come back to her. But give me an hour of your time now,"

"It's a deal," he said, putting his tools to one side. "Thank you for being so understanding."

Over the meal, Louis admitted his fears. "I was quite nervous earlier, afraid when I took the first stroke. But I can do it, Katie, I can do it." Remembering the angel, he smiled. "Though I need practice." In a whisper and almost as an afterthought, he said. "I can do it."

Katie heard the words and thought; as if there was any doubt. Why else had they come all this way if it wasn't to follow a dream and find out who they were?

He made the mistake, in his elation of carving again, to share what he had done that weekend with a fellow carpenter. But the man's response disheartened him.

"You're just a man playing about with a few knives and a bit of wood in thy workshop." That's how the fellow described it when he told him about the piece he was carving. It was a blunt Yorkshire response that didn't endear him to his fellow worker. It crushed him a little. It was rather depressing that his skill was seen as a hobby in the 1970s, did the man have no soul?

Did they only work for the payday? Some did, that was a fact. Food had to be put on the table and bills paid, and there was satisfaction when a job was complete, but where was the creativity, the artistry? It made Louis sad.

After that he kept his 'hobby' to himself.

Privately, he decided when he had enough work to exhibit, he would apply to the local galleries. He'd been given a gift and he was going to use it, and it was the only way he would be able to sell his work.

He found there was a network of artists in the area and they helped him source different woods of walnut, mahogany and cherry. It was slightly more difficult to carve these woods, but the finish was well worth the effort. As a general rule, the best wood to use came from the 'leafy' hardwoods; silver birch, willow or sycamore that grew readily and easily in woodland that surrounded his town.

Fashioning furniture would have to wait. He needed to hone his skills again, but he would make a start for Katie, who had admired the rocking chair at The Royal Oak. Louis resolved to try his hand at it as soon as he could. Another test he must pass. His idea of making furniture to sell when they had sufficient funds was probably years away.

That didn't stop him from designing the things he wanted to make. Soon, a whole stack of sketchbooks loitered on the coffee table with his pencils. When he wasn't outside in the workshop, he was scribbling in them. Katie admired his talent; it pained her that his dreams would have to wait, but that was life. They had only been here a short time; Rome wasn't built in a day.

Three months later he had four new carvings; two in lime, one cherry and one oak. The spirit in nature was being released by his clever hands. In June, a new plaque appeared in the bedroom; squirrels with acorns, dormouse on wheat, a single blue tit and swallows resting on the wing. The wood was lime. Its white finish against the golden walls thrilled Katie. She placed it next to the Angel, his first piece. The others were wrapped and stored in the workshop.

Louis' first piece of furniture came into the cottage not long after. It had reinforced his belief in himself and his crafting skills. He had felt nervous when started it, but like the bed that they lay in every night, this was a token of his devotion for Katie. The new rocking chair, designed and built by Louis, was sitting by the fireplace. The central panel up the back was carved. In low relief, a whole variety of fish swam among the waving seaweed; crab and mussel shells were scattered in the mix. And, if you looked very carefully, a small seahorse was half-hidden in the bladderwrack and sea lettuce.

Louis had placed it by the fire, ready for Katie's return from work at The Royal Oak. It pleased him, to watch her response to his gift to her. She was so obviously delighted. He had carved it so that two blank panels outlined the sunken central carved one. There would be nothing to dig into her back, it had been thought out beautifully. Her only comment was, that when she sat in it, she hid his work. He could have kissed her. In fact, he did. Louis had hidden his trademark, the small butterfly, under the seat. His secret. He couldn't leave his work without, his mark.

40

Louis was on the back foot. He had got back late from work and the one thing they couldn't afford was not to be on time for the dinner at The Royal Oak. Katie was already waiting for him, showered and dressed in that little black dress she had worn at the Avondale almost a year ago. She looked fabulous, if just a little impatient.

It was ten minutes before 7pm. In just forty minutes the first course would be served. He had to get a move on. Doris and Harry would be waiting for them, and he couldn't let the team down. He knew that the new chef had been recruited from a top hotel in Harrogate. Tonight was going to be special occasion for all of them, and a glimpse of what was to come.

Fifteen minutes later, Louis was half-dressed; he'd shaved and was looking into the dressing room mirror, splashing some aftershave on his face, when he saw movement out of the corner of his eye. Why he didn't automatically turn around he didn't know.

The mirror reflected the bed, and his headboard was in full view. The carving was moving as though being stretched and pulled, and the image of a face was emerging. What he saw was impossible. It just couldn't be. She couldn't be here. But it confirmed his worst fear. It was Sophia.

He stiffened at the sight for a second and his hand, ready to apply the lotion, stayed still at his cheek. Then, determined not to make any movement that would alert her to the fact that he had seen her, he carried on patting his face and saw the look of surprise when she noticed him standing there. Quickly, she withdrew into the dimension behind the wood. He could hardly believe what he was seeing. How on earth had she been able to enter his sanctuary?

He was even more shocked that he wasn't totally surprised; was that why he hadn't responded? There had been incidences when he thought that maybe, just maybe, she was around. Accidents had happened that could not be fully explained by logic.

'What a fool I've been,' he thought angrily. He had been so wrapped up in starting a new life with Katie that when suspicion had crept into his head, he had pushed it to one side. He had dismissed the pulls of doubt and the specks of suspicion over the past year. He shuddered to think how long she'd been there hiding in his kingdom, listening to their intimate conversations and more. It sickened him. How long indeed, and then it hit him; she must have blended with Katie when she collected her compact from Avondale Hotel. It was after that day that Katie had become somewhat changed, more absent-minded and had lost time in deep thought. He had thought it was because he'd put pressure on her, but now! She'd been cold all the time. Oh Lord! The virus they'd thought she'd had, was Sophia. It was so obvious now. Sophia had travelled with them to Leeds, then lived at Little Bourne with them and had come back here using the bed to travel. He remembered the van trouble that John and Larry had had. His shoulders slumped. It was all so clear now that he'd seen her.

Sophia had gained access to his sanctuary, his special place. He felt a kind of panic. Butterflies were busy in his belly. He must get her out of the kingdom and back to Avondale Hotel, but he had no idea how he could achieve it.

Downhearted, he perched on the bed. He must do something. It crossed his mind that if he got her to hallowed ground, she might cross over to wherever she really belonged. He remembered that in his day a murderer could not be buried in a churchyard or graveyard. Maybe that was why she was trapped, as he had been. It was a possible explanation.

"Are you nearly ready?" Katie's voice came loud and clear into the bedroom.

"Coming," he muttered.

His attention far from the evening that was in front of them, he finished dressing, then a terrible thought struck him. He had seen Sophia, not felt her but seen her. What did that mean?

He thought he knew. He was in a borrowed body and that body must be starting to die. A great weight swamped him. He had been feeling tired lately but he had been working long hours, so he had expected it. He was living a mortal life but he had known all along it wouldn't last forever. Now, he had more reason to have his sanctuary back and the visitor evicted.

He reached across to the headboard; his hand hovered over the carving unsure whether he really wanted confirmation of what he knew in his heart to be true. The warm wood offered itself to him; it was part of him and seemed to urge him to touch its surface.

Fear tightened in his throat as his hand reached out and touched the rich surface. It was warm to his touch but didn't yield. The wood had refused him. It wasn't ready to open up to him yet. Great relief surged through his body. It was the first time he was grateful to be wrong. His eyes filled; he wiped the tear away. Thank God he wasn't facing his greatest fear. It wasn't his time; not yet.

He touched the dog's tail and smiled. A rush of gratitude flushed through him. His dog, man's best friend, would be waiting on the other side for him in due course.

"Lord," he muttered out loud. "Has Sophia met my dog before me?"

Oh God! What am I to do about Sophia? This new problem had landed his lap. For a full, glorious year he had shared life with Katie and a love that would last for eternity. And now it appeared that Sophia had shared a lot of that time too. It was so stomach-churning and depressing.

How was Katie going to take it when he told her?

He shuffled on the bed sighing. He had been ready to die, and seeing Sophia brought it home to him how precious life was. He was feeling vulnerable. He hadn't planned to be trapped in Mike's body. That was an accidental miracle, and all lives come to an end. His was not an exception to that rule, except that he would find himself back in his netherworld in his kingdom.

When the time came, it came. The two great truths about being mortal were; you were born and you died. The walk between those truths made that person, good or bad. At least he had tried to be honest and caring to his fellow beings. He hoped he had been fair to Katie as well. They could share love as they had before he was given this living shroud. It would be as she slept, in her dreams, if she wanted that. God, he hoped she would. Love extended beyond death, of course it did, but physical love was so precious. Would she cope with the difference? A raised voice shook him out of his despondency.

"Louis are you ready? We're going to be late." The impatient tone in her voice flooded into the bedroom, bringing him up short. His thoughts had locked him to the spot and his hand was still touching the wood. He pressed it once more, just to make sure. It didn't move.

"I'll be right there." Turning off the light as he left, pausing at the door. He gave their room a last look. He was possessed by the thought that this cosy bedroom was no longer a place he wanted to share with Katie. Their privacy was gone; Sophia was hiding in the background. What was he to do?

There was no pleasure for him at the special dinner; hiding his worries behind a smile he laughed politely at Harry's jokes and tried hard to keep up with the small talk around the table when his mind was still on the image coming out of the headboard. He saw Katie watching him; she had obviously noticed he wasn't quite himself and there was concern in her eyes from across the table.

The courses came and went in regular intervals over the two hours; the food smelled smelt good and the presentation was excellent. Doris and Harry both agreed that it had been exceptional, though their clients at The Royal Oak would expect it to look less pretty on the plate and be a larger portion. Louis half-listened to the comments around the table but, in truth, he couldn't even taste it. His head was full of thoughts about how to tease Sophia out of his world and out of their lives. Katie, Doris and Harry had enjoyed the evening; it had been a success and Maurice had been given the seal of approval.

The evening was coming to an end; coffee and chocolates had finished the meal. Louis was gazing at the brown dregs at the bottom of his cup, lost in his thoughts building himself up to tell Katie what he had seen. Together, he hoped they would work out how to get rid of the unwanted ghost.

The walk home was going to be shocking for Katie, but it couldn't be put off. Once back at the cottage, everything they said might be overheard, and that would never do.

SOPHIA

She'd heard them talking about going out for dinner and there had been no sound of movement beyond the wooden veil for some time. She decided to take a peek into the bedroom before roaming around the cottage to see what they'd been up too. Not that there was ever anything exciting going on, at least not up to now.

It was a shock when the first thing she saw was Louis using the dressing table mirror to splash sandalwood cologne on his face, but luck was with her; he was facing away from her. She thought, resentfully, he's preening himself. He was a good-looking man, but not as handsome as her angel. She knew Louis would try to remove her from his kingdom if he could, but now she wanted to stay. Her lover had found her in that special place; it was vital she was there when he visited. She pushed back beyond the veil; content that Louis hadn't seen her.

It pleased to her know that Louis and the woman had no idea that she snooped into their belongings and roamed the cottage when she was bored. And she was bored. Bored to tears and lonely; maybe that was why she made the mistake of emerging before she had heard the front close shut with its inevitable clash when they left.

Her beautiful man had disappeared again; back, she supposed, to his own dimension beyond the thin fabric that separated his world from hers.

When he came, he made her feel special and wanted; he understood her and they made love tenderly under the Tree of Life. She loved his touch, his voice, his passion, but in the moment when she thought he was ready to stay with her, he disappeared; left like a thief in the night taking her heart with him.

She was left empty and alone. What if he didn't return? anxiety bit into her. Restlessness ruled when he wasn't with her.

The door banged. That was the signal, the sound she had been waiting for. She was free to wander around the cottage. The smell of the living in that space made it easier not to feel so lonely. But wandering around the cottage was not bringing her comfort like it usually did. Her angel had gone and she felt bereft.

Nothing would satisfy her tonight. Lost in her grief, just one question was ringing in her head; how had Louis managed to become human again? Envy filled her as she touched surface after surface, her hands partly disappearing into the sofa, chairs and table. She trailed her hand over the vase that was filled with roses, her favourite flower. Heads of red, pink and white; their delicate petals had opened up and should have been sharing their perfume with the whole room. But there was none. She became irritable. How could a rose not have a fragrant smell? Her fingers clutched at one of the heads to bring it to her nose, but they passed through it. She leaned over the blooms but it made no difference. She couldn't smell anything. What good were they without perfume? she thought angrily. She supposed that the Katie woman had bought them and she didn't like that either. Hatred hovered over the table, hatred from her heart surged out through her body down her arm, and into her fingers that were touching the petals.

'Die, why don't you die.'

She watched the flower change, each translucent petal of pink started to shrivel, turning brown as it did so. She had a powerful urge to laugh; it made her giddy to have this sort of power, it was magic. With malice she touched each rose one by one, enjoying the spectacle of death that played out before her eyes. Laughing, she gathered herself, dancing a jig around the table with its dead centrepiece, her laugh becoming louder with each step until she danced to the bedroom and returned to the kingdom. A surprise awaited her. Her beautiful angel had returned.

41

It was a warm night, considering it was the middle of September. The long days of daylight were slipping away as they moved towards autumn. Dusk had been settling over Ravensend when they walked down to The Royal Oak. Thursday wasn't the ideal day to be out for dinner, with work the next day but it was near enough to the weekend to regard it to be so. The weather had been exceptional that day and it was a glorious Indian-summer evening.

Three hours later, Louis was helping Katie on with her light coat for the walk back to the cottage, unsure how he was going to approach the subject of Sophia. The white fluorescent street lighting sent a cold sickly glow down on the faces of those who were out and about, but it gave light and they needed it tonight. The moon was waning in the dark sky; not surprisingly it gave little overall illumination as they started to make their way up the street back to the cottage.

"What's the matter?" she had asked him, after walking barely fifty yards. She stood still catching his arm, stopping him in mid-stride and turning to look him in the face under the harsh brightness of the street lamp. Louis averted his eyes; his shoes had suddenly become interesting.

"It's serious isn't? Louis talk to me."

"I do love you," he returned defensively, finding her face with his eyes. "It's about Sophia," he stumbled on, his words spilling out with the urgency of needing to share with her. "I didn't want to spoil the evening for you, but tonight, while I was getting ready in our bedroom, I saw through the reflection of the mirror the face of Sophia emerging from our headboard."

At last, it was out. The last three hours had been purgatory holding the bad news in.

Katie's face turned even whiter under the street lamp's glare and her eyes widened with disbelief. He caught her hands as they flew to her mouth, muffling the moaning sound that escaped from her at the shock of his news.

"What do you mean?" she whispered.

"Sophia pulled back into the kingdom when she realised she was not alone."

"Sophia's in our room, in our bed? God! How?" Katie searched his eyes for an answer.

"I've thought about that and I think the how is easy. Do you remember last year, when you left your compact at the Avondale Hotel and we went to collect it? Shortly after that you thought you had caught a virus, remember how cold you were? It lasted weeks. I think she blended with you then."

"That can't be right. Surely, that means she...she has been with us for over a year." Katie suddenly felt the need to sit down. "Oh, Louis, my knees are giving way." She clung to him, her head resting on his chest, and his arms supported her as he held her to him.

"She used me, didn't she?" It wasn't a question; it was a statement.

"Yes, my darling girl, she did." He kissed her head and squeezed her extra tight.

"Look, why don't we go back to The Royal Oak, find a cosy corner and talk about it? We can't talk at home, not now."

Katie agreed by the briefest nod of her head, then, hand in hand, they returned to the pub. They found a table away from the bar and were relieved that neither Barry nor Doris was serving just then; questions would have been asked about their return and right at that moment they only had questions for each other. Questions with no answers.

They settled on an old-fashioned ginger beer to sip. Served in tall glasses with ice, it sat untouched in front of them as they talked in muted voices.

They searched their memories of the last year, their visit to Leeds and the first time Katie had a loss of time, and how she had worried that she was developing something nasty. Instead, unknown to her, she had been harbouring Sophia inside her; the sinister ghost that had already tried to kill her. She thought about all the mood changes she had suffered, and the fight with Debs that was so out of character, that led her to leaving the Echo. Katie had been so ashamed of her behaviour even though she hadn't remembered it. Had Sophia used her as some form of entertainment? It was uncomfortable to think that she had carried Sophia. She had never suspected the ghost lived within her. It had never occurred to her that Sophia was responsible for her ills. Katie had been confident that she was miles away in the Avondale Hotel and was of no danger to them.

Glory! What fools they had been. Sophia had crept into their lives through her, had been around as they shared love in his bed. Katie's stomach turned over at the thought and she felt a little sick. She was reminded of when Sophia had used her body while she was sleeping to make love to Louis. She had been used again and again by Sophia and the thought of it all was giving her a headache.

And now their unwanted visitor had found her way into Louis' kingdom. How she had gained access was a puzzle and they could only assume she was popping in and out at her will. Everything had changed. What they thought was their castle and a place of safety was gone. It was obvious that they couldn't talk openly at the cottage anymore. Where did they go from here?

Katie's were filling with tears. Anger surged though her. She would not bow to a ghost; Sophia mustn't be allowed to destroy them. Despite her fine thoughts, it was impossible to know how could they stop her. That was something they had to face and get to grips with.

Louis could see Katie getting upset as they unpicked more of the previous year. He held her hands, desperate to comfort her. She was the victim. He could kick himself; why the hell hadn't he recognised what seemed so obvious now?

The sights and sounds that surrounded them in the lounge bar were not entirely lost on them. The patrons, laughing, talking and drinking and generally enjoying their night out, seemed to mock their mood. The situation was intolerable but only they knew. If those people heard them talking of ghosts, they would probably think them mad or soft in the head. Hunched over the table, they kept their voices low as they carried on assessing the last twelve months. Louis shuddered; she could have killed them both with her tricks. Sophia was a menace in every sense of the word. Being wilful and dangerous was her hallmark.

Mouser wandered into the room, strutting along as though he was totally in charge of the whole establishment. Eyeing Katie in the corner of the room, he made a beeline to her for some affection. The cat had taken a shine to her and often followed her about while she was working.

Mouser's fur tickled her skin as the cat rubbed against on her shins. Somehow its touch soothed her.

"Hi there, cat," she said, bending down to oblige him by tickling him on his neck. He stretched it up in loving response. Not entirely content yet, the cat took one glorious leap, landing on her now exposed lap.

"This cat behaves more like a dog," said Louis, while Katie quietly enjoyed the loving attention the pet was giving her. Mouser managed to break some of the gloom in their conversation and lifted their mood. Taking a sip from his glass, Louis was pleased to have a diversion from the intense conversation. A soft purring sound from deep in the throat of Mouser was like a muted lullaby to Katie as she snuggled her head against his.

"Oh Lord, Louis!" Her eyes looked over the tall glass to him. "Do you remember how Mouser reacted the day after we moved here? And those nightmares that Doris had… do you think?" She stopped mid-sentence. Louis' eyes said it all.

"So, Sophia used Doris as well! The cat must have sensed the deception; that's why it spat at Doris." The cat had dashed under a table to hide; he remonstrated with himself that he hadn't even had an inkling that his ghostly wife had been here. He had missed so many pointers. They had to put a plan together, however outlandish. Somehow, Sophia must be exorcised and sent into the next world so she couldn't harm anyone else.

Mouser, still curled up on Katie's knee, seemed determined to stay close to her.

"Silly cat." Katie muttered, with a half-smile on her face. "You can't stay there for long; closing time in a few minutes."

On cue, Doris appeared behind the bar, a sure sign that the five-minute bell was about to be rung. A look of surprise covered her face when she saw the two of them sitting in the corner of her lounge bar.

"Oh dear, that's torn it," remarked Louis, watching Doris come from behind the counter and walk over to see them.

"Thought you'd gone home already." Her sharp eyes and instinct recognised that something was amiss. "Is everything alright?"

It was good to have friends, but their problem was not one they could share with Doris. Instead, they smiled and raised their glasses. "Just wanted a quiet drink before we walked home."

"That's good," she said, relief on her face; it was as though she had expected a problem from them regarding the meal they had earlier. "Harry will be here in a minute, we had a meeting in my snug," she offered as an explanation. "The food was good tonight. I think we have a winner with Maurice."

She looked at the sleeping cat and shook her head.

"I see Mouser found you."

One ear twitched and then the other. On hearing Doris's voice, the animal uncurled himself, lifting his head before abandoning Katie's knee, jumping down onto the red carpet and stretching out his back; then he sidled over to Doris, pushing his head and body against her, demanding to be noticed and waiting to be stroked.

"You're supposed to be looking after my cellar and chasing the mice," Doris said reproachfully, yet a smile hinted at the corners of her mouth and she obliged Mouser by bending down and giving him a good rub on his belly. As if obeying her orders after being petted, he bounded off in the direction of the bar. Doris followed in his path, her parting comment to the couple was,

"Got to sound the bell. Harry will here in a minute, probably drop you home, see you."

Harry appeared at the sound of his name. "Hi, I thought you had gone ages ago." He inclined his hand towards Doris. "She's about to shut up shop. Want a lift home?"

The bell rang; time to leave. It had been quite an evening and it was getting late.

Louis nodded in acquiescence. "That's very kind of you."

"Nonsense, it's on my way."

It crossed Katie's mind that Harry and Doris had become rather close over the last six months. Were they more than good friends? She hoped so. She looked at Louis. He was her soul mate and she rather liked the idea that everyone had a soul mate waiting somewhere. Why couldn't Harry be Doris's?

Her wishful thinking was pushed aside. Nothing had been resolved that night, and how they would proceed had been left in mid-air. It was time to go home, knowing that their uninvited guest would be there, perhaps listening to every word they spoke. Katie was feeling the strain; her legs didn't want to carry her. Harry was his usual charming self and the ride home was brief and swift and better than walking. Good Nights were said and they waved at the departing car.

With some reluctance, Louis turned the key in the door of their home and they edged in. How could they sleep? But sleep they must and they must act normally. Sophia couldn't know they were on to her. Every word they spoke would be guarded; nothing would be normal. The prospect was awful. They were unprotected and would be until they found a solution to the Sophia problem.

42

Returning to the cottage that Thursday evening confirmed to Katie everything that Louis had told her. Her fresh roses, bought two days ago and so carefully arranged in her best vase, were quite dead. It was a shock and quite unnerving seeing the flowers crumpled, their brown heads bowed and facing down to the polished wood of the table, their reflection in death staring back. When they had left that evening, the flowers were the centrepiece of the dining table, looking beautiful in their splendid colour. There was no rational explanation as to why they should have died unless a vindictive supernatural force had had a hand in it.

Seven days later, they were both feeling rather worn. It had been an awful week for them. They were tired from lack of sleep; tossing and turning, their dreams were alarmingly full of being spied on, and when they were awake they guarded every word, in fear of Sophia picking up that they were aware of her presence. The only time they could speak freely was when they were out of the cottage. Unable to be themselves and uncomfortable in their home, they resorted to eat out as much as possible down at The Royal Oak. The food was good and a bottle of wine slid down easily but the worry stayed. Any comfort they might have found in making love was no longer possible, but they did hug each other every night, tightly holding on to the love they shared in the bed with the carved relief of the Garden of Eden on the headboard.

Down at The Royal Oak, Doris was keeping tabs on them. Something was up, she was sure of it, but she could hardly start asking them questions. But it was strange. To come to dinner once a week was fairly normal for young couples without children but she was seeing them in the restaurant every other night, except Sunday because it was closed.

Katie and she were friends as well as employer and employee, but they never had time to stop and chat about ordinary things. When they did talk it was usually about business. She couldn't come out and interfere, but Doris liked the couple and wanted to help.

Katie had been aware of searching looks from Doris and her hovering, as though there was something on her mind, over the last few days. Did she want to talk? If it had been about the business, Doris would have already brought it up, but Katie couldn't help feeling she was being watched by her. It was almost as bad as being at the cottage, except she knew Doris had only good intentions while Sophia was downright evil. Hadn't she already tried to kill her?

It was the Thursday night, exactly one week later, when they agreed on a plan of sorts over dinner.

They talked and talked until they were weary and realised that the only way they could encourage Sophia out of hiding was to entice her out, by taking her to a place that they thought she wanted to go to. The night they had dined at the Avondale Hotel, Sophia had used the waitress in the restaurant to blend with so she could show herself to Louis. It occurred to him that the house was possibly the only place that would interest Sophia. It was her home and she had haunted it long before they had happened on it.

Sophia's memories were there, the portrait of her mother hung looking down from the staircase into the vast reception hall; her father and her garden would draw her back to the place, Louis was sure of it.

There was no other place that was connected to her except the cottage and apart from the honeymoon period of the first six months after they were married, she had never really settled there. The grass was always greener elsewhere. She never had enough to occupy herself without her garden and she would never mix with the neighbours, even those who were well off. Sophia had become a social outcast with her own class because she had married him and he still felt guilty about that. It was little wonder that she had been lonely and angry and that the marriage started to fail.

Nevertheless, if she didn't want to go back to the Avondale Hotel, they would be stuck with her and he couldn't bear thinking about that.

Katie suggested that they might sell the bed, but if they did would they lose his kingdom forever? Louis knew he couldn't sell it. If and when he died and was released from this living shroud, he needed it as his retreat – but not with Sophia in it. Would it ever be free for him to return to?

They would have to try getting Sophia back to her old home, and, sadly that meant that Katie would have to be her travelling mode.

"I'm so sorry, Katie, it's the only way. We are going to have to tempt her out of the kingdom to blend with you. When we get to the Hotel, we should have afternoon tea or something just to give her time to realise what she is missing by staying at the cottage."

"Well, my love she can't blend with you," replied Katie, in a hushed and rather pessimistic voice. "You're already taken. God! I hate it, I don't want to be used again." There was panic in her voice, and a look of complete revulsion on her face.

"I know, love, but look at it this way we are using her this time. We will be aware, if not in total charge, and we can't be any worst off than we are now."

"It makes me so nervous, but I don't think we have any choice. Stay close to me all the time, won't you?" Her eyes were brimming with tears but, somehow, she held them back; she had to be strong.

"I'll be with you forever, I promise."

"When shall we go?"

"How about Monday? It's a quiet day for both of us. The weekends are so busy for you and you can't let Doris down now The Royal Oak is building a reputation for service and good food."

"So be it; in three days. Let's hope it works."

"We can only try." He smiled in false confidence, and taking her hand lifted it to his mouth and kissed it. She smiled back, her eyes betraying how she really felt. She felt trapped in the situation and in danger and yet there was no alternative but to face it and see it through.

SOPHIA

It was Sunday evening. Her beautiful man had left her again and she was lonely, so she slept, hoping for his quick return. But she never knew when it would happen or how long he would stay.

Sleep was the only answer; to push away the empty void she was in. The sights and sounds of the meadow in the kingdom no longer kept her interest and since she had met her man she couldn't be bothered with her garden. She wanted excitement not the dullness of the ordinary.

Sophia had been brought out of her slumber by loud voices coming from the sitting room. She heard her father's name, Robert Pennock, in the conversation and it piqued her curiosity. She left the safety of her hiding place and stealthily moved through the bedroom and to the doorway.

Louis and Katie were sitting by the fire. It was early evening. They were drinking wine and looked settled in for the night in the deep embrace of the armchairs. It all appeared so cosy and another moment of jealousy flooded through Sophia. Louis had loved her like that once. She stared at Louis' face. His dark eyes were filled with tenderness for the creature that was sitting opposite him. How she hated her. She saw Katie as a rival; she wouldn't allow that dowdy woman sitting opposite him to have him. Sophia never could bear to share anything, even if she didn't want it any more. But he had rejected her and for that he must pay as well. She had them in her sights. There would be no reprieve when the time came and it was coming soon, she could feel it.

Louis could not only sense her presence as a cold current of air filtered into the room but he could also see her shadowy shape standing in the doorway. Knowing her eyes were watching them, he didn't falter and kept the conversation going, hoping he appeared relaxed and normal.

"I always liked old man, Robert Pennock. He was fair and generous and because he was a self-made man he understood where I was in the world. Everyone needs a bit of luck and he was mine."

Katie nodded. "He must have been very special for the age you lived in."

"He was. I couldn't have had a more understanding father-in-law. He spread the word about my talent to friends and colleagues, boasted about the shutters in his home, he helped make my name. I can only think of him as my benefactor."

"And tomorrow we'll be eating back in the room with your shutters for afternoon tea," said Katie, smugly. She was thinking ahead and hoping that by then Sophia would be engaged with the house again and out of their lives.

It was then that Louis had a thought, if they were going out there was something he wanted to do, but he had not had time to fit it in the his busy work schedule. And it was on their way.

"Katie, would you mind taking a detour tomorrow? I would dearly like to visit the church and the graveyard. Ever since we got back, I've kept meaning to go, but haven't had the time and it's September. It's an anniversary. I didn't tell you but Massie died in September, though I can't remember the date – or year if it comes to that. I do remember it was the end of summer and I had him buried in St Mary's churchyard. We could set off early and visit the church. You've never been up there and it's a bonny little church. I would like to find his grave and lay flowers on it. Would you be okay with that?" He went on, only pausing for mouthful of wine. "We should be able to find the grave, and it would be good for me to leave some flowers on it as a token of remembrance, don't you think?"

Katie wasn't quite sure what to think. He had never mentioned anything up to that point other than the agreed plan and afternoon tea.

It was going to be a strange day tomorrow, thought Katie. Louis had sprung that on her. "How silly of me not to realise you would have relatives there. Of course, we must and we'll buy flowers on the way."

SOPHIA

The conversation had been a surprise. How obliging these two dolts were; she would be taken back to her home the next day, courtesy of the Katie woman, without them ever knowing. She was triumphant. Tomorrow was the day she had been waiting for; to return to the house, to have noise and movement again, to be entertained by the guests that lodged there, to watch and haunt as she wished. She would be glad to leave the quiet of the cottage and the kingdom behind, realising that her beautiful man would find her wherever she was. Contented, Sophia slipped back into the bedroom and through the headboard. Now, she would have to wait and listen for them to come to bed, then she would act. However, it didn't satisfy all her hopes: she still desired their deaths.

The chill left the room as soon Sophia did; Louis was able to relax as he felt her leave. He raised his glass, nodding to Katie, and, after taking a sip, mouthed 'She's gone.'

So far so good. Now he was sure she would attach herself to Katie. He prayed that their plan would work and that his darling girl would be out of danger by tomorrow evening. For, while Sophia was haunting, he feared for Katie's life; she was only safe now because Sophia needed to blend with her, but once she no longer needed to use to her, what then? Her unpredictable temper could explode at any time. Please God, he would be rid of her soon and his kingdom would be cleansed of her soul.

Neither Louis nor Katie was particularly hungry. The wine had part-killed their appetite and their nerves were on edge too, not knowing how the next day would play out. The mere thought of eating made Katie feel sick but, in her wisdom, she insisted they have a snack. Drinking on an empty stomach was never a good idea and having a hangover in the morning was definitely not on. The bottle of wine they were sipping was, with its twin, keeping cool in the fridge door. When Katie went in to collect it to top up their glasses, she also grabbed a chunk of cheese, tomatoes, celery and grapes, crackers from the cupboard, plates and knives and carried them back to the sitting room on a tray.

"Here, darling." She offered him a plate and knife after she had set the tray down on the occasional table. "Cheese and wine for supper, will it be enough or shall I make scrambled eggs?"

"It will be fine. Thanks." He looked up at her, wondering how he had been so lucky as find her. His chest tightened at the thought that she would have to carry his demented wife's spirit again, the same one that only a year ago had tried to drown her in the bath. He wished that he didn't have to put her through it.

They toyed with the cheese, pushing it around their plates, only managing a morsel or two and nibbling on the crackers as they finished the chilled wine. They were too wired to sleep and yet they must. Louis picked at the grapes before standing up and marching to the fridge. The single bottle that was left was chilled and ready to drink. He lifted it out of the door found the corkscrew and carried it into the sitting room where Katie was sitting staring at the fireplace, hunched up and deep in thought.

They were literally marking time before going to bed.

"I've brought more refreshment," he topped up the empty wine glasses. "Here, have some more wine for a little Dutch courage and who knows? Perhaps it might help us to sleep."

"Amen to that," said Katie, wondering how she would ever sleep, waiting for her body to be used. One glass led to two and before they knew it, the last of the second bottle was emptied into Katie's glass. Taking it to her lips, she drank deeply. All sense had retreated and hangovers were forgotten. "Oh! Bugger it." And she downed the glass in one go. "Show me to my bed, my man," she ordered. "I think I might just sleep now."

Sophia heard the footsteps coming into the bedroom. The night was hers. In a little while she would blend with the woman and come the morrow she would be taken back to where she rightfully belonged. She felt a surge of happiness. She had been patient. Everything comes to those who wait.

43

When Katie woke, she felt chilled but not ill. Coming up from her sleep, she remembered the plan that she and Louis had made. Lying next to her man, she scanned his sleeping shape. Her thoughts were in turmoil. He loved her, she knew that, so much so that he wouldn't have asked her to carry Sophia if it wasn't absolutely necessary. The chill on her skin told her it was just like before, only this time she knew what her problem was.

Louis stirred. The light from under the curtains filtered into the room, offering a bright day. He turned over to look Katie and saw her strained face. So, Sophia had blended with her. His heart went out to her; she nodded and he knew. His compassion for her was overwhelming; he reached out, pulling her and her uninvited visitor to him, and held Katie so tight she could hardly breathe. He closed his eyes, hugging her, not wanting her to see his distress for her. When this was over, he thought, if she agreed, he would take her back to the south away from the dark spirit she held. This was all his fault. His pride and his dream had taken over. Why had he wanted to see inside Avondale Hall? If they had turned away, none of this would have happened. In the south, she would be safe.

Breakfast was somewhat strained, conversation was guarded, but they had avoided hangovers from the wine they drank the night before, and the coffee tasted especially good.

It was a little after 10am when they set out to buy flowers for Massie's grave. The red roses they purchased from the corner shop had just arrived, according the girl behind the counter, and were still in bud. Katie thought about the ones that had died on her dining room table and hated the thought she was carrying such a vindictive spirit.

At breakfast time, the day had promised to be good, and it hadn't disappointed them. The sun was giving off autumn warmth in its rays and the sky was blue. It was everything they would have wished for in a September day; a good day to search a graveyard.

They collected the car and drove to the church. It had once been situated on the edge of the village, now new streets and houses surrounded it.

It was little wonder that Louis had all but forgotten where it was; no matter, they pulled up and parked by its boundary wall near the lych gate.

Gargoyles and saints looked down from the roof of the stone and flint church with its square tower. It stood quietly in well-kept grounds, aloof from the everyday toils of the town; someone took great care to keep it tidy.

Looking over the walls, Louis could see the headstones standing proudly, marking the last remaining resting place for the dead; they surrounded the church on all sides. Most graves looked as though they were tended. Little pots of flowers were dotted around making the place look almost cheery. Katie and Louis passed through the arch of the lych gate, with its decorative beams and tiled roof, Katie could see it was very old, dating perhaps from the church's first foundations. She stopped to look at a plaque and read that a church had stood there since 1100. She wondered how far back the graves went. History was here under the soil with the people who had worked and died from centuries ago. With no plan of how the graves were laid out, they would have to search the grounds and read every headstone until they found Massie's resting place.

It was a painstaking task to search the graves, names, dates of birth and death, husbands, wives, and children. The newer headstones, clustered together behind the church, didn't go beyond 1950. It would seem there had been no burials after that in this section, and so they were of no interest to them. The older graves were scattered around the rest of the grounds, with the great and the good buried near the body of the church, to be nearer to God it was supposed. Memorials made of marble and stone, flanked with a wrought iron decorative edging, were elegant in their solemnity and reflected the status of the occupants close to the church that had sheltered them for centuries.

Headstones on the other graves were weathered, some crumbling with age and covered with a rich lace of white, yellow and green lichen. They held the ordinary souls from the village. They were close together, row on row, and reached the outer boundary walls. The names and dates on many of these had been worn away, making them difficult to read. Louis was patiently going from stone to stone, but as yet had not found his father's resting place.

Katie wandered to the porch and was curious to find out who was laid to rest in the ornate sarcophagi near it. Still clutching the flowers she'd bought to lay on Massie's grave, she called to Louis who was searching near the boundary wall, to come over to look at a particular black marble grave.

He came over at her behest.

"It's Robert Pennock!" she declared, as Louis joined her, and pointing to the engraving along the edge of the sculpture, the text in old English. It looked flowery compared to modern writing with the font and different spelling but there was a no mistaking the name.

"So it is."

Louis stood still as he looked at the black marble monument. It could have just been installed yesterday. It was in good condition, unlike the headstones he had just been inspecting. With a slight nod of his head, he acknowledged the figure that appeared to be sleeping with a tasselled cushion under his head. He read the legend. He had been a generous benefactor to the church, their schools and the dame school for teaching working class children before they were old enough to work. 'A man who should be remembered.'

"It's very grand and he was a good man. Come on, we still have more graves to view before we head off to the Avondale."

"Perhaps we could leave a single flower, I'm sure Massie won't mind." Katie hung back as Louis turned to head off. "I'll be there in a minute, I'll just leave a rose."

"Good. I approve." He moved off, back to his task.

Katie felt strange as she unwrapped the flowers to select one for the grave. She stopped. The sun had warmed her; she lent her face to its gentle caress and she was grateful. She laid down the rose and turned and followed Louis.

Still hidden within the woman, Sophia heard her father's name being spoken. What did it mean? Her father was here; where was he?

Were they back at her home? If so, she could disengage from this harlot.

Deciding to take a look at what Katie could see and taking over the body for a moment, she used Katie's eyes.

The elegant monument with her father's name on it was laid in front of her.

So that's why she couldn't find him in the house. His earthly remains were here and not in the garden where she had lain. She was overcome emotion. Forgetting all about returning to the Hall, Sophia left her host and fell, draping her spiritual body over the black marble hugging the cold stone where her father had been put to rest and sobbed.

A grey mist descended, wrapping itself around Sophia and obscuring the daylight. A strange sound, similar to a penny whistle, played in her ears. It got louder, developing into harpsichord music. Her tears stung her face; she lifted her head, peering in the mist, searching into the fog to see beyond it. A faint spot of soft light was starting to grow in front of her. With it came a sweet sickly smell and the music in her head got louder. Her nostrils were filled with the scent of roses, the flower that meant so much to her, roses that still held their perfume.

The light grew stronger. Her eyes saw a shadow appearing in the mists of the fog; its shape formed before dispersing and forming again, as though struggling against some invisible force to be seen. Finally, a man's shape with no face was visible; it was an outline she knew, a shape she loved from happier times. Her father was at last close to her.

She reached out to touch him but the grey dust in which he was formed only moved as her hand passed through it; the shape re-formed and she heard her father's voice, loud in the music that throbbed in her ears.

"You broke my heart, daughter. You killed Louis in his sleep. You were not like your wonderful mother who was kind and generous. What kind of a person had you become?"

His words hit her as powerfully as his fist would. There was bitterness in his voice. It clawed at her heart; the words had been spat at her. Never in all her life had her father admonished her. He had been her beloved father; why was he talking this way?

It hurt, cut her to the quick. He didn't understand that she had been so lonely. She'd lost everything when she married.

"Why can't you see?" she pleaded to the evaporating mist. "Louis was the star of the village. I was only his wife, an accessory, someone to grace his home. But society ignored me. I had nothing. It took years to realise I should never have married him even though I did love him. His work was everything. It shut me out. I felt so desolate and abandoned. What had I left? I thought he was going to leave me. For weeks he had been distant and indifferent. I couldn't face the disgrace of being swept aside. He had to die. What choice did I have?"

She waited for an answer, but he gave none. The shape was dispersing, melting back into the grey dust. It scattered, the soft light faded completely and the music stopped.

Suddenly, she was left in the soft September sunlight sitting by her father's grave. Poison filled her, and she was empty of all the love she had for him. Anger raged red. How could he reject her? She was his only child and he had always loved her. How dare he? Bile burnt her throat; her eyes filled with blind hatred. Her hatred turned again to Louis, as she spied him by the boundary wall. How dare he be alive and walking in the sun? He was the reason her world had been turned upside down. She pushed herself up, turning all her attention to where Louis and Katie were searching, still looking for Massie's headstone.

"Where are you my beautiful man? I need you," she screamed at the top of her voice, letting out a wail that sounded like an animal in great pain.

44

The dark grey, granite stones stood on uneven ground, and though most graves were well tended, firm and upright, others were partially dislodged, leaning at dangerous angles, some in of danger of toppling over. Who looked after them? Louis could only guess. Perhaps the congregation of the church were the ones who tended and cut the grass, proud of their community and unable to let the grounds go to rack and ruin. He was grateful for their diligence; it made his quest so much easier not having to fight weeds and stinging nettles.

The years had taken a toll on many of the gravestones. Those that stood out by the boundary wall had been affected the most by the wind and rain; the writing by the stonemason's hand was almost illegible.

The graves were a testimony to the harsh life many had suffered in his time. It almost broke Louis' heart that so many family headstones bore the names of infants that had died before the age of two. Life could be cruel; measles, whooping cough, a poor diet and bad sanitation were all contributors to infant mortality.

Louis and Katie kept their voices muted and respectful; it seemed only fitting as they wandered in their search on consecrated ground, afraid that by moving through the graves they were disturbing unseen souls, who were listening to their conversation, as they read the names on the headstones.

Like everything else in Ravensend, the place and the graveyard had changed over the years, and it took some time to find the stone that bore the name in italic script of Massie Parker. Like so many others, it was almost illegible when Louis came across it. The badly weathered stone was holding only half of his father's name. He looked beyond the lichen coat it wore to the broken letters of Massie's name and felt pride. "So, this is where you are."

His brave and caring father had been a gentleman in every sense of the word, and had set Louis on the road to a life well away from labouring in the fields, allowing his son's natural flair and skills to develop under the wings of a master carpenter.

The slab was in a bad state, crumbling away; time had not been kind to it. It stood with a lopsided lean, where it had been placed over a hundred years ago. Louis looked down at it, touching it gently; he tapped the headstone thoughtfully as if trying to reach his father through the stone, but his thoughts were no longer in the graveyard.

"Shall I leave them here?" inquired Katie. Louis hardly heard her speak because his thoughts had turned to The Royal Oak and the back bedroom where the rocking chair that he had crafted for his father lodged, with the quilted throw. A lump gathered in his throat, and his eyes misted over. The past might be the past, but time cannot remove the deep love and affection that a child has for a parent. Standing there in silence, by the boundary wall, staring at the granite stone, he felt the pain of loss all over again. A tear ran down his face; he swallowed hard to hold back the rest that were waiting to flood out. Katie saw the tear and turned away to give him privacy. She knelt and placed the flowers next to the crooked stone. He needed a moment or two to come to terms with meeting the past with the present, and all the emotions that came with it. She walked a few steps away to give him space.

Staring across the graveyard at nothing in particular, she noticed something was happening, something strange near the porch of the church where she had left the rose. A light wind had crept in and was circulating the church grounds, but, by the monument, it was whipping up the dust, making it dance, twist and turn. It soared to the height of a small child before collapsing as the wind dropped, settling the particles back where they came from.

At the next gust more dust and dirt were picked up. It was amusing, like watching a dust ballet performance without music. Katie was mesmerised as it repeated the dance again. With the next gust it gathered more dirt and soil, and the blackish shape grew taller than before. Katie felt there was a master puppeteer somewhere, pulling some invisible strings on the dirt puppet for her amusement. It was now almost as tall as she was. She had heard of dust devils before but had never seen anything like this.

The wind cried and the wail became stronger; it was growing louder as the particles of black soil began to thicken. The dance ended with a twirl, changing into a vortex; the cry became a howl and the body was growing in size; wider, broader and denser. She suddenly felt threatened by the twister that had formed by Mr Pennock's grave. It grown in size to stand almost as tall as Louis.

The warmth had gone out of the day though the sun was still shining. Coldness crept around the gravestones, suddenly bringing a chill to her skin. It was then she realised Sophia had left her, she had been so preoccupied with the search she hadn't noticed. She felt an arm around her shoulders. Louis had noticed the spectacle too; he was staring at the dust devil, puzzlement on his face. She was glad of the comfort of Louis' strength besides her.

They were rooted to the spot, hypnotised, watching the twister grow.

"What *is* that?" Katie asked, pointing at the phenomenon that was increasing by the second. "It's getting bigger, it can't be a tornado, not here in Yorkshire, can it?"

It was not so much a question; more a statement. Worry lay heavily in her voice as she searched for Louis' hand; finding it, they linked together, watching the whirling dust move as it started to creep forward. They saw the evil gathering speed through the graves, dashing towards them. Now the 'tornado' had grown as tall as the church roof. The noise of it was deafening as it increased its mass.

Louis could feel her; Sophia wasn't hiding in Katie any more, she was out there somewhere in the graveyard; but he couldn't see her. Where and how was she hiding?

Was she responsible for this huge dust devil? As the vortex came nearer Louis knew that Sophia was within it. He must stay close to Katie; protect her if he could. The twister came fast, dropping the temperature with ice twirling in the dirt. The freezing menace was closing in and it consumed them in its track.

A thick black swirling mix of grit and ice stung their faces. Instinctively they used their hands to protect their skin from the sandpaper effect, breaking their bond. The mix had separated them.

The choking dust filled their noses and mouths; their eyes were shut tight against the force. It stung their faces like a swarm of wasps might, coiling around their bodies, finding any bare skin it could. Katie was afraid to open her eyes for fear of being blinded. If only she could see Louis. Her soul was crying out for him; right at that moment she needed him. She felt like a rag doll, frail and weak, unable to cope with the ferocity of the wind and all it brought.

Although they stood close together, the debris was dividing them. He wanted so badly to shield her, but it was no good. The mix became thicker and every particle hurt as it bit into their faces. The screaming wind with the dark earth had won, singling out Katie with its denseness, forcing itself between them until they were divided. She couldn't cry out, but she did try to push her hands through the dirt-barrier to reach Louis. He was near; she knew that, just beside her somewhere, but out of reach.

Where are you, Louis? her inner voice cried out, as fear touched her heart. She could feel icy fingers pressing through her skin as if trying to touch her soul. She was terrified at the sensation, before she was lifted off the ground by the wind.

The particles stopped attacking her, and a space had developed between her and the spinning mass. Involuntarily, she opened her eyes and saw a face of a demon looking back at her. The face of the young woman was so like the portrait she had seen in the hotel, a year ago. Sophia. Louis' wife. The spirit who had used her, who had tried to drown her. The cornflower blue eyes staring at her were changing. A black disc replaced the blue, her mouth curled up in a smirk, opening up just enough for Katie to see a forked tongue flick out and in and out, before it found a part of Katie's face that was unprotected. The tongue trailed across Katie's cheek; the sting was like that of a jellyfish's tentacle. It left a red weal behind it and pain that stretched up into her head and down into her neck.

Invisible hands were pulling at her, snatching at her hair, attacking the clothes she was wearing. Her head was knocked backwards, her hair was grabbed by invisible hands that pulled her into the twister's stream. She couldn't fight them. Their force lifted her up like a fairground balloon. Rising upwards, she felt the grip of huge icy hands on her ankles. With a force more powerful than the wind, they spun her body through the noisy spinning wall and with a mighty heave Katie was thrown out of the twister. She landed on the headstone of Massie's grave. The stone, which had stood there for over a century, was dislodged with a frightening force, tipping it at an even more precarious lean.

Katie never saw it topple; her neck had been broken when she had struck it. A dark form uncurled itself from the dust, hovering over the still body. To make doubly sure that Katie was dead, it pushed the dislodged granite over. The headstone fell to one side, missing the body but glancing the back of Katie's skull crushing it. Blood pooled under her head, making a red halo that surrounded her lovely face. The roses that she had respectfully laid for Massie were scattered around her head. The dark form, with the bloated smile, opened its snake-like mouth wide and laughed, before stepping back into the dark world of her making, ready to settle the score with her husband.

The smell of decaying roses hung in the air and in the dust that surrounded him. Louis was trapped inside a tube but his body was protected from the whirling particles. The wind shrieked at him as it took the dirt on a merry spin. In and amongst the black moving wall, red eyes were peering at him. The spirits of lost souls joined the wind and sang with it. They twirled around him in the mix, letting their presence be known, threatening but not touching him. His heart sank, heavy with worry; what was Sophia up to this time? The confined space he was in had grown; he looked up but couldn't see the sky. If he reached out, would he be able to find Katie and touch her? She would need the reassurance that he was still here beside her. But as he tried, more demons joined the others, opening their eyes to stare at him. There was no way he could force himself through their barrier. He felt defenceless, up against a force he didn't know, a force that was stronger than him. What was he to do?

"Katie, can you hear me?" he shouted, hoping she would hear above the volume of the shrieking wind. "Answer me, please answer me." Straining his ears, he listened but he wasn't rewarded by the sound of her voice. How was he going to escape from the centre of this phenomenon? Sophia was behind all of this. As long as she hadn't hurt Katie.

Suddenly Sophia was there, emerging from the throng of lost souls with a broad smile on her face. Her friends closed rank behind her. There was no way out. Her eyes flashed through slit lids, as she looked him up and down. He felt cornered; a spasm of pain went through his body.

The army of chaos had helped to create the phenomenon that she had hidden in. They approved of her attempts to steal and kill, and the more Sophia had slipped into their ways the more they liked her and the more her soul belonged to them and to their master. She felt more powerful than ever. Having just killed the woman had lifted her spirit. She wondered if she should tell him that his harlot was dead; it would tear his heart out. She suppressed a giggle. In the dimness of the black funnel, she was set on removing Louis from his host, effectively killing him again. In her tormented mind she saw herself possessing the body and gaining a life for the one she lost; the thought of living as a man amused her.

The time had come to steal the body Louis was using. She would claim it once she'd killed her cheating husband. She wanted to live again, claim her prize, and in the next moment she tried to invade the space that Louis occupied in Mike's body.

The fight was on. She allowed the wall to close in. Louis was struggling to breathe with the dust she directed at him. It passed down into his lungs and attacked the heart he shared in Mike's body. He could feel the strain on it. In what seemed like a long few minutes, but was barely seconds, he recognised that the heart was in danger, the beat was irregular and it started to spasm. Pain shot down his left arm.

Burning with vengeance, Sophia pushed herself through the veil of flesh that was Mike and sought Louis. He could feel red-hot fingers tearing at his spiritual body. He was at a loss as to how he could to stop her. Then, to his complete shock, she was there inside Mike's living shroud with him. Her hatred and anger spilled over as it twisted around his spiritual body. It was then that he heard the insane laughter and her voice filled with hatred.

"I told you if I couldn't have you, no one would."

What did she mean?

Mike's earthly body couldn't take two spirits fighting within it. The heart stopped, ejecting the two souls, and Mike's dead body fell to the ground. The end had come to Louis' borrowed mortal life.

Louis' spirit had been released but Mike's body hadn't accepted her; her hopes were dashed. The disappointment showed clearly on her face and she blamed Louis. In his ghostly form, he saw her displeasure. She had failed. She turned to attack him but Louis was now able to hold her in spirit and he held her wrists so she was unable to strike him. There was madness in her eyes and her pupils were dilated. The colour red replaced the cornflower blue he had known.

The feeling of malevolence was growing within the dark cocoon he was trapped in with her. She called for someone but with the noise of the wind it was difficult to hear the name. He thought he heard angel and was confused. The eyes had disappeared from the dust walls, but he could feel evil in the air. The vortex surrounded both of them, wailing, the wind increased and with it came with an odour he knew. It announced the arrival of a fallen angel. He couldn't dismiss it. The devil preyed on the weak, fed on fear, hatred and broken souls, roaming the planet as he did; searching out the malcontents, the power-hungry, the warmongers; tricking the lonely and sad, the envious and angry into his trap.

He remembered the red eyes of the fiend he had seen seventy years ago and saw the same in the eyes in Sophia. Disgusted, he released her hands and pushed her away from him. She responded with more laughter. The madness in her voice raised the hairs on the back his neck. Changes were taking place in front of his eyes. Her mouth gapped open, leering in a lopsided grin; a bright pink forked tongue flicked out, aiming for his face. She darted towards him. He side-stepped her lunge and pushed her into the swirling dust. She came flying back, her face full of fury. She didn't seem to realise that her form was still changing and her legs were shrinking, being replaced by stumps with hooves. Anger and hatred, jealousy and malice poured from her. All her beauty had been wiped out by her destructive soul; he was seeing the real Sophia, but the image he saw shocked him to his core.

Her beautiful man came when he was called; he was hungry and ready to collect more souls. A demon with a sincere smile and eyes that spoke of love and passion, he hid his real identity. In disguise, he was handsome, but a fallen angel was still a fallen angel, causing havoc wherever it went, devouring, and feasting before moving on. Sophia trusted him. He joined them, pushing into the space, revealing himself to her looking like a god. His dark curls sparkled with glints of gold, and his smile widened before he bent to take her in his arms to kiss her. He caressed her for a moment, stroking her hair with his bronzed hands, looking deeply into he eyes, Sophia was giggling like a schoolgirl who had just tasted her first kiss. Louis was forgotten. The demon ignored Louis as though he wasn't there. He knew Louis' soul didn't belong to his underworld and he couldn't touch him.

All pretence gone, the angel with the red eyes locked in on Sophia. Together they blended, laughing as they joined. The black and gold masculine form extended itself around Sophia's body, growing quickly in both ways until her body was completely obliterated from Louis' sight. The volume of their laughter rose to a crescendo before it stopped abruptly. The couple were evolving; burnished scales and skin appeared and vanished in the mix. The evil covered her entirely; the strange moving mound on view to Louis looked like thousands of shimmering beetles, crawling and ingesting her bit by bit, until they totally consumed her. Shock and disbelief filled his senses.

Having fed on her hatred and anger, the demon and his friends started to dissipate, clearing the air and removing the twister with them.

The vortex scattered, Louis dropped from it, hitting the ground to witness a scene that – had he not been already dead – would have killed him. His darling girl was sprawled out, twisted in a vision of death. He could see the back of her head had been shattered and she was gone. Her red blood, still wet, had made a halo on the green grass and there were roses laid around her face. The sight of it would never leave him. Once again, he had been robbed of his love, and it looked as though the headstone he had bought so many years ago for his father had become the tool that killed the love of his life.

Mike's discarded body lay next to her. The body had lent him life, allowed him to be mortal for a year with the gift of touch and taste that were now lost in his spirit life. He had come home to find his roots; instead, he had brought death to Katie.

As he stood looking at the ghastly scene, the pain he felt was overwhelming. He knelt beside her body and felt a great void opening up in his heart. How was he going to survive without his darling girl? His head bowed down in grief looking at her lovely face. Even in death she was beautiful.

He was becoming aware of a tugging on his body. There was tightness in his spirit and a giddiness that was strange to him. Something was pulling at him, a small tug at first, but the tugging was becoming stronger and he had no control over it. He was being pulled away from the scene of pain, cast through the air, shooting forward at a terrifying speed like a stone from a catapult, pulled by the bed he had died on.

His blood that stained it so long ago was calling him back. He was returned to the place where he started.

45

Lori and Joe's world had fallen apart, after the knock on their door that Monday evening. The police officers had been kind. Offering condolences and a kind of bereavement service. It was all too much for them to bear. The police didn't seem to know what had happened; only that the two bodies were found in the churchyard. And it looked as though there had been a terrible accident.

Lori and Joe had clung to each other when they were told. The shock was devastating. Lori felt that a knife had twisted in her heart, the pain struck down to the deepest depths of her soul. She had never thought that she would have to bury her child, her beautiful, clever daughter. It was all wrong, it couldn't have happened; she should have gone first. Numb with grief on hearing the news, it completely wiped all their emotions away. They couldn't even cry; to let out the scream that was locked inside them. The words of the police cut deep. It was something that they would never get over. Their sweet lively daughter was dead.

Lori was in denial, she had spoken to Katie on the Saturday, and although she was not as chirpy as her usual self, she had assured Lori, that everything was going well. The new extension to The Royal Oak had been a success, which made her job more secure, and the new chef Maurice, whom she didn't like, was good at his job. Doris had been right about him. And Louis was as busy as ever, working hard. He had carved some wonderful pieces for their home, and had made her a special gift, a carved rocking chair. Katie had been so pleased to share it with her, and was looking forward to their first visit, to show it off, which they promised, would be soon. Now it was all too late. Where had the year gone?

They were very confused when the police told them that the man's body had been identified as Mike Develin, but had gone by the name Louis Parker.

Mike was the man, that shared the house with Katie in Little Bourne. The one she had told them had left the Echo. They had never guessed that Louis was Mike when they met him at Christmas. Why the secret? why had Katie kept it from them?

Now Katie and Louis were both dead and they would never know the answer. The numbness of grief overtook them; the mystery would wait. They heard the word inquest. Yes, that should give some clarity to how this accident happened. What else could it be?

As the weeks rolled on, they couldn't quite come to terms with the fact that Katie had been deceitful to them. They promised themselves, when they felt stronger, they would go to the north and see if they could solve the puzzle.

The walk to the shops on Sunday mornings was just part of her routine now. Getting out of her bedsit, that was so dismally shabby and depressing, was essential; her landlady made it plain she had little interest in it, other than collecting the monthly rent. Buying a Sunday paper with the glossy supplements and walking down to the local café to drink a milky coffee suited Debs after a week at work. She could at least pretend that one day she would have the money to enjoy some of the goodies that were advertised in there.

With the correct change already in her hand she pushed open the door of the convenience store that sold broadsheet newspapers. She heard the ring of the bell alerting Jack to a customer and he came out of the backroom and greeted her with a smile.

"Good morning, young lady, I saved you your usual read." He pulled a bulging folded newspaper stuffed with plastic covered magazine, from one side of the counter, passing it to her with one hand and taking payment with the other.

"Thanks, Jack, I am a bit late this morning, it's been a busy week and I slept in." She made her excuse and turned to the door, escaping before any small talk started. She was longing for a strong coffee.

Two doors down from Jack's shop, the smell of coffee hit her senses; she turned the corner into the next road and approached the small but busy 'Coffee Lounge'. She hoped that she would find a seat free; panicking a little because she wasn't usually as late as this. Through the windows she could see people at every table, sipping a beverage and reading the morning news.

She was quite downcast at the prospect of going back to her empty flat, but as luck would have it, a couple stood up to leave, right there by the window. Quickly she entered the noisy café and sat heavily on the now vacated leather chair. The woman who was leaving smiled at her. "I kept it warm for you."

Debs smiled back. "Thanks, it's just what I need." Settling down, she blessed her luck, and waited for someone to come over and serve her.

Life was so dull, especially at work. She had never thought that she would miss Mike or Katie; it was over a year ago since they left the Echo. She had got rid of Mike, but in her heart of hearts she knew she had not been totally blameless in that disastrous date with him, and then Katie had gone too. Regret at her behaviour towards Katie still stung when she thought about it; after all it was Mike that had hurt her.

Katie had moved on and Debs had stayed at the paper, but it had been a hollow victory. The work place had not been the same since, and her so-called friends had cooled towards her.

She didn't have a boyfriend now and she was lonely. Her dreary bedsit needed a facelift. She should move on, but didn't have the money to pay for the sort of home she wanted. She needed to share like Katie and Mike had. If only she had a good friend.

She almost jumped out of her skin when a voice asked. "What can I get you?" She had been so absorbed in her thoughts that she had quite forgotten where she was. Suddenly all the noise of the café surrounded her; she was with other people but still felt alone.

"A milky coffee please."

"Anything to eat?"

Debs looked over to the specials board, an English breakfast was quite reasonable, and coffee was included in the price. And it was still morning, just. She would treat herself; it would count as lunch as it was fast approaching noon.

She ordered the breakfast from a very young waitress with heavily made-up eyes and black hair. Dracula would have a tasty morsel with that one, she thought.

"I'll bring it over, my lovely," responded the girl in a singsong voice, rushing back to the kitchen with the order.

Who was she calling my lovely? Thought Debs, and why, were Mike and Katie on her mind? It was work! Perhaps changing jobs and finding a new career would help; a new life away from here. There were too many unpleasant memories jogging at her brain.

The green leatherette chair gave slightly as she moved to get more comfortable; her hands struggled to open the plastic to get the magazine out so she could read the fashion pages. She always read them first, then the horoscopes, before putting the broadsheet flat on the table to study what had been going on in the world at large.

By the time she had perused the fashion and seen what the journalist thought might be next spring colour and the autumn collection that were becoming available in the shops, she realised her clothes were hopelessly out of date; she needed to find some money to spruce up her wardrobe. As she finished the page, the young waitress was back with a plate of hot food and a steaming milky coffee.

Fifteen minutes later, Debs was feeling much better. The food had lifted her mood. The September sun was shining through the windows, blue sky replaced the dull grey clouds. The world looked a better place and she would settle down and read her paper in depth. Debs ordered more coffee when the girl came to take away her soiled plate.

Hiding the waxy checked tablecloth from view she spread the newspaper out and started reading the front page. It was full of politics as usual; the same old stuff was reported over and over again, but nothing seemed to change, no matter who ran the country. She turned the page.

The girl came back quickly. The cup rattled in the saucer as she laid it down on the edge of the table. The bill was discreetly tucked under the base of the saucer, just sticking out enough for Debs to see it.

But Debs hardly noticed it or the drink that had been put down, until the girl interrupted her thoughts. "I've put your bill under the saucer, Miss."

Debs murmured her thanks without looking up. A headline had caught her eye on the inside page. She reached out automatically lifting the fresh hot drink to her lips, while still scanning the paper.

MYSTERY DEATHS IN NORTH YORKSHIRE OF FORMER JOURNALISTS FROM THE HOME COUNTIES.

Police are looking into the mysterious deaths of a young couple who died on the outskirts of the small northern town of Ravensend. They were found lying next to each other among the graves in the grounds of St. Mary's Church, six days ago on September 24th. It is thought that Katie Brown known as Katie Parker tripped over on the rough ground while visiting a grave and fell onto a headstone that dislodged with the force of her fall. It would seem whilst she was on the ground the stone toppled over, catching the back of her head and killing her instantly.

Sports Journalist-turned-carpenter was identified as Mike Develin who had worked for the Hertfordshire Echo, before he moved to Yorkshire. He was also known locally as Louis Parker, changing his name, when he became a carpenter. He suffered a massive heart attack. It is thought, it was probably caused by shock, at seeing his partner killed in front of his eyes.

Some locals, who saw what happened, described it as a small tornado in the graveyard. It appeared out of nowhere, lasting for less than five minutes, hovering rather than moving over the graves, before dissolving back to dust. It is thought it may have happened about the same time that the couple were visiting the graves, and may have contributed to their deaths in some way. No other damage was reported apart from the toppled headstone in the graveyard. There will be an inquest.

No scientific explanation could be found.

Police are asking if anyone has further information to ring the police helpline.

Debs burnt her mouth as she took a sip of hot coffee; it shocked her but not as much as the shock she had reading the paper. Those people, that couple, were her colleagues, her friends, until Mike had dated her. But dead! Surely not? Had he changed his name because of her, because she had ruined his reputation? She would never know.

Her mood swung back to depression; tears were not far away. Sorrow filled her, not just for the deaths but because it was too late to make amends, too late to take some of the blame. She could never sort out their differences now. Her skin swept with a cold chill; someone had walked on her grave. She gave an involuntary sigh, and wiped away a tear. The meal she had just enjoyed lay heavily on her stomach; she felt sick and thought she might just vomit.

She had never expected something like this to happen. All her anger and the resentfulness she felt towards Mike suddenly died too.

Later that day, a few miles away, a couple sat watching the 6 o'clock news on tv.

A male presenter behind a desk was reading the news in a monotonous voice; the couple were enjoying their evening meal from trays balanced on their knees. It was all the same old stuff, doom and gloom around the world. The French had tested an H- bomb in the Pacific Ocean; Mexico had experienced an earthquake, in which approximately 500 people had died, with many more displaced; twenty Trade Unions had been expelled from the TUC. The world was a mess.

Their topside of beef with roast potatoes and vegetables was delicious and the red French wine they were drinking was sitting in long stemmed glasses on the coffee table. It was an ideal way to spend Sunday evening.

The report of two journalists killed in the town of Ravensend made both of them stop, mid-bite. Their meal, forgotten, they were suddenly concentrating on the report of the town they had heard of through Katie.

The voice droned on.

'In the small town of Ravensend, two bodies were found six days ago, September 24th, in the local graveyard.' A camera shot of the graveyard, with the church in the background, panned out, swinging round to show the local anchorman with a microphone in hand. Standing next to him was a police officer, ready to give the country his version of events.

'At present this is an ongoing inquiry. The circumstances relating to the deaths are still unknown. The woman is believed to be Katie Brown, a former journalist from the Home Counties, who called herself Katie Parker. The man who was found near her body has been named as Mike Devilian, sometimes known as Louis Parker. A post-mortem will be carried out to ascertain how they died.

It's thought a headstone toppled over and struck the woman. The man, known locally as Louis, may have been going to help her when he suffered a massive heart attack and died. If anyone has any information, we ask that they come forward and get in touch'

The camera panned back to the reporter. 'Doris Hardaker, the owner of, The Royal Oak, a hotel and bar in the town, employed Katie Parker. She is shocked at what has happened to her friends. She stated that the couple were reliable and happy living in the north. Why they were at the graveyard was a mystery to her. They would be missed. That is all we have at this time.' The camera shot was back in the studio and the news rolled on to the other issues.

The couple were left shocked, gravy congealing over the food going cold on their plates. Their mouths dropped open; they were speechless.

Turning to his wife, Mac was the first to recover. "I never knew he was called Louis, did you?"

She was already wiping away tears from her eyes, "Oh, Mac, how awful. Our Katie and Mike, going all that way only to die."

Then, not holding back, she sobbed that she had lost her friends.

Mac could feel his eyes filling with tears too. He hurriedly took his tray and left the room. It wouldn't do for her to see him cry.

46

He'd been pulled through what felt like a vortex at such a speed that when the journey stopped suddenly, he felt quite giddy.

Released from Mike's living shroud he found himself back at the cottage, a prisoner of the bed that bore his blood. Stained as he died over a century past, it had called him back. He had known this day would come but he had never thought it would happen the way it had.

The pain he was carrying was crucifying. The last image he had of his darling girl was something that he could not get out of his head. Her poor body sprawled out amongst the graves, roses and a sticky halo of her own blood around her beautiful thick chestnut hair. Lying next to her body was the one he had occupied. The body that had fit him so snugly that Katie said she could hardly distinguish the difference between him and Mike.

"Oh, Katie." A large moan escaped from his mouth that sounded more like it came from a wounded animal than from the soul of a human spirit. He curled up on the floor next to his bed, his arms wrapped around his legs, his head rested on his knees. He didn't move for some time. Immersed in his own grief and pain until his heart was almost at breaking point, he looked at the bed, his bed, their bed; The bed where they had made love, with a passion that had been wholeheartedly shared. His chest heaved as he threw back his head and, with a full arch of his body his arms raised and his hands clenched into fists that punched the air, he screamed. The scream pieced the room; it was followed by another and another until the full depth of his anguish was released and his tears fell, hot tears that stung his eyes and ran down his face. He was alone again.

He threw himself onto the bed, wanting to be close to where Katie slept, wanting to inhale her perfume. That perfect scent that lingered in Katie's hair might have been left behind on her pillow, and he pushed his face into it. The scent was faint but it was there. Lying with it he sobbed with the pain that was raging through him. When at last the tears stopped, he put the pillow back with a reverential touch. It wasn't wet; there was no damp patch on it, no sign of his tears.

Why would there be? he thought. He was a ghost again.

He looked at the headboard and saw the tree. The two images stood as they always stood, but between them was the newest carving of a dog. In his pain, he had quite forgotten about the extra image he had carved, and right now he needed some company. Would the wooden veil be ready to admit him back into his kingdom?

Oh, my God, please let me in. Gingerly, he put the flat of his hand onto the carving and pushed gently. The wood moved in response to his touch, much like opening a door. His world was waiting for him and a four-legged companion would also be there behind the façade.

It had been an oversight not including animals in his world when he carved the headboard. Katie amended what he had overlooked in his kingdom, she had the power of imagination that proved magical and she brought birds and bees to his world. She had made it live and now because of him she was dead. His sorrow deepened.

He longed to feel affection and comfort from a living creature and having carved a dog with curling tail in the wood, he wondered what breed of dog was waiting. In a few seconds he would know and meet his new friend for the first time. Together they would share his otherwise empty world and ease the pain of grief.

The headboard opened its arms for him; his kingdom was ready for his return, inviting him to walk the path that led to the tree. A spread of sunlight rushed into the bedroom lighting the way back to his world.

Walking up the path, and seeing the sun shining through the branches as it always did, pained him. He resented it. How could his sun still shine? It had no right to be so bright pretending that his world was happy. Didn't his world know that she was dead? Didn't it understand his sorrow?

The tree was heavy with ripe fruit hidden amongst its leaves, fruit that was never picked or eaten, that hung as pure decoration. His shoulders slumped. The fruit was not needed, had never been needed, was superfluous. It sat there looking rosy, and so tempting yet he would certainly not have need of it; he would never be hungry again.

He felt another body blow. In the last year he had got used to being mortal, to tasting food and drink, feeling hot and cold, to making love with his darling girl. More loss to come to terms with; further grief, extra pain, burdens that he would have to get used to.

The dog, which looked like a golden retriever, appeared to be sleeping, lying in the shadows of the tree. One ear twitched as it heard the crunch of footsteps making their way towards him on the dirt path. Its head rose ever so slightly, listening and taking notice of the man, assessing the character of Louis with its large brown eyes. The mouth opened as if to smile, greeting its creator. A pink tongue loped to one side as the animal leaped up and came to greet its master. Its body bursting with energy, it danced and pranced around, greeting him like a long-lost friend. The tail wagged with the force of a small sandbag, catching Louis on his legs and, despite his low mood, he loved the welcome.

Louis suddenly felt uplifted, the pain in his chest eased and he couldn't help smiling as he bent a knee to stroke the excited animal. He was almost knocked off his feet by the weight and enthusiasm of the dancing dog. Wrapping his arms around the neck of his new best friend, Louis tried to avoid the wet tongue that was being delivered to his face. But in the next moment he was knocked over and rolled under the tree while trying to defend himself from the cosh-like tail of the dog. It flopped beside him and placed its head on his master's chest, looking with soulful eyes into his eyes. Despite his misery, Louis found himself laughing and patting the dog's head. His next job, it would seem, was to find a name to suit his boisterous pet.

A bird on the tree above his head caught his eye. The blue tit hopped from branch to branch before taking flight in the direction of the mountains, Louis' eyes followed the small bird's flight over the meadow, and the mallards flying in formation overhead. A lump rose in his throat. Katie had brought those to his world; every time he saw them, they would remind him of her. The birds and bees, dragonflies and swallows belonged to her thoughts, her imagination; not his.

Sadness returned, sitting there with the nameless dog beside him. Together they looked out over the meadow, watching the small movements of the insects and listening to the song of the stream that sang as it passed over the rocks, bubbling on its way to the mountains.

With his dog by his side, Louis wrapped himself in all the warm memories he could muster. He had loved and he had lost. He hugged the dog close to him. The dog's sad eyes looked up at Louis and a cold nose nuzzled his face. The retriever's coarse tongue licked Louis' face, wiping away the soft salty tears. In spite of himself Louis felt grateful and he smiled. He scanned the vista, relooking at his creation and there, in the distance, the white walls of the half-hidden cottage attracted his eye. It glistened in the sunlight like a white flag. Then he saw a wisp of grey smoke curling up as it left the stone chimney.

He was stunned. In all the years he had spent in his retreat, smoke had never been seen coming from the cottage. Confusion filled his already aching head but then curiosity overcame him; he must find out what was going on. His stomach knotted with tension. Could it have something to do with Sophia? Had he been mistaken and she had escaped from the demon? Perhaps her soul was still walking the earth and perhaps... he pushed the thought to one side. He could never be with her. Hell was where she belonged; she couldn't be here.

Jumping up, he squared his shoulders ready to investigate down at the white cottage with all its possibilities, possibilities that he would rather not think about. The dog was on his feet, standing alert in anticipation of some movement, waiting for the command to go. Louis started down the track and the dog matched his pace. Passing through the fields and meadow, together they marched with purpose towards the white building. Little by little the house grew as they neared its boundary until, at last, they were standing in a garden of roses, a garden that Louis had never seen before, made by Sophia's hand in front of the whitewashed wall of his cottage. She had left behind something quite beautiful. Her love for flowers, especially roses had at least brought out the good in her, the good he knew when he married her. How had it all gone so wrong?

She couldn't be back here, surely? His fears rose. He thought he had seen her devoured by the demon, but if he was mistaken and she was inside the cottage waiting for him, what was he going to do? A chill went through his body. She had killed his darling girl, his soul mate. Now, he was shaking. It was going to be impossible. He couldn't allow her to be here yet how would he get her to leave? He had tried to take her back to Avondale Hall, if only he and Katie hadn't visited the graveyard. His concerned dog knew something was very wrong and nuzzled Louis' hand, while making a soft whining that sounded like sympathy.

With one last glance at the rose garden, it was time to be courageous, time to investigate inside the cottage and solve the mystery of the smoke. Louis was full of trepidation. What would greet him?

It was only a short walk to the front door but it might have been miles. His legs were weighty and reluctant to get him there quickly. His dog led the way, running forward before coming back to Louis to hurry him on. He was a champion thought Louis. No fear, and encouraging him to step up. There! The dog had earned his name; Champ.

The oak door was slightly ajar when they reached it, as though it was expecting visitors and was welcoming them in. Louis could smell wood smoke from a log fire but stopped short of going in. The dog stopped too; sitting at the door, it yawned, looking at Louis for instruction. Louis was listening intensely but couldn't hear a sound from inside. The dog sniffed the air and decided that there was no danger. Before Louis could stop him, the dog pushed at the door and let itself inside; all Louis saw was its rump and a tail disappearing into the hall.

Louis heard a voice, soft and low from within. "There you are, I wondered where you'd gone?" A woman's voice. One that he couldn't quite recognise.

Oh my God! She's here. He froze.

The interior looked dark, so unwelcoming.

Disillusioned and discouraged, he hung his head. This was his world. It belonged to him. This couldn't be happening.

Champ's head suddenly appeared, peeking around the door as if inviting him into the room beyond, before disappearing again back into the heart of the cottage.

It was time; he pushed the door back to allow him in to face his fate. Turning through the small hall to the door of the sitting room, he stopped and stared at the scene that confronted him. It was the last thing he had expected to see.

Seated in a rocking chair by the fireplace, looking relaxed and serene was his darling girl. His heart leapt with joy. It overwhelmed him. All his anxieties dissolved, the weight of grief lifted, his heart was as light as a feather and he felt quite giddy.

Katie was on her feet and across the room before he had chance to say 'Hello'.

Her arms locked around his neck and she was kissing him hard; Louis wrapped his arms about, her kissing her back. He could hardly believe he was there, touching her, caressing her. How was it possible?

Not to be outdone with affection being given out the dog tried to squeeze between the couple to be petted. They obliged him, stroking and patting him, which only made him demand more. They laughed and pushed him to one side as, hand in hand, they headed outside. They made their way to the tree, with the dog dancing about them all the way there. Sitting on the grass, in the shade of it, they held each other contentedly until Katie was ready to tell her story.

"It was all so awful, wasn't it? I flew out of the twister and hit the gravestone. Then I was floating in a white mist. A soft light surrounded me, I felt peaceful, I had no pain. I think I knew I had died. In the mist a brighter light imposed itself onto the space I was in. It was beckoning me into it; there were no words but it was imploring me to enter it, but I couldn't leave you, my darling. I remembered that you refused to pass through the light to the next dimension, so, like you; I turned from it, hoping that my connection to your world would bring me to you and it did. I woke here in this cottage and waited for you. I knew you would follow me here, even if it took time. I knew you would come, and I would wait for you forever."

And forever was exactly what they both would share together.

The bed was sold. The new owner was named as Doris Hardaker, of The Royal Oak, Ravensend. North Yorkshire.